THE SENTRY

Atop a crumbling rampart stood a sentry, weapon in four-fingered hand, partly clothed...its snout instinctively twitching at the scent of the man and woman walking toward its city.

Berkley books
by David F. Bischoff

DAY OF THE DRAGONSTAR (with Thomas F. Monteleone)
STAR FALL
STAR SPRING

DAY OF THE DRAGONSTAR

DAVID F. BISCHOFF <u>AND</u> THOMAS F. MONTELEONE

BERKLEY BOOKS, NEW YORK

DAY OF THE DRAGONSTAR

A Berkley Book/published by arrangement with
the authors

PRINTING HISTORY
Berkley edition/May 1983

ISBN: 0-425-05932-4

ACKNOWLEDGMENTS

The authors would like to thank the following people
for their invaluable contributions to this book:

Stanley Schmidt
Victoria Schochet
Melissa Ann Singer

and

Dr. Charles Sheffield

For CHARLES SHEFFIELD,
gentleman genius

DAY OF THE DRAGONSTAR

PROLOGUE

SOMETHING MOVED BEYOND the Barrier.

The sound stirred Garr from his thoughts and the dreamy half-sleep which had overtaken him. Guard duty was usually so monotonous, it was easy to not remain alert. A lonely business, being on the night cycle . . . and standing sentry during just that portion of the night when most of one's fellows had locked themselves in the Dark Fold.

Now Garr was fully awake, listening. Something stamped through thick jungle, the sound of its great hind claws crushing undergrowth harshly. Whatever it was, thought Garr, it was big and it was coming close to the Watchtower. A ravenous cry pierced the blackness. Garr tensed. The beasts were getting bolder. Despite the boring nature of Dark Watch duty, more reports were being logged concerning beasts roaming closer to the Barrier. Though most waited till dark to begin their feeding, several species had begun to learn to feed during the day—much to the distress of the maintenance crews who worked on the fortifications during the hours of light.

No light now, thought Garr as he peered over the edge of the Tower. The thing below neared his position, masked by the darkness. Anxiously, Garr tugged the latch of the Weapons Cage. Wakened, the tiny beasts within chittered and hissed. Garr didn't like waking them up, they complained so. But he didn't want to take any chances. With a gloved hand he reached in and grabbed one quickly. Dealing with squaves was second nature to a warrior. Upon detection of his scent, the specially bred lizard quieted, sheathed its needle claws, and wrapped its rudimentary wings close to its narrow body. Upon touching it, Garr felt the immediate subliminal contact of master to beast. Instinctively, the squave stiffened into firing position as it was brought up into the night air. Garr placed it into his Launcher. He cocked the bow, and trained it upon the sound's seeming origin. The polished wood of its stock felt slippery as he traced its contours down to the trigger. He leaned over the edge of the Tower, which loomed high above the great wall of the Barrier. He wanted desperately to hang his lantern over the edge and shed some light on the creature. Always best to know the enemy. But Headquarters advised against attracting the beasts to lanterns if it could be avoided.

The sounds grew louder. Snapping branches. Muffled clumps of heavy hand-claws. Wheezing, bellows-like breathing. It was down there, coming closer.

Though it was his calling, Garr hated Watch duty in the Towers. You were so confined. So alone. And nobody closer than the next Tower down the line—more than two hundred ems distant on either side. That is, except for the Prowl Beasts, and Garr never felt very comfortable around them without their trainers nearby.

There was no communication among the Towers other than by lanterns. A green light flashed each hour, downline to the right, if everything was secure. A red light shone anytime that all hell was breaking loose. You just always hoped there would be time to rig that red light and flash it.

Scraping sounds. The rasp of claws against the wood and stone base of the Barrier.

The damn thing had picked up his scent, thought Garr. It

2

was trying to get up at him. He could hear the beast mewling as it clawed at the base of the great wall. Too dumb to know that Garr was beyond its reach. Garr was grateful the walls of the Barrier were so smooth and steep. However, when any of the big carnivores got worked up into a real feeding frenzy, they did not exhibit such traits as cunning or patience to try to figure out how to deal with a wall. They just hurled themselves against it.

Unconsciously, Garr stroked the scales of the squave nestled in the wide groove of the launcher. Garr avoided the sharp spine that grew from the creature's head, which injected enough poison to stop just about any medium-sized beast. Arrows were available, but the squaves were much more effective. Voracious little creatures, with the help of a Launcher, they could be hurled at beasts at sufficient speed to pierce the toughest of hides. Even if they were not accurately fired, they could use their tiny wings to guide them toward the beasts. As often as not, squaves were killed in the process, but if the beast were not quick enough, a squave could, with the help of its claws and needle-sharp teeth, burrow quickly into a beast and have a marvelous feast.

The really large creatures were fortunately too massive, too ponderous, to attempt any serious climbing of the walls. The only damage the really big bastards ever did was an occasional stumble against the masonry, knocking loose mortar and buttressing. More work for the maintenance crews.

That was the real problem, thought Garr. The Barrier itself. It was so old, so terribly old. Built so long ago that even the Priests were not certain of its true age, parts of it were always decaying, weakening. That, plus the prowling of the beasts, had required the systems of Watchtowers, which were strung along the great wall like beads on a string. All the way around the world.

More clawing, snarling. The creature was getting frustrated. He sounded like a good-sized carnivore. Peering over the edge, down into the murky jungle twenty ems below, Garr was unable to see anything. Even when he held the lantern over the edge at arm's length, there was not enough illumination to penetrate the black night. But the beast needed no light as long as it could smell its prey. . . .

3

The noises from the moist darkness increased. Guttural, slavering sounds. From deep in the thing's throat came the sounds of mindless hunger, of meat-gulping urgency. Claws scrabbled crazily against the stone.

What was going on? *He'd never heard one of them act so persistently, with such determined commotion. Straining, he thought he saw the faintest of reflections and movements, but it was so dark below that the jungle could have been a bottomless pit. A pit of nightmares. They loved the darkness, where they could slither up behind you and—chomp!—that was the end. Just thinking of it made Garr's scales sit up on edge, his nostrils flare involuntarily.*

Suddenly, the scraping sounds ceased. There was a pause in the beast's rapid, panting breath. For an instant, there was a silence in the jungle below: no small animal scuttlings, no clicks and murmurings of insects. Nothing. When one of the beasts was stalking, all the crawling and flying things seemed to vanish.

Another sound. It was walking away, Garr thought as he perceived footfalls on the matte of the jungle undergrowth. The footfalls stopped. Garr heard unnatural groaning sounds—the strain of wood and bark as a tree was being uprooted, and the sucking up of thick mud as its roots were pulled from the wet floor. A muffled crash sounded as the tree smashed through the undergrowth. The beast must have been so crazed with hunger it had stumbled into something, thought Garr. Soon it would be lost in the black depths, however, and there would be no danger. He brought the lantern in off the edge of the Tower, easing his grip on the Launcher, but still drumming his three fingers nervously against its solid stock.

Just as he was beginning to relax, new sounds floated up. The beast was still *there. Its breathing increased, rasping the air. A new sound. Something was being dragged across the vine-tangled brush of the forest.*

His scales tensed once again, his thin tongue whipping constantly in and out of his mouth. Garr listened, wondering what was happening below. Waiting in the darkness was too passive; he had to do something.

Pulling a rag torch from his supply chest, Garr struck his flint. The torch soon blazed with an oily flame, casting a blood-

4

red glow upon the sparse interior of the Tower. Just as he leaned over the edge, holding the torch in his right forelimb, something jarred against the base of the Barrier. Something massive and heavy thundered against the Tower, shaking Garr from head to tail. The rag torch fell from his grip and fluttered downward.

As the fire penetrated the darkness, Garr saw the thick trunk of a tree leaning against the Barrier, extending above the base of the Tower itself. The torch fell to the jungle floor, lighting up lush green surfaces . . . and something else.

A brief glimpse of something tan, or grey, moving quickly to avoid the heat and light. Then scrabbling sounds of claws against rough bark.

The torch flared once before going out. In that instant Garr saw how close the beast was, how terribly close. He felt himself thinking of when he was young . . . just reaching intelligence level after a savage youth surviving the wilds where he'd hatched. He remembered vaguely moments like this, staring into the face of death. Yet somehow, he'd always escaped. . . .

Garr stared down at the creature, as if under a spell, his eyes locked in upon the thing which stared up at him with great eyes like flat yellow pools. It lunged forward. The eyes grew wider. Powerful hindlegs gouged into the tree bark. The thing surged upward in a final savage thrust.

Garr raised the Launcher in his hands, knowing he would not be quick enough. There was a flash of white teeth in the dying light, the glow of the lantern. The beast's mouth opened wide, as if unhinged, and closed quickly, snapping the Launcher and the squave in half, and taking off Garr's right forelimb in an instant.

The attack had been so swift, so surgically clean, that Garr had felt nothing. His nostrils flared as he took in the full scent of the beast's dead-blood breath. The great yellow eyes flicked and the jaws snapped once more.

It was the last thing Garr ever saw.

CHAPTER 1

2027 A.D.
COPERNICUS BASE: IASA LUNAR COLONY

"WE'VE GOT a problem," the Professor had said on the phone.

The statement woke Colonel Phineas Kemp up fully. Problems were his meat and potatoes. That was why he was Colony Commander here, as well as Chief of IASA Deep-Space Operations. Problems were worth getting out of bed for at such an early hour.

"Does it demand immediate action? I came over as soon as I could," Colonel Kemp said tersely, hiding his enthusiasm.

Professor Andre Labate, Director of the Lunar Observatory, stood over a bank of consoles, glanced at the illuminated display screens; his mind had drifted away from the conversation. "Uhmm . . . no. No, it's not exactly of *that* nature, Colonel." Evidently the Astronomy Chief had been awakened early as well. His wavy grey hair was mussed, his off-duty clothing disheveled. Kemp seemed to tower over the small man, even though he was not a tall man himself. He just cleared the height limitation for astronauts at 1.8 meters. His erect posture and well-proportioned, muscular body gave the impression of a tall *presence*. Despite his haste to get to the Observatory from his quarters, Kemp wore a fresh uniform. He always looked crisp and professional. Sharp, clear-eyed, alert. That was the ticket. He wore his dirty-blond hair fashionably long. His nose was sharp and hawkish, accenting his thin-lipped, firmly-set mouth. At thirty-seven years old, Kemp was the ideal media-image IASA astronaut. He worked very hard to maintain that appearance.

Impatiently, Colonel Kemp cleared his throat and waited for Professor Labate to continue. The fellow had an irritating flair for the dramatic pause. Probably a throwback to his days in lecture halls.

"A problem, you said. . . ."

Labate blinked, then nodded. "Oh, yes. Fascinating, all of this. Well, now. Let me give you some background information first. One of my graduate students. . . ." He pointed to a dark-haired young man seated at a console across the room—the only other occupant of the Observatory. "Name of Boucher. Robert Boucher. He was on shift here about an hour ago. We've been running some routine measurements on the Tarantula. . . . You know, the Great Looped Nebula. It's in the large Magellanic Cloud in the Constellation *Doradus*. The biggest we know of its kind, with a diameter of eight hundred light-years."

Speaking with soft urgency, Labate moved his hands about as though in some scientific sign language. His thin grey eyebrows rose and fell emphatically. "Now," he continued—and though Kemp knew some of what he was saying, he let the man tell his story unimpeded—"part of our project concerns photometric analysis. We set up a large array of aligned photometers, each focused on a small, sequential feature of the Nebula, each comparing radiation output from hard U.V. out to the near infrared. Three-micrometer cut-off. Each photometer covers a small arc of the sky. Do you follow me so far?"

Kemp smiled patronizingly and nodded. He shifted his weight

8

casually and leaned against the edge of the computer console behind him, keeping his stare intent despite his feeling. *This couldn't be that important. An interesting astronomical discovery. No crisis.*

"We were getting reams of good hard data. Fascinating results, but totally reasonable. Until tonight."

"Okay. I'll bite. *What* happened *tonight?*" Finally it was coming out. He'd discover why the priority-intercept line had buzzed him from a deep sleep and he'd been summoned here.

"I'm getting to that. My grad assistant, Boucher, was sitting right here, monitoring the displays, when he noticed an unexpected *peak* on one of the photometers in the array."

"Indicating what?"

Labate shrugged. "Any number of things. Boucher immediately checked the most obvious—instrument malfunction—but he couldn't find anything wrong. Could have been some kind of stellar eruption—a nova in Tarantula—but it was so brief we had to discount that kind of explanation." The older man drew a breath, exhaled. "Boucher logged in the peak and continued to monitor the system, until he noticed that other photometers in the array were producing *peaks at regular intervals.* The display was linear for all intents, and each peak was equal in strength. Now Boucher's from Princeton—he's here on an IASA Fellowship—and he's one of my better assistants. He immediately considered the possibility that the instruments were not picking up a disturbance within the Great Looped Nebula, but something far closer, something moving *in front of* the field of view. Follow?"

"Meteor storm? New asteroid?" But no, Kemp thought immediately.

Labate shook his head. "Not very likely. Although whatever it was that was producing those photometric peaks was probably quite large, it's doubtful it could be a meteor swarm—too far away, not enough density. And we didn't like the idea of an asteroid because the photometer array is aimed so far off the ecliptic."

"A comet, then." Jeez. This was getting to be like Twenty Questions. Kemp hated games and could not hide the impatience in his voice.

Smiling, Labate clapped his hands together. The sound was

9

sharp and surprising against the soft hums and general low noise of the room. "That's very good, Colonel. *Very* good. All evidence seems to point towards a comet, doesn't it? Indeed, that is what young Boucher imagined. Boucher's comet indeed. The lad was ecstatic." He chuckled, gazing over fondly at his astronomy student.

Kemp surmised the obvious. *"Not* a comet then."

"Odds are very much against it," Labate said crisply. "Unless it's like no comet any of us have ever seen. Boucher called me about an hour ago, several minutes after he picked up on the peaks. We ran a spectroscopic analysis of the object, continued tracking it, and finally compiled a rough set of orbital elements. It's heliocentric, no doubt about it."

"Did that clarify anything?" This *was* strange. Something in a solar orbit. Any object large enough to peak a photometric array might be very large indeed. Something that big, hurtling down the gravity well towards the sun.....Perhaps this was a problem, or could become one.

Labate nodded. "A few things. The object is following a fairly classic cometary, orbital pattern, close to parabolic. Its distance, when sighted, was about eight hundred million kilometers—about the same as Jupiter's orbit. Spectrographic analysis gave us Fraunhofer absorption lines, which was odd, if it was going to be a comet. We then checked for Doppler shift on the sodium D line, as part of the range-rate measurement. As you know, there's no absorption to speak of between here and Jupiter's distance."

Sounded right, but Kemp was not totally sure of the implications. His knowledge of astronomy and astrophysics was comprehensive, but only on the survey level. He was about to ask Labate to clarify when the old man began speaking again, this time more excitedly, his hands twitching even more animatedly.

"So we ran some spectrographic comparisons and found that the orbital spectrum was an *exact match of the solar spectrum*, slightly shifted by Doppler effect. Do you understand what that means?"

Kemp had played along so far, but he was getting weary of this. Phineas Kemp could be as polite as necessary to humor anyone, but he wasn't by nature a mild man prone to gentleness for its own sake. He knew how to wield both politeness and sternness. Both played a part in leadership, and it was the latter that he began to employ now, with steely efficiency.

"I'm not sure I do, Professor. But if this is indeed as important as you think it is, you had better stop playing teacher and start filling me in with the straight scoop."

Blinking and cringing a bit, Labate seemed a little surprised at the rebellion of his temporary student.

"Well, I'm not *sure* what it is, mind you. But it appears to be something very large, and with a highly reflecting surface. Smooth enough to produce photometric peaks whenever that smooth surface faces the sun and reflects back the light. Whatever it is, it is probably engaged in some kind of slow, but regular *tumbling* motion—hence the regularly spaced and timed peak intervals."

"I see . . . and this behavior is unnatural for any known solar system bodies?"

Labate shook his head. "There's nothing out there that *we* know about with an all-wavelength better than .99, Colonel. *Nothing!* And don't forget those first-look orbital elements. It has come in from a long way out. Maybe as far as Pluto."

Kemp looked away from the Professor, glancing absently at the banks of instruments and displays within the Lunar Observatory. Beyond the instruments yawned a large observation bay window which presented a view of the sloping shelf upon which the Observatory rested. Spreading out into the main depression of the crater lay the sprawl of dome-structures which comprised the Lunar Colony. Beyond the Colony, the short horizon of the moon edged out the velvet-black sky. Somewere out there, thought Kemp, an object was hurtling towards the sun . . . towards mankind.

"How long before you'll have some more hard data?" he asked Labate.

"Not long. Another hour and we will have enough to make some more correlations. If the object has an unpowered orbit, we will have a good lock on it. We will have velocity, period, eccentricity, semi-major axis . . . maybe even its size and mass."

"Right," said Kemp, employing all his authoritative manner. "I'm going to have to put a security blanket on this project. I'm sure you're aware of that, aren't you, Professor?"

Labate sighed. "I was expecting it. I'd be surprised if you didn't."

"How about Boucher? We can't let this information slip out. Could get in the wrong hands. Has he been in contact with anyone since the beginning of this business?"

"Absolutely not. Only me."

"Very well. I want you to assume command of this operation. Boucher will be assigned to you, and will remain here. I'll have Rheinhardt provide you with meals and some security personnel, if this thing drags out to a few days and you two need sleep. In effect, you're going to be confined to the Observatory."

"I practically live here anyway. Boucher, though. . . ."

"We'll have to issue some kind of cover story for your confinement. Security will take care of things. From now on, all communications to and from the Observatory will be classified and on Security Intercept. I'm going to convene a meeting of the Joint Chiefs right away . . . that is, as soon as you get the rest of the hard data collected. When you tie down an orbit, I want you to present the information to the Staff." Kemp adjusted the collar of his uniform, cleared his throat. "Now, tell Boucher I'd like to have a few words with him. . . ."

CHAPTER 2

WITH A TENTATIVE SMILE, Becky set the plate down before him. "Best I could do at such short notice," she said, wrapping her dressing gown tighter around her slim body.

"Thanks," said Kemp. He picked up a piece of toast and began to munch it between sips of steaming, aromatic tea. He scanned the preliminary readouts that Professor Labate had provided.

"Joint Chiefs of Staff meeting in an hour, huh?" said Becky, settling down with her own plate of soy-sausage and scrambled reconstituted eggs.

"Yeah." The hard facts had come in, and they'd been absolutely incredible. Labate was going to present them to the meeting, implications and all. That was going to be some meeting, all right. "You stuck around just to find out what was going on, right?"

"I stuck around because I fell back to sleep, Phineas." Her

dark and attractive Semitic features lost their smile. "I just happened to overhear—"

"And you're just dying to know what all the hoopla is about. I know you, my dear. I don't blame you. I'd be the same way. But frankly, this is classified stuff. I can't tell you."

She wiped her long black hair away from her face and glared at him, ignoring her meal. "You know, Phineas, you're probably the most tight-assed man I've ever met. I truly resent your lack of trust in me. I want to talk about it. It goes deeper than just this and—"

Kemp cut her off with a single cold and curt word. "Later."

She blinked her dark brown eyes in a vexed manner, and then settled down into a surly silence over her breakfast.

Too bad she'd stayed the night. This wouldn't have had to happen. Rebecca Thalberg was the one person he really didn't like to treat this way. But the qualities he admired most in her—curiosity, intelligence, and a cute womanish stubbornness—were also the things that caused them to occasionally lock horns. Still, he loved her. She was different from the other women he had known. And Kemp had known plenty of women. They were attracted to his rugged good looks, his abrasive, cocky demeanor, his status as a rising star...a man to be respected and listened to. A man in *control*. But Kemp's affairs with women had always managed to be such ephemeral, casual liaisons. The women had never seemed to be able to delve beneath his surface, and he'd never sought to know them in any other way than physically. Rebecca was different. She'd met him will to will, and demanded that he know her as a person. Kemp had chosen to do just that, and there were moments, like this, that he regretted that.

Still, she was a beautiful woman. He liked the way her raven hair was parted in the middle, with little curl or additional arrangement—the way it framed her oval face. He liked the way her high-breasted body shone with health and warmth. She was the Coordinator of Copernicus Biomedical Division, clever and intelligent, gentle and loving...and sometimes a royal pain in the ass.

He played with his eggs as he concentrated again on the figures, reading them over again to make sure his eyes hadn't played tricks on him.

A large unidentified body was entering the main plain of the solar system at an oblique angle, out near the orbit of Jupiter, approximately forty degrees to the ecliptic. Cometary orbit with a period of about two hundred years. Velocity, thirty kilometers per second, increasing as object approached perhelion, closest position to Earth before heading back out.

The thing was some kind of cylinder.

Three hundred and twenty kilometers in length.

Sixty-five kilometers in diameter.

And it wasn't a comet, either. Labate's mass estimates indicated that neither was it a solid body.

Question was, just *what was* the thing?

He swallowed the last of the tea, packed the papers together, and placed them in his briefcase. He pushed the half-eaten breakfast away and stood to go, still feeling baffled and excited and . . . somehow, distant. If Labate's wildest notion were reality . . . the thought just took one's breath away.

"You're not finishing?" Becky said, trying to take the sourness out of her voice. She wasn't one for holding grudges, though when her temper flared, it was scorching.

"No. I'm sorry, but I'm just not hungry. This is pretty important stuff, Becky. I . . . I *do* wish I could tell you about it, but—"

"I know. You're a stickler for rules. Especially for your *own* rules. Never sleep with your girlfriend more than three times a week; it takes too much time and attention away from work otherwise. Never take more than a half-day a week off. People depend upon you. Never say 'I love you' other than when absolutely necessary. Makes your lover too smug and self-assured and hard to handle. Have everything in control. Never let loose of too much emotion. Kemp's Commandments." She spoke blithely, with no bitterness.

"I do love you. You know that."

"Do I? Hmm. I guess the only reason I put up with your crap is that I love you too."

"Rotten luck, right?" Relieved, he let go of a boyish grin.

"For me, maybe. You seem to handle yourself pretty well."

"Thank you for staying, Becky. Thank you for breakfast." Almost reluctantly, she accepted the invitation of his open arms, hugging him softly and firmly.

15

"One promise." she said.

"Which is?"

"You'll tell me what all this was about at least one minute before you are officially allowed to."

"I think that can be arranged."

The shuttle whined to a stop. Phineas Kemp jumped onto the subway platform. The terminal was almost empty at this early hour since the night shift—a skeleton crew anyway—was still on duty, and the day-personnel were probably still sleeping. Kemp took the elevator to the top floor of the Admins Dome, the only level located on the lunar surface.

As he entered the office complex, he nodded curtly to the security woman on duty. He walked straight through to his office, adjacent to the conference room. Soon that chamber would be occupied by the Joint Chiefs, sealed off from the rest of the base under a Level One Security net. Kemp knew that he should be preparing some kind of introductory speech, something to quickly explain the nature of the emergency conference, but the words would not come to him. Instead, thoughts of his father kept interfering. Kemp tried to temper those memories by asking himself how his father might handle the impending situation. The old boy had indeed had quite an effect on him, Kemp thought, smiling with a touch of sadness.

Kemp walked to the broad, curving slope of smoked glass, the executive-sized window which gave him a spectacular view of the northern quadrant of Copernicus Base. Roughly a hexagon in design, the Colony was a series of domes and geodesic structures connected by underground tunnels. Eighty percent of the Colony was located beneath the surface of the crater basin, partially for protection from the infrequent meteoroid showers, but primarily because it allowed a more efficient use of lunar construction materials. Copernicus Base was the oldest permanent lunar settlement. Hard to believe it would soon be celebrating its thirtieth anniversary. During that time, it had grown from its original complement of twenty-eight men and women to its present permanent population of eight hundred and sixty. Copernicus was the first extraterrestrial Small Town, containing everything from a general store to a village barber shop.

Kemp supposed that the Base would remain the crowning achievement of technology until the L-5 Colony progressed beyond the planning and financing stages and actually began construction. At thirty-seven, Phineas Kemp was proud to have been placed in charge of Copernicus. An honor, yes . . . but he always felt that his appointment had also been a testament to his exemplary record as an astronaut. His record of space "firsts" would never be equalled, and he often imagined that his name would find a place in the history texts beside Lindbergh's, Gagarin's, and Armstrong's. There had been a time in Kemp's career when he thought about this kind of paper immortality so much that it seemed to be his consuming passion, the driving source of his energy and competence. His father had always wanted him to be the best—the best at *whatever* he attempted— and he had dedicated his life to that end.

But now, as Kemp sensed the age of forty rapidly approaching, he also sensed a subtle change in his attitudes toward life in general, his *own* life in particular. Some of the things which had seemed so important earlier had lost their fascination. Priorities were slowly shifting, rearranging themselves in his mind, and there were times when Phineas Kemp felt insecure, actually felt unsure about how he would conduct his future affairs.

Smiling, Kemp shook his head slowly as he stared up at the blue-green jewel that was the Earth. His colleagues perceived him as astute, authoritative, decisive, unshakably calm, and ambitious. He did not want them to alter their opinions one jot. And yet . . . he was getting tired—tired at such a young age. It almost seemed criminal to him. He thought of his father, and how that man had driven himself and his small Canadian semi-conductor company to the heights of the industry, wondering how embarrassed he would feel to know his son was . . . what? Growing *bored* with over-achievement? *Impossible! Bullcrap!* the old man would have said, and Phineas would have agreed with him.

But something was happening to him. Things were changing. He thought it might be Rebecca. . . . Perhaps that "urge to settle down" his mother had confidently assured him would strike him someday was slowly sinking its sedentary hooks in.

Kemp looked down at his watch. They were all late. He'd

been the only one on time. Typical. They'd all feel pretty bad when they discovered the importance of the meeting. Something had to be done immediately, before Ramadas Khan Base got word of this business. That could be a very sticky situation. He glanced again out the observation port. The Earth, covered with angel-hair wisps, hung several degrees above the horizon. It looked so close that one might be able to reach out and touch it. His home . . . but he'd never be able to appreciate it again. No. Almost instinctively, he knew that his destiny lay somewhere beyond the Earth, in the stars. He'd known that, or sensed it rather, since his early adolescence when his father helped him build a telescope from the Edmund Scientific Company. After all the hours in the dusty basement, grinding lenses, machining the fittings, mounting everything, it had been such a joy to take the instrument out into the crisp, black night in the back yard, where the universe peered down at him. Some called it a sense of wonder, of coming to terms with the boundless cosmos, but Kemp called it a sense of destiny.

The intercom chimed.

"Security, sir. Doctor Labate, Major Rheinhardt, Doctor Kolenkhov, and the rest of the Joint Chiefs of Staff have just arrived."

Kemp closed his eyes almost solemnly, thinking of Labate's closing words to him: *"Yes. Yes, Colonel. It looks that way. Some kind of spaceship. Chances are good. An* alien *spaceship."*

Kemp said, "Send them in, please."

CHAPTER 3

LIKE A GIGANTIC INSECT, the *Astaroth* hung in the blackness of space, hovering silently.

The general symmetry of the cylindrical ship was broken by a series of three-dimensional trapezoids—the outer bulkheads of its great ore-holds. The bow comprised two command blisters which resembled multifaceted eyes—further enhancing the insect-image of the enormous vessel. Within its hull labored the ore-crushers, the processors, and the furnaces. The *Astaroth* was a self-contained factory in space which provided metals and alloys to the IASA moonbases and Bradbury Station, the Mars colony.

On the belly-side of the ship hung a series of launch-bays—each platform holding two- and four-man ships. These smaller crafts, official^{...}signated as SP2's and SP4's, were nicknamed "Snipes" by the miners. The little ships were employed primarily as surveying/prospecting vessels and were crammed with all manner of detection and measurement gear. Shaped like teardrops with the point-ends truncated, the Snipes were powered by small but efficient MHR reaction engines. They had exceptional range and maneuverability, and were equipped with retractable "grapples"—servo arms which allowed the Snipes to attach to the rough-contour surfaces of asteroids and ferry them back to the *Astaroth*'s ore-holds for crushing and processing.

At launch bay six, Peter Melendez and "Big Chuck" O'Hara climbed into their Snipe, sealed the hatches, and waited for bay-decompression and subsequent ejection into space. They had, only minutes previously, been ushered from Major Franco's office after receiving concise, if mysterious, orders.

Neither man had spoken since entering the ship, other than to verify pre-launch checks on their consoles, but when the routine task had been completed and final countdown had commenced, O'Hara nudged his partner and put a hand over his throat-mike. "What do you figure's going on?" he asked in a husky whisper. O'Hara was a large, beefy man. His face was round and freckled, his complexion always on the florid side. He looked like a hard drinker and would have been if IASA regulations were not so strict about such things. It had been more than five decades since man had entered space, and more than two decades since the frontiers had been opened up for the common man—the blue-collar, workaday types who would build Earth's extraplanetary empires. Big Chuck O'Hara was one of those men. He was a miner, with a miner's view of the world, whether back on Earth or out in the asteroid belt.

After hearing O'Hara's question, Peter Melendez only shrugged, then indicated that they wait until their mikes were not patched directly into the *Astaroth*. Melendez was almost a perfect opposite of O'Hara: small of frame, delicate features, soft-spoken, and well-educated. He had been working on a post-graduate degree in Sociology at Cornell several years ago when he abruptly had become bored with it all. He'd acquired a wanderlust which had eventually led into space—the IASA Mining Division being the only branch of the service which would accept him. After a quiet life of safe, dilettante experiences, Peter Melendez had decided he would cast it aside for a sample of the rugged existence of the "new frontier."

As the countdown ebbed away, Melendez glanced over at his partner. He had been running missions with O'Hara for more than three months, and Peter was growing tired of the man's abject boorishness. Their cabin conversations comprised little more than O'Hara's running monologues about women and tales of his physical prowess in fights.

Melendez was beginning to think that the new frontier was not so very new after all, and he had been having thoughts of going home. But now his blood was up. Something odd was going on, and Peter was curious to know why Major Franco had sent them out on a very secretive recon mission.

A lurch. A sudden assault of G-forces. The Snipe catapulted from the launch bay. Automatically, the engines cut in, stabilizing the craft. The intersect coordinates had already been keyed into the Snipe's on-board computer, and the little ship began burning through the darkness towards a predetermined rendezvous point. For the moment, at least, O'Hara would have little to do in the way of piloting the craft.

"Pretty strange, isn't it?" croaked the bigger man, rubbing his mouth with the back of his hand the way he did when he hadn't had a drink all day.

"I guess so," said Melendez, pretending to be carefully examining his consoles of detection and recon gear. "Wait a second, will you?"

The radio crackled in their headphones. "SP2 double A, this is Big Mother. We have an A-OK launch here. Do you copy?" Major Franco's voice.

"We copy, Big Mother," said O'Hara. "Launch is nominal, and we are locked into programmed flight."

"Stand by, SP2 double A. Further instructions to follow. Out."

O'Hara flipped off the radio and looked at Melendez. "Now tell me, what do you think is goin' on? And what'd you mean— you *guess* so?"

Peter Melendez looked up from his consoles. O'Hara's face was a mixture of curiosity and intimidation. "I don't know what to make of the secrecy, if that's what you mean. We're supposed to run a recon mission. You know as much as I do."

"Which ain't much," said O'Hara. "And I thought you college guys were supposed to be so smart! You don't know nothin'...."

"Hey, knock it off, will you?" Melendez attempted to keep the anger from his voice, hoping that an honest plea for something approaching camaraderie might be successful.

"I'll tell you what *I* think. I think it's them friggin' A-rabs. They've probably got some kind of ship out here in our territory."

"I doubt it," Melendez responded. "The TWC doesn't have any ships that can operate this far out."

"Then what the hell is it we're supposed to be lookin' for?"

Melendez sighed. "You heard what Franco said. Copernicus picked up some kind of object in this quadrant and they want a close-up look. That's *all* he said, for God's sake."

"Well, I was just thinkin'.... You don't think they'd send us out here to do anything ... you know ... *dangerous?*"

Melendez shrugged. "How the hell do I know? I mean, look at our *jobs*. They're not exactly what I'd call 'safe.' "

Their helmet phones crackled again as Major Franco's voice cut in: "Okay, SP2 double A, our telemetry is affirmative for a Number One intersect. Autoguidance until you achieve a visual contact. Manual after that. Do you copy?"

"We copy that," said Peter. "Can you tell us what we're going to be making visual contact *with?*"

"Negative. When you get within range, I'm told you won't be able to miss it. That's all I can tell you right now. Proceed on course. When you make visual, you will be patched in to a Priority Channel with Copernicus on a scramble-sequence. You will have to validate before beginning the transmission. Frequency 204.8. Do you copy?"

"We copy," said Melendez. "What is present ETA?"

A brief pause. "For visual, or course intersect?"

"Either one will do."

"ETA for intersect is thirty-two minutes. Can't give you visual...."

"Why not?" Melendez did not like the tone in Franco's voice.

"Sorry, SP2 double A. I can't talk about it. We are standing by for visual confirmation. Big Mother, out."

"Roger, Big Mother," said Melendez, flipping off the transmission key.

"He can't talk about it," said Peter. "That's crazy, isn't it?"

O'Hara harrumphed. "Ain't the only thing that's crazy. Like how come they picked you for this mission. Me, I can figure. . . . I been with this outfit for almost ten years—they *know* I'm good. But you! You ain't been space-boomin' for more than a year or so."

Melendez smiled. "I learn fast, I guess." He did not really feel like talking to his partner, especially when he was in one of his argumentative, aggressive moods. Peter Melendez *did* share O'Hara's apprehension concerning the mission, but he did not want to talk about it. They would know what they were looking for soon enough. He stared through the forward port into the endless velvet night.

Neither man spoke for several minutes. There was tension in the atmosphere of the small ship's cabin, but Melendez was able to ignore it by directing his thoughts outward, to the possible reasons for the recon mission. It *was* possible that the brass had picked up a TWC ship in the vicinity. Was it armed? Disabled? Maybe no one knew what it was doing out here. The thought was troubling. The Third World countries were not very advanced in space technology. Indeed, the only thing they had actually accomplished was a lunar settlement. Aside from the two IASA moonbase installations—Copernicus Base and Tsiolkovskii Base, both staffed by the combined space agencies of North America, Europe, and the Soviet Union, there were two other permanent colonies: a fledgling enterprise recently established by the Chinese—Dua Ho Chang, and an older installation erected by the Third World Confederation—tagged the TWC. That base was called Ramadas Khan and it was the final glorious breath of the TWC, having been built soon after the close of the twentieth century, when the emerging African nations and the Arab political estates were at the peak of their power. Within the intervening quarter-century, however, after the oil-depletion leverage of the Third World had been exhausted with the extinction of petroleum, the TWC became a second-rate political influence in global affairs. Since that time, the TWC had clung to their moonbase, recognizing it as a final vestige of their past glory, even though they were partially dependent on the IASA for logistical and technological support.

If it was a TWC ship, though, why were they sending out a Snipe? wondered Melendez. Tensions between the IASA nations and the TWC persisted, to say the least. In fact, there was an unspoken tradition of hostility, and several "incidents" within the past decade could have easily escalated into direct military confrontation, had not the diplomats of the involved countries been quick to ameliorate the disputes. True, the world did not hang in such precarious balance as in the previous century. But the utopian vision of political and economic harmony among nations was still quite distant.

As far as Melendez knew, though, the TWC just didn't have the hardware to get out here. Their Deep-Space vessels were obsolete and their telemetry equipment was ten years behind state-of-the-art.

So what was it they were going after?

Melendez's thoughts kept tumbling over and over, and he wanted to verbalize them, but talking to O'Hara was not fruitful, to say the least. The man did his job, and that was all.

Checking his watch, Melendez realized that they were within fifteen minutes of ETA with the object. He stared absently through the port, into the bottomless pit of stars, remembering how it had been when he'd first ventured into space. He had since overcome those early feelings of fear and insignificance but there remained a sincere *respect* and a sense of wonder about the universe. Melendez felt that he truly appreciated the vastness of the galaxy, the implications of the hundreds of millions of suns which burned in the darkest of nights. Here he was, a speck of bone and blood, a smear of chemicals crawling across this immense canvas. A cold, insensitive place, it made you appreciate the only true warmth in the universe for human beings—the warmth of *other* human beings.

Something flickered on his long-range scanner displays. The instruments were picking up an object. Other sensors were also flashing into screen-brilliance. A solid object of incredible proportions. . . . Melendez keyed in a request for some preliminary figures.

The display blinked. Numbers appeared.

Distance from object: 4100 kilometers. Mean dimensions

of object: 321.45 kilometers by 64.78 kilometers.

Melendez re-keyed the request. Couldn't be anything out there *that* big if it was a ship. Theirs *or* ours. Surely, if it was an asteroid, the Survey would have known about its existence a long time ago, especially if it was off the ecliptic.

The display screen blinked. The same numbers reappeared. Melendez checked again, just to be certain before contacting the *Astaroth*. No error. Whatever it was, the Snipe was gliding toward it at a speed of six kilometers per second.

"Hey Chuck. Look at this," Melendez said in a soft voice.

O'Hara looked. "What the hell is it?" His tone of voice had changed from condescension to something milder.

"Don't know. We're not in visual mode yet. But it's damned big. We should be seeing it soon...."

"You'd better get the *Astaroth*...."

"Yeah." Melendez keyed in his mike. "Big Mother, this is SP2 double A.... Do you copy? SP2 double A, calling Big Mother...."

"Big Mother here." Major Franco's voice swept through the phones.

"Major, we have scanner-contact." Melendez read out the incoming data. "Visual will come momentarily. It's *big*, Major."

"Affirmative, SP2 double A. I have orders to patch you directly to Copernicus now. Good luck, gentlemen. Big Mother, out."

Static crackled, followed by a series of bleeps and clicks as the scrambler codes activated. All transmissions from the Snipe would now be beamed hundreds of millions of kilometers back to the moon. Traveling at the speed of regular radio waves, communication from the asteroid belt to the lunar surface would have required a fifteen-minute time lag between transmission and reception. Thus, an inquiry and the reception of an answer would consume a half hour of real time. Communicaton over the immense distance within the solar system would be frustrating if the IASA were constricted by the old laws of relativistic physics. Indeed, it was the discovery of the tachyon—that particle zipping along at hyper-light speeds, incapable of deceleration *below* the speed of light—which had made Deep-Space Operations feasible. Deep Space communications were accomplished by means of a tachyon wave-generator.

Peter Melendez keyed in the proper frequency code, which would validate the Priority Channnel transmission, and waited.

At Copernicus Base, it was early afternoon. Business as usual for the majority of lunar base personnel. Almost eight hours had passed since Phineas Kemp had convened the meeting of the Joint Chiefs. Only a handful of high-echelon Copernicus staff knew of the as-yet-unidentified object. Kemp was pleased with the efficiency and smoothness of Oscar Rheinhardt's Security operations.

Copernicus Base hummed with the life of the hive: farmers, mechanics, technicians, scientists, administrators, pilots, all busily engaged in their duties, all necessarily unaware of the drama about to unfold in Deep Space, thought Phineas Kemp.

Attired in his Informal Officer's jumpsuit, he paced back and forth in the Communications Center, waiting. Waiting and brooding. The room was empty except for Major Alterman, Director of Communications for Copernicus Base—one of the few personnel briefed on the current Security topic. The room was bathed in a soft darkness above, illuminated only by the operational lights on the consoles. It was cool and quiet with the relaxing murmurs and thrums of smoothly functioning machinery permeating the atmosphere.

In contrast, Kemp felt tense.

The image of the reactions of the Joint Chiefs to Labate's pronouncements still registered in his mind. Kemp realized they were merely reflections of his own awe. The words reverberated.

"*. . . initial sign of its presence was a series of luminosity peaks. These peaks were caused by the specular reflection of solar radiation off the surfaces of the object—*flat *surfaces,*" Professor Labate had told them. "*The intervals between reflectance peaks indicate that the object is rotating about a principal axis of inertia. It's an immense cylinder, tumbling end-to-end through space as it approaches the sun. Whenever the flat ends of the cylinder face the sun, we get a bright flash of reflected radiation and light. Spectrometer readings suggest that it is of a metallic substance of uniform characteristics. The object is emanating some kind of VLF electromagnetic field. So far we have not been able to identify its nature, although*

*the parameters indicate something of a fairly large order, well
within the limits defined by a controlled fusion reaction."*

They'd immediately realized the implications of that. Kemp's
own words had almost been superfluous. *"A ship. Evidently
been there in orbit for a sizable amount of time. Some product
of an alien civilization."*

The expressions of the others had changed rapidly, passing
through stages of shock, flickering briefly through a spectrum
of awe and confusion, finally settling into acceptance. Excited
acceptance.

Security measures previously implemented by Kemp had
been reinforced by Oscar Rheinhardt, Security Chief. No doubt
neither the Chinese or the Khan Base had any idea of what
was out there. Their equipment was not as good. Still, they
could take no chances. The discovery was of immense political
importance, to say nothing of scientific significance. Officially,
the Observatory claimed it had had a hardware crash on the
machinery pertinent to the discovery, and were awaiting repairs.

Because it would take an estimated four weeks to reach the
object if they deployed one of the ships in the lunar area, it
had been decided to use a DS mining operation in the approximate vicinity of the object's closest approach to the asteroid
belt. Two ore-processing ships were within range: the *Astaroth*
and the *Cassandra*. The Mission Commander of the *Astaroth*
was a former crewman of Kemp's—Major Altimiras Franco.
He could be trusted. The Joint Chiefs had agreed.

He was in charge of the first operation with the chance of
contacting an alien intelligence. How about that, Dad, Kemp
thought to himself as he waited. How about that.

Alterman looked up, his beard strangely underlit by the
instrument lighting. "Colonel, we've just gotten word from the
Astaroth. Their Snipe reports instrument-contact with the object
and Major Franco is patching us in."

Finally! thought Kemp, turning quickly and returning to the
central console. He slid into a chair next to Alterman, strapping
a throat mike to his neck quickly. "Thank you, Major. Ready
when you are."

"The Snipe's just keyed in his scramble-sequence. Go ahead,
Colonel."

"Copernicus Base, calling SP2 double A. Do you copy?"

"This is SP2 double A, Copernicus. Spec-5 Peter Melendez on the com. How is my signal, Copernicus?"

"We copy, Sp2 double A. This is Colonel Phineas Kemp, Melendez. What have you got for us?"

As the Snipe crewman repeated his initial data material, Kemp nodded to himself, then signaled Major Alterman to contact Security Chief Rheinhardt, Scientific Operations Chief Marcia Bertholde, and Gregor Kolenkhov, Chief of Support Operations, a summons which would bring them immediately to the Communications Center from where they waited on stand-by, quite close.

"We copy that, Melendez," Kemp said. "You should be getting a visual any minute now. In the meantime I want all instrument-data on telemetry ASAP."

"Roger, Copernicus. Stand by, please."

Panels on the console began flashing and blinking within three seconds. Display screens began accumulating rows and columns of data. Kemp nodded to himself as he spoke again. "All right, SP2 double A, we have a copy on your telemetry. Copernicus Base is standing by until you have visual confirmation."

"We copy," said Melendez. "SP2 double A, standing by."

Kemp leaned back in his console chair and exhaled slowly. The feelings of tenseness mixed with ennui had been extinguished—at least for the moment. Memories flashed through his mind, and he briefly recalled scenes from his years in space. The claustrophobic cabins, the eternal night always threatening to swallow you up, tension as thick as the smell of your sweat. Kemp remembered and he wished that it was *him* in that Snipe, drawing close to the unknown object.

A door slid open at the far end of the chamber. Turning, Kemp saw the other members of the Staff enter quickly. The expression on their faces betrayed anxiety mixed with excitement.

Kemp motioned them over to the console, and began to explain the current situation.

After keying out the throat mike, Melendez turned to O'Hara. "Kemp! Colonel Phineas Kemp. Commander of Copernicus Base, and he was talking to *us* on Priority Channel."

O'Hara was staring straight ahead, as though afraid of what he might see looming from the darkness. "I don't like it," he said softly. "We've been thrown into something big, Melendez. Why else would the top brass be interested in what we're doin'?"

"Yes. My feeling exactly. For once in my life, I think I agree with you." Melendez smiled to relieve the growing tension, but O'Hara was in no mood for it. The larger man grimaced and returned his gaze to the forward viewing port.

"Jeez! What's *that?* See it? Something just flashed!"

Melendez had trouble speaking. "Yes. We're closing in on it. Relative velocity down to five KPS plus. Hang on. . . ."

O'Hara obeyed, then breathed deeply several times, nervously rubbing his lips with the back of his hand. "Bigger every second. Christ almighty, that's it! Look!"

Staring into the speckled night, Melendez concentrated on something shining with grey-whiteness . . . a metallic glint. The object appeared to be a rectangle, much longer than it was wide, growing larger. As the Snipe homed in on the object, the resolution became more clear, the configuration more distinct.

An immense cylinder. Slowly tumbling, end over end. . . .

O'Hara cleared his throat. "I seen a lotta rocks in my time, but I ain't seen nothin' like that. Ain't no asteroid, that's for sure."

Melendez realized he was gawking. "I'd better get Copernicus back on line." Unsteadily, he keyed in the mikes, and spoke his identification, following it with: "We have a visual."

"We copy, SP2 double A. We have your current velocity at 5.3 kilometers per second. Distance from the object 2.67 thousand kilometers. Do you copy that?"

"Affirmative, Copernicus," Melendez said after a glance at his readouts. "Do you suggest deceleration and manual control at this time?"

"Affirmative. Cameras on, now. We want to *see* that thing."

"I'm switching to VOR transmission immediately."

The instructions were quickly punched into the instruments. In addition to the omnifrequency scanners, sensors, spectrometers, and other analyzing instruments, three high-resolution Hitachi-Kodak VOR cameras zoom-focused on the object. One

29

camera transmitted crystal-clear images in the visible spectrum, while the others produced infrared and ultraviolet images.

"All right, SP2 double A. We have a signal. Good hard line. Continue to monitor your telemetry and approach the object on manual."

"Switching, " said Melendez as he nodded to O'Hara, who punched out the autoguidance and assumed control of the small ship.

"SP2 double A standing by," he said, then keyed out the throat mikes. The cylinder was already much larger, he noticed. Its dimensions were staggering . . . and they still had more than a thousand kilometers to go! "How's it going?" he asked O'Hara.

"Fine." O'Hara did not look at him, but continued staring at the cylinder which floated silently ahead of them.

It *was* hard to keep your gaze away from the object. Now that its shape was clearly discernible, it was obvious that it was no natural formation—asteroid, meteor, or even a monstrous chunk of frozen water or gases. A perfect cylinder—hundreds of times larger than the tallest building. Impossibly large, thought Melendez, yet there it was filling up the viewport with its bulk. The thought kept hitting him over and over: something this large, so cleanly devised, had to have been designed. *Created.*

The notion could hardly mesh with his acceptance, and yet before him was all the evidence he needed.

"Oh, Jesus, I don't believe it. I *don't* believe it," said O'Hara, his voice soft, almost reverent. "What the hell *is* it, Melendez?"

"I think you know about as much as I do, O'Hara." A shiver of awe ran down his spine.

The VOR transmissions burst upon the Communications Center screens. Phineas Kemp and the Staff members stared at the images silently, unable to speak. Growing larger, clearer with each second, the representation on the computer-enhanced screens was obviously of an intelligently conceived and constructed object. Kemp could see the first details and markings along the dull, metallic surface. One end of the cylinder was flat and almost featureless, but the opposite end, when it tumbled past the camera's field, revealed large conical things, superstructure and tank-like formations. *Engines.* Engines capable of propelling the monstrous ship across impossible distances among the stars. No other alternative. The ship was not of Earth's stellar system—humankind had already established that it was alone in Sol's collection of planets.

"It *is* a ship," whispered Marcia Bertholde, beginning to look every bit of her forty-nine years. Smoke coiled up from her cigarette, coiling like DNA molecules near her face.

Kemp nodded. "Yes."

Rheinhardt's aging, wrinkled face looked grim. "If you laid it on its side it would stretch from Washington to Manhattan."

Kolenkhov shifted his ample girth uneasily in his seat, hands clasped together as though for a wished-for drink. "What are you going to have those two men do, Phineas?" he asked. "It might be dangerous."

"Observatory data indicates that the object has been locked into that cometary orbit for a long time. The orbit is *very* stable, and the period is precise. Aside from an undifferentiated electromagnetic field—which the Snipe's instruments are picking up *here*"—Kemp pointed to a column of readouts on one of the console's screens—"the object seems to be dead in space, although the scanners indicate a precise axial spin. Probably for artificial gravity inside."

"A derelict?" asked Rheinhardt.

"I don't know," Kemp said slowly. "All I'm saying is that it *appears* to be a derelict. It could have been orbiting the sun for God knows how long."

"Is it safe for those men?"

Kemp looked back at Marcia Bertholde. *"Safe?* How should *I* know? We're in a hostile environment, Marcia. What the hell is 'safe' out here?" He sighed, suddenly sorry he'd snapped like that. "Listen everybody. I don't know what we're dealing with any more than the rest of you. All I know is that we have a chance for an extreme close-up recon of something that appears to be an extraterrestrial object. A *ship*. And we can get a first-hand look at it! I intend to *get* it! If anybody has any objections, I want to hear them. *Now.*"

No one spoke.

The Snipe had come so close to the object that its viewing ports were totally filled with the greyish-silver expanse of its hull. The stars and the darkness had been matted out, effectively removed from reality. It was though the Snipe were preparing to land on the surface of a planet.

"Let's get the hell out of here!" said O'Hara. "We got their pictures. . . . Let's scram."

"I have to call Copernicus first."

"Jeez, I could use a friggin' drink. . . ."

"I could too, Chuck. I could too." Melendez patched in moonbase Communications and voiced the proper contact words.

"We copy. Your telemetry is excellent. We estimate distance at one-forty kilometers. Put in for a matching orbit. I want recon within five hundred meters of the surface, relative velocity less than a hundred kilometers an hour. Can you handle that?"

"We'll try, Copernicus."

"Good luck."

"On-board computer has matched orbit coordinates, Copernicus. Stand by . . . matching orbits." At that moment, the controls were momentarily removed from O'Hara as the autoguidance speeded the vessel to obey the orders.

"Continue close-approach to five hundred meters. Surface-scan velocity One hundred KPH," Colonel Kemp's voice spoke in Melendez's headphones. The thought of coming that close to the immense ship threatened to unnerve him. He concentrated on his instruments.

"Affirmative, Copernicus. Match orbit velocity in five seconds. Stand by."

O'Hara switched off his mike. "Crazy! Friggin' crazy!"

Melendez tried to wave him off, then switched off his mike. "Look, will you keep an eye on the controls, goddammit."

"Listen, Melendez, if there's anybody *inside* that thing, they might not like the idea of us pokin' around out here."

Calming his voice, Melendez said, "Think for a minute, will you? Anybody that is capable of building something like this ship, or whatever it is, doesn't have to be afraid of us. They've probably been aware of *us* a lot longer than we've been aware of them."

"Then how come they haven't sent out no welcomin' committee?" O'Hara's eyes widened. His forehead glistened with sweat. "How come!"

"I don't know," Melendez responded. "Look at the size of the damned thing! I mean, maybe we're so insignificant to them that they don't even care. We're like a little bug crawling along the side of a skyscraper."

The helmet-phones crackled. "SP2 double A, what's going on up there? Everything all right?"

Back to Priority Channel. "Affirmative, Colonel. We have achieved match orbit, and will be assuming manual control. Altitude twelve hundred meters and closing."

"Roger, SP2 double A. At five hundred meters, begin recon toward the closest end of the cylinder."

"Altitude seven hundred meters and closing, stand by. . . ." said Melendez, gazing over at O'Hara, who was nervously controlling the descent of the Snipe. The big man's face was flushed. He was covered with perspiration. His hands trembled slightly.

"Copernicus, we have reached altitude. Close-approach recon beginning now. Instruments are tracking. We have a positive make on all systems. Do you copy?"

"Affirmative. Make your first pass along length."

"Roger, Copernicus. Please stand by." Melendez swallowed with difficulty as he watched the metallic grey expanse of the object sweep past their viewports. An endless stretch of metal, so smooth it could have been polished on a jeweler's wheel. Occasionally the featureless, alien plain was broken by an unidentifiable contour—a housing, a small dome, a piece of superstructure that could be an antennae system, or perhaps even a weapons system. There was no way of knowing.

O'Hara was handling the controls as though in a trance. His eyes stared straight ahead, out at the surface of the vessel. It loomed so close it looked as though one could reach out and touch it. He thought that he might be able to do something to assure O'Hara that they were not in any danger.

"Copernicus, this is Spec-5 Melendez. I was wondering if I might ask you a fairly important question? Important to us, especially."

"Colonel Kemp here. Go ahead, Melendez."

Melendez smiled slightly. He'd long ago discovered that the best way to handle a problem was to attack it straight on. Ask the right questions; get familiar with the authority figures;

don't be afraid. He'd ask what he wanted to know, not caring about the responses he might get as much as his ability to establish a position for himself.

"Thank you, sir," Melendez said. "You see, my partner and I have been wondering just what it is we're scanning. I mean, does Copernicus have any idea? Have you made contact with it?"

"Negative, Melendez. We don't know any more than you. Attempts to communicate with the object on every conceivable band and frequency have been made. All negative. The only signal we detect is a general field display, which indicates some kind of internal activity. We don't know what kind of activity, and we were hoping that you might be able to help us find out. Continue lateral scan, Melendez. We will forward further instructions as necessary. Standing by."

O'Hara pulled his throat mike off and cast it across the console. "They don't care about us!" He continued to stare straight ahead, rocking in his seat, whispering softly to himself. "Christamighty, O Christamighty!"

Poor guy, thought Melendez as he assumed control of the Snipe as well as the instrument monitors. The thought struck him that O'Hara might try something crazy, and he doubted if he had the physical strength to contain him.

He shook the notion from his mind, checked his instruments, and concentrated on the object. Its surface seemed more cluttered now, as the Snipe edged along its length, away from the bow. Configurations and shapes were scattered across the expansive hull, which Peter noticed was turning slowly on its longitudinal axis. He considered reporting this to Copernicus Base, but realized that the scanners would have long ago relayed this movement back to the moon. The rotation did indicate something: the instigation of an artificial gravity *within* the vessel by centrifugal force.

An old idea, but a sensible one, included in the original colony designs of O'Neill back in the last century. This concept made sense, considering the fact that it was alien. The inhabitants might require a gravity-dominated environment so that they might endure the long spans of time needed for interstellar flight.

An alien ship. The phrase resonated in his mind. Hard to

accept. It stretched his mind to the point of snapping. He could understand why O'Hara was tottering on the point of hysteria.

As the Snipe continued its longitudinal course, Melendez noticed a general increase in the complexity of superstructure on the hull. Small hexagons seemed to be placed in clusters of six at regular intervals. Antennae and other unclassifiable projections sprouted in abundance.

"SP2 double A, this is Copernicus. Accelerate to five hundred klicks a second and continue longitudinal course. We want to get a look at the aft section. . . . Do you copy?"

"Copy!"

The Snipe lurched forward under the power from the ship's thrusters, and the landscape of the hull glided by quickly. Melendez guided the ship silently towards the opposite end of the great cylinder. As the Snipe drifted past the end of the cylinder, he felt an instant of vertiginous fear. The maneuver was not unlike driving a car off the edge of the Grand Canyon.

Copernicus, this is SP2 double A. UCR should be giving you pictures of what looks to be the business end of this thing. I'm plotting a transectional course across the diameter. Do you copy?"

"We copy, SP2 double A. Continue on changed course. We *are* standing by. . . ."

Melendez checked his instruments, then stared down at the gigantic funnel-shaped structures which passed beneath the Snipe. They were engines. Immense engines. Literally hundreds of the inverted cones were grouped in clusters of ten. The dimensions were deceiving, for although they looked small in comparison to the bulk of the ship itself, Peter knew that even one of the cones, placed next to the Texas Triangle towers, would make those buildings look like a stack of children's building blocks. He wondered what energies had flowed from these great engines, what kind of force had once collected here.

O'Hara had calmed down considerably. His lips were moving, but he made no sounds, and the rocking motions had slowed to almost nothing. "How you doing, Chuck?"

O'Hara looked at him, but said nothing for a moment. His eyes were blank and lifeless. "Just get me outta here."

There was nothing to say to that.

As the Snipe reached the end of the transect across the

cylinder's diameter, Melendez radioed in for further instructions, which called for another longitudinal scan. Keying in the maneuvers, he guided the little ship past the edge and into position. The delicate fire of the retrorockets responded as Melendez played his control console like a musical instrument.

Some people thrived on moments like these. Others collapsed under the pressure. Phineas Kemp knew there had already been a surfeit of make-or-break moments in his own career . . . and yet, here was another one laying heavy on him. He looked carefully into the faces of the Staff Chiefs, hoping to find an answer, finding nothing.

What should be done?

"Gregor," he said softly. "How long before we can get a reliable analysis of this data?" Kemp waved an arm at the display screens.

The Russian shrugged noncommitally. Gregor was a good friend. A large, going to fat man, he obviously enjoyed the pleasures of a "Western-oriented" style of living. Over the years he had acquired a taste for good California wines and straight poker. Smiles came easily to his Slavic features, but none were forthcoming now. "Not long. An hour or two, if we put enough good people on it."

"They'll all have to be cleared through Security," Rheinhardt reminded him sternly.

Kemp nodded. "Gregor, give him the names you want. Oscar, get those clearances immediately."

"And the men in the ship?" Marcia Bertholde said.

Kemp turned and faced her, retaining his stoical expression. She was a hard one, Marcia was, just waiting to get him through a chink in his armor. She was ruthless and ambitious. But she was also extremely efficient, almost indispensable, in her assigned duties.

"I haven't forgotten them, Marcia." He turned to Kolenkhov. "Gregor. I'd like to get a molecular sample from that thing's hull. What's the feasibility?"

"Shouldn't be a problem. The Snipe's grapples have metal samplers in their tool gauntlets. The miners take rock samples with them all the time."

"Right. We'll give it a try and then get those fellows back

to the *Astaroth.*" He leaned over the communications control. Switched it on. Spoke.

Melendez jumped as Colonel Kemp's voice cut through the cabin's silence. He responded immediately.

Kemp continued. "Listen, Melendez, we have one final task before breaking match orbit. It's been suggested that you can use the soil-samplers on your ship's grapples to get us a molecular sample of the object's hull. You'll have to key in a match for the object's axial rotation. Can you do it?"

Eager to please, Melendez spoke without pausing to consider any possible danger in the request. "Affirmative, Copernicus. On-board has necessary matching capability. Not too different from attaching to a spinning asteroid. We've put down on rocks with worse rotations than this."

"We copy, SP2 double A. Proceed on longitudinal course beyond the aft-end superstructure. Select a suitable touchdown by visual. We will monitor via VOR. Good luck. Copernicus standing by."

O'Hara continued to stare out the viewport, mumbling to himself. Probably better this way. If the big man realized what was coming next, he might short-circuit.

Checking his boards, Melendez began to decelerate, then keyed in a matched orbit request based on the Euler spin parameters of the object. The ship's small computer responded immediately as the durations and designates for thruster-fire appeared on the display screen. Melendez had a moment now to reflect on this final phase of the mission. He kept wondering about *who* might be inside that giant ship . . . and how they might feel about earthmen pouncing on their outer hull and scraping around. A little close-up snooping was one thing. But actually touching down . . . ? That might not be such a good idea.

On the other hand, here was his chance for real achievement. Physical contact with an alien ship. The dream of adventure he'd had for space was now being realized. He'd be a hero.

He could go back and face Caroline now, with a solid and substantial reason for leaving Earth. Maybe she'd understand after this. . . .

The display screen stabilized, the on-board ready for the

complex maneuver which would bring the Snipe down.

"Ready for touchdown," he said.

"We copy. Proceed with caution."

Punching in the instructions, Melendez watched the hull configuration grow larger as the tiny Snipe began its descent. He could see patterns in the collection of hexagon shapes, noted the formations of dome-like blisters spaced evenly across the hull. He saw seams in the metallic surface which might be hatches, and thought of radioing in his observations, before he realized that the Copernicus was seeing it as well.

"Altitude one hundred meters and closing."

The Snipe attained the angular rate coordinates and was now descending at a Sixty-two-degree angle. A large expanse of hull stretched out ahead of the ship's flight path. Melendez thought it would be a good touchdown site.

"I'm within fifty meters of the surface, Copernicus. Do you suggest a hover-attitude or complete touchdown? The grapple has a five-meter range."

"Attempt complete touchdown. We want to be sure of the sample."

"Roger. Eighteen meters and descending."

O'Hara grabbed his shoulder. "Get us outta here, kid. They're gonna kill us."

Ignoring him, Melendez watched the hull of the giant ship rise up to meet them. He could see that its metallic surface was burnished and scored from the abrasions of countless particles and micro-meteorites. How long had this thing been drifting through space?

As the Snipe approached a flat area, Melendez noted movement on the hull.

"Copernicus. Something's moving down there. One of those little domes. Peeling back...."

There was a pause. Then: "We have it on the VOR. Cancel touchdown. Repeat, cancel touchdown and get out of there."

As Melendez reached for the proper key on his control panel, a brief burst of light flashed beyond the viewport.

The blister on the alien ship's hull had disappeared, replaced by an array of parabolic dishes, which immediately converged their beams to intersect with the oncoming Snipe.

The beams of intense energy from the array wrapped the

prospecting ship in a ring of dancing fire. The heat of contact vaporized the outer hull instantly. Decompression blew out Melendez's ears before he could even scream.

The explosion swept him into blindness, then nothingness.

In the black silence of space, there remained a small cloud of debris. Metal fragments. Ash-like swirls of particles. The cloud retained a vague orbit around the gigantic vessel, dissipating gradually into space.

CHAPTER 4

MINUTES FROM IASA JOINT CHIEFS OF STAFF
MEETING, August 15, 2027
(Partial) SUBJECT: ARTIFACT ONE
CLASSIFIED—TOP SECRET
FOR GOVERNMENTAL EXECUTIVE USE ONLY

(Excerpt) FAX SHEET SUPPLIED BY DR. ANDRE
LABATE

RELEVANT INFORMATION

Semi-major axis of orbit: 35.33 Astronomical Units
(highly eccentric perihelion 24 million kilometers)

Orbital period: 210 years

Stability of orbit: unknown, although backward integrations for a hundred thousand years suggest very high stability

Axial rotation period: 360 seconds

Electromagnetic activity: undifferentiated

First Order of Business: Colonel Phineas Kemp exonerated from blame for deaths of miners Charles O'Hara and Peter Melendez. General agreement that SP2 double A destroyed by automatic, unmanned defense system accidently triggered. Still no response from within object (code name, Artifact One).

Second Order of Business: Discussion of security measures (see attached complete report from Security Chief Oscar Rheinhardt).

Third Order of Business: Announcement of plans to intercept Artifact One with a Deep-Space Probeship as soon as possible. Crew of eight to be launched within thirty-six hours, with three objectives:

1. Neutralize defensive systems of Artifact One.
2. Gain access to ship's interior.
3. Analyze and determine feasibility of attaching continuous impulse engines to craft, to guide it back to a geo-lunar synchronous orbit for further intensive study.

Fourth Order of Business: Selection of crew complement. Duties and suitable individuals selected.

Mission Command Pilot:	Douglas Fratz, Lt. Colonel, IASA
Back-up Astrophysicist and Navigations Specialist:	Michael Bracken, Lt. Captain, IASA
Tactical Engineer:	Ian Coopersmith, Captain, IASA
Assistant Tactical Engineer:	Thomas Valdone, Lieutenant, IASA

Weapons Specialist:	Dr. Gerald Pohl, US Army
Exobiologist:	Dr. Amos Hagar, civilian
Communications Officer:	Alan Huff, Lieutenant, IASA
Biomedical Specialist:	Dr. Rebecca Thalberg, IASA

"No," said Kemp, "I won't have it!"

"You were outvoted, dear love," said Becky, smugly walking ahead of him. She had to go back to her apartment to get ready for the trip, then to her laboratory to select the equipment she needed. She could use this spot of adventure. Get away from the drab, sterile Copernicus hallways like the one she walked in now. Get away from Phineas Kemp, and at the same time *prove* herself to him. Clearly that was what was necessary in this war of love in which they were involved. She couldn't convince him to play her way, with warmth and vulnerability, intimacy, and sharing. She had to show him that she was his equal in the things that counted to Phineas Kemp, namely ambition, strength of will, and accomplishment.

Kemp grabbed her arm. "Wait. Will you talk for one minute? There's still time to change your mind."

She swung around to face him. "I'm going, Phineas, and there's nothing that you can do to stop me! I'm the best-suited person on the moon for that position. And I want it!"

She paused for a moment, a bit surprised at Kemp's expression. It wasn't stern or demanding. It was actually soft, almost pleading. Since those poor miners had been killed, he'd been like a rock. Hardly a word from him. He hadn't *touched* her, and he'd repulsed any efforts she'd made to comfort him, damn him. He didn't seem to care much that two lives had been lost—only that his plans had been fouled. Becky could understand his preoccupation. What she couldn't understand was why it seemed to obsess his every waking and sleeping moment, and why he wouldn't let her share some of the burden. He was a self-sufficient bastard, and he'd rather die than show *anyone* that he felt human emotions in times of military stress. Even his lover.

Now, though, there was something like hurt in his attitude.

Hurt—and extreme worry. "Look, Becky. I love you. This has been rough for me. If I had to fret about your safety. . . . I mean, this could be a *very* dangerous mission and. . . ." She was astonished. She swept back her hair and stared straight at him disbelievingly. Was he actually showing honest emotion? Had she managed to tug it out of him? "Well, if I'm thinking about your welfare all the time . . ." He glanced away from her. ". . . I just wouldn't be able to fulfill my duties here at Copernicus properly."

She blinked and dropped her mouth a bit with vexation. Then she spun about and began walking again, faster this time.

He was in excellent physical condition, and it only took a moment for him to catch up with her. "Hey! What did I say?"

"Phineas, I accept the fact that you care more about this blasted job of yours than you care about me. Just don't shove it in my face. You won't have to worry about me." She turned on him quickly, frowning. "I'll just make sure I don't make the mistake of that Snipecrew and follow the more stupid of your orders. My number *one* exercise of that resolution will be to ignore your demand that I don't go on the mission."

He cringed a bit, as though he had been slapped. Stunned, he took a step back. Then his face hardened: his neck muscles tensed. "Very well, Becky. I . . . I'm sorry to try and persuade you against doing what you want. I'll see you before you leave." He turned around and began to walk away. "Maybe."

"Phineas. I didn't mean to phrase it that way."

He ignored her, and continued walking, his footsteps echoing softly in the corridor.

Becky sighed shallowly. Men! They refuse to open up, and when you desperately try to get some emotion out of them with a jab, they reel and then run away from you! Why the hell had she gotten involved with Phineas Kemp, surely one of the worst of the lot! For two years she'd been seeing him, and it had always been this way, never improving. Why? *Why?* Because he was handsome and strong? He was that, certainly. Something melted inside of her when she looked at him. Because he was good in bed? Yes, that too. The best she'd had as far as endurance and technique went. Because he reminded her of her father? Very much so. And at least Phineas never slapped her around.

Because of all those reasons, and because she respected him for his competence. Trusted him. He never lied. Maybe it was because he lacked the imagination, but still it was a sight better than a lot of men she had known whose egos and relationships were propped upon an elaborate structure of dissembling and self-delusion. But above all, there was a part of her that helplessly *surrendered* to him, immersed itself deeply in his being when he was around. It was deep and it was love, no question. He said he loved her too, and perhaps he did in his way. But he refused to surrender to her, give himself to her as she did to him.

So, she figured if she gave him a taste of his own medicine, showed him she was fully as competent as he, *competed* with him (oh, how he relished competition), they might at least be able to begin to discuss things on equal terms. God, how condescending he was sometimes. . . .

Oh, dammit! Don't even think about the self-righteous jerk, Becky told herself. Do what you want to do, she thought as she reached the lift which would take her to her apartment.

She *did* want to go on the mission, and not only to prove herself. Indeed, she felt a sense of awe about the thing. As a specialist in biology and space medicine, extraterrestrial life had always been one of her consuming interests. To think that she was going to have the opportunity to actually examine evidence of it!

She concentrated on this as she entered the lift, struggling very hard not to think of Colonel Phineas Kemp.

For the first time in their relationship, she wanted to think of herself first, herself as the most important person in her life. It was difficult to do that when you were in love with someone, she knew, but there always comes a time when you have to stop thinking about the other person to the exclusion of your own happiness. Just how happy was Phineas Kemp making her anyway?

A tough question to answer.

She reached her apartment level, left the lift, and walked slowly down the corridor to her door. Palming the lock and entering the small living space, Becky paused to look around the room. A picture of Phineas on the dresser portrayed him in his best media-image—waving to the the cameras as he

45

emerged from an orbital lander, holding his helmet jauntlily under his left arm, an award-winning smile on his comely face. It was the Phineas Kemp that the world knew well; Becky wished there was a more personal, warmer side to Colonel Kemp that she alone knew.

She had grown up with a father who had little time for his children. He worked on Seventh Avenue in Manhattan's garment district, spending sixty to seventy hours a week building his financial empire. He built it and died of a heart attack by the age of fifty-six, and Becky often mused that the most important thing he had ever said to her was "Pass the salt" when they were seated together at the dinner table. It is often said that people choose mates in relationships that are close to the templates of their most influential parent. Could it be that Becky's father, by his very indifference to her, had influenced her more than her overly protective mother?

An interesting thought, that.

Becky had always been more of a cool thinker, respectful of the rational idea, the empirical approach to problem solving. She prided herself in being of the scientific bent all through school, but she secretly feared that she was suppressing her emotional side. In fact, when she really analyzed herself objectively, she suspected that she was a closet romanticist, that she really needed someone to be sweet and sappy with. She wanted someone who remembered anniversaries and silly little things, someone who sent her flowers for no reason at all, someone who gave from the heart without being asked first.

And it wasn't that Phineas Kemp was not capable of those kinds of things. No, it was simply that they never occurred to him. Becky knew that he would normally try to give her anything she asked for; she was simply tired of having to go through the motions of asking.

What happened to spontaneity? To pleasant surprise?

Her decision to go on the *Heinlein* had been a bit of spontaneity, hadn't it? And if it wasn't pleasant for Phineas, it had at least been a surprise.

She smiled at this last thought, then began wondering why she had pushed so hard for the mission slot. Was it because she wanted to prove something to herself? Or maybe prove something to Phineas? Perhaps the real reason was something more subsconscious—a means of drawing Phineas out of his official shell, of making him demonstrate some concern for her. . . .

Well, he had certainly done that, although not in the way she had really wanted. She wanted support from him, some sign of belief in *who* she was, not merely as a desirable woman, but as a person of self-worth and professional ability.

As she lay on her bed, staring up at the ceiling, she began wondering about the mission itself for the first time. She had not really considered how dangerous the exploratory journey might be. It was funny how the mind worked—placing emotional and psychological needs in the highest priorities, and in the process, forgetting about the real physical dangers.

What did she really expect to gain from the *Heinlein* mission? Becky sighed to herself and rolled over to stare at the blank face of the bulkhead.

CHAPTER 5

IT TOOK ALL of Ian Coopersmith's professional training to stay calm, to continue concentrating on the problem before him and not the immensity and majesty of the thing called Artifact One. There it was now in the viewscreen, lending part of its relflected light to the dimness of the IASA *Heinlein's* control room. Scattered about him, either in their flight positions or simply strapped down to observe, were the other members of the expedition, the lights from the screen and the control boards playing over their intent features in odd patterns. He'd come to know them all in the days of the journey. Traveling in space tended to do that with a group. You learned your insignificance real quick against the backdrop of the universe, and you let more of your defensive barriers down to others, if only for the company that was so vital.

Coopersmith stared down again at his operations panel, wanting to check his figures again, but knowing they were right. A trace of the old neuroticism again, huh chappie? he asked himself.

In this situation, who could blame him?

Lieutenant Huff leaned over and said in his usual mild voice, "Channel clear, sir."

"Right. Thanks." Coopermsith cleared his voice, and snapped on his headphone mike. "Copernicus Base. This is the *Heinlein*. Coopermith here."

He glanced over his shoulders and gave a wink of reassurance to the others. That was important at this point, and Coopersmith tried to maintain a spirit of bonhomie with everyone to try and relax them. All except two remained expressionless. Doctor Hagar was frowning with intense concentration, as though it was his will power alone that made this expedition possible. He'd said almost as much once, allowing that if it weren't for his efforts amidst the public in the past years, the space program might have been extremely curtailed. The bounds of the man's egotism never failed to astound Coopersmith. He studied science the way a person obsessed with geneology might study his family tree, and with the assumption that he was indeed at the uppermost branches of intelligent development. Doctor Thalberg smiled pleasantly at him, which was a welcome relief. He could use *that* kind of space medicine anytime.

"Affirmative, *Heinlein*," came a voice, deep and crackling, from the speaker grille. "What is it, Captain?"

"We are prepared to start the disarming operation. Request check on telemetered data. Do you get a good make on the visual?"

"One moment, *Heinlein*."

Coopersmith waited along with the others in silence.

Waiting, thought Coopersmith. There was a lot of that in Deep Space.

They'd waited awhile to get here. The IASA Planetary Probeship *Heinlein* had hurtled through the light-shot darkness of space on a course here that formed a great quasi-linear trajectory. Powered by high-thrust, continuous-impulse Lukodyanov engines, the ship had made a continuous-thrust hyperbolic transfer to rendezvous.

The *Heinlein*, by IASA standards, was a moderately large ship—more than a hundred meters in length. Since it was a

Deep-Space vessel which would never fly in any planet's atmosphere, no thought had been given to aerodynamic design. The control section, located at the bow, resembled the head of a mako shark, but without the smoothed edges. Below the forward viewport yawned a large ram-scoop, which enforced the shark image. Trailing off behind the control section was a thinner, rectilinear fuselage which contained fuel cells, crew quarters, equipment hold, launch bays for planetary probes and lander, life-support modules, and the energy converters. Beyond the fuselage, at the aft end, were the engines—large conical funnels in four groups of three. All along the hull, ungainly superstructure dishes and radio-receiving parabolas were placed. In terms of sophistication, the *Heinlein* made the old LEM modules of the first moon landings look like the Wright Brothers' gas-powered kite.

As grand a vessel as the *Heinlein* was, it was dwarfed into insignificance alongside the alien cylinder. So immense was Artifact One, that if viewed from a distance, the *Heinlein* alongside appeared no larger than a dust-mote trying to attach itself to the alien hull.

As they waited, Commander Douglas Fratz just gazed at the ship, shaking his head slowly. "My God, those engines. . . . Can you imagine the *thrust* they must have in them?" His voice was surprisingly soft for his build, which was large and muscular. He wore his reddish-blond hair long although it was beginning to thin at an early age. He sported a neatly trimmed beard that looked like a chin strap to keep on his hair. He'd accompanied Colonel Phineas Kemp on the first manned probe to Pluto, earning a commendation for his service during the long, arduous journey.

"I think what interests IASA most," said Coopersmith, "is the drive."

"Hmm?" returned Fratz.

"Drive!" Doctor Hagar said, like a teacher talking to a small child. "Interstellar drive! By what method did this ship get here? Obviously, the intelligence that constructed this was also able to figure out how to cheat the speed-of-light barrier. If we get ahold of that"—His voice was excited—"the universe will open up to us. Mankind will spread to distant planets, as we were meant to. A glorious dream, fulfilled."

"Yeah," said Fratz. "The glorious dream that I want to fulfill right now is to complete this mission and get out of here alive. You can spread your seed over the stars as much as you want, Hagar. I just want to keep my ass intact."

Coopersmith and Thalberg were the only ones to laugh at that. But inside, Coopersmith agreed entirely with the commander. He had a wife and a family who, he'd long since realized, were a lot more important to him than his job. Coopersmith was a tall, tightly-constructed man of forty-two. His bronze-tan complexion was not born of sunbathing, but of his parentage. His father had been a British factory worker, and his mother a West Indies Black who'd worked as a salesclerk in London. *"You've more than a touch of the tarbrush in ye, Ian,"* his father had once told him. *"Your mum and me dumped the whole bloody barrel on ye!"*

"Yes, well, that's what all of this preliminary stuff is about, isn't it, Commander?" said Coopersmith.

Using the coordinates and telemetered data from the ill-fated *Snipe*, Captain Coopersmith had guided Fratz along the hull, delicately scanning the alien surface in search of anything that appeared to resemble an entrance hatch, or perhaps a launch bay. After a careful survey of the ship's surface, several likely configurations were located, mapped, and more intensely studied.

If Artifact One possessed more than three hatchways, they were well hidden. Coopersmith would have preferred to enter at one of the ends, but no accessway was immediately apparent. There were, however, hatches in the middle of the cylinder, each of a different size.

An intense study of the device which had destroyed the *Snipe* had advised the IASA to equip the *Heinlein* with a phased array of active screens which should effectively neutralize the amplified light weapons of the alien ship. After an in-depth survey, Captain Coopersmith selected the best landing and entrance site for the *Heinlein*'s lander module. The first step, however, was to disarm the geometrically placed blisters which covered the hull.

Coopersmith and his assistant, Thomas Valdone, had assumed that the defensive blisters were arranged in the observed pattern because each had limited range. To test this theory, dummy probes—small gas-powered rockets—were directed towards the hull. Within twenty meters, a tight beam of light flicked out from the closest blisters. End of rockets. Coopersmith's theory seemed to test true. And so he devised a battery of small, shaped thermonuclear warheads with controlled explosive characteristics, protected by energy screens. By computer guidance, each warhead was directed to a defensive blister within range of the selected entrance hatch. The controlled explosions should, theoretically, eliminate the defensive blisters without causing more than superficial damage to the alien ship's hull, thereby providing a safe work-corridor for the landing module and the EVA team which would be working to open the hatch.

A risky operation, this, mused Ian Coopersmith. Although all available data indicated that the alien ship was dead in space, and had been so for an indefinite amount of time, there was no guarantee that an extraterrestrial intelligence was not observing them and would interpret the shaped-charge explosions as acts of aggression.

Colonel Kemp had pointed out, though, that there had been no response from the alien vessel to any human communications attempts. There was no alternative but to attempt entrance by force. Quite simply, it was a risk which had to be taken.

The warheads were armed. All that was necessary now was word from Copernicus Base.

It arrived.

"Affirmative, Captain. Colonel Kemp's given the go-ahead. Anytime you guys are ready."

"Launching warheads now. Stand by, Copernicus...."

Coopersmith nodded to Commander Fratz, who keyed in the launch order to the *Heinlein*'s on-board computer. The ship shuddered slightly as the warheads were launched. Instantly, tracking instruments displayed their data on the console screens. Small, three-dimensional blips closed in on a schematic representation of the targets. No one spoke save for Coopersmith, who reported the closing distances in a half-whisper: "Trajectories are on-line...closing nicely...twenty meters and closing...ten...we have detonation!"

In the vacuum of space, the explosions on the surface of the alien ship transmitted no sound. They looked like brilliant crimson buds suddenly blossoming. The display grids of the console flickered as the sensors collected new information. Coopersmith could see that the first phase of the operation had been successful. The controlled explosions had obliterated the defensive blisters without seriously affecting the alien's hull.

"Copernicus, this is Coopersmith. So far, so good. Scanners indicate no loss of pressure on Artifact One. We are launching a dummy probe. Stand by."

Fratz waited for Coopersmith's nod, then keyed in the launch. Heads turned to watch as the small torpedo-shaped probe, equipped with shock-absorbing landing legs, slowly descended toward the surface of the alien ship. No one spoke as it closed within range of the defensive systems. Closer and closer it descended until its automatic devices fired off a short burst of retrofire and the probe settled gently upon the surface, holding fast with magnetic seals.

"Copernicus, we have a touchdown!" cried Coopersmith, exultant.

"Affirmative, Captain. Congratulations," returned the communications man from Copernicus.

The crew cheered, and Coopersmith swept off his communications helmet, and turned blue eyes upon the company.

"I do believe that we're next!" he said.

Ian Coopersmith kept his thick, dark hair cut short for moments such as these. Long hair could be rather a problem sometimes in an EVA suit. Coopersmith tried to keep his problems down to bare minimum.

"Ready, Valdone?"

The dark Italian turned amused eyes and Sicilian nose toward Coopersmith. "I've been ready for this for a long time, Captain."

Coopersmith gave him a thumb's up signal They donned their helmets and switched on the life-support equipment.

After a quick jump through the airlock of the *Heinlein*'s number one lander, which had drifted down from the Probeship and effected a perfect landing near the outlines of what appeared to be an entrance bay, they floated cautiously down to the hull.

Led by Coopersmith, they carefully walked with magnetic boots across the surface of the alien ship. The lander—which

looked to Ian rather like an overfed tarantula—waited patiently
behind them.

A historic occasion, thought Coopersmith. Yes indeed. Man's
first physical contact with an extraterrestrial craft. But there
was no trumpet fanfare, no live TV coverage to Earth's billions,
no eloquently-rigged speeches for the history books. There
would be time for such things later, maybe. History books were
not on Coopersmith's mind as he appraised the contours of the
hatch below their feet.

The outlining seam of the hatch was quite large: approximately ten meters wide and fifteen high. Several small rectan-
gles that measured slightly more than two meters each were
on each side of the hatch. Their function or relationship to the
larger, seamed configuration was not clear. Coopersmith used
a sensory instrument which resembled a fluoroscope: Mark 8
Betatron Scanner, which allowed the user to view the interior
of metallic objects of varying degrees of density and opacity.

Incredible, thought Coopersmith. An airlock quite compa-
rable to IASA design.

Although he and Valdone weren't able to determine how to
operate the entrance electronically, the Scanner did allow them
access to the mechanical system of the lock. By cutting through
the hull with torches at the control-point, they were able to
open and close the outer hatch manually. The entire procedure
took five hours. Best to work slowly and cautiously, Coopersmith reasoned. Each step in the operation was being fed
back to Phineas Kemp at Copernicus.

At last, the large hatch slid open to the right, revealing a
flat, featureless platform. Coopersmith entered a chamber which
was roughly fifteen cubic meters. The metallic walls had a
slightly burnt-blue cast, and were buttressed by support girders.
At the opposite end of the chamber, Coopersmith could see
the outline of another hatch. Presumably, the other end of the
airlock. At a height of approximately five meters, next to the
hatch, was a set of three levers, inset in a meter square shadow-
box. Coopersmith assumed these to be the controls which operated the interlocking set of hatches.

Floating up to inspect the controls, he wondered why they
were so inaccessible. The logical explanation was obvious. The
aliens who built this ship were at least several times larger in

scale than humans. The thought was an unsettling one. Coopersmith did not dwell on it. He concentrated instead on the immediate task.

"'Copernicus, this is lander one," he said in his British accent. "Coopersmith here. We have successfully entered what appears to be a standard airlock chamber. We're going to try some experimenting. Stand by, please."

"Affirmative, lander one. Proceed with caution." Colonel Kemp had taken over the communications. The man was probably tense as a coiled spring by now. His voice sounded small and very far away.

Coopersmith indicated to Valdone that he was about to touch the controls. "Valdone. Get back out on the hull by the lander. Tell Bracken to be prepared to lift off if we have any trouble."

Valdone signaled agreement and floated slowly from the airlock, positioning himself on the hull near lander one. The far-away sun glinted off his faceplate as he stared in at Coopersmith.

Exhaling slowly, Ian Coopersmith studied the three levers, each as large as a cricket bat. They were color-coded. Red. Yellow. Green. God, thought Coopersmith. But there was no way that the alien color system meant the same as the human code. He followed that assumption and tripped the red lever.

Nothing happened.

Coopersmith reached for the next lever. "Negative on the first control, Copernicus. Trying number two, here. . . ."

Slowly, soundlessly, the outer hatch slid shut.

"That's got it, Captain," said Valdone, floating by the outer hatch, watching it seal Ian off from the outside.

"All right," said Ian. "Let's try it backwards, and make sure I'm not sealed in here permanently."

He pushed the lever back to its original position and the hatch began opening again. "Bull's eye!" said Valdone. "Looks like we're in business."

"Okay," said Coopersmith. "I'm closing it down. Valdone, come inside. Let's see if we can get the other hatch to work."

He rethrew the yellow lever and again closed the outer hatch. Trying the green control resulted in no change, but only momentarily. Slowly, the sound of gases rushing into the chamber became audible.

"Copernicus, this is Coopersmith. I'm getting what appears to be pressurization of the first chamber. Stand by."

Less than a minute passed before an electronic chime sounded in the chamber. Coopersmith presumed it to be a signal indicating the proper pressure.

"Captain, we've got an atmosphere in here. Want to run an analysis?" Valdone drifted down to the deck, where they had secured their instrument packs.

"Right, Tom. I'll notify Copernicus." He switched over to the patch-in with the lunar base once again. "Colonel, we've got an atmosphere in the lock. Valdone's running a check on the make-up now. Please stand by."

"Hey. Now that's really something. Listen to this, Captain. Nitrogen, oxygen, carbon dioxide, trace argon, and a little water vapor. Pressure about a thousand millibars! That's incredible."

"Ah, Copernicus. This is Coopersmith. Atmospheric analysis indicates nearly Earth standard mix. Breathable for us anyway. Pressure is close to sea-level averages. Temperature approximately fifteen degrees Centigrade."

"We copy that, Coopersmith. Exact data will come in from telemetry. Proceed with entry operation." Jesus! They'd all expected an *alien* atmosphere.

"Roger, Copernicus. Stand by." Coopersmith shut down the radio link and stared for a moment at the control panel and the large hatch. Thoughts which he had been able to keep from his mind would not leave him now. The full impact of where he was and what he was doing suddenly struck him.

Staring at the blank hatch, Coopersmith's mind *unhinged* for a brief moment. He saw visions of strange beings standing on the other side of the entrance, waiting to greet the naive Earth folk who had bumbled into their ship like moths into a spider's web. He thought of London's Surbiton, where his modest rowhouse lay jammed in with a thousand others like itself, where his wife Leticia and his son Nathaniel lived and worked, knowing that they would only know his company in six-month chunks of time.

Suddenly, Coopersmith was aware of movement to his left. Turning quickly, he saw Thomas Valdone beside him, staring at him. "You okay, Captain?"

"Yes . . . yes, fine, I was . . . just thinking about something."

Valdone smiled. "Yeah. I know what you mean." The engineer looked at the flat imposing surface of the hatch. "I'm pretty scared too. I . . . I don't know, Captain. I've grown up loving the stars. And now. . . . Well now all I want to do is go back home and be safe. Here, in the thick of excitement. Thomas Valdone! Privileged man! My old man . . . my old man is gonna be real proud of me. My momma too. My wife didn't want me to go. I kinda wish I'd listened to her." He sighed. "But still, Captain, if you . . . just let go, you know, accept all this immensity. You kind of lose yourself, and the fear ebbs a little. It becomes awe. Know what I mean?"

"Valdone, I wouldn't have any other man along with me."

"Thanks. Well, I guess we better give it a go, huh?"

Coopersmith turned and reached for the third lever, pulling it down. A low humming sounded as the inner lock door slid left. Both men stared into the darkness beyond as though peering into the mouth of some great beast. Valdone produced a powerful light-torch from his utility pack and flicked it on. The broad beam of light pierced the blackness, revealing a four-sided corridor leading away, like a mine shaft. No markings or features showed on the walls except for two parallel rods, attached at frequent intervals along the surface, that ran into the dark. Also spaced at regular intervals were small struts, protruding from the parallel rods. If you looked at it long enough, you could see that it was a multipurpose ladder, an aid to climbing "up" the long corridor.

Valdone grabbed the first rung.

"Wait a minute. Come on back. I'm going to depressurize and bring in some of the others."

As Valdone worked his way back onto the airlock, Coopersmith reclosed the hatch with the now-familiar controls. As the outer hatch reopened, Ian turned to his assistant.

"You stay here. I'm going back in the lander with Bracken and assemble the others. It's time to get in there and see what makes this thing tick."

An hour later, the entire exploration team was assembled in the first chamber of the Artifact One's airlock. Commander Fratz and back-up pilot Bracken remained at their stations aboard the *Heinlein* and lander one, respectively.

"Right, then," he told the group, after letting them ogle the airlock for a moment. "We've got something to breathe inside, believe it or not. Once we close the second lock, we can discard the EVA gear. However, I want everybody to wear LS-rigs in case of an emergency. Stay close together and keep your radios *on* at all times. Keep your sidearms *in* your holsters. No one is to draw arms without my authorization. Clear?"

It seemed to be. Everybody agreed, either immersed in wonder or obviously touched with anxiety. "Friends," he announced. "I give you Artifact One!"

The proper levers were manipulated. The chamber pressurized. The inner lock opened. Lanced by the concentrated power of everyone's electric torches, the dark corridor appeared less forbidding, and much more like the functional access to the ship's interior it was.

One by one, the members of the team entered the corridor, until the last, Doctor Pohl, a lanky, red-faced man, floated through. He gave the all-clear. Coopersmith closed the interior hatch, instructing all to divest themselves of the cumbersome, Deep-Space environment suits.

Pulling off his helmet, Ian Coopersmith smelled the air. It owned a cool, antiseptic quality which, while not offensive, seemed alien in his nostrils. Perhaps it was merely psycho-suggestion that gave it that scent. Still, it seemed odd.

He waited until everyone was ready. They all wore field jumpsuits, backpacks, and emergency life support modules strapped to their chests. The LS units had collapsible face-masks which could supply water and oxygen for several hours.

"Huff, patch me into the *Heinlein* link," Coopersmith said as he grabbed onto the ladder leading upward into the belly of the alien ship.

"You're on, Captain."

"Copernicus, this is Coopersmith. We have entered the air-lock assembly without a hitch. There appears to be an access corridor leading up into the main body of Artifact One. We're going up now. Stand by."

After receiving the go-ahead from Kemp and his lunar team, Ian led the group upwards. The scraping of their boots on the metallic rungs and their labored breathing penetrated the surrounding hollow silence. The corridor, under the influence of Artifact One's artificial gravity, appeared to be going straight "up"—actually toward the geometric center of the cylinder. The distance they traveled was approximately a hundred meters, ending on a ten by ten-meter platform fronting an entry hatch directly above their heads.

When everyone had gathered on the platform, Coopersmith relayed their progress and position back to Copernicus. Receiving another go-ahead, he ordered Huff and Valdone to open the hatch manually by means of two interlocking gear-wheels. The sound of metal, moving smoothly, filled the chamber. Instead of sliding into the bulkhead, like the previous ones, this hatch opened vertically. As the hatch parted, a bright seam appeared, as if there was an intense light source immediately beyond it.

Everyone tensed momentarily. The two men paused as Coopersmith held up a cautionary hand.

"Right," he said, climbing the short ladder leading to the hatch. "Keep your sidearms ready, just in case there's an unfriendly reception committee. Not likely, that, but we'd best be ready for anything. I'm going in first. Then Valdone. If that goes well, Thalberg, Pohl, and Hagar follow, in *that* order. Huff, you bring up the rear and establish a homing beacon at this hatch just in case there's a maze of passageways. I want everybody to lock into the beacon. That way nobody gets lost. Also, Huff, I want you to maintain the link through the *Heinlein* back to Copernicus. Everybody got that?"

Coopersmith looked at the party. Pohl's mouth was ajar. He breathed heavily. Hagar's fingers twitched nervously. Huff was stolid and alert. Valdone licked his lips expectantly. Thalberg's eyes were wide and dark.

For the first time Coopersmith realized just how beautiful those eyes were as they looked up toward an unknown future.

He turned back to the hatch. "Here we go."

CHAPTER 6

THEY STOOD UPON a small rise of earth which overlooked a sloping meadowland. This faded away to a marshy swamp and, finally, a lagoon. To either side lay the edges of a dense, lushly green forest. Warm and muggy, the air was full of steaming, organic smells. Looking to the horizon, it was hard for Ian Coopersmith to accept what he saw. He read a similar emotion in the faces of the others.

There *was* no horizon.

The tropical landscape of jungle, river, and sea stretched endlessly away until it *curved upward* and over them, filling the sky, *becoming* the sky, sixty-five kilometers distant, curving, curving back behind them in an endless roll. The entire interior of the gigantic cylinder ship was a living world of rich loamy soil, swamp, forest.

Light streamed down from a brilliant source. It was so bright and intense that it hurt Coopersmith's eyes, as though he were staring at the sun. Quickly, he flipped down the sun-shield goggles on his LS helmet.

Running the entire three hundred and twenty-kilometer length of the cylinder, hanging almost magically in the zero-gravity center of the rotating world, burned a thick rod, a seemingly solid column of light and heat which filled the world with artificial day.

A feeling resembling *deja vu* swept Coopersmith. He'd dreamed of standing in a place like this. His vision had been instilled in him by the dreamers who'd planned a space colony fitting this concept on a much smaller scale, filled with cities and parks, not wilderness. This was *alien*. And it was *huge*. Seeing it from the inside made him realize just how large it really was.

The group stoood about him silently, almost reverently. Coopersmith knew they were feeling just the way he did.

Without a word, as though speech might somehow break the magic spell of the place, Coopersmith led them down into a reedy meadow, feeling the spongy earth give slightly beneath his boots. Coopersmith studied the odd terrain, feeling twinges of uneasiness, as though the party were violators of some ancient tomb. Mist hung shroudlike over the lagoon. Odd gurgles sounded. Insects thrummed, their buzzings and chirpings cutting through the thick, humid air.

They walked upon rusty-colored, weed-choked earth. Bright green vines crept around trees. Small herb-like growths proliferated. There was no grass. On both sides of the clearing, all the way down to the marshes, walls of forest stood in green shadow. Palm-like cycads squatted in uncounted numbers, their thick boles and trunks like unstaved barrels, accented with light brown cones. Giant tree ferns exploded with deep green fronds and fresh shoots. An *alien* wood, though Ian Coopersmith. Never seen before by man. Large, black-limbed conifers grew here, along with sparsely needled evergreens—primitive pines and spruces, tall proto-firs and cedars, thick cypresses which seemed to reach out like tentacled creatures, unbranching hemlocks black and pencil-thin. Presented before them was a skyline of fiercely stark, immobile life. A jungle of steaming shadows so thick, so densely crowded, that it appeared impossible to clear a path through such a natural barrier.

Forever distant, insects hummed constantly. This forest must *teem* with life, Coopersmith thought. Life amidst the broad leafy boughs of the ginkgoes, amongst the soaring redwoods. This was a world never silent, a world fiercely alive.

Something screamed, piercing the stillness of the air. Like the cawing of a crow, the sound came to them, and then was suddenly choked off, swallowed and lost in the forest's depths. The cry broke into everyone's thoughts, pulling them from their private worlds of perception. They were once again aware of one another. Time had been slipping away from them in this strangely timeless place, Coopersmith realized.

He turned and faced the group. "Somebody sure went to a lot of trouble to do all this."

Nervous smiles. Pohl coughed. Rebecca Thalberg adjusted the straps of her backpack.

"Hard to believe we're really *seeing* it," Thomas Valdone said, dropping down to one knee, cupping a handful of loose soil and plant life in his hand. "We're really *here!*"

Amos Hagar, the brash exobiologist and world-famous media personality, stepped forward, smiling. "Captain, this is the most important discovery in the history of mankind! Do you realize what this is! What we've found!"

Gazing stoically at the enthusiastic Hagar, Coopersmith said, "I think so," very dead-pan. He'd never liked Doctor Hagar. The man used the media to popularize science, true, but in doing so he watered it down, sugared it to make a palatable drink for the public to swallow. Hagar was known for his gushing enthusiasm and unbounded optimism, his high-flying prophecies about contact with alien life-forms.

Coopersmith noticed that the others were intently watching Hagar, caught up with his burst of childish wonder, awaiting his next pronouncement. Obviously relishing an audience, even here, Hagar stepped away and prepared to address the group, the smile building on his round face. He gestured wildly, the way some Victorian actor might execute a Shakespearean soliloquy. "Look around you! It's a lost world. . . . *The* Lost World! Look at those trees!" He pointed towards the forest. "Cycads! Ginkgoes! Smell the air! We are standing in the midst of the *Jurassic* age . . . an exact duplicate of the environment of Earth as it was one hundred and sixty million years ago!"

"How can that be?" asked Rebecca Thalberg, her long dark hair curling beautifully out from the edges of her helmet. "How old is this thing? This . . . ship?"

Hagar spun, almost dancing like a small child in a toyshop. "Anything which can be conceived can be possible. You can't ask such a question, Doctor Thalberg . . . you must simply accept what undeniably *is!* Look around you!"

Which set off a flurry of comments and questions from the rest of the group. This continued for a few minutes before Coopersmith called them back to order. "All right. Wait a minute. We don't know any of this for sure. And we aren't going to know until we start conducting ourselves like a scientific team. Huff . . . set up your communications gear right here near the hatch. Everybody keep your helmet-phones *on*. Doctor Pohl, Doctor Thalberg . . . I think you both have some instruments which can get us some hard data. I think it's time we started doing that. . . ."

All of the team resumed their professional attitudes, except for Hagar. He seemed piqued at having lost his audience.

Ignoring the man, Coopersmith continued delegating duties. "Valdone, you and Hagar will accompany me. Get out the cameras and the recorders. I want everything down on record. And Huff . . . ?"

"Yes sir, Captain." Alan Huff's voice came over the helmet-phones crisply. Coopersmith liked Huff. Young, very bright, Huff was extremely dedicated. Although he had not known him as long as he'd known Valdone, he trusted the man's sincerity and obligation to duty.

"Patch me in to Copernicus. They must be going crazy, wondering what happened to us."

Huff made the proper radio links, enabling Coopersmith to detail their incredible discoveries to Kemp and staff. Audio and visual signals from the portable camera gear were telemetered back to lunar base. After a pause no doubt caused by astonishment, Kemp cautioned them to stay close together. Alan Huff was ordered to remain with the homing beacon.

Slowly the group of five advanced across the small clearing toward the marshland and the lagoon beyond it. Coopersmith and Valdone carried their .50 caliber sidearms drawn. The others handled the recording and analytical instruments.

The ground became soft under their feet as they traveled. The insect chirpings paused infrequently, as though the world had briefly become aware of their presence and was watching them.

Something moved overhead.

Soaring past the glare from the central rod, a dark shape glided easily over them. A smallish, bat-like thing, it headed toward the lagoon, where it skimmed perilously close to the calm surface of the water.

Hagar followed its flight with his camera, trying to keep it in focus. The first sign of advanced animal life, everyone watched it.

"Pterosaur of some sort," said Doctor Hagar. "Looking for its lunch, probably. Funny. Not quite as I had visualized the species."

As if on the cue, the first Pterosaur's appearance heralded the arrival of more silently gliding creatures. The last in this lazy formation tilted its pointed head and peered blankly at the humans below. Its pointed beak slit slightly, and Coopersmith caught a flash of tiny teeth as it emitted a high-pitched screech. It followed the flight path of the others down to the lagoon.

"Incredible," Valdone whispered. "Just incredible!"

Hagar spoke much louder. "This must have been some kind of . . . of *specimen ship*. An interstellar laboratory. The builders of this ship . . . they must have visited the Earth *so* long ago! A hundred and sixty million years ago. They stopped and picked up samples of Earth's life forms. No wonder—"

"But what happened?" interrupted Rebecca. "It's still *here*."

"*Something* happened," returned Hagar. "I don't know what. An accident? A malfunction? Maybe a disease wiped out the crew, I don't know. But the ship never left our system. It's been here all this time . . . the creatures in it probably developing. Here all this time. *Waiting* for us."

Valdone laughed. "I wouldn't exactly say, 'waiting.' Looks like it's been getting along pretty well *without* us."

"What's that?" said Coopersmith. He pointed to the left, past an extension of the forest where it abutted with the shallows of the swampland ahead. Indistinct movement beyond the fronds and vegetation . . . something slow, as though traveling with stealth. The shapes beyond the forest peninsula ventured into the clearing. Three large creatures, standing on their hindlegs, waddled awkwardly to the water's edge.

Dinosaurs.

"Jesus," said Valdone. "I don't believe it."

Coopersmith waved for silence, then spoke in a low voice into his helmet-mike. He checked with Copernicus of the quality of the transmission, reporting briefly also on what was taking place. Four other dinosaurs of the same species appeared at the edge of the swamp, all kneeling down on the shorter forelimbs to drink from the placid, reedy surface.

"Iguanodons," Hagar said. "Not exactly like we imagined them but close enough. Evolution *is* taking place amongst these creatures. These are herbivores. Probably harmless as long as one of them doesn't fall on you."

Studying the herd of dinosaurs, Ian Coopersmith remembered their pictures in his books as a child, and shook his head. Iguanodons. They were massive creatures. With dark brown hides, thick, fleshy legs and bellies, they stood on their hindlegs and balanced on thick immobile tails. At least four meters tall, they were. Twice a man's height, and probably hundreds of times heavier. Their heads were large, making their small eyes appear even smaller. Their throats hung down from their jaws in loose folds of dewlap. Their movements slow and deliberate, the Iguanodons required a long time to properly right themselves on their hindlegs after dropping down to drink.

Quietly, Coopersmith and the group closed to within a hundred meters of the creatures without disturbing them. Then suddenly one of the taller ones, now resting on his back legs and tail, raised his snout as if testing the scented air. Instantly, the Iguanodons' movements quickened. Acting on a silent signal, the herd began moving away from the swamp, away from the humans and toward the lagoon, where a gentle, sloping beach reached down to touch the waters.

"They've smelled us," Hagar said. "Strange scent's going to drive them off."

No one spoke as they watched the herd attempt to hurry away from the area. It was almost comical to see such massive, ponderous beasts waddling along, their tails and hindquarters wobbling in a swaying, rhythmic motion. The last Iguanodon had struggled to its feet, weaving slightly as it regained a delicate balance, and started after the others. It had hardly taken a step when the quiet scene was broken by the furious crackling and rustle of foliage from the forests' edge to the left. A tannish blur of movement broke from the shaded tree-barrier. Something large and quick and almost twice the height of the lumbering Iguanodon.

Quickly, the intruding dinosaur lunged for its waddling prey, pouncing upon its back. For an instant the two creatures hung in their bizarre frieze, balanced, not toppling, the dark, muddy brown hide of the prey in sharp contrast to the attacker. It was a large biped with heavily muscled thighs and large splayed hindclaws. Its long, thick tail, whipped back and forth like a cat's as it hunched over the Iguanodon, trying to hold its rubbery flesh in tiny foreclaws. The Iguanodon fell forward, slapping into the swampy earth with a muffled thud, emitting a weak, bleating cry like a wounded bird. Now the carnivore, a Gorgosaurus or something closely akin to that class, went for the kill. In a moment so quick Coopersmith could bearly follow, its great jaws opened, flashed a razor set of teeth, and snapped viciously into the Iguanodon's flanks. It stood partially upright firmly digging its curved taloned feet into the bulk of the victim. Then it ripped and jerked its head from side to side. Under the savage attack, the worried flesh of the Iguanodon gave way, and a great bloody flap was torn from its side. The Gorgosaurus raised its head, holding the cattle-sized piece of meat in its teeth, tossed it slightly, and snapped its jaws once more. The entire gobbet of flesh disappeared into its mouth, slipping down slowly, distending the carnivore's throat as it passed.

"Good Christ," Valdone said.

"Let's get out of here, Captain," Rebecca said. She was backed up by a chorus of similar opinions.

"No, wait!" said Doctor Hagar. "We're safe here . . . he can't see us or hear us. He's busy with his food and *will* be for quite awhile."

The Gorgosaurus jammed its open jaws into the ravaged belly of the Iguanodon, tearing out another red section of still-quivering flesh. The Iguanodon trembled feebly under the weight of its killer, but to no avail. Its life fluids seeped from the gash in its flank and its small bird-like eyes slid shut. The Gorgosaurus ripped and tore, its jaws snapping mechanically. Pieces of hide and red muscle pulled loose from the stilled prey. The feeding was a frenzy that did not stop, as the great lizard head of the killer plunged again and again into the warm flesh. Soon its snout was coated with glistening blood, and still it fed.

Rebecca Thalberg cringed away from the scene. Horror and repulsion showed in her expression. Coopersmith read her unspoken pleas to him.

"All right, people, we'd better be getting out of here. We're not—"

"Captain! Captain!" The voice of Alan Huff screamed hysterically in Coopersmith's helmet-phone.

Quickly turning, the group rushed through the reedy terrain of the meadows, swinging back to the right towards the clearing and the rise where Huff had positioned himself. As they approached the entrance hatch area, Coopersmith saw two smallish dinosaurs, no taller than a man, racing towards Alan Huff. Huff knelt on one knee, pistol at arm's length, ready to fire. The dinosaurs were bipedal, long legged, with thin, pointed tails, their bodies tapered up to large-jawed, big-eyed heads. Rows of sharp teeth glinted. Their small forelimbs seemed to dangle helplessly as they ran. Like giant birds, they half-leaped, half-strode across the clearing with the speed of thoroughbreds, filling the air with crow-like caws. Even from the considerable distance, Coopersmith could see the panic in Huff's eyes as he raised the gun and fired off three quick shots into the closest dinosaur.

The volley struck the racing predator in the throat and lower jaw, instantly exploding its flesh in a shower of pink mist. It staggered forward, losing its balance. Shaking its fearsome head, it spattered blood and small fragments of bone into the air. But still it plunged forward. The second dinosaur, untouched by the explosive bullets, plunged past the first and leaped in the air like a kangaroo, its hindclaws flaring, crushing into Huff's chest.

The communications man managed one last shot, fired wildly into the air, before the beast was upon him. Huff was thrown on his back under the greater weight of his attacker. As Coopersmith's group closed in, they could only watch in horror as the first dinosaur, a Compsognathus, raked its hindclaws across Huff's abdomen, splitting him open like a piece of over-ripe fruit. Instantly, the ripping and tearing began as the snapping jaws pulled Huff apart. The second, wounded predator leaped into the bloody fray, finishing the kill.

Hoping he was still in contact with Copernicus, Coopersmith spoke into his helmet-mike, barely repressing a yell. "Huff's dead! The place is crawling with dinosaurs. We're getting *out!*"

Valdone fired pistol rounds at the two dinosaurs. Doctor Pohl and Rebecca Thalberg fumbled with their weapons, finally adding to the volley of explosive slugs. The air was filled with gunshot reports and the hideous, keening screams of the dinosaurs. Coopersmith tried to control his thumping heart and trembling body. Carefully he took aim with his pistol and fired.

New sounds filled the air. Loud bellowing, like that of wounded cattle. Sharp cracking barks . . . as though from the mouths of giant bullfrogs. What had only moments ago been a placid, pastoral meadow abuzz with insects singing was transformed into a slaughterhouse reverberating with death screams. Coopersmith followed the bellowing sounds and saw a nightmare emerge from the walls of forest to the right. The others saw it too. For a moment, the sound of gunfire was only an echoing memory.

The sounds of battle had aroused it.

The smell of blood and death had attracted it.

The half-dead, shell-riddled carcasses of the two Compsognathus lay crumpled over the remains of Alan Huff. It was first drawn to this carrion. But as it staggered from the forest, it paused and looked at the five humans, barely fifty meters away.

For a moment, they stared at one another, the humans and the Allosaurus—eight tons of killing machinery. From head to tail it was more than twelve meters long. Standing on its powerful, pylon-like legs, it towered above them at a height of eight meters. Its hindlegs rippled with muscle-tonnage, sheathed in a yellow-brown leathery hide. Its forelimbs twitched, closing its three-digit claws instinctively at the sight of prey. Its great head, weighing perhaps a half-ton, turned slowly, so that it could study the humans with its large saucer-eyes. Its lower jaw hung open, dripping saliva, its throat heaving from the furious beat of its breath. The nightmare head dipped, bobbed, and weaved, displaying a row of dagger-teeth, a death's head smile.

Then it raised that head, nostrils flaring, testing the air, smelling the carrion smells and the new smells, the new prey. It bellowed once again, and dropped its head, hunkering down, extending its tail almost straight, horizontal with the ground. The great legs moved, and it streaked forward, covering the distance between itself and the humans in two-meter strides. For such a massive creature, it was inconceivable that it could move so quickly. Yet its motions were smooth and fluid, co-ordinated beyond belief.

Coopersmith and Valdone stood their ground just long enough to empty the clips of the weapons. The shells ripped through the Allosaurus' thick hide with little apparent effect.

It bore down upon them like a steam locomotive.

Rebecca Thalberg ran by Coopersmith's side as the group split up in different directions. Ian and Thalberg to the left, toward the distant forest edge. Valdone, Pohl, and Hagar back toward the marshlands.

This tactic seemed to confuse the giant carnivore. Seeing the prey suddenly divide and separate, it slowed its charge, tilting its ugly head, as if contemplating the movements. Valdone kept running, but Hagar paused for an instant, spellbound by the immense creature which closed in on him. The Allosaurus had shaken off the distraction and was now continuing on a straight ahead course. Valdone screamed at Hagar, even turned back to fire two rounds into the thing's head, uselessly.

As Hagar shook free of his paralysis, the beast was upon him. Dipping its head, with little break in its gigantic stride, it snapped Doctor Amos Hagar, world-famous author, media personality, and deliverer of deadly *bon mots*, into its terrible jaws. Hagar did not even have time to scream before the razored teeth closed upon him, slicing him cleanly in half. The parts tossed briefly into the air before being wolfed greedily into the beast's maw. Swallowing as it lumbered forward, it bore down on Valdone, who was laboring against the spongelike marsh-land which seemed to suck his boots down.

Coopersmith and Thalberg ran mindlessly toward the for-est, a glimpse of Hagar's death urging them forward. They ran until Coopersmith's mouth and nostrils felt afire, his legs ached. His mind flooded with thoughtless, boiling chaos. Naked panic. He could feel it in Rebecca as well. The dark green wall of the forest bobbed and jerked before his eyes as they ran.

As they reached the forest, crashing blindly through rough-edged fronds of low-lying ferns, Coopersmith paused, sensing a moment of safety. Reaching out, he grabbed Thalberg's arms, pulling the woman close to him, dropping to his knees. "Wait," he half-cried, gasping for breath. "Wait!"

They turned and looked back towards the marsh where the Allosaurus had just overtaken Valdone. Rebecca looked away, but something kept Coopersmith's eyes on the grisly scene. The great beast had actually run over Valdone, stamping him into the soft earth. Now, in a hunting frenzy, the creature savagely clawed at the ground with its hindleg, digging up great clumps of earth, pulling out the mangled remains of Coopersmith's colleague. A bright red mass stuck to the beast's right foot. Slowly, it bent down, examining it for an instant, then snapped it up in two quick bites. A lump formed in its throat, which quickly slid from sight down its gullet. A helpless rage filled Coopersmith. He felt fear and hate and despair all at one time.

"We've got to get back to the hatch," he said finally, shaking Thalberg, making her turn and listen to him.

"We can't make it. Those other things. . . ."

Coopersmith looked back towards the hatch. The two cadavers of the Compsognathus had already attracted a crowd. Bird-like carrion eaters had descended upon the bodies and were already feeding. The air above the pile was smeared by a swarming black cloud of insects. The forest noises filled their ears, occasionally pierced by the cries of other predators, aroused by the scent of the kill, which filled the air.

The Allosaurus, having finished with Valdone, stood near the edge of the marshland, pausing to pick its teeth with its forelimb claws. It looked almost dainty as it stood, flicking and pawing at its jaws. Then it held its snout high, trying to pick up the scent of the others. Thus it stood, motionless for a moment. Then it slunk indecisively off toward the other edge of the forest. Coopersmith watched it, wondering where Doctor Pohl had gone.

"It's moving off. Come on . . . we've got our chance right now. Stay close to the trees and we'll work our way closer to the hatch."

"Captain, look!" Rebecca pointed up and across the small meadow to the rise where Huff had been attacked. New shapes had emerged from the forest. Two more bipedal dinosaurs similar to the one they had seen attack the Iguanodon. . . . Gorgosaurus, Hagar had called them.

The two new beasts ambled boldly onto the scene, instantly scattering the carrion-eating Pterosaurs, the insects, and a small crowd of diminutive, pale-skinned dinosaurs that looked like ostriches. The Gorgosaurus advanced, their mouths open, jaws drooling, bleating out warning cries. They rushed up to the carcasses and the remains of Alan Huff to begin their ritual of ripping, tearing, and greedy gulping of flesh. There was no way Coopersmith and Thalberg could hope to get past the newcomers.

Nor was this their only problem. The Allosaurus was emerging from the edge of the forest, pounding toward the smaller carnivores.

Then Coopersmith saw Pohl, creeping along the outer foliage. Why had the man left the safety of the trees? Gerald Pohl glanced back skittishly as he moved along. Perhaps another meat-eater was converging on the scene, and Pohl was escaping *that* one.

The Allosaurus paused, catching some small movement in the corner of its vision, tilting its large head towards the forest edge. Though the great beast was quite stupid, evidently not having evolved much—like the crocodile—in the last hundred million years, its senses were not dull. To be an effective killing machine, to be able to keep such a massive, energy-burning body sated, the Allosaurus had to be extremely adept at catching prey. So it possessed keen vision, sensitive smell, acute hearing. It stood now watching the tiny toylike man scamper along the outermost trees.

Plenty of time for the kill.

Doctor Pohl continued to half-run, half-stagger away from the dark forest. He ran with the mindless panic of desperation, which showed in his movement. Deeper in the forest, Coopersmith saw a shadowy form following him.

He was making a desperate dash for the safety of the hatch.

Pohl charged toward the spot where the two Gorgosaurus snapped and shoved at one another over the final morsels of the ravaged bodies. The scent of blood and ripped-open bowels was thick in the air. It smelled of feeding time. Coopersmith watched the Allosaurus observing Pohl running toward the other beasts, its dim brain no doubt trying to understand what kind of prey would rush into the jaws of its attackers.

The two Gorgosaurus paused in their bloody repast, thrusting their snouts upward, catching the human scent. Turning, they seemed to grin. They bellowed with killing-joy. As they began their smooth, loping strides toward the man, Pohl fired three shots at the closest beast, one shell striking the back of its throat. A lucky shot, it exploded the thin layer of bone beneath the creature's brain. Evidently, the shock of impact jellied the nerve center, killing it instantly. The Gorgosaurus lurched forward, falling on its snout, its hindlegs and tiny forelimbs twitching convulsively. Seeing this, its companion fell upon its fellow to rip a large piece of warm flesh from its still quivering thigh.

Doctor Pohl had pulled up, and was struggling to slap a new clip into his pistol, trying to think what to do next, when a giant shadow crossed his path. Turning, he saw the steel-muscled bulk of the Allosaurus towering above him, gliding quietly and quickly over the soft earth. Lowering its head, it opened it jaws. Pohl fired his sidearm wildly before rolling to the left. The light tan hide blurred past him. Scrambling to his feet, running out from between the feeding Gorgosaurus and Allosaurus, he did not look back.

Ahead of him, angled off to the right, was the entrance hatch. He was not more than fifty meters away. Gerald Pohl staggered forward, leaning, half-falling, to sustain forward motion. Coopersmith held his breath for the man . . . then gasped as the Gorgosaurus sprang from its meal and bounded across his path.

"Pohl!" Coopersmith cried. "*Run*, man!"

Pohl did not seem to notice the creature until it was directly above him. He tried to dodge, but to no avail.

Open jaws dropped over his head and shoulders.

Coopersmith averted his gaze as Pohl was decapitated. Never had he imagined such slaughter, such mindless killing and feeding. Rebecca grabbed him and began sobbing and shivering in his arms. She gasped for breath. He wished he could join her in the physical release.

A bellow.

Coopersmith looked up. The Allosaurus was advancing upon the Gorgosaurus. The two dinosaurs faced each other, barking and hissing in an attempt to scare each other off. Neither apparently wanted to fight as much as it desired to feed. Slowly the smaller Gorgosaurus backed away, turning to finally sidestep off toward the forest.

The Allosaurus threw back its head, rejoicing in its triumph with a final roar of primordial joy. Then it ambled up to the remains of the dead Gorgosaurus, and began to rip and tear with reptilian gusto. Coopersmith watched it feed for the better part of an hour. He held Rebecca Thalberg, who was now quietly sobbing. When the Allosaurus finished its bloody meal, it slowly settled down, reclining over the skeletal carcass of the victim. Coopersmith knew that it would now fall into a heavy doze—a half-awake torpor, while its great body labored to digest the feast.

Not forty meters from the hulking beast lay the entrance hatch and safety. After seeing the quickness of the predators of this world, the unmerciful death they held in their claws and jaws, Coopersmith knew that he would not risk trying for the hatch as long as the Allosaurus remained close at hand. He felt defenseless against the hostile world they had found. It was an arena of twisted nightmare, full of God-knew-what-else beside the dreadful things they'd already seen devour their companions.

"C'mon. We've gotta move a little farther back into the foliage."

Rebecca wordlessly obeyed.

They slid past the brushing vegetation, crawled over fallen trees for some minutes.

Something rustled in the forest behind them. Ian tensed.

"What is it?" Rebecca asked.

"I don't know. The smell of blood keeps drawing more to the area. Not safe back there now. That's why we're moving on just a bit."

"What about the hatch?"

"No way. The big fellow's out there sleeping it off. I don't want to wake him up." Ian patted her protectively on the shoulder. For a moment, she relaxed. Then she gazed upwards.

"Ian. Look. . . . Look at the light. It's getting dark! Oh my God, no. . . . It's getting *dark!*"

Coopersmith studied the junglescape and noticed that the colors seemed a bit more saturated, that the shadows were deeper, darker than they had previously been. Flipping down his goggles, he stared up at what he could see of the light rod in the far away center of the cylinder.

It *did* seem dimmer. More solidly defined.

He held Rebecca for a moment after flipping up the goggles. "You're right. The light source must be timed, automatically, so that it produces a natural cycle of night and day."

Rebecca shivered. "Ian, I don't think I can stand it here in the darkness. . . ."

"Let's get away from the clearing. The safest place would be up in some high branches. Can you climb a tree?"

"Sure I can," she said, almost indignantly. She was recovering her spunk. Good, thought Coopersmith. She'd need it.

They stood and walked cautiously farther into the cooling shadows of the forest as darkness descended. The world was again lulled into false serenity by insects.

A cry of hunger pierced the growing darkness.

CHAPTER 7

CHRIST, what a wretched headache he had.

Phineas Kemp seemed wrapped in a thick mist of preoccupation as he sat in an uncharacteristic slouch before the Command console. All around him, voices blended in a babble of shouts. Confusion and shock and even a hint of panic stirred through the room, like the echoes of his own mind. The headache had been there before all this. Now it pounded like the voice of doom.

The Deep Space radio crackled with the voice of *Heinlein* pilot Fratz, but Phineas was not listening. He kept replaying the sounds of the final attack by the Allosaurus on his crew. *Rebecca*. Visions of her mauled swam in his brain, as violently as the ache there. Becky! No. . . . Not Becky!

He managed to remain calm. So far no final verification, no *proof* that she had been killed. She might have escaped. . . .

"Colonel Kemp. . . . ?" Communications Officer Alterman said.

"Yes? What is it?"

"I've got Commander Fratz on hold, sir. He's awaiting further instructions."

"Oh, yes. Of course," said Kemp.

He'd been in the Mission Command Center when the *Heinlein* crew entered Artifact One. Kemp and the Chiefs of Staff had shared the astonishment of the crew's finding. A little world. . . . A lost world. . . . A *model* of the Jurassic period of Earth, perfectly preserved. Incredible, inconceivable. . . . And yet they'd seen it with their own eyes, heard its savage sounds.

They'd watched helplessly as the crew was overrun by the carnivorous beasts.

Kemp expelled a shivery breath as he flicked the transmission switch on his console. "Kemp here. Go on, Fratz."

Fratz's voice was strained. "Colonel, we've completely lost contact with the exploration team. Do you want us to go in?"

"Negative, Fratz. You and Bracken are not equipped to deal with the situation in there. We're going to need some fairly sophisticated weaponry and defensive rigs to handle those lizards."

"What about my crew!"

"I think. . . . I think we have to presume that they are beyond our help at this point. At any rate, I don't want to risk the loss of more lives and equipment. I want you to remain in matched orbit with Artifact One for twenty-four hours. If any of the crew have survived, that should give them enough time to reach Huff's communication gear and contact your ship. If they contact you, request further orders from Mission Control. We'll be studying the situation down here. We'll keep you updated. That's it for now. Copernicus out."

Fratz signed off, leaving Phineas alone with his thoughts. He was of two minds about sending Fratz and Bracken into the alien ship. There were arguments for both courses of action, but Kemp was not emotionally prepared to discuss them at the moment.

Someone slapped him on the shoulder and sat down. It was Gregor Kolenkhov. "My friend, I cannot believe this. How can we have seen what we have indeed seen. By Lenin's Tomb, I have never heard of such a thing!"

"Who could have anticipated anything like this?" asked Kemp

rhetorically, shaking his head. He was getting groggy from lack of sleep, having been up for the last twenty hours. He wondered if he could fall asleep knowing what was happening out beyond the orbit of Mars.

"But what the hell *is* that thing?" said Kolenkhov. "An alien ship full of *dinosaurs* . . . it's absurd . . . it's unreal."

"But it *is* real, Gregor. We *know* that it is, and we must deal with it as such." Phineas looked about the room, where the other Chiefs were standing about talking, obviously unsure as to whether or not they should intrude on his conversation. Phineas had the feeling that even though he must get approval from the Joint Directors, everyone was looking to him for the solutions—even though he had thoroughly fouled up the first two attempts to deal with exploration of Artifact One. What was it the Americans always said—three strikes and you're out? He had a feeling that they were correct.

"Where did it come from?" asked Kolenkhov. "That's what keeps eating at me. What *is* it?"

Kemp looked up at his friend, trying to push the troubled thoughts from his mind. "I've been thinking about it," he said slowly. "Labate figures that it could have been in solar orbit for a long time, right? Why not for about a hundred and sixty million years?"

"That's impossible. What kind of civilization could have built a ship, or *anything* for that matter, that could last that long?"

"It's not impossible," said Phineas. "Artifact One is a completely self-sufficient *world*. It could be equipped with servomechanisms and systems that are self-repairing. It could be a robot-ship that is capable of existing indefinitely. As for the dinosaurs, the answer seems rather obvious—it's some kind of 'specimen ship' that visited our world back during the Jurassic. The alien crew, whoever they were, probably outfitted the interior of the ship with the suitable atmosphere, and then picked up samples of Earth life-forms. It would seem probable that the ship is capable of creating a variety of planetary environments, depending upon what world the aliens visited."

"Big-game hunters of the galaxy," said Kolenkhov. "Incredible. But you might be right. . . ."

"The big question remains, though: Who were the aliens

who built that ship, and what happened to them?"

"You mean why didn't the ship ever leave our solar system after picking up the animals? Why is it still here after hundreds of millions of years?"

"Yes. As perfect-seeming as Artifact One might appear to us, something must have gone wrong. Either with the crew or with their interstellar drive. A plague perhaps, which could have wiped out the crew? Some kind of equipment failure? I don't know. . . ."

"Maybe this isn't the time to be worrying about it, my friend."

"You're right," said Kemp. "I've got to answer to the Joint Directors for this fiasco. Six more people killed and time is running out."

"Running out for what?"

"The closer that thing gets to the sun, the faster it is accelerating. The closer it comes to us, the more chance that the Chinese or the Third World will detect its presence. I don't have to tell you how bad it would be if either of them got their hands on that ship."

"What do you have in mind?" Kolenkhov asked.

"I don't see where we have much choice. Whether or not the *Heinlein* does make contact—we *have* to send another ship out there, Gregor. We've got to intercept that ship and bring it into our own backyard, and we've got to do it fast."

"What about Fratz and Bracken?"

"I don't know. If I keep them out there, waiting for something that might not happen, it seems to serve no purpose. But if another ship is dispatched to intercept them, they could help the new crew get things operational."

"If you're asking me for my opinion," said the large Russian, "I would let them stay there. Just in case. . . . You never know."

Kemp shook his head in thought. "I have to think about it for a while. Everyone is kind of in a state of shock right now. It's probably not a good time to ask for rational observation or advice. Nobody could have predicted anything like this. . . ."

Neither man spoke for a moment. The silence that hung in the Mission Control Center was a heavy cloak which threatened to suffocate everyone. The Communications Chief, Alterman, broke the silence. "Colonel Kemp . . . I've got a message from the Joint Directors. They would like to see you at once. Executive Conference Room in Admins."

Kemp grinned ironically. "Well, I can't say I haven't expected this...."

Gregor Kolenkhov stood up and put his large, beefy hand on Kemp's shoulder. "Listen, my friend. It might not help matters, but you can tell them that all of us are behind you a hundred percent."

Smiling, Kemp shook his head. "Thank you, Gregor. I hate to admit it, but I'm feeling pretty isolated right about now."

Kolenkhov picked up the feelings beneath the words and his expression changed from cheeriness to a grim embarrassment. "About Becky...I don't know what to say...except that perhaps we have no confirmation that she was...was lost."

Kemp shook his head. "I...I shouldn't let my emotions get in the way, Gregor, I'm sorry."

"Phineas, please, you have nothing to be sorry about. Our lives are not controlled by graphs and computer readouts. It's *okay* to *feel* things, you should know that."

Kemp shook his head, knowing that Kolenkhov was correct. The man had inadvertently touched upon one of the greatest problems in Kemp's life. Becky was constantly bugging him to let himself go, to *feel*. Now he wondered if it mattered anymore. "All right," he said finally. "Thank you, Gregor. I suppose I should be getting over to Admins. Take over for me here, would you?"

"Of course."

The conference room table was lined with the four Joint Directors and Oscar Rheinhardt of Security. No one else was present. They waited until Kemp had entered the room and took a seat at the end of the table. He felt as though he was on trial.

Director Johl cleared his throat before speaking. "We would like to take this opportunity to tell you how shocked and sorry we are to have to meet with you under these conditions. However, I want to stress at the beginning that we do not hold you responsible for what happened to the *Heinlein* crew."

As the others nodded, Kemp thought to himself that he did

not care what the Directors felt—because he held *himself* responsible for the disaster. That was what counted. But all he said was: "Thank you, sir. I understand completely."

Johl nodded and continued. "The reason for the meeting is obvious, Colonel. What do we do now?"

Phineas paused for a moment, reflecting on what he had said to Kolenkhov privately. They had been his true feelings on the operation and he saw no reason to veil them when speaking with the IASA Directors.

"The way I see things, sir, there is nothing we *can* do . . . except to try again. I suggest that we outfit one of our biggest ships—one of the Outer Planets Class like the *Goddard* or the *Von Braun*—and get a team of the best specialists available. We go out there for two reasons: to search for survivors, and to rig Artifact One with some high-thrust engines so that we can steer it out of its present orbit and guide it back to Earth. We can put it into Earth-moon L-5 position, where we can study it indefinitely. I don't think I have to explain the scientific, as well as political, importance that alien ship represents."

Everyone at the table nodded thoughtfully. Chris Alvarez looked at Kemp, then spoke. "Is this suggestion of yours feasible, Colonel? Do we have the equipment and the know-how to pull it off?"

"Once we have assembled our personnel, we can run a variety of feasibility-scenarios through the computers. Then we would have a few optimal probability models to choose from. I'm convinced that we can handle it. Now that we know what we are up against."

Several of the other Directors discussed Kemp's plan among themselves, as though he were not present. He could not detect anything negative in their considerations. Everyone seemed to be of the same basic belief—that they had no choice but to continue to deal with Artifact One. There was simply no way that humankind could ignore the presence of such an incredible discovery.

"Time is our worst enemy at this point," said one of the Russian Joint Directors. "You must begin assembling a crew for the second mission immediately. How long would it take?"

"Under normal conditions, I would not launch a Deep-Space ship the size of the *Goddard* without at least two weeks of preparation, but we don't have that kind of time. We must launch within seventy-two hours to ensure that we intercept with enough time to outfit Artifact One and revise its flight path."

"Is it possible to mobilize in that short a time?" asked Nelson Johl.

"I'm going to need a lot of help," said Kemp.

"You'll get that," said Alvarez.

"What about Security?" asked Phineas. "How are we going to cover the kind of activity that will be going on around here? Copernicus Base will be turned upside down in the rush to get that ship and crew ready."

Oscar Rheinhardt cleared his throat. "I've been giving that some thought, Phineas. That's why I've been invited to attend this little get-together. The official line of the *Heinlein* mission was a preliminary survey of a large rogue asteroid on a close approach with the Earth. I can prepare a statement for the media and for the general staff on Copernicus that should satisfy even the most curious."

"Such as?"

"Well, I'll get together with Professor Labate, and have him concoct some data on the rogue asteroid. We will say that there is a possibility of close flyby with the moon, and that we are sending another ship out there to either divert the course of the thing, or rig it with some H-bombs and blow it to hell and back."

Kemp shook his head. "It sounds a bit shaky to me, but I don't suppose we have much choice. There may be some level of panic among the general population if they think there's any chance of their colony being perturbed by a gigantic piece of rock."

"We will try to downplay the dangerous aspects of the possibility, saying that as long as we act quickly, there will be little cause for alarm. That should cover the need for triple-shift preparation on the launch."

"All right, Oscar, I suppose I should not try to tell you how to handle that end of things." Kemp laughed shortly. "I'm going to have enough problems, I think."

There followed a lengthy discussion of how the mission should be coordinated and what responsibilities for launch prep arations would be handled by whom. Kemp was frequently asked for his advice, and gradually a well-formed, concise plan was hammered out. The selection of specific crew members was held off until the other items had been dealt with, but finally the subject was reached. Phineas had several people in mind, and it was agreed that if Copernicus and Tsiolkovskii did not have the right specialist for the right job, then they would be summoned from Earth on the next shuttle.

"There is only one more thing," said Phineas, "that I have not discussed with you." He looked at the small group of Joint Directors, waiting for the right dramatic moment.

"And what is that?" asked Chris Alvarez.

"I thought you would have expected it, or perhaps even asked me about the possibility," said Phineas. "But since the subject has not come up, I think I should clarify my position on the matter."

"And what is that, Colonel?" Nelson Johl tapped his briar pipe into a large glass ashtray.

"It has been agreed that I should be responsible for the selection of the officer to be placed in charge of the second mission . . . and I have been thinking about who would be the right person for the job." Phineas paused and cleared his throat. "And I think that the best person for the job is Colonel Phineas Kemp."

CHAPTER 8

THE MAN WAITED.

Though it was the quietest time of the evening in this part of the large lunar colony, the man could hear the occasional clatter of footsteps. So far, one of his fellow colonists had actually used the stairs by which he waited. But there was nothing unusual about finding a man in a stairwell, having a smoke. Smoking was not permitted in the corridors. The stairwells, however, had drafts and therefore, though still legally off-limits to lit cigarettes, it was general knowledge that if you didn't have a private compartment to poison your lungs in right on hand, you could use the nearest stairwell.

The man let the cigarette burn in his hand. He despised cigarettes. Smoking them, however, was a good reason to loiter here like this, waiting for his contact.

The cigarette burned down to the filter. The man stubbed it out in a tiny portable box, which also held the ashes.

He took out another, sighed, and lit it.

"Bring one for me?"

Startled, the man spun around. The Quartermaster was regarding him from just above. He gave the man a smirk, and joined him.

Feeling guilt as heavy as ever, the man handed over the documents in his briefcase. The Quartermaster began to thumb through them after accepting a cigarette.

Another secret meeting, thought the man, only hours after the Joint Directors meeting. Out in the depths of space, the alien vessel hurtled on down the gravity well towards the sun, while the *Heinlein* and its abruptly depleted crew hung nearby, watching and waiting. At Copernicus Base, all necessary personnel had been put on triple-shift status as preparation for the launch of the *Goddard* got into full swing.

The man wished he did not know what he knew.

But then . . . well, there was Jimmy to think of, wasn't there?

He was quite high in the command hierarchy of Copernicus Base. With more than thirty years of service in the IASA, he was beyond reproach and suspicion. Yet he was the most highly valued espionage agent for the Third World Confederation.

More than ten years ago he'd been approached by the TWC with an offer that was difficult to refuse. The agent's son was employed as a Reclamation Engineer in East Africa; he would be assassinated if the agent did not comply with TWC demands. All very simple. Direct and straightforward—two attributes which were *not* hallmarks of the Third World confederation— and yet it worked perfectly in this particular instance. For ten years, the IASA official had served as a leak-proof pipeline to the Intelligence Division of Ramadas Khan Base.

The second member of the meeting was, on the surface, a Quartermaster for Ramadas Khan Base. Each month the TWC Quartermaster checked through Security at Copernicus to receive vital supplies carried to the moon in IASA shuttles. It had been more than a decade since the TWC technology had been outstripped by the Copernicus and Tsiolkovskii Space Programs. Without logistical and economic support from the IASA, Ramadas Khan would be as empty as a ghost town.

Each month the Quartermaster met with an IASA official concerned with him, under the auspices of the Lunar Free Trade

Treaty. Later however, he would meet with his more important contact, from whom he received other vital supplies. It was a simple fact of life that governments did not live by bread alone.

"What do you have to tell me?" the Quartermaster asked. The man was of a dark complexion. He wore a self-satisfied smile on his handsome features.

"There have been few developments since the Snipe was destroyed by the alien ship," the IASA official said quickly.

"Have you heard from your son lately? I understand he is doing well . . . for now."

Dammit. The guy *knew* something was up. Perhaps he had another informant, only on a lower level. "All right, there has been something new." Reluctantly, the IASA official explained the disastrous voyage and discovery of the *Heinlein,* and the resultant plans of the Joint Directors to launch a larger ship to intercept Artifact One.

"Do you feel they can do it?"

"Definitely."

"When do they plan to launch?"

"Within fifty-six hours."

"Of course, you must understand that my government will want one of our people on board that ship." It was not a question. The TWC Quartermaster grinned unctuously.

"Yes. I understand."

"Can you arrange that?"

"I don't know. Security clearance will be very tough."

"But you *can* arrange it, *can't* you?" Again, there was no suggestion of a question.

"I . . . think so."

"That is good. Good for you. Good for us. And of course good for your son, who is doing such a nice job in the Republic of East Africa."

The IASA official did not speak for a moment. "You know, I've always hated this. You people have never made it easy for me to be sympathetic to your causes. I don't mean the threats and the reprisals. That's part of being adults in an adult world. It's just that you all seem to be such a bunch of humorless, cold-hearted bastards."

"You do not seem to object to our humorless, cold-hearted money," said the Quartermaster, frowning. "You look at us through the distortions of your own culture, and therefore you do not understand the motivations that fuel us. That is the way it has always been. You should know better than most that we have suffered greatly within the last two decades. Our ancestors who fought and schemed so hard to bring our people to greatness would be very displeased with us now. Do you know how terrible a feeling it is to achieve the pinnacle of global power— only to have it snatched away by forces beyond your control? My people are accustomed to suffering. It is a part of a long, bloody heritage. But we will not tolerate humiliation."

"Since when is oil depletion viewed as a humiliating tactic? Even back in the eighties, your leaders knew that their stranglehold on the world economy would be short-lived. It is now time to pay the piper."

The Quartermaster flung his half-smoked cigarette down and stepped on it angrily. "Don't get wise with me! I am not here to argue political and economic ideologies. I am here because the survival of the Confederation depends on people like *me*."

"And me, unfortunately. If you didn't have a flock of scared stool pigeons puking their guts out everytime you rang the bell, your wonderful Confederation would be back in their mud-huts and desert tents where you belong."

"Flattery will get you nowhere. My people are quite proud of the simple beginnings from which we have come. The fact you and your governments fail to accept is that things will never be so simple again."

"I see. . . . Once you've had a taste of the good life, there is no returning to the Garden of Eden."

"You could phrase it like that. You with your penchant for simplistic Western fables. Nevertheless, my people have learned quickly the ways of the world. This latest discovery will be the key to our own renaissance. The governments that control the power of the ship coming toward us can control their own future. My people are destined for that power. We mean to have it by any means."

"Whatever you say. Just make sure my son stays healthy. If anything happens to him, you can bet I'll turn myself in and blow the whistle on you."

"We keep our bargains. I must go now. The supply vans will be loaded. Just remember that my people will want one of our agents on board that second mission. I don't think I should have to remind you what the consequences would be if you do not comply."

"You will kill my son . . . go ahead and *say* it. You've said it so many times before, why be gentle at this point of the game?"

"Very well. We will kill your son. Satisfied?"

The IASA official looked away. "We'd better break this up now."

"We will meet again at the next shipment?"

"Do I have a choice?"

"No. Goodbye."

The Quartermaster departed quickly and quietly, leaving the troubled TWC agent to ponder what must now be done. It would not be difficult to place a Third World operative on board the *Goddard*. There were several men and women in Deep-Space Operations who qualified for the assignments, and who would be beyond suspicion since they had never been asked by their government to engage in any covert activities. TWC Intelligence, seeing the growing need for an extensive espionage network almost twenty years before, had been placing operatives within the IASA with regularity. Some of these operatives had never been utilized, but they were always available if needed.

Somewhere beyond the orbit of Mars, Artifact One spun in toward the sun. The IASA official considered the implications of what he had been asked to do, and wondered if the life of his son was worth the trade.

Sleep would not come easily tonight, he knew.

It was business as usual for Marcus Abdul Jashad. His orders had taken him to Paris, the famed City of Light, and he regretted that he would be having such a short stay in what—even *he* was forced to admit—remained one of the most beautiful and fascinating cities on the planet. Yes, his stay would be unfortunately brief, but such was the nature of his business.

He sat by the chair at the window of the Hotel Internationale, a soaring glass tower which overlooked the promenade to Versailles, the age-old site of meetings, treaties, and summit conferences. Later that morning, delegates from the European

Economic Alliance would be conferring with the leaders of the Third World Confederation in a mini-summit enclave. The white men of Europe would be sitting down with the darkly-complected ministers of the TWC to discuss issues of the day, said *Le Monde*. *Issues of the day!* thought Jashad. *How quaint a phrase!*

These Europeans were so smug, now that they were no longer under the thumb of the petroleum cartel, of the TWC. Our day in the sun has been too swift, sweet but fleeting, thought Jashad. And now the old men of his alliance were knuckling under to the fierce economic pressure being brought to bear by the rich, influential nations of the West and the East. There was an ugly attitude brewing in the camps hostile to the TWC that now it was growing time to pay the piper. In the last quarter of the twentieth century, the Arab and African states had called the tune, and the whole world had danced. But now, the oil was practically gone, and what was left was not wanted. Their base of power obliterated, the TWC was falling on hard times, and was beginning to kowtow to the whims of the other nations of the world.

It was an unthinkable position to Jashad, and the hatred for the white man and his technology burned deep in him. He sucked deeply on an Egyptian cigarette, exhaled, and then broke into a coughing spasm. A large clot of phlegm became dislodged in his chest, rocketing up his throat. Jashad caught it on the end of his tongue and wiped it away with the tip of his index finger. He stared at the dark, sticky mass for a moment, considering that he should again try to quit smoking, and then flicked it away contemptuously. It struck the filigreed wallpaper of the suite and clung to it like a living thing. Jashad smiled at his minor gesture of defiance, and took another deep drag from his cigarette.

Checking his watch, he saw that it was almost time. He moved to the bed, where his suitcase lay open. First, he removed a case of what appeared to be Cuban cigars, each wrapped in a thin aluminum tube. He opened the case and began opening the cigar tubes, shaking out of each a false top which contained a cut-off panatella tip. Then he began to screw together eight of the tubes, fitting their micromachined threads into one another until he had the barrel and chamber of a weapon. From his camera bag, he removed the handgrip from his Nikon system and fitted it to the barrel. A trigger-assembly was concealed as part of a bartender's kit, and a high-powered scope masqueraded as a telephoto lens. Even the shrewdest customs agent would never see a weapon among such ordinary objects. Jashad's ammunition was always supplied by local agents—inevitably more than enough for his assignment—and he especially enjoyed the kind presently provided. It was a caliber hollow-point explosive shell which left no doubt of any impact outcome. Even a shot to an extremity such as the arm or leg caused such massive shock to the body that the victim's heart and nervous system was instantly jellied. It was a shell which the American CIA listed as "very high on the 'lethality index.' "

Jashad grinned as he thought of the typically Western governmentese while loading the clip into his weapon. They were such fools! Did they really think that the younger factions of the TWC would let the old men roll over and play dead? There comes a time when all things must admit their age and decrepitness, a time to move over for the young jackals . . . or be devoured by them.

Again, he returned to the window, where he had cut a small hole in the thermal glass, large enough to admit the barrel of his weapon. He sat down in a chair and watched the promenade where already the French gendarmes were lining the streets and barricades, where the motorcycle patrols were forming an advance guard for the limousine column now advancing upon the old palace. Through his scope, it was as though the steps to Versailles were twenty paces distant, and Jashad smiled at the absurd simplicity of this assignment. In all the years of paranoia and high technology, nothing had been effectively done to prevent the efficiency of one man with a gun.

Calmly he watched for the approach of the silver, turn-of-the-century Rolls Royce of Ada Kadan Mrundi, the Economic Minister of the TWC, and the elder statesman of the Confederation. When Mrundi had been a young man, he had been a fiercely respected leader of Third World objectives, a hero to young boys who called him by his tribal name—"The Simba"— the great lion. But now, the Arab leaders had become disenchanted with their African ally and feared that he would lead them all down a primrose path to economic strangulation at the hands of the white men. The *Jiha* had decided that Mrundi must be eliminated publicly so that the whole world would know that the TWC was not ready to roll over and play dead.

And who else but Marcus Jashad would be the one selected for this monumental task, this important message to the world? Was he not the premier specialist in such matters in perhaps the whole world? To some, he was an international hero, to others, an international criminal. He smiled at the thought. It did not matter what the world thought of him. He knew his job and he knew it well. One of the best, yes. . . .

And then, out of the morning mist, came the procession of armored limousines. Through his scope, he watched for the silver Rolls, catching it glinting off the sun's rays, following it carefully to the front of the palace. Checking his clip and the firing chamber, he drew in a breath and held it, watching the magnified figures of security personnel caper about the opening doors to the vehicles. And then Mrundi was visible in gaily colored tribal robes, surrounded by the press of his body-guards so that only his shining bald head was visible in their midst.

There would only be seconds before he was carried into the mirrored halls of the palace. Only seconds for the job to be done, but that was all Jashad required. He squeezed the trigger twice and the weapon recoiled silently as the shells raced to their mark. Jashad grinned as he watched his work through the scope. Mrundi's shining bald head suddenly exploded like a piece of over-ripened fruit and his party of bodyguards were sprayed with a fine pink mist, expressions of shock upon their faces.

Withdrawing the weapon from the tiny hole in the glass, Jashad dropped it to the floor, where it fell silently onto the carpet. He changed his clothes deliberately, wishing that he had a woman at his disposal. He always felt a need for a violent sexual release after an assignment such as this one, and on some lucky occasions he had been able to punish a young one with his excess energies. The younger the better, he thought with a smile, as he put on dark glasses and left the suite.

By the time he reached the lobby, there was already a subtle hum of confusion and a tinge of fear in the throngs which were moving out into the street. Calmly, he joined them, assuming their mask of a apprehension and morbidity, and moved as close as the gendarmes' barriers would allow. He watched the follow-up until the ambulances and the police vans made it impossible, and then he simply disappeared into the crowd.

That evening he was in a small fishing village on the coast of Portugal where he would be meeting his contact—a small yacht which would take him across the Mediterranean to Alexandria. At last he would have his rest and his reward—they had promised him *three* ten-year-olds this time. It would be a pleasant cruise indeed.

But when the dinghy pulled up to the shoreline, Jashad could see that something was wrong. He was an expert at reading the faces of men, and he could see that the *Jiha* captain who greeted him carried an unexpected message.

"What's wrong?" he asked as he climbed aboard.

"You know that there's been a change of plans?" The captain's expression was of mild confusion and surprise.

"Not really," said Jashad. "You tell me."

"Something important has come up. A change of plans, and you will be needed immediately."

Jashad felt a rush of outrage shoot through. "Is this how they repay me for such a cleanly executed job! When?! And where?!"

The boat slipped into the oily black waters towards not a yacht, but the sleek, low-profile lines of a military gun-boat. The *Jiha* captain shook his head. "I'm sorry, Marcus. But we need you *now*. You are going to the moon."

CHAPTER 9

THE STEAMY HEAT of the Jurassic forest hung about Ian Coopersmith. He half-reclined in the broad, firm fronds of a towering, prehistoric fern, where he and Rebecca Thalberg had spent the night in a kind of half-sleep punctuated by the nightcries of predators and prey. It was the morning of their seventh "day" on board Artifact One, and Ian was gradually learning necessitics for survival in the harsh, uncompromising environment of Earth's long-ago past.

Thirty-two kilometers above his head, running the length of the gigantic cylinder-ship, stretched a burning rod of heat and light. Coopersmith had assumed that it was some kind of gigantic fusion reactor—a p-p reaction—perhaps being fed by induction of interstellar hydrogen. Possibly the power source was something more exotic, like the new power kernels—Kerr-Newman black holes with McAndrew shields—or maybe the theoretical quark modulator made fact. Coopersmith could not be certain, but any civilization that could build a ship as magnificent as Artifact One could not be limited from developing *any* kind of technological miracle. The illuminator, as Ian had come to refer to it, operated on a roughly twelve-hour cycle—simulating a never-ending sequence of artificial days and nights. The temperature varied by less than ten degrees Centigrade by Ian's estimate between the days and the nights, but it was enough of a difference to produce temperature gradients along the length of the cylinder and produce cyclic forms of "weather."

Although Coopersmith had been a tactical engineer for most of his professional career, he had a modicum of survival experience in the outdoors, thanks to vacations spent camping in the American Northwest. Though he was not expert, he possessed enough knowledge to have, thus far, kept him and Thalberg alive. Water could be found in stream-fed lakes, underground "springs"—which in reality must have been vast storage tanks and recycling systems—and, if need be, swamps or rainpools. Food was found in a large variety of greens and fruit-clusters that they observed the herbivorous dinosaurs eating. Early on in their wanderings, Ian decided that they would eat no fruits or seeds that they did not see the lizards consume themselves. So far, at least, they had not poisoned themselves. On the second day, he discovered a mineral deposit of flint, which he used to chip at the steel edge of his belt-buckle, and from that point on, he and Rebecca had fire if they needed it. She had kept reminding him that they would require protein in their diets to maintain their stamina and strength, and the fire would help make left-over carrion from a felled herbivore more palatable.

They had their first taste of Iguanodon on the fourth day, and to their surprise, it was not the taste-horror that had been imagined.

During their week in the jungle lowlands, Ian had been able to make some elementary observations about the behavior of the dinosaurs, which had helped them survive. It seemed as though the daily routine of life among beasts was a never-ending cycle of feeding, sleeping, copulating, and eliminating. The fleshy herbivorous creatures such as the Diplodocus, Iguanodon, Brachiosaurus, and Trachodon remained near the swamps, rivers, and lakes, and seemed to do most of their feeding and copulating during the day-cycles. In their numerous encounters thus far with the herbivorous dinosaurs, Ian had noted that the large creatures were quite skittish and almost afraid of the humans—when they noticed them at all. It seemed that the plant-eaters possessed such low levels of intelligence that they usually failed to detect Ian and Rebecca even when they blundered into their midst. They seemed to depend more on their sense of smell and hearing than on sight, and were only dangerous if you remained in their path as they clumsily waddled along.

The carnivores were another story altogether.

Having seen how quickly and savagely the Gorgosaurus and the Allosaurus had devastated the exploration team, Ian and Rebecca had a fearful but healthy respect for the meat-eating species. From long-distance observation, Ian had noted that the predators normally were less in evidence during the middle of the day-cycles, and it was not uncommon for them to be found lying in a clearing, dozing loudly at these times. The carnivorous dinosaurs did their principal feeding at night, relying on a super-keen sense of smell, remarkably sharp night-vision, and incredible quickness. Ian reflected upon his early books of childhood on dinosaurs which often referred to them all as lumbering and slow. Nothing could be further from the truth in regard to the meat-eaters—they were swift without a doubt. It was difficult to sleep for the first few evenings because of the nocturnal feeding habits of the predators, and the darkness was constantly being shattered by their savage cries, and the bleating, sheep-like sounds of their victims being literally eaten alive.

Because of the feeding patterns, Ian and Rebecca had taken to spending their nights in the highest trees, usually protored-woods, giant ferns, and the occasional large ginkgo. They could easily find something taller than the largest of the meat-eaters, which would be approximately ten meters. At least Ian had not seen anything larger than that, but he could not be sure that some truly monstrous Tyrannosaurus did not prowl only in the darkest of nights, and had yet to be seen by them. He did not wish to think about such things.

It had been bad enough adjusting to the sounds of the night, especially when they would be anchored into the treetops, held in by "safety harnesses" which Ian had fashioned from vines, and some large beast would stagger into their particular tree, shaking them from their half-sleep with earthquake immediacy. There had also been one occasion when two bipedal carnivores (Ian had not the presence of mind, nor sufficient light, to identify them) had smelled them as they slept in the high limbs of a proto-redwood. The scent of such helpless, fear-struck morsels had driven the carnivores into a mindless frenzy, for they remained at the base of the tree for almost the entire night, endlessly attempting to scale the tall, thin tree. Leaping, ripping, and tearing, they continued until Rebecca was driven to the edge of hysteria. They had no choice but to hang in the darkness, hoping that the terrible claws would gain no purchase, that the knife-edge jaws would not come flying up out of the damp night. As the dawn had grown closer, the two predators gave up their attempts and searched for more accessible prey, but when Ian descended from the tree an hour after the day-cycle had begun, he was shocked to see the deep gouges in its base, literally thousands of claw-slashes left as a monument to the savage intensity of the hunters.

They had spent the first three days trying to retrace their panicked flight through jungle back to the entrance hatch where they had first come upon the beasts, but this had proved fruitless. They had entered the Jurassic forest at nightfall, and spent several maniac-hours running mindlessly through the darkness, climbing trees only to find them unsuitable, or searching for outcroppings of rock that might have a small fissure or cave. Ian and Rebecca had failed to identify and remember any significant landmarks that might have helped them recognize the approximate location of the small clearing by the swamp, and the smaller knoll where the hatch had opened. There was the additional problem of learning to plot one's position on a landmass that had no celestial features other than the longitudinal shaft of energy going down the center of the ship. This was good for achieving a "north-south" orientation, but little else. With a landmass that curved away and up in both "east" and "west" directions, it was difficult to readily deduce one's position.

After three days of wandering hopelessly through the interior, Coopersmith had suggested that they not continue to search for the hatch. It was possible that it had been accidentally closed by the inadvertent actions of some dinosaur, or perhaps some automatic mechanism had sealed it after some predetermined amount of time. If it did remain open, it was doubtful that he and Rebecca could find it without risking a terrible death. From his observations, Ian had learned that the most dangerous places to be were near the marshes and lakeshores—for it was here that the herbivores huddled for food and drink, and that drew the predators. The hatch, as Ian reminded her, was perilously close to a natural feeding ground, and he would just as soon avoid it as not.

His reasoning was not unsound, because it was only logical to assume that Copernicus Base would eventually send another exploration team into the ship, and that if he and Rebecca could survive until the next team arrived, then they would be saved. Ian further reasoned that the best way to remain alive would be to do those things that would keep them as far from the predators as possible.

And so on the fourth day, they had begun, at Ian's suggestion, following the topography as it sloped gradually upwards to a highland of sorts in the direction of the ship's engines. The higher ground seemed safer, since the rivers ran down to the lakes and marshes below and drew the dinosaurs with them. It had been Coopersmith's vague plan to work their way toward the rear end of the ship in the hope of finding some sign of entrance into engine rooms or perhaps the alien crew section of the ship. If they could gain entrance to the business-end of the ship, they might be able to use the communications equipment to contact Copernicus. If that proved impossible, they would at least have a haven from the predators of the interior.

They had traveled in a "southerly" direction, using the illuminator as their rough guide, for three days, and with each passing cycle they learned more about the magnificent world within the ship. The world-shaping aliens had been meticulous in their reconstruction of an early-Earth environment. Ian and Rebecca passed gorges, mudflats, raging white-water rivers, placid streams, impenetrable forests, jagged peaks in the highlands, and even volcanoes in various stages of eruption. The interior was a miniature Earth in every respect save the land mass, which curved and hung above their head some sixty-five kilometers distant. It was, in one sense, a primitive paradise. Ian found that he had mixed feelings about a world so untouched by the hands of man.

He stirred slowly as he came to full consciousness, feeling the tightness of the vine-harness he had fixed the previous evening. For the first few hours of the day-cycle, his muscles would be screaming at him, in defiance at being shackled to the limbs of the trees. Looking up several branches, he saw Rebecca sprawled and tied upon the broad fronds of her own limb. She was still sleeping and he hesitated in waking her, though it was important that they use all the daylight hours wisely.

"Becky...." he said softly. "It's time for breakfast."

The dark-haired woman jumped fitfully and was instantly awake. She looked down at Ian with large brown eyes. He was surprised at how attractive she looked after a week without a proper bath, hair conditioners, and the other things which women put to such good use.

"Ooh, God... I can't believe I'm still alive," she said lazily.

Ian chuckled as he began unfastening his harness. "Are you fully expecting to wake up one morning and discover that you're *dead?*"

Becky laughed. "No. I want to wake up and find that this has all been the proverbial bad dream, and that I am back home in Copernicus."

"Why Copernicus? Why not go the whole hog, as they used to say, and be back in Kansas?"

"Ian Coopersmith... I do believe you're setting me up for the old 'Toto, I have a feeling we're not in Kansas anymore' line...."

He smiled impishly. "Well, maybe I was..... Sorry about that. Do you need some help getting untied?"

"No, I've got it. What did you say about breakfast?"

"I just said it was *time* for it. Never said a word about what it was going to be."

"As usual. When are they going to start providing menus around here?" Becky pulled the last vine away from her, and held on tightly to the thick limbs which supported her, slowly inching towards the trunk of the giant fern.

"I think they've been serving the same menu here for a long, long time," he said. "Come on, let's get down and see what we can find. Some scrambled Pterosaur eggs, perhaps. Or maybe some nice fresh leftovers...."

Ian worked his way down the tree's trunk, then waited for Becky to follow. She was quite agile and plenty strong for someone her size. As far as taking care of herself, Ian felt that she was doing a more than adequate job. She rarely had trouble doing any of the tasks that needed to be done. In the week they had been thrown together, Ian had come to respect and admire her. On the few social occasions he had met her when she was dating Phineas Kemp, Ian had to admit not being too impressed by Rebecca Thalberg. She had seemed somewhat pushy in social situations, and had the annoying habit of constantly reminding people that she was a top-flight surgeon and Biomed specialist. Ian now wondered if being under the penumbra of Kemp's many accomplishments made Becky feel impelled to assert her own individuality in any way she could. . . .

As she reached the loamy, sponge-like soil, Ian was already glancing about warily, listening for the sounds of heavy footfalls and thrashing foliage. The forest seemed quiet for the moment and he suggested that they shoulder their few supplies and move out. For the last day they had been heading across a rise in the land that was now beginning to slope downward toward what appeared to be a very lush, green valley. From the heights of the treetops Ian had seen a large river cutting through the center of a depression. He would have preferred to avoid the valley because of the higher dinosaur population that would be found near the waters, but the valley seemed so vast that it would take them several extra days to circumvent it.

They gathered primitive fruit-blossoms and large seed as they traveled "south" until they chanced upon the lower half of a small bipedal dinosaur's carcass. It was hanging in the tangled branches of a thicket, and was untouched except for the teeth-marks which had separated it from its head and shoulders. Ian assumed that the little fellow had been bounding along the night before and had unfortunately hopped into the jaws of one of the big boys. Having dined on the upper half, the predator must have lost the rest of its meal in the undergrowth, and rather than root it out, had moved on for larger, more satisfying prey.

At any rate, Ian quickly skinned and dressed the muscular thighs of the creature and prepared a fire. They would have to eat quickly since the scent of the cooking meat might attract some meat-eater who had not yet collapsed into the torpid, digestive state of the day-cycle, or perhaps one of the beasts who were getting smart enough to realize that there was ample opportunity to feed well during the times of light.

After finishing their "protein supplement," as Becky sardonically referred to their carrion meals, they kept moving into the thicker foliage of the downward-sloping terrain, until they reached a rocky outcropping, a ragged ledge which looked down into the river-valley.

Ian suggested that they rest for a moment among the rocks, since it was a fairly secure position. He sat peeling the rough, prickly skin off a gingko blossom, preparing to suck up some of its pulpy juices, when he spotted something down in the carpet greenery below their position.

"Now what in bloody hell is that?" Ian pointed to a spot far below them.

"What is it? Where?" Becky moved down beside him and followed the line of his index finger.

"See those white things? Way down and to the left of those yellowish tree-blossoms, or whatever they are. Those white patches...they almost look like they could be geometric shapes...like *buildings*."

"Buildings? Are you sure?"

"I don't know. We're too far away at this point, but I think we should investigate, don't you? It's in the same general direction we're headed."

"All right." Becky drew in her breath slowly. "I guess it doesn't matter what we do.....We're trapped here anyway."

"Oh, come on now? It's only temporary, I assure you. They're probably sending out another ship already. If I know Kemp, he probably has every man in Deep-Space Operations in on this one. We'll be rescued...all we have to do is keep ourselves alive, that's all."

As he dozed in the shade, Rebecca watched Coopersmith.

His well-shaped, muscular chest rose with steady regularity, his finely sculpted nostrils flaring as he exhaled the rich air. Some kind of insect buzzed by. Becky swatted it away. The man deserved a rest. She would see that he had it.

Surprising how much she'd come to like the guy.

Helping to keep her alive in this dreadful place was certainly a factor. But she'd come to admire him for more than his capabilities for survival. Despite the grimness of their situation, he'd managed to maintain his sense of humor. He could be a charming, engaging conversationalist when he cared to be, and, seeing their ordeal weighing on her mind as well as body, he used that talent often to cheer her up during meals, or when they strapped themselves into high branches and chatted while waiting for the sleep of exhaustion to overtake them. He seemed to brim over with an optimistic view of every situation. Obviously Coopersmith was not a man used to failing. His confidence had helped her no end. She'd come to depend on him emotionally, despite herself.

She used to resent people like Coopersmith—always cheery, always finding silver linings in the darkest of clouds—but when she found that his personality and world-view was infectious, it helped lend her strength and hope.

And he was damned attractive physically, too. Sometimes when she looked at him she felt . . . unusual. It was pleasant but troubling . . . and she tried to concentrate on other things.

In their conversations, she'd learned that Ian's mother had been a West Indian Black and his father white and British. That explained his rich dark complexion and somewhat angular Caucasian features. He spoke his English with a curious blend of accents—Island, London, and Houston—which she found increasingly charming. Coopersmith was big, strong, competent. His love for perfectly running machines and weapons-systems seemed to be shared with his respect for the human body, which he believed was a perfect biological mechanism. A disciple of stringent diet, he'd told her of his practice of always getting plenty of exercise. He practiced meditation as well, which seemed to instill in him a pleasant, almost Zenlike acceptance of the relationships between man, machine, and nature.

No, she'd never met a man quite like Ian Coopersmith.

He opened his eyes suddenly.

"You're staring at me," he said.

"Sorry. I like looking at people, and you're the only other human being around."

"I suggest that you keep your eyes elsewhere," he said good-

103

humoredly. "Or some creature might decrease the human population of this place by two."

"Okay, smarty. But it's my turn for a little shut-eye."

"And my turn to watch you."

"Now, now. Practice what you preach."

She lay back on the soft ground. The thought of his eyes on her was intriguing.

When their rest-period was over, they continued on across the highlands and slowly descended toward the river-valley. Ian paused every so often to get his bearings in relation to the illuminator and the relative position of the white objects he had seen from the heights. As they dropped lower into the dense foliage of the forests, the white things that might be buildings were often lost from view and Becky depended totally on Coopersmith's sense of direction. It was easy to see how they had lost their way in the first place and had been unable to find the entrance hatch. Even after Ian had claimed to have worked out a simple orientation method, and had attempted to explain it to her, Becky continued to feel hopelessly lost.

They continued downward for the better half of the day-cycle without incident until they stepped into a small clearing bisected by a small, shallow brook. There was a wide expanse of mudflat which flowed down to the water, covered with a variety of sizes of saurian footprints. Most of them were no larger than a man's, although there were several sets of deep, taloned prints, which suggested that predators favored this spot as a good feeding ground.

As Ian and Becky broke through the brush at the edge of the clearing, intending to use the brook as an opportunity to refill their water rations, Coopersmith stopped suddenly, putting his hand to his mouth in a pantomime of silence.

"Goddamn!" he whispered. "I didn't see that bugger until we stepped clear. Be quiet and don't move!"

"Where?" asked Becky, looking beyond Ian, but seeing nothing.

"There. By those trees. He's almost the same color as the brush. . . ."

Becky saw it now, and her breath caught for a moment in fear.

Concentrating on picking out the beast's natural camouflage from the flora, she could now see the bipedal dinosaur. It was a theropod of the Gorgosaurus family, although she was not certain of its exact species. From where they stood it appeared to be about twice a man's height and many times his weight. Sprawled upon its back, it half-reclined against the bole of a large conifer. Its small forelimbs stuck up and away from its grossly distended belly and its head was tilted back at an odd angle, mouth slightly parted while clouds of insects buzzed about its meat-flecked teeth to steal some scraps.

"Is it dead?" whispered Becky.

"No, I don't think so. Sleeping off a big meal, I'd say. Big torpid bastard. . . ." Ian shook his head, and slowly drew his sidearm from his holster. So far, he had been careful not to waste ammunition, and still had more than thirty rounds in his jumpsuit pockets. His Magnum pistol handled .44 calibre exploding slugs, which he assumed would do lots of bone-damage to anything struck at close range. But considering the thickness of the carnivores' skulls, Ian had figured that the best place to fire at an attacker would be in the vital area just below their small forelimbs but above their bellies.

Holding the Magnum ahead of him, he motioned Becky to follow him slowly and quietly along the edge of the mudflat, and away from the sleeping hunter. Gradually, they added distance between themselves and the beast until they reached the other side of the clearing. Ian paused to check their position against the illuminator and then entered the forest again.

"Just walk slowly and steadily. We'll be all right if we keep quiet and don't wake him up."

Becky nodded and kept moving. They threaded their way through the ranks of proto-firs and giant ferns as the thrumming sounds of the never-silent forest enveloped them. It was difficult to imagine that one could grow accustomed to the steamy, redolent forest and its machine-like buzz of life, but as Becky followed Ian, she realized that she *was* getting used to the thick, damp greenery of the Jurassic world. Even though one could stumble upon a walking nightmare at any time, even though the millions of species of insects, leeches, and slugs were waiting to have a bite of your warm flesh, you learned how to live with it. The old adage about humans being the most adaptable of creatures seemed true.

They walked carefully into the valley for another fifteen minutes without speaking. "Are we safe now?" Becky finally asked.

Coopersmith shrugged. He was still carrying his Magnum in his right hand. "Who knows? The more distance we put between us and him the better, but we might be walking straight toward one of his cousins. You never know in this business. . . ."

Just then, there came a loud bellowing noise which seemed to split apart the heavy, humid atmosphere of the valley. Tracking the source of the sound, Ian stared through the thicket of trees, watching for some sign of movement, some change in color or the light.

"What is it?" asked Becky.

"I don't know . . . as usual, I guess. Doesn't sound like one of the meat-eaters, though. Too high-pitched, you know?"

"I'll take your word for it. Hope it doesn't wake up Sleeping Beauty. . . ."

"We'd better keep moving in any case. It sounded like whatever it is is off to the right. Let's just try and steer clear of it."

They moved off again, more wary than before. The bellowing sounds increased, and were soon joined by similar sounds farther away. If Ian didn't know that the beasts were so stupid, he would have considered that the creatures were communicating in some fashion of hoarse cries.

He mentioned it to Becky, who smiled but said nothing.

Ten minutes passed and it seemed to Ian that they were drawing closer to one of the bellowing creatures. He stopped and peered off among the trees. Something large was thrashing about among a group of cycads and ferns. "Look! There he is! See him?"

"I remember him," said Becky. "Stegosaurus, right?"

"That's the one. What's the matter with him, do you suppose?"

The dinosaur was running about in a tight circle like a cat chasing its tail. Its large-humped, plated back swayed to and fro as it moved, pausing only to bellow its singular cry. Each time it would be answered by another beast, presumably another Stegosaurus.

"You know, Ian, I think you might have been right. I think they are talking to one another. . . ."

"That's ridiculous! They're as stupid as turnips!"

Becky smiled. "And I think we've been wrong calling this one a *he*. . . ."

"You mean—it's a mating call? You know, you might be right, Becky. Maybe we should stay for a moment. This might be interesting."

"You want to play voyeur to a coupling of lovestruck Stegosaurus?" Becky laughed.

"Now, wait a minute! Don't you know that one of the burning questions of science has always been, 'How in bloody hell did the dinosaurs *do* it?'" Coopersmith smiled, his bright teeth in sharp contrast to his dark complexion.

"Hmm, I suppose you're right. Are we safe here?"

"Safe enough, I'd think. If their cries of passion get too loud, I would suspect that they would attract meat-eaters to themselves before us."

"Do you *really* want to watch?" asked Becky.

"Why, certainly! This is valuable paleontological research! My God, woman, you're making me sound like some kind of pervert. . . ."

"Oh, Ian, I was just kidding you. *I* want to see this as much as you do. I wonder what they do with those spikes on their tails?"

"Move them out of the way, I hope. Look, here comes her young prince now. . . ."

Beyond the stand of trees, they could see a larger, mottle-skinned Stegosaurus, lumbering towards the female, pausing only to make that odd bellowing sound. When he approached the female, she stopped her frantic chasing of her own tail, and allowed the male to join her in the strange dance of love. They followed each other's tails for a few moments, their bellows transformed into bleating noises that almost dripped with anticipated passion. Closer and closer they drew to each other, their circling dance slowing until the two awkward beasts had almost stopped. While the female shifted uneasily from one foot to the other, the larger male changed positions so that, although he was still facing opposite her, his hindlegs were even with hers.

Suddenly the female dropped over on her side, lifting her

spiked tail up and away from her suitor. Seeing his lady in such a submissive and obviously seductive position, the male moved closer to her until he could lift one of his thick hindlegs over hers, half-straddling her. More soft bleating sounds, and the two ugly beasts attempted to copulate. The eventual congress took some doing. Ian could not help but chuckle as he watched the male repeatedly fail in his efforts to complete the job.

"I'm glad it's become a bit easier for the rest of us," he said. "Would sort of take all the fun out of it, wouldn't it?"

Becky smiled. "I daresay, Ian, I think you're right."

The Stegosaurian union, once effected, was brief and perfunctory. Apparently neither member of the species took much delight in the performance, and were following some atavistic urge, rather than seeking any relief from tension. In fact, once finished, the male hobbled away from his lover without so much as a backward glance, leaving her to struggle awkwardly to her stubby feet alone.

"Well, that's one more burning question laid to rest," said Ian. "Of course, that was only one species..... We've got thousands yet to record."

Becky laughed. "I think you *are* a pervert...."

"I never thought I'd *ever* be accused of being kinky with dinosaurs!"

They laughed for a moment as they watched the female finally gain her feet and walk off lazily to search for a soft spot to lay her eggs.

"I don't suppose we have to worry about waking up that predator back there, not if all that racket didn't do it," said Ian. "But I think we should keep moving nonetheless. What do you say, my dear?"

"I'm just visiting here. I follow you."

"This way, then," said Ian. He was beginning to feel more and more comfortable around Rebecca Thalberg, and he knew on another level that an easy, cooperative relationship between them would be a plus in terms of their survival. It was possible that he could become physically attracted to the small, raven-haired woman, but he tried to keep such thoughts from his mind. It was when you started letting your mind drift away from priorities that you got yourself into trouble....

They walked farther into the river-valley, pausing only to have a light "lunch" of seeds and fruit. Finally Ian estimated that they had traveled far enough to get a closer look at the white objects seen from the highlands. He selected a tall cycad, and nimbly scaled it, getting as close to the top as possible so that he might peer down into the deep green carpet below them. As he scanned the lowlands, he was shocked at what he saw.

Just breaking the line of treetops about ten kilometers distant were the unmistakable signs of intelligent life—the tips of three large pyramids, glistening brightly under the light of the illuminator. Ian's pulse jumped as he strained to make out some detail in the structures. His first impression that he had seen some kind of buildings had been correct. It was somehow more unbelievable than the rest of the crazy world they had discovered.

"Becky," he called down. "You're not going to believe this . . . but I think we've got some company in here."

She looked up and watched him as he worked his way down from the tree, waiting until he jumped to the soft earth before speaking. "What're you talking about?"

"There's some kind of buildings ahead. I saw the tops of them—look like pyramids to me. It might be a city or a temple or something. . . ."

"But how? Who built it?"

"I don't know, as is the usual state of affairs. But I suggest that we find out what we can before it gets dark. I've taken a new fix on the position, and it looks like we have about ten klicks walking ahead of us. You feel up to it? I'd like to get there before the night-cycle."

"Do you think there's any . . . *people* there? Would it be dangerous?"

"I'm asking myself the same questions, but somehow, I don't think it would be any less safe than where we are now. Let's get moving, what say?"

It was not a city.

Three limestone-block pyramids—three-sided configurations—were arranged to form the points of a large isosceles triangle, all bounded by the remains of a two-meter block wall. The jungle had done its best to completely overwhelm the ruins and had done so quite efficiently. All that remained of the wall were a few bare patches which Ian cleared by cutting away the thick mat of vines and creepers that covered it. The pyramidal structures had, at one time, been built with step-configurations like the South American temples or the Mid-Eastern ziggurats, but now they were crumbling down, under the constant pressure of gravity and the creeping growth of the forest.

It was impossible to determine how old the structures might be, but Ian estimated that they were very old indeed. He found it curious that there were no remains of statues or any friezes, reliefs, or any other stone-work that would give some clue as to the identity of the builders. From an engineering standpoint, the pyramids were not works of inspiration or architectural finesse, and seemed to be only a few orders above the primitive constructions of Stonehenge.

Rebecca sat upon the lower steps of one of the structures watching Ian poke about in the thick undergrowth, still searching for any clues to the mystery.

"Could there possibly be *people* here?"

"We can't assume that from what we have here, Becky. This only tells us that at one time, probably a long time ago, there *were* people here. It doesn't look like they've used this place for a hundred thousand years, if you want to know the truth."

"Could they have been neanderthals or . . . australopithecines?"

"You mean those fellows Leakey found? I doubt it. . . . The latest data puts humankind on the map around ten million years ago. That's still a hundred and sixty million years after the dinosaurs. No, that's not too likely."

"But maybe they *evolved!* Right here in this ship, the way they did on Earth."

"You mean the little protomammal and tree shrew bit? Hmm, I suppose that could have happened, but isn't all that predicated on the demise of the lizards? I haven't kept up with that sort of thing, but I seem to have the idea that most scientists feel that the Earth passed through some kind of planetary disaster period that caused the demise of the dinosaurs, and that was the only way a new order of creature—the mammals—ever had a chance to get started. *After* the dinosaurs had been eradicated."

"And. . . . ?"

"Well," said Ian, looking off into the darkening shades of green beyond the walls, "that obviously didn't happen here. I mean, the dinosaurs dominated the Earth for a *hundred million years* or so. That's being a success under anybody's terms. Whatever wiped them out on Earth never had a chance to do it up here, and as you can see, they are still going strong. If there *are* any tree shrews or protomammals, or whatever you want to call them, crawling around up here, I haven't seen any. And even if they're nocturnal, it seems obvious to me that all the big fellows with the scales and the nasty dispositions have been doing a good job of keeping them in check."

"That still doesn't tell us who built these ruins."

"No, it doesn't. But it only leaves us two possiblilities: either the alien crew, having experienced some kind of technological problem in the control section—famine, mutiny, etc., all following naturally afterwards—had struck out inside their giant terrarium simply to survive. Maybe they lasted for a few thousand years, or whatever, but with the loss of their technology through the generations, until their descendants were a bunch of primitives who eventually died out . . . or, the second possibility, which is that during all this time, in this controlled biosphere, some species of dinosaurs evolved to sentient levels. . . ."

"My god, Ian, is it possible?"

"Is anything *not* possible? That's the question, isn't it? But there's a problem with that theory, too."

"What's that?"

"Well, where are they? These intelligent dinosaurs, I mean, if they survived as a species. I mean, they have had lots of time to evolve, and they should have been able to dominate this whole little world after all the *millions* of years."

"They could be *anywhere*, Ian. We haven't even begun to cover the territory inside this ship. For all we know, we might be wandering around in one of their game preserves or 'national parks.' "

"By God, that's a sobering thought, isn't it?" He smiled and sat down beside her. "It's getting dark. The cycles are about eleven hours and forty minutes each. Days and nights used to be shorter on Earth."

He watched her as she gazed up at the dimming illuminator. She really was a fascinating woman. She'd been opening up a lot to him, telling him about her life. She'd taken the intense academic and professional course in life, and now, in the face of the possibility of death, she wondered if she had made proper choices. Parts of her seemed, in this alien hot-house, to be blooming.

"Maybe they're up there," she said, pointing past the halo of the rod, beyond the sky, at the landmass sixty kilometers above them. A thick haze kept everything there indistinct. "Maybe we're just in the wrong part of town." She turned to him. "Well, what do we do now besides survive?"

"I was thinking that maybe we should stay here tonight. Maybe linger for a few days."

"Ian. I can't believe how scared I am."

"Well, that's an emotion we're both sharing. Look, my dear, I've told you. We've just got to make the best of it, that's all. I'm frightened of dying . . . especially in the manner that most creatures die in a place like this. But I'm also frightened of finding some of the answers to our questions. I mean, I'm not sure I *want* to know what all this bloody nonsense *means*."

"You mean that there *are* some things that man was not meant to know?" Becky smiled half-heartedly.

"No. Not *that* rubbish. I mean I'm not sure I can mentally or physically deal with the underlying truths about this ship and everything that's in it. At least not *now*, while I'm trying to stay alive. There's such a thing as *too much*, you know. Too many mysteries. Too many questions. After a while, you just don't care anymore. . . ."

"Now you're starting to sound like me."

"Am I? Good God, we can't have that, can we?" He put his arm around her, surprised that she felt so tiny and frail. She responded to his touch by leaning into him. He felt the soft warmth of her body against his chest. Ian had almost forgotten how good it was to hold someone, the reassurance it gave. He thought immediately of his wife Leticia. Would he ever see her again? He thought of all the intimate moments they'd shared, the way, sometimes, they'd almost *think* the same way, finish sentences for one another. A pang swept through him. . . .

What the hell was the use of anything? Scientific inquiry. Status. Achievement. Fidelity. All the things he'd worked for all his life. Under the glare of the illuminator, amidst the smells and the sounds and terrible beauty of this savage paradise, all his civilized values seemed . . . distant.

What was happening? What was he thinking about, really?

He switched his attention toward thoughts of the timetables they were dealing with. It had been seven days since they'd been stranded inside the ship. Even if Copernicus had mobilized another ship within that week's time, considering the increasing velocity of the alien vessel, the tricky navigational maneuvers, the speeds necessary of the IASA ship, and the additional difficulties of finding him and Becky, it was going to be another thirty to forty days before they could hope to be found.

A *long* time to simply survive. A *long* time to live with someone like Becky, becoming close, sharing. . . .

Becky stirred lightly. She seemed to nestle closer against his chest. "That's nice," she said.

"What's that?" he asked softly.

"Feeling you holding me, that's all. I'm so glad you're the one that made it, Ian. I don't know if I could have held everything together without you."

"Yes. You would have. We can do amazing things when we have to."

"Maybe," she said. "But you've made it a lot easier. It occurs to me that I've never thanked you."

"*Thanked* me? What for?"

"For being so *competent*. I guess that's the right word. And . . . for being such a—God, I sound so old-fashioned, but—for being such a gentleman."

"Oh, I think I know what you mean. Somehow I don't think being a gentleman will ever go out of style. Not with the right people, anyway."

"Are we the *right people*, Ian?" Becky looked up at him. He found himself falling into the depths of her brown eyes. Odd feelings stirred in him. He knew what was happening. Should he resist, or not?

"I don't know, Becky. But I think so."

She put her arms around him, pulling him even closer. "I do too," was all she said.

Ian looked up to see the illuminator growing dimmer, now only a dully glowing amber. Shadows fell across the landscape like dark pools. the green of the forest became more intense. The sounds of life scurrying for survival hummed in the air about them. Something woke up screaming and hungry in the distance, but Ian barely noticed.

In that first moment of intimate contact, Becky asked herself, over and over, the same questions. They flashed through her mind in a heated rush, mingling with the initial stirrings of passion. *Why are you doing this? Do you really want this? What is he going to think of you?*

She quickly decided that it did not matter. That *nothing* really mattered except staying alive, and that anything else was just some icing on the cake. She and Ian had been forced to be so close in all other ways since being marooned inside the strange ship, so close that a sexual intimacy seemed to be the most natural thing to happen. She knew that he had been entertaining fantasies. Becky was no naive child; she knew men's basic needs and drives.

All these thoughts, she knew, were her super-ego's final flashes of restraint or rationalization for what was happening. But the thoughts were growing fainter now, becoming gauzy and insubstantial as she allowed her senses to override everything else. She could feel her hands, her fingertips, digging into the firmly muscled flesh of Ian's back, pulling him close to her. At first, she detected a moment of hesitation on his part, as though it occurred to him to resist her. But then there was the sag of relaxing muscles and the embrace of his arms around her waist.

His jumpsuit was damp with perspiration and humidity, and as he slowly nuzzled his cheek against her neck, she could feel the prickles of his beard, the smell of his sweat. She closed her eyes, perhaps out of fear of gazing boldly into his, and turned her face upwards to meet his lips. She was surprised to feel the gentleness of his kiss, the tentative touch before pressing closer. Becky parted her lips slightly, and felt his tongue slip into her—and a shot of fire burned through her body, slowly at first, then curling and snaking its way, tingling, out to her extremities.

She heard herself speak his name softly as they parted briefly to take a breath. "You wanted this, didn't you?"

"Yes, of course," he said awkwardly, "But I didn't know about you. . . ."

Becky smiled. "Well, now you do!" She kissed him, and this time her tongue slipped past her lips, probing, teasing. She lay back against the large, smooth rock behind, sinking into the spongy ground cover, and Ian settled down beside her. The expression on his face was one of excitement and fear, and Becky understood how he was feeling—the awkward passion of the very young, or perhaps the very guilty.

No time for guilt now, she thought. Tomorrow we may be dead. . . .

Reaching out to the zipper of his jumpsuit, she pulled it down. The fabric peeled away from his bronze skin, the firm pectoral development and taut stomach. As though hypnotized, Becky watched the zipper descend, revealing Ian's mesh briefs, his swelling penis beneath them. He carefully slipped out of the sleeves of the garment and pulled her close to him, and she let the tight curls of his chest hair tickle her face. He was a very masculine man, hard, firm, sinewy. In that respect he was like Phineas, although he was taller and heavier than her lover.

He kissed her again, longer this time, and with less of the tentativeness of before. He unzipped her jumpsuit with confidence, pausing to tease her softness with a brief touch before continuing, until it was down to its stop just above her pubic mound. As he slipped her jumpsuit away from her shoulders, she felt a new tingle of exhilaration rush through her. God, it had been so *long* wearing these clothes! How good it felt to be free of them! She undid her brassiere, and let him lift it away from her, as though they were participating in an age-old ritual. She smiled to herself at the thought—perhaps it was just that. To feel her small, firm breasts free from the constraints of the halter, to feel Ian's touch upon them tenderly, gave her another rush of passion. She could feel her nipples growing hard in the anticipation of his touch, the tingly God-I-can't-stand-it pleasure of them being moved easily, playfully under the flick of his fingers. . . .

And then he was pulling her up, silently gesturing that she

get to her feet. Slowly she rose with him, embracing him as the sounds of the primitive world thrushed and hummed around them. She was losing contact with the outside world, the harsh killing world of their prison, falling into the hot whirlpool of desire. Kneeling, Ian unbuckled their LS boots, and she kicked hers away as she stretched out, arching her back, feeling air play upon her wet shining flesh. He put his hands on her waist, sliding them down to her bare hips, and she could feel the surrender of the jumpsuit's dampness, clinging but falling away from her. In one smooth motion, her panties and the leggings of the suit fell away from her and she stepped out of them.

She was suddenly extremely conscious of her nakedness, not merely to Ian, but to the hostile gaze of the primeval world. It was in itself an exciting sensation. It was a daring, exhilarating gesture. A defiant thing of fear and desire. And now he was standing before her, his own jumpsuit having dropped away, and for a long moment they simply stood staring at each other. First into each other's eyes, then dropping downward, taking in the raw, primitive beauty of their bodies enveloped in the lush green growth of the jungle.

Ian's body was shining from the patina of sweat which coated him like a sweet oil. He took his breath in deep gulps, and with each breath, tiny muscles in his chest and neck rippled. He was a beautiful man, and she hoped that he found her body as exciting as she found his. She moved to him and they embraced, and she could feel the hot column of his penis pressing and throbbing against her soft stomach.

Still embracing, they sank once again to the floor of the jungle, feeling the smooth sponginess of the ground cover tickle their bare skin. Insects buzzed and cavorted about them, perhaps excited by the strong emissions of sexual scents they were giving off, but Becky didn't care.

He ran his index finger down the center of her body, pausing to tease and tantalize until he reached the edge of her pubic hair. She arched her back, raising her mound up to meet his touch, and she could feel her juices overflowing already, running down the crack of her ass. And when he touched her, merely *touched* her there, at the source of her wetness, she exploded, coming so strongly that her vaginal compressions were almost painful. Oh God, it was never like this!

And then he was letting his fingertips lightly dance upon her softest parts, bringing her up and over again. He kissed her there, playing with her lips with his tongue until she simply wanted to die. Time had become a forgotten thing, and she floated in a netherworld of total, endless feeling.

She finally pleaded with him to stop, to enter her and fill her with all of him. Slowly he reacted, again teasing her, only this time with his penis, until finally he was inside her, slipping and sliding without effort, and she felt like a fountain, a geyser of passion and total wetness, total heat.

When he came, she could feel the muscles of his upper arms, which held her tense like corded rope, straining yet holding back from crushing her. He cried out and the sound seemed to linger in the damp stillness, and Becky lay there savoring it, thinking that Ian Coopersmith was one very beautiful man. . . .

CHAPTER 10

THE PHONE AT Doctor Mikaela Lindstrom's desk rang with a strident sound of urgency. Looking up from her proofreading of an annual report to the Board of Directors, she answered the phone with a distracted air.

"Hello?"

"Mikaela?" asked the very familiar voice.

"Yes, what is it, Matte?" She could detect a tension in his voice, even though he had only spoken her name. It was as though she could feel the nervous energy in the silence of the phone line.

"I've got to talk to you..." said the male voice. "I've got something to tell you, so that...so that you won't be too shocked when you get home tonight...." The man paused to suck in a desperate-sounding breath.

Mikaela's warning sensors immediately went off in her mind. She and Matte had not been getting along terribly well lately, and he was a high-strung, dramatic artist-type, who had several times threatened suicide since they'd met. Her heart began beating at double-time and her hands were instantly perspiring.

"Matte! What's wrong? What is it?"

"I had to do it, Mikaela. . . . I couldn't stand it any longer!"

"Matte, stop this obscure talking! What is the matter? What're you talking about?!" She fought to keep panic from creeping into her inflection.

"All right, I'm sorry, Mikaela, but this is hard for me to explain." There was a long pause, and she could hear the flare of a match, of a cigarette being ignited, drawn upon, and exhaled. She decided that she would wait him out. "After you left for work this morning," he finally continued, "I had some friends come over. They helped me. They helped me to move my things out. I'm leaving, Mikaela. I've got to get away from you. . . ."

The words poured out of him in a rush and struck her with the force of a physical blow. Something was forming a lump in her throat, threatening to cut off her breath. "Oh, Matte . . ." she heard herself saying. "Why? Why didn't you tell me what you were thinking? What you wanted to do? . . . Where are you now?"

"I *couldn't* tell you," he said sadly. "I was afraid of having another scene, Mikaela. I can't take any more of that kind of thing. Staying up into the middle of the night, crying jags, making up when we both know that everything was not settled. . . . I just had to get out!"

"Where are you, Matte? Do you want to meet somewhere and we can talk about it?"

"No, no meeting . . . no talking. Not now anyway. I'm at a friend's house, but I don't want to tell you where. I . . . I don't want to see you for a while, Mikaela. It's just too hard for me to handle."

She paused and took a deep breath. "Did you take *everything?*" It was a stupid question, but it had just come out of her.

"Yes. One of my friends brought a truck. . . ."

"Listen, Matte, I know that it's been hard for us," she said, not thinking of what she would say next. "We're so different, you know. . . ."

"The difference between art and science," he said with a half-hearted laugh. Then a pause before continuing. "Look, Mikaela, I really don't want to talk about it right now....I just want to be alone for a while. I've got some thinking to do. I just didn't want you to come home tonight and find all my stuff cleaned out, find the apartment...like it is now. I just couldn't do that to you...."

Her impulse was suddenly to lash out at him, to attack him for pulling such a noble bit at the end. *He runs off like a rat escaping a sinking ship, and then he tries to make it seem he's doing me a favor by calling to warn me!*

But she said nothing like that. She too was weary of the relationship, the tempestuous nature of their lives together. She was too cool and rational, and he was too sensitive, too explosive.

"All right, Matte, if that's what you feel you must do, I certainly can't stop you. I'm shocked, but not really surprised, I guess. There were some things about us that were very good, but I know there were other things that were quite bad. Perhaps you are right to do this thing. Perhaps you are the stronger of the two of us. I would probably have let it drag on indefinitely."

He sighed on the other end of the line. "The sex, Mikaela....The sex was good, but that was all." He laughed mockingly. "Despite what the rest of the world might think, we Swedes don't live on sex alone, right?"

Mikaela could say nothing. She listened to the fidgeting silence at the other end of the line.

"I think I'd better go, Mikaela. Good-bye...."

"Will I see you again?" she asked, but the connection had already been broken. She replaced the receiver to its cradle, and stared at the papers on her desk—for an instant her mind was a total blank. No thoughts. Only feelings. Feelings of loss, of disorientation. Pain.

The door to her office opened and her secretary peeked in. "I've got those articles you wanted Xeroxed, Doctor Lindstrom. Do you need anything else before I go to lunch?"

Mikaela continued to stare at the clutter on her desk. "No thank you," she said softly. "That will be fine for now."

The door closed and Mikaela was alone again. Alone. The word flared brightly in her mind. She would go home to her apartment and find it defiled. Parts of it ripped out forcibly and the empty spaces looking like open wounds. She was a strong-willed woman, and although she had deep feelings and strong convictions, she sometimes had difficulty showing them. It was shyness more than being aloof or condescending, but in social situations, she was quiet and not very effusive in her warmth or eagerness to entertain.

She loved her work in paleontology, and had been a spec-tacular student, researcher, and author as her young career had taken her quickly to an upper echelon position with the Institute for Biological and Paleontological Research. Before she had begun her thirtieth year, she was respected throughout the ac-ademic world as an authority on prehistoric life, particularly the dinosaurs. Her career and her future were assured, but she wished that her personal life had even half the signs of such stability.

Although she was not afraid of men, or sex, or any of the binding commitments that a one-to-one relationship demanded, she had been unable to find the right person with whom to share her life and interests. Her latest attempt had been Matte Elster, a twenty-eight-year-old abstract painter, who had met with only limited success in the whirlwind competitive circle of the European avant-garde. He would have never admitted it, but her success and *his* failure in their chosen fields was one of the largest problems in their faltering relationship. Male ego, thought Mikaela, it was such a fragile and precious thing, and yet the world seemed to run on wheels that were greased with it.

There came to her a feeling of terrible emptiness, and she knew that she didn't want to go home and face the physical emptiness of her apartment. She wanted to run away. Away from everything. Her job, her duties, her friends. It was a desperate feeling that was stronger than she had ever felt before. Whenever this happened, and it had happened several times before, she came to realize an important facet of herself—each time a little more emphatically. The most important thing in her life was not her research, her success, and her security. It was a far simpler thing, but far more difficult to attain—the love and respect of someone intimate.

Shaking her head, she cut off the daydreams and returned her attention to the papers on her desk. She wondered if she would have the strength to get through the day, through the dull busy-work of the annual report to the Institute's heavy-weights.

The phone rang suddenly, and she paused before answering it, thinking that it might be Matte, calling to say that he had reconsidered, that he was sorry. She considered what she would say to him, and whether it was all worth it in the long run.

"Hello," she said tentatively. "This is Mikaela Lindstrom." She did not usually answer so formally, but she wanted Matte, if it *was* Matte, to see that she was business-as-usual.

"Doctor Lindstrom, this is Christopher Alvarez. I am one of the Joint Chiefs of Staff for the IASA—the International Aeronautics and Space Administration."

Mikaela was surprised to hear the crisp tones of the old gentleman on the line. She was familiar with his name, but had never met him. She was confused and could not imagine what such a high international figure would be calling her for. "Yes, Mr. Alvarez, what can I do for you?"

"Quite a bit, I hope, Doctor. Something has come up which is a very sticky problem for us here at the Administration and we may be needing your expertise. I have already cleared this with your superiors at the Institute, and all I now require is your acceptance of the mission."

Mikaela cleared her throat. "Mission? I'm afraid I don't understand."

"Quite simply, Doctor Lindstrom, we would like to have you on the next shuttle to our Lunar Base of Operations at Copernicus."

"You mean on the *moon?* You want to fly me to the moon?" Mikaela almost laughed as she mentally recalled the old love song of the same words. In light of what had just happened in her personal life, it sounded even more absurd. But still she was shocked and mystified by the proposition.

"Yes, indeed, Doctor. We are assembling a team of specialists in various fields, and yours is one that will be vital to the success of the mission. I am afraid that I cannot say anymore on the telephone, because of security requirements, I'm sure you understand."

"Oh yes, of course. . . ." *The moon! They want me to go to the moon!*

"Well then, if you are interested in my somewhat mysterious

offer, I would like you to be in our Headquarters Building in Brussels tomorrow morning at 10:00 A.M. We will be having a briefing session at that time, at which point you may officially accept or decline our offer. Can I count on seeing you there?"

She paused, brushing a wisp of blond hair from her face. Things were happening so fast that she was not thinking correctly. Her curiosity was raised to the nth power and now she could do nothing but accept, believing that everything had indeed been approved by the Directors of the Institute. She told Mr. Alvarez as much, and he promptly ended the conversation, sounding very pleased with it all.

Mikaela replaced the receiver and again her mind was a confusing whirlpool of thoughts. Swiveling in her chair, she looked out the window of her office, which overlooked the city of Stockholm. She looked past the modern office buildings and intrusive geometric shapes to the island in Lake Malaren where the picturesque, old part of the city remained placid and punctuated by the rising spires of stone cathedrals. Such a beautiful city, she thought, and how different it would be on the moon. . . .

Could she withstand the claustrophobic lifestyle? Perhaps. Could she pass up such an opportunity—a chance to do exactly what her less rational side desperately wanted, that is, to *get away* from everything? No. It did not matter what the IASA wanted with her; she would go to their meeting and she would accept their offer. Better that she simply leave everything for a while. Restructure her feelings and her priorities, and start over. After all, she thought, I am young and attractive; it's not the end the world.

Smiling for the first time that morning, she picked up the phone and dialed the Director's Office. It was time to make some of her intentions public.

CHAPTER 11

TRYING TO EXPEND purely nervous energy, Colonel Phineas Kemp sat at his command console and punched up another complete set of calculations for the trip. Then he'd do a maintenance check, he thought, sipping at coffee as figures and diagrams began to blink onto his readout screen.

He sure as hell was going to make sure *this* expedition was successful, he mused, ignoring the activities of the other members of the crew.

Looking like a floating petroleum refinery, the *Goddard*, with its improbable configuration of spheres and superstructure, had just accelerated from lunar orbit on its intercept course with the *"Dragonstar."* Phineas Kemp had not been pleased when Marcia Bertholde had coined the term for the alien starship. He preferred the more functional title of Artifact One. However, the more lyrical, romantic minds had prevailed. To them, *Dragonstar* was so beautifully apt a name for the alien ship. Even before the *Goddard* was launched, the new code name had been almost universally accepted.

Like the *Goddard* 's smaller counterpart ships, the Outer Planets Probeship was equipped with Ludodyanov ram-impulse engines. Constantly accelerating at about one Earth gravity, the *Goddard* would achieve a velocity in the neighborhood of three million kilometers per hour before decelerating and matching the ever-increasing orbital velocity of the *Dragonstar*.

Phineas Kemp had installed himself as Mission Commander of the *Goddard* 's voyage. He had supervised the crew selection and every detail of the mission plan. Although the primary objective would be to commandeer the *Dragonstar* and bring it into a stable L-5 orbit, he had acceded to the requests of the Joint Directors to include several paleontologists and biologists (shuttled up quickly from Earth) so that some preliminary studies could be made of the specimen-jar environment of the Earth's early ages. He could understand the excitement and desire on the biologists' parts, but the real importance of the *Dragonstar* was what was hanging off the ass-end of the ship—engines which had carried it to Earth's solar system from God-knew-where. Light-years distant, to be sure, and Phineas could hardly wait to have IASA's engineers crawling over the innards of that ship. The secrets waiting for humankind were immeasurable, and, thought Phineas, whoever it was who bestowed such a gift on the world would be forever remembered....

But there he was thinking of his damned ego again. Would he ever get out from beneath the thumb of his father and the old man's expectations? It was times like this that made him doubt it.

There *was* another reason why Phineas has assumed command of the *Goddard*. It was a reason he had shared with no one, and rarely himself. Rebecca Thalberg. Plain and simple, there was part of him that considered the voyage a rescue mission because he refused to believe that she was dead. The logical part of his mind kept telling him that as long as there had been no positive verification that she had been killed in the initial havoc (and there had *not* been), he would continue to believe that she might have escaped. The thought of never seeing Becky again troubled him in his conscious mind and in his dreams, and he cursed himself to realize that it required a tragedy of this proportion to make him *see*, to make him *feel*.

And so, even though he had selected his crew for the primary objective—twenty engineers and EVA riggers, plus the three paleontologists—Phineas still had twelve (including himself) highly-trained astronauts with planetary exploration experience. Twelve physically and mentally tough men and women who could form a small, extremely capable expeditionary force. Phineas dreamed of leading them, armed with sophisticated weaponry and survival gear, through the interior of the *Dragonstar* in search of Becky.

He would certainly have the time for it, he thought. Once the initial surveys and preliminary explorations had been conducted, and the out-rigger engines had been attached to the alien vessel's hull, there would be plenty of time for extracurricular activity. It would be a long trip back to lunar orbit, and everyone would need something to keep himself occupied. Mikaela Lindstrom, the chief paleontologist from the Institute for Biological and Paleontological Research, and her two assistants, would be busy with their dinosaurs. Robert Jakes, the chief engineer, and his men would keep tabs on their jury-rigged tugboat operation. Phineas would be providing security for the rest of the crew, planning a search and examination of the alien crew quarters, and perhaps sending out a few exploratory teams.

If Becky was alive, he would find her.

He finished his coffee and examined the readouts again.

The *Goddard* accelerated through the emptiness of space, her computers constantly reassessing her position in comparison to that of the *Dragonstar*, and guiding it into an oscillating trajectory that would sweep in grandly alongside the giant alien vessel. The weeks passed quickly for the crew as they prepared for a quick, well-coordinated assault on the spinning cylinder. Phineas Kemp conducted briefing sessions and contingency-plan meetings at regular intervals. The crew was bombarded with every scrap of information known about the *Dragonstar* until every man and woman knew the vessel and their job connected with it as well as they knew their most secret thoughts. There would be no screw-ups this time around. Three strikes and you're out, Kemp had told them, and it was time for a home run.

As the *Goddard* closed in on its target, Kemp had all of the crew as excited and anxious to get moving as a high school football team the night before the Thanksgiving Day game.

All except one.

His name was Ross Canter. He was one of Doctor Jakes's Assistant Flight Engineers. Tall, thin, and somewhat emaciated looking, Canter was considered one of the best men in his chosen profession. He had a slightly Mediterranean aspect, a fact which he attributed to his mixed parentage of Israeli and Irish, which was borne out by the fax sheet in his Security Clearance file.

That information was, of course, incorrect.

Ross Canter, whose real name was Pierre Rassim, was a member of the Third World Confederation's Intelligence Division—known simply as the *Jiha*—although his contacts with his superiors since joining the IASA fifteen years ago had been extremely infrequent. He was part of a vast community of global spies and agents whose existence was acknowledged by all participating countries and alliances, but whose individual identities were not always known. It was said that espionage was quite boring in the long run, and that it was not the pulse-quickening life described in popular films and novels. Ross Canter would agree with that completely. In his years of service to the *Jiha*, he had never been called upon to do anything, other than file his "progress reports" on a regular basis, which served only to allow his superiors to know that he was still alive. He often assumed that he was being watched, monitored so to speak, by other agents so that it could be known if he was being unconsciously swayed by the "other side," but he had never been aware of any surveillance.

In actuality, Canter had to admit that the first place had been waning as he grew older. It was said that age makes more conservatives than speeches, and he tended to agree with the aphorism. As an engineer with IASA, he concluded that he would have been doing a similar function in the TWC, and that he loved his work as much as a man should. Therefore, he supposed it did not really matter which government he worked for, since he was in the long run, an engineer and not a spy.

The only factor, in fact, which had kept him loyal to the Third World Confederation was the kindnesses and story-telling abilities of an old man named Ahmad Nesrudah. Canter had been a small boy living with his parents in Beirut during the outbreak of the near-disastrous Oil War in 1998. The Lebanese city was practically leveled in the course of the action, and there were hundreds of thousands of war-orphans, of whom Canter was one of the more fortunate.

Ahmad Nesrudah had been an Iranian Oil Minister during one of that country's various political/religious ruling regimes, but he had possessed the good sense to vacate the area before it became personally dangerous. When his wife and remaining children were killed during a series of surgical bombings, he set out to replace his family with an orphan son. Finding the young Pierre Rassim in a Unesco Center, Nesrudah adopted him and transported him to his private villa in a small Saudi town, where he was revered as a teacher. The boy grew up under the sharp and intelligent care of the old man. He was taught to trust no one but himself, to arm himself with knowledge, and to respect the ancient Arabian traditions.

Old Ahmad seemed to delight most in telling the boy stories of the Arab terrorist groups of the latter half of the twentieth century—a time when he had been more politically active himself. It was then that the Third World became recognized as a force to be dealt with, and it was only because of the glorious efforts of their ancestors. It was the first time in almost a thousand years that the noble culture which had its roots in the Ottoman Empire had raised itself and challenged the supremacy of the Europeans and the upstart Americans—mere children in the world of culture and antiquity.

Ross Canter/Rassim had loved the old man dearly, and had many times sworn to him that he would never betray the ideals in which he believed. After attending the University of Palestine, he entered the *Jiha,* and was sent to Chicago, where he began living his false identity, living the life of a secret agent, waiting for the moment when he might be called to serve the ideology of the TWC and the memory of old Ahmad Nesrudah.

The moment had finally arrived.

Phineas Kemp sat in the Command chair as the *Goddard* approached the long-awaited rendezvous. "This is Colonel Kemp on board the *Goddard*. Calling Commander Fratz...Come in..."

The radio crackled for a moment before Fratz's voice came

through. "Good afternoon, Colonel, we've been expecting you. Sorry that I don't have anything to report . . . but things have been quiet since—"

"We figured as much, Commander. Stand by for docking. . . . You can go to automatic any time now. Report to the Command cabin when you're on board."

"Yes sir. . . . Docking procedure sequence starting now. Stand by, *Goddard*."

Once the smaller *Heinlein* had linked up with the larger ship, Kemp intended to have Fratz and Bracken pilot the *Goddard*'s landing module, since they were the only ones with anything one might call experience in landing upon the *Dragonstar*. Kemp wanted to waste no time in getting the mission under way, and had already assembled the first part of the team in the transport bay of the lander. He had been over the recordings Coopersmith and Bracken had completed on the alien hatch opening sequences and the descriptions of the "ascent" to the surface of the inner world of the alien cylinder. Phineas planned to lead the first group of ten into the *Dragonstar*— their first objective to establish a secure base camp, and then begin disarming the defensive systems of the outer hull so that the engine-rigging could begin.

He looked at the impossibly large expanse of the alien ship through the main viewscreen and shook his head. Even though he had seen the VOR recordings uncountable times, and had watched the cylinder grow larger and larger as the *Goddard* approached, it was still difficult to accept how immense the thing was. Phineas's ship was more than two hundred meters long, one of the biggest ships in the Deep-Space Division, and it was like a flea preparing to land on an elephant's back in comparison. The *Goddard* was so close now, that that cylinder was no longer recognizable as a ship—its endless surface stretched in all directions like the surface of a medium-sized moon. The details of its hull stood out in the sharp relief of sunlight and shadow. Phineas sat watching the screen, thinking that this gigantic *thing*—this ship of monsters—would not beat him. It was his for the taking, and he would not fail.

"Excuse me, Colonel, but Fratz is on board now," said the Assistant Flight Commander.

"Tell him to get up here on the double."

Phineas looked back to the screen, trying to imagine what it would be like inside the *Dragonstar*. Until this moment, the thought of being frightened, or even apprehensive, had not touched him, but now as the moment grew nearer, he felt the bottom dropping out of his stomach. He wondered how he was going to hold up under the pressure. . . .

Fratz entered the cabin just then, and Kemp was glad for the escape from his thoughts. He quickly briefed him on the landing procedures and gave Fratz a chance to offer any additional advice that might be helpful. After a short discussion of technique, both men left the cabin—Fratz to enter the Command chair of the landing module, Kemp to the transport bay.

The first group into the lander included Lindstrom and her two assistants, Kemp, and six other astronauts. Everyone wore standard EVA gear and carried with them large survival packs with the gear they would need once inside the *Dragonstar*. Kemp and his men also carried equipment racks and a field generator which would be needed to rig up an electomagnetic "fence" around the perimeter of the base camp. In addition, each man and woman was equipped with a sidearm *razer*, which looked very much like the Bren gun of the previous century, although it fired a concentrated beam of heat energy instead of standard slugs. The paleontologists had objected to carrying the weapons, but that was before Kemp had allowed them to view the recordings of the tragedy of the first expedition.

Standing in the transport bay, Kemp spoke into his helmet radio. "We're secured down here, Commander. Any time you're ready. . . ."

"Stand by, Colonel. I've commenced separation. . . . It's not a very long trip."

There was a soft metallic thud as the lander broke away from the *Goddard* and began tilting over to the proper touchdown attitude. Kemp studied the faces of his team, looking for traces of fear and uncertainty. There was no place for it now.

"We are descending now, Colonel. One hundred and fifty meters, and closing. . . . Stand by. . . . Seventy-five . . . fifty . . . stand by. . . . We have touchdown."

Just as Fratz spoke there was a clang which traveled through the superstructure of the lander. Kemp was suddenly aware of the pull of his magnetic boots against the bay floor as the centrifugal forces of the rotating alien ship attempted to push him away from the lander's deck. He decompressed the bay, watched as the door slid open to reveal the large rectangular seams of the entrance hatch. To the right of the hatch, Kemp saw immediately the burned out panel which Coopersmith's team had cut away with a razer-torch, to reveal a series of manual controls. Phineas eased his way down to the surface of the hull and began motioning for the others to follow, while he walked carefully and slowly up to the manual override controls. Although the levers looked a bit large for easy manipulation by the human hand, he had no trouble activating the airlock system and he breathed a bit easier as the outer panel of the lock slid open soundlessly.

"Okay, everyone. Inside the chamber. Slowly, please. That's it . . . one at a time."

The team gathered inside the first chamber of the lock, which was quite large, and could accommodate twice as many in comfort, then watched Colonel Kemp enter. He kicked free of the metallic flooring and floated up to the lock control panel on the inside of the chamber, then slowly reached for the yellow lever.

Just as Coopersmith had reported, the outer hull panel slid shut, sealing the team in total darkness until Kemp turned on his utility lamp. He reached up and touched the green lever, which activated the atmosphere/pressure cycling. The sound of gas entered the chamber and everyone stood silently, listening until an electronic chime sounded. Kemp reached up and pulled the final lever, a dull red in color, and the sound of machinery humming could be heard as the inner door slid open to the left.

"All right," said Kemp. "Turn on your utility lamps, and follow me. Up ahead here is an access shaft. The rails are handholds with some evenly-spaced struts to use for your footing. I want you to all assemble on the other side of the airlock and discard the EVA gear, then get yourselves outfitted for the trip up this shaft. Be careful on the ascent, and be sure to give the fellow ahead of you enough room. Now, let's get started."

The group filed into the shaft and Kemp followed them, closing the airlock and making certain that the air pressure was all right before unlocking his EVA helmet. The others followed his lead, and soon everyone was stripped down to their tight-fitting coveralls and radio helmets. Each member of the team shouldered his or her survival pack and lined up for the long climb, but waiting for Phineas to take the lead. He noticed that no one spoke, although there was more than the usual amount of coughing and throat-clearing.

Phineas climbed the hundred meters up to a square platform, but long before he reached it, he could see the blazing square of light that was the open entry hatch—the place where Alan Huff had been attacked while transmitting the audiovisual signals back to Copernicus Base.

"All right, attention. . . . I'm on the landing platform below the hatch. I want everyone to assemble here before we go up. The hatch is open, and extreme caution is the order of the day. When you get up here, draw your sidearms, but keep them on safety until ordered otherwise."

Kemp stood off to the side and watched his team slowly join him on the platform. He kept looking up through the hatch where the bright light of the ship's interior burned whitely. From his angle, it was impossible to discern anything clearly, but his imagination was filling in what the eye could not yet see. His pulse was pounding in his ears, and it seemed so loud that he was certain that his helmet-mike was picking up the sound.

When the last man had clambered up to the platform, Kemp signaled the Command cabin of the *Goddard*. "This is Kemp. . . . We've reached the entry hatch to the interior and we are preparing to go topside. We will provide visual as soon as some defensive perimeters have been established. Stand by, *Goddard* . . . we're going up. . . ."

Kemp climbed through the hatch and stared about the clearing. A feeling of *déja vu* swept over him as he looked across the clearing, to flanking walls of proto-firs, cycads, and redwoods, to the sloping marshland and mudflat where the first team had recorded the waddling herd of Iguanodons. In the hazy distance, the mottled foliage of the landscape curved upward towards the halo-like glow of the central illuminating rod. No horizon. It was a heart-stopping sight, even though Phineas had been prepared for it, and it made all those "artist's conceptions" pitiful in comparison.

Slowly, he climbed up to the soft, spongy turf, listening to the chittering, humming sounds of this world. Motioning for the rest of the team to follow quickly, Kemp moved down off the small knoll and found the remains of Huff's communications gear. Some of the metallic parts were already showing signs of corrosion in the humid atmosphere, and the plastic casings were laced with tiny teeth marks—little predators testing out anything for a possible meal, he assumed.

But that was all. There was absolutely no sign of Huff's body, nor any of the others. Apparently nothing was wasted in this world of primitive instincts. There was a distant scream in the air. Looking up, Phineas saw a dark shape far away, gliding like a kite in the misty sky. The intruders had been spotted and the signal was going out. He wanted no repeat of the previous team's experience.

"We've got to move quickly," he said to everyone through the radiophones. "There'll be plenty of time for oohs and aahs. Let's get that fence up. . . ."

Phineas was pleased with the efficiency with which his team operated. They could have been in Central Park for all the attention they paid to the Jurassic wonders all about them. Within ten minutes they had staked out a large circle in the clearing approximately a hundred meters in diameter. The enclosure was circumscribed by a series of "fence-posts" placed at regular intervals along the eight thousand-meter circumference. Each post was a miniature field-generator controlled by a central transmitter, which operated in synch with the posts on either side of it. Anything that attempted to pass between the posts would do two things: set off an alarm, and get itself hit with three hundred thousand volts at stunning amperage. It was a simple "force-field" security barrier, which could easily be foiled by intelligent espionage elements, but would be extremely effective against any predatory dinosaurs.

The power was turned on, the perimeter tested and found to be working perfectly. Phineas felt immediately more at ease once the team was secure, and relayed the information back to the *Goddard*. He ordered Doctor Jakes and his team of engineers and riggers to begin disarming the *Dragonstar*'s defensive systems, so that installation of the impulse engines could begin as soon as possible. Using a refined version of Coopersmith's original methods, Jakes' team should be able to have the first engines in place within forty-eight hours.

Two days inside the *Dragonstar* passed quickly. The base camp took shape quickly with inflatable structural domes which served as crew quarters, supply huts, infirmary, communications headquarters, research labs, and power stations. The collection of domes and superstructure seemed wildly incongruous with the lush surroundings of the forest and the marshlands— the ultimate anachronism—but the *Goddard* team soon established a respectful rapport with the environment and the animals which were drawn to the small human incursion upon their world.

For Mikaela Lindstrom, the interior of the *Dragonstar* was the fulfillment of her dreams. An encapsulated world of the past, which would forever put to rest the theories and arguments concerning the early geologic periods of life on the Earth. She was totally grateful to have been included in the mission to the *Dragonstar*, and though she and her two assistants would barely begin to investigate the myriad secrets of the Jurassic wonderland, she would at least have time, during the return voyage, to map out a system of inquiry.

It was not long after the force-field had been erected that the first dinosaurs were seen. Coming up from the misty regions of the swampland which sloped down away from the base, a group of three herbivorous creatures called Camptosaurus, half-walked and half-hopped toward the encampment. Mikaela watched them as they approached cautiously, recording them with a small videocube camera with an adjustable telephoto lens. The dinosaurs were less than two meters tall and resembled kangaroos in general body shape, although their heads were quite birdlike. Their coloring was a mottled green that was almost an exact duplicate of the color of the foliage that grew close to the swamps and lakeshore. The creatures did not come all the way up to the electrified perimeter of the camp, but veered off within a hundred meters of it to pluck juicy blossoms from some of the low-hanging branches of cycads.

The swamp and marshland proved to be a favorite watering hole and feeding ground for a majority of herbivores. Within the first two days Mikaela and her crew had been able to record and observe the habits of a variety of animals—Trachodons, Brachiosaurus, Iguanodons, Ankylosaurus, even several monstrously huge Brontosaurus and impossibly-long Diplodocus. In her earliest notes, Mikaela had observed that there was very little contact between different herbivorous species, and that the plant-eaters generally avoided animals not of their own kind. But this was a gentle aversion, rather than the blind, panicked flight expressed whenever the scent of a predator was in the air.

Since the waters attracted many plant-eating dinosaurs, it was also natural that the carnivorous dinosaurs would enjoy good hunting in the same region. Although Mikaela and her crew soon discovered that most of the feeding took place in the early hours of evening and darkness, there were still many occasions during the day-cycles to observe the meat-eaters at work. She was impressed and terrified at the sight of some of them. Massive, strong, and surprisingly agile, the meat-eaters were nightmares come to life. Many of them, like the Gorgosaurus and the Ceratosaurus, had thick hides of bright colors—oranges, yellows, pale greens—since they had no need for the safety of camouflage. The largest carnivore she had yet seen had been an Allosaurus considerably larger than any ever found in fossilized form. It looked as though it was the same creature that had attacked the first expedition, and Mikaela assumed that the carnivores exhibited some degree of territoriality in their hunting grounds. Among the species of meat-eaters, she observed no direct combat, although there was a definite hierarchy of species, mostly defined by size and ferocity. Most simply, the smaller fellows gave the larger fellows a wide berth and a first chance at any prey that might be felled. She also noted that some of the smaller predators traveled and hunted in packs like wolves. The relatively small, quick species like the Compsognathus, Velociraptor, and Deinodon could be seen in the early evening hours racing about the perimeter of the camp, rushing up to the force-field at full speed, only to be knocked senseless by the energy screens, then stagger to their feet and try again. Mikaela was amazed at the savage intensity with which even the smallest carnivores hunted and fed. She had witnessed their neighborhood Allosaurus bring down a fat, slow-moving Hadrosaurus with incredible agility, covering several meters with each stride of its massive legs, pouncing upon the victim's back and crushing it to the ground. Pinned, the Hadrosaurus was helpless as the Allosaurus literally tore its body into bite-sized pieces. The beast fed until its stomach became so distended that it could hardly stand erect, then slowly rose from the carcass and stumbled off into the forest, where it would sleep for a day or two in the depths of a digestive stupor.

But the attacks of the Allosaurus were tame when compared to the horrible tactics of the marauding packs of Compsognathus, and especially the odd little dinosaur called the Deinodon. The latter creature was no more than three meters long, standing just higher than the average man, but was one of the most distinctive-looking bipedal dinosaurs. Its head was similar to the Gorgosaurus or the Allosaurus, and was full of sharp, ripping teeth, but its legs were much leaner, ending in two large toes and a third digit which had evolved into a twelve-centimeter, sickle-shaped claw. Its other remarkable feature was its long tail, which always protruded horizontally to the ground, as though held rigid by thick musculature or fused tail vertebrae. Equipped thusly, the Deinodon was an incredibly agile, terribly lethal creature. Mikaela had watched packs of three and four of the species *running* through the edges of the forest and across the clearing below the base camp at speeds approaching that of a thoroughbred horse. From what she had seen thus far, the Deinodon was the speediest predator of all. It could run down any prey with impunity, whereupon it would perform its special kind of death-dealing. Once it ran its victim aground, the little dinosaur would hold the body away from it with its longish forelimbs, then balancing one leg and using its rigid tail as a balance-pole, it would employ its scythe-like third claw to slash open the prey's belly, effectively disemboweling it with several deft strokes. This procedure was done with such swiftness that the eye could barely follow it. The sharp-teethed jaws snapped up gobbets of warm flesh with equal speed and efficiency. To see a small pack of these killers take down a large Trachodon and butcher it within minutes was an experience not soon forgotten.

In addition to its chilling hunting techniques, the Deinodon had also been seen galloping into the middle of a meal being enjoyed by one of the really big predators such as the Gorgosaurus and literally steal the food from its huge jaws. It would perform this dangerous feat at full speed, snapping a chunk of warm flesh from the forelimbs or snout without breaking stride. The larger carnivores, though angered they might be, were usually so startled that they almost never gave fruitless chase. It was like a game the small predators played, and it gave credence to the idea that all dinosaurs were not the dull, dim-witted creatures formerly imagined. More than once Mikaela thought she detected the bright sparkle of cunning laughter in the small killer's eyes.

Her observations also cemented the still-raging controversy of warm versus cold bloodedness in the dinosaurs. She had been working on the observations and calculations when Phineas Kemp entered her laboratory dome.

"How's it going, Doctor Lindstrom?"

She looked up and saw the colonel. Blue eyes as bright as neon, sandy hair, and square, all-American jaw (though she knew he was from Canada). He was not a tall man, but he was trim and well-muscled, and quite handsome in the old-fashioned sense of the word.

"Oh, good evening, Colonel Kemp."

"You can call me Phineas, if you'd like."

"That would be nice," said Lindstrom. "I never was very high on formality. Everyone calls me Mickie... but I prefer Mikaela."

Kemp laughed. "I can't even *tell* you what they call me! Behind my back, that is...."

Mikaela smiled and gestured that Phineas take a seat at the lab table where she was working.

"I stopped by to tell you that we will be sending out an expeditionary team in the morning—well-armed, of course— and I was wondering if you and your assistants would like to accompany us?"

Mikaela brightened and smiled broadly. "You were wondering?! My god, Colonel... I mean, *Phineas*.... Ever since we got here, I've felt like a little kid outside the window, waiting for the candy store to open!"

"Yes, I'd rather expected that," said Phineas, smiling. "I hope you understood my reasons for keeping everyone inside the perimeter. I thought it would be best if we secured the outside hull and got the outrigger engines in place before tackling the interior."

"Are the engines ready?"

"Just about. Jakes says that the final emplacements will be made this evening. After that, all that will be necessary will be to secure the *Goddard* and *Heinlein*, patch in some computer-guidance to the outriggers, and we're on our way. We should be firing the engines by tomorrow at mid-day."

"How long will the return voyage take? Am I going to have much time to explore the rest of the interior?"

"I'm not sure yet. . . . We only have some of the preliminary figures and projections at this point. It depends on how well the *Dragonstar* responds to course changes and deceleration. We're moving along at pretty good rate right now. It's going to be a tricky operation for awhile. No one's ever piloted a ship this big before."

"No, I don't suppose they have. . . ." Mikaela looked at Kemp and wondered if he was really that serious and wrapped up in his work, or if he was trying to "make conversation." He did not act as if he was in any great hurry to leave, and she was of two minds about his intrusion on her thoughts and notes.

"Have you made any interesting discoveries or observations yet? I see that you've found plenty to write about, even by just watching them beyond the perimeter."

Mikaela wondered if Phineas Kemp was actually interested in her notes, or whether he simply wanted to get into her pants. She hated to think of men in those terms alone, but her experiences with Matte and other men had taught her that most of them preferred to get physical first, then bother to get to know you later.

She decided to give the colonel the benefit of the doubt. "Well, since you've asked," she said with a calculated smile, "I *have* come up with a few things that knock the hell out of the old ideas about the dinosaurs being reptiles . . . at least like the reptiles that we are now familiar with."

"You mean that business about the hot-bloodedness?" said Kemp off-handedly.

Mikaela's face must have revealed her shock that he would know something about her work.

Kemp smiled. "My dear Doctor Lindstrom, just because I

am a lantern-jawed astronaut does not mean that I am a total dolt in terms of anything other than trajectories and g-forces. . . ."

"I *know*, Colonel, it's just that I didn't expect very many people to—"

"To be interested in paleontology? Mikaela, when I was a boy, I think I read every book ever printed on dinosaurs! Those big buggers used to fascinate me. Used to dream about them still being alive somewhere in the world, and that someday I'd find them, or that one night, one of them would amble up to my bedroom window and peek in to have a look at me with his big yellow eye!"

Mikaela laughed along with Kemp, and she felt herself blush.

"I'm sorry," she said, after a slight pause. "I guess that when you get so immersed in your work, you can sometimes forget that there are other people around who might understand and appreciate what you're doing."

"Yes, I know the feeling. I think it's a common problem with people who really love their work. Sometimes they can let it get in the way of the *people* in their lives."

"You mean the old 'love me or love your work, but you can't love both' routine?" Mikaela smiled and shook her head. "Yes, I've been down that road a few times myself."

"Well, I wasn't trying to get into anything personal," said Kemp quickly. "It just seemed like the appropriate thing to say. . . ."

"Oh, I see," said Mikaela. She noticed that he was a bit edgy when she relaxed the conversation. She had heard some of the crew members talking during the voyage about the colonel being involved with one of the missing people on the *Heinlein* expedition. He was probably having trouble dealing with the whole mess, and she decided she should respect his wishes and simply back off.

"Well, anyway, let me tell you what I've found out so far. . . ."

"About the dinosaurs, you mean?"

Mikaela smiled. "Yes, of course." She shuffled through her notes for a moment. "You see, it was generally believed for so long that the dinosaurs were just giant lizards that it was also assumed that they were cold-blooded, like the reptiles on

Earth today. But reptiles are dependent upon the environmental temperatures for their own body temperatures. And even under optimum conditions, true reptiles can only produce about a *twentieth* of the amount of energy than hot-blooded animals, like mammals, of the same body weight."

"And the bigger the body of the reptile, the *more* energy would be required to move it."

"Of course," said Mikaela. "And just in a couple of days, I've seen creatures like the Deinodon and the Compsognathus who move so quickly that they could not possibly be reptiles."

"But if they're not lizards, then what are they?"

"That's what all the research will really be about. Can you imagine what we'll learn when we can actually dissect a few of these animals? My feelings are that they are either a totally extinct class that resembles our modern reptiles in appearance only; or that they were a part of the reptile family that was hot-blooded and simply died off. We'll find out lots of things before we're done . . . now that we have this floating zoo."

"*If* we are careful," said Phineas. "That was one of the things I wanted to tell you about. When the expeditionary teams go out, I want you to realize that our first objective will be to search for any trace of the *Heinlein* team who might have survived. Scientific research will be secondary at this point, and I want you to understand that, okay?"

"Yes, that's quite clear. Are we going to be going out on foot?"

"Maybe for the preliminary excursions. But I'm planning to have several omni-terrain vehicles assembled, plus an ornithopter which will be able to fly in the contained atmosphere of the cylinder. There are some tricky vortices and gravity gradients that we will have to play with before we really know what we're doing."

"Well, don't worry about me and my people, Phineas. I promise that we will be cooperative. Nobody will go running off into the grinning jaws of old T. Rex." She smiled and closed her notebooks, sensing that their talk was almost at an end.

"Speaking of T. Rex . . ." he said as he stood up. "I haven't seen him yet, have you?"

"No, but I'm not surprised. Most of his fossil remains have

been found in less densely foliated regions. He seems to have preferred hunting in more open territory, most likely because of the trouble he might have had squeezing between all those redwoods in the thick parts of the forest."

"That's something good to know," said Kemp, reaching out to take Mikaela's hand, shaking it lightly. "Very well, then, it was good to have a chance to talk to you for a bit. We'll be assembling at oh-eight hundred hours. See you in the morning."

"That'll be fine, Phineas. And thank you. Good night."

Kemp smiled wanly, turned, and left the lab. Mikaela smiled to herself, thinking that she found him attractive in an odd way. There was something about his ram-rod mannerisms that didn't seem right. There was probably a lot more to Phineas Kemp seething about just beneath the surface, waiting to be unleashed, and Mikaela had the notion that she might be the woman to do the job.

Ross Canter entered the airlock of the *Goddard*, along with his co-workers on the outrigging project. As a flight engineer, he had not been dangling in space on an umbilical to do the actual labor on the engines but had acted as a supervisor and inspector of the work. The engines themselves were not as much of a problem as the proper placement and method of securing them to the hull and structure of the alien ship. It would have been much easier to have simply located the alien control section of the ship and used the on-board engines. Of course, Canter knew that there would be a whole new set of problems involved in something like that. It might be near to impossible to figure out how the engines worked without risking the destruction of the entire vessel; or it might all be in vain, since one of the most probable reasons why the ship was orbiting the sun dead in space was some kind of engine failure.

As Canter entered the ready-room, where he and the others slipped out of their EVA suits, he realized how thankful he was to be almost finished with the job. He did not like EVA work, just hanging out there in the bottomless pit of space. It gave him a bad case of vertigo, especially when he was looking down the endless length of the *Dragonstar*. It was like he was falling outwards all the time.

The *Goddard* and the *Heinlein*, docked together to form

one ungainly ship, had been attached to the side of the alien hull, and after a few more series of tests, Doctor Jakes and his men would be firing up the engines and the alteration of the *Dragonstar*'s orbit would begin. According to Canter's timetable, that would be just about the right time to sabotage the communications centers of both the *Goddard* and the *Heinlein*. Once the later phases of the operation had commenced back on the moon, there could be no more contact with either ship.

He had gone over the plan of action in his mind many times, and he was confident that he would be successful. It was incredible when he thought about it ... how easy it would be to do the job. In fact, having seen how far along the outrigging project had gone, maybe now was the best time to do it. Canter hung up his EVA suit in the locker and left the ready-room, walking quickly up to his crew quarters to pick up the few tools he would need.

Since he was a flight engineer, it was not unusual for him to be heading down the main corridor to the service module section of the *Goddard* with a tool belt dangling from the waist of his jumpsuit. No one paid him more than the usual attention of saying hello or simply nodding. Canter smiled back as he passed the few members of the skeleton crew on board either of the ships. Almost everyone was kept occupied either outside the alien ship, or down inside at the base camp.

After passing through the hatch to the service module, he locked it securely behind him, and paused to study the layout of the module, making sure that it coincided with the schematics he had brought with him. The module was one of the main ganglia in the nervous/electronic system of the ship. All the support and tactical systems for the *Goddard* originated here. Canter stood in the midst of a vast array of wiring, plumbing, modular paks, and harnesses, which would have stymied anyone without the explicit knowledge to understand it all. Canter traced the ventricular harnesses strapped along the bulkheads to the main bank of modular paks. Following the color-coded schematics, he located the pak which contained the monolithic micropressors in charge of Deep-Space tachyon communications. He pulled a small tool from his belt, a magnetic-driver, and unlocked the communications pak. It was so easy, he thought. A twist of the wrist, pull out the modular assembly, and the *Goddard* was deaf and dumb.

Placing the pak in his breast pocket, he stepped back and took his miniature welding-torch from his utility belt. A few deft strokes of the superheated beam of the torch and the bus-bar connectors for the modular pak were fused into slag. Even if Stores had replacement modular assemblies, no one would be able to repair the damages in time.

Canter put away his tools and left the service module, passing through the main corridor without being seen. He passed through the docking-collar lock into the *Heinlein,* which at the time was unoccupied, Fratz and Bracken having been reassigned to duty on board the *Goddard.* Canter had even less apprehension as he entered the service module of the smaller ship, where he disabled its communications facilities with ease. *This is for Nesrudah,* he thought to himself as he finished the job. He did not allow himself to think about what he was doing beyond that simple aspect. He had long ago learned that you only got yourself into deeper trouble when you tried to grapple with the implications of actions which were beyond the scope of your understanding. He only knew that he had been called upon to do a specific job, and that it was not his place to reason why, as the old poem said. He would leave that to his superiors.

When Canter returned to his cabin on board the *Goddard,* he lay back in his bunk and smiled to himself, satisfied that he had done his part so well. With any luck, he would not even be suspected, much less caught. Besides, he thought, pretty soon old Kemp will have a lot more than a saboteur to be worrying about.

CHAPTER 12

CAPTAIN FRANCIS WELSH had been a Mission Command pilot in the IASA since the early days of lunar colonization. He had seen the face of the far side of the moon transformed by the hands of man, and at one time had played a large part in that transformation. But as he grew older, he found that the Deep-Space Division was planning to phase him out of the program, systematically replacing many of the older Mission Commanders with young, fuzzy-faced kids. Well, that was the way it always was, thought Welsh, but he didn't let them put him out to pasture without a fight; he had, in effect, kept them from doing it by transferring to the Mining Division of Copernicus Operations. His many years of training and experience were just the ticket to get him a command on one of the big ore-processing ships. That had been more than four years back, and he'd been serving in that capacity ever since. It was all in what a guy got used to, he often thought, but what the hell. It

145

sure beat going back down to Earth where things were as crowded and confusing as ever. "Screw those poor bastards," Welsh often said. They didn't know what they were missing out here.

The name of his ship was the *Andromache*, the first of its type to be outfitted with ram-impulse engines, which made it one of the fastest industrial-class ships in the IASA. It was a big ship, almost two hundred meters long, mostly superstructure and modular ore-holds. Those twenty ore-holds were actually miniature landing modules which could be detached from the main body of the ship and guided down to the lunar surface to be unloaded. Aft of the ore-holds were the crew quarters, the launch bays for the Snipes, and the Command Module. All the way at the rear lay the Lukodanyov engines which had revolutionized Deep-Space Operations and made asteroid mining a feasible, profitable endeavor. Captain Welsh loved his ship, even though it wasn't much to look at and had none of the media-glamour attributed to the interplanetary exploration ships.

At the moment, he had the *Andromache* in a halo orbit above Ramadas Khan, the TWC lunar colony. Having recently transhipped ore and refueled at Copernicus Base, Captain Welsh was finishing up a routine delivery to the logistically helpless Third World colony. Since the Black and Arab Confederation had no ships capable of Deep-Space Operations, they had arranged through a series of treaties and agreements to be supplied by the IASA. Captain Welsh often wondered how those agreements must have stuck in the craws of TWC leaders, since the situation was a total reversal of the petroleum cartel dictating policy to the rest of the world during the last three decades of the previous century. Served the bastards right, thought Welsh. If they hadn't been such sons-of-bitches about the energy problems of the past, maybe they wouldn't be getting screwed so badly by the IASA now. He wasn't sure how much the TWC paid for shipment and delivery of supplies, but he was positive that they were paying up the hallowed ying-yang.

Checking his control panel, he saw that the on-board screen indicated that there was only one more ore-hold module remaining to be re-docked into the *Andromache*. Then it would be time to head out to the Belt again for another two-month stint. His crew, three officers and sixteen miners, were already on board, preparing for the three-week trip to the asteroids.

Flipping on his radio, Welsh called the TWC receiving dock. "Ramadas, this is *Andromache*. . . . What's the hold-up on that last module? Any trouble?"

There was a pause before his phones crackled slightly and an accented voice replied. "No problems, Captain Welsh. The last of the ore has just been dumped. Launch of Module-18 is scheduled in ten minutes. Please standby. . . ."

"Ten minutes? What the hell's the delay for?"

"Sorry, Captain, but we have a slight malfunction. One of the launch bay doors is sticking. We have a crew working on it, and are promised that the problem will be corrected momentarily. Please stand by. . . . Ramadas out."

Welsh turned to his flight assistant, Lieutenant Knapp, a large, bearded, burly character who looked as though he would be more at home behind the helm of a New England whaler. "Can you believe those clowns? They're always screwing up something, aren't they?"

Knapp laughed, but said nothing. Their conversations about the TWC were a familiar routine. Welsh hated them; it was as simple as that.

". . . they did a lot better," Welsh was saying, "when all they had to worry about were their camels and their spears. . . . They got no business out here in space when the people in their own countries are still eating each other. . . ."

"C'mon, Captain, it's not as bad as all that," said Lieutenant Knapp.

"No, I guess you're right. I mean, what's a little famine and pestilence? It makes life more interesting when you're watching it from within the palace walls."

Knapp checked his timepiece. "I think we'd better check in with them again. We've got to go through check-out with Copernicus before lunch. Linkowski gets pissed when we throw off his schedule. . . ."

Welsh shook his head in mock disgust. "Yeah, I'd better find out what the hell's going on." He flipped on the radio and called Ramadas Khan.

"We are very sorry for the delay, Captain Welsh," said the accented voice. "The problem has been corrected and we are preparing to launch. Please stand by. . . ."

"Wait a minute," said Welsh. "Just a goddamned minute! Patch me in to my Module pilot, Ramadas. . . . Give me Spec-5 Burcroff. . . ."

"One moment, Captain. . . ." the radiophones crackled with static, an ever-present sound which Welsh always ascribed to TWC inferior equipment.

"What's the matter, Captain?" asked Knapp.

"Something funny's going on," said Welsh. "I hailed Burcroff and he's not responding. He's supposed to be in Command Cabin while they unload."

"Jesus, what do you think's up? Should I notify Copernicus?"

"No, not yet. I don't want to do anything that will get everybody upset . . . not till we know something for sure." Welsh hailed Ramadas again. "This is Captain Welsh on the *Andromache*. What's going on down there?"

"I'm sorry, Captain. We just checked on your Module pilot, and found that he has taken ill. . . ."

"What? What the hell is wrong with him? Let me talk to him?"

"I'm afraid that's impossible, Captain. Your pilot is unconscious. We have a physician with him at this very moment. Please stand by. . . ."

Welsh cut off the channel, and turned to Stuart Knapp. "This is a lot of bullshit! Call Copernicus and tell them what's going on."

As Knapp called Copernicus Base, Welsh's phones crackled again. *Those slimy bastards! What now?* "Andromache, this is Ramadas. . . . Spec-5 Burcroff is having some kind of seizure. We have notified Copernicus, and requested that we have one of our own pilots return Module-18 to your ship. . . . Do you copy?"

"Yeah, we copy," said Captain Welsh. "Stand by, Ramadas. . . ." He turned to Knapp and spoke softly. "Did you get a confirmation on that from Copernicus?"

Knapp nodded. "Yeah, Linkowski's blowing his frigging mind. He says to get that Module docked and get checked out. He's got a shuttle coming in and he's one flight-controller short today."

"You mean I'm supposed to let one of those dumb monkeys

put his hands on one of our Modules! Is he crazy?"

Knapp shrugged. "He's already given them confirmation to ferry it up. . . ."

"Goddamnit, Stu. . . . I don't like it. Something's going on!"

"*Andromache*, this is Ramadas. . . . We have confirmation of launch. Stand by for rendezvous with Module-18 in minus three minutes. . . ."

Welsh banged his palm against the Command console. "Those sons-of-bitches!" He flipped on the radio. "That's affirmative, Ramadas. . . . We copy here. Do you have a status report on my pilot?"

"Affirmative, *Andromache*. We've sent him to our infirmary. He is conscious and the physician says he will be all right. . . . Stand by. . . ."

Welsh turned to Knapp. "We're going to be a man short, it looks like. Tell Copernicus to have a shuttle ready to bring us a back-up while we're going through check-out. Also, you'd better have Linkowski log a report with Security. I don't like the sound of all this shit. . . ."

"Security? You sure, Captain?"

"Yeah, do it." Welsh flipped a key and watched the schematic on his screen. The ore Module was approaching his ship on a perfect course, and he was surprised that the TWC pilot was that good. Within twenty seconds, he would be aligned with locks and be drawn in automatically by the computer-guidance.

"Module-18, ready for docking," said an unfamiliar voice in his phones. "Do you copy, *Andromache?*"

"We copy, Module-18. Auto-guide should be taking over just about now . . ." said Welsh, watching the screen, just as another thought came to him. Cutting off his mike, he turned to Knapp again. "Stu, call Rappaport, and tell him to get his ass down to the airlock for 18. Have him call me if anything looks funny. . . ."

Knapp nodded and used the intercom to the crew section.

A green light flashed on his screen, indicating that the Module was locked into the superstructure. Welsh continued to watch the screen, and was surprised to see that a yellow warning bar began flashing—an indicator that the ore-holds had been opened from the inside, facing the airlock which ran along the main corridor of the ship.

"What the hell's going on? Somebody just opened the hold on Module-18." He radioed the Command Cabin of 18, and got no response, and he felt a fist tightening around his stomach. It was a sixth-sense feeling that something terrible was about to happen. "Stu? Any word from Rappaport?"

"No, Captain. . . ."

He keyed in a channel to Copernicus quickly. "Linkowski, this is Welsh on the *Andromache*. . . . We've got a problem up here, do you copy?"

"You're goddamned right, you've got a problem, Welsh. . . . You're throwing me off schedule, and—"

"Screw your schedule! I've got an unauthorized airlock entry on Module-18. I want you to—"

He was interrupted by a klaxon blaring through the ship, sounding a general quarters alarm. "What the hell—? We've got a general quarters in here, Linkowski! Get a Security ship scrambled!"

"Captain, I'm not getting any response below decks," said Knapp.

Welsh felt the rising jolt of panic that was surging through his heart and up the back of his neck. "Linkowski?! Did you copy that last transmission? We've got big trouble up here. Our little brown brothers have given us a-shot in the ass!"

Welsh's phones crackled for an instant as the Copernicus flight controller started to reply, but Welsh was not listening. The hatch to the Command Cabin had been opened behind him and he had swiveled around to see what was going on. Three men dressed in olive green jumpsuits, LS-helmets, and face-shields stood on the threshold.

They were holding weapons at their hips.

"Captain—!" Stu Knapp had started to get out of his chair when the first slugs caught him in the chest. His uniform blossomed red. He was thrown back against his console, eyes still open, but seeing nothing, ever again. Welsh started to move as the two men rushed him, the closest swinging the stock of his weapon against the side of his head.

Captain Francis Welsh didn't even have time to see stars before blacking out.

When he regained consciousness, the three men surrounded him. Lieutenant Knapp's body lay near the hatch. One of the intruders was sitting in his chair, his face still hidden by the faceplate of his helmet. One of the other men leaned down, sticking the weapon of his gun under Welsh's nose.

"A thousand pardons, Captain Welsh...but I regret to inform you that your ship has been commandeered by the TWC."

The words sunk into Welsh's numbed mind slowly and for a moment he didn't react. He looked up at the anonymous figure, trying to ignore the weapon in his face. "Why? What do you want? What's happened to my crew?"

"Your crew is dead, Captain. We have already left lunar orbit."

"What for? Where are we going?" Welsh shook his head, put his hand to a damp, pulpy gash on the side of his head. He couldn't believe what was happening. The thought of his crew being killed was absurd. It couldn't be true....

"It is not necessary that you know the nature of this mission. We have already reprogrammed your navigational computers, and you will not be needed in that capacity."

"Then why don't you kill me too, you bastards?"

The man chuckled behind his faceplate. "An engaging idea, but I have decided against it, Captain. We shall keep you alive in the event of an emergency, since your knowledge of this ship may prove helpful...."

"Well, you may as well shoot me now, because I wouldn't help you for all the shit in the world...."

Again the unseen chuckle. "We shall see about that." Turning to the third man, the leader spoke again. "Take him to his cabin and keep him under guard. And get this body out of here...."

Welsh was pulled to his feet and escorted from the Command Cabin. He was tempted to turn and go for the man's weapon. Go out in a blaze of glory and all that crap, he thought. But then another thought struck him. A thought that was far simpler and more logical: *screw it*, he thought, and began laughing softly to himself.

Stanley Linkowski, Copernicus flight controller, stared uncomprehendingly at his screens. The *Andromache* had fired her engines and slipped quickly from lunar orbit. There was no response from her by radio and the Security shuttle which had been launched to rendezvous with her was left far behind in the wake of a full-power thrust of her ram-impulse engines.

Alarms were sounding in the Tower and men were screaming and running around all over the place. For a moment, Linkowski could think of nothing other than the fact that he had committed a supreme foul-up and that they were going to have his ass in a crack for it.

One of his assistants had tapped him on the shoulder to tell him that he had a call on the Priority channel. As though in a daze, Stanley picked up the phone.

"Yes? This is Linkowski...."

"What in hell's going on over there?" said a violently angry voice.

Stanley recognized the voice of Gregor Kolenkhov, who was in charge of Copernicus Base while Kemp was off on a mission.

"Doctor Kolenkhov? I'm sorry, I'm not sure... I think we've had one of our ships hijacked."

"No shit!" cried Kolenkhov. "I want you to track that ship and get me a projected course as soon as possible. How in the hell did you let something like this happen, dammit!"

"I'm short-handed today, Doctor, and I...." Stanley fumbled for the right words but nothing would come to him. It was going to be a long day....

Within the hour, Copernicus Base received an official communique from TWC Headquarters in Mecca. The crux of the message stated that the Third World Confederation disclaimed any responsibility for the armed take-over of an IASA vessel. They attributed the incident to the work of an underground terrorist organization calling themselves the Lunar Liberation Collective, and said that the TWC had no idea why the *Andromache* had been hijacked.

Diplomatic relations between the IASA Alliance and the TWC became strained to the breaking point as accusations and threats were hurled back and forth. There was the usual groundswell of public outrage, but nothing was actually done of any consequence in the geopolitical arena.

In a hurriedly assembled meeting of the Joint Directors of the IASA, Gregor Kolenkhov explained what was known about the hijacking incident. "...and although we have not made this known to the media, the tracking stations have confirmed course projections for the *Andromache*." He paused to clear his throat, and look each of the Directors in the eye. "It appears as though the ore-ship plans to rendezvous with the *Dragonstar....*"

"Oh Jesus...!" said Christopher Alvarez.

"But how could they know?!" said Nelson Johl. "This is impossible...."

Kolenkhov shook his head. "Impossible, I'm afraid it's not. Apparently, the security-leaks problem is more severe than any of us could have imagined. It is obvious that the TWC, despite their claims to the contrary, have known about the alien ship and realize its value as an economic and political tool, and that they plan to assume control of the vessel."

"Is there any way we can catch them? Stop them?"

"It is quite doubtful. The only ship capable of overtaking them is the *Clarke* enroute to the Mars Installation. We are planning to re-route it and arrange for course rendezvous, but they will be at least a week behind the *Andromache*. Besides, the *Clarke* is an exploratory ship, not a military vessel. The crew is for all intents and purposes unarmed."

"What do we know about the group that took over the *Andromache?* How many men? How heavily armed?"

Kolenkhov shrugged. "We know practically nothing. The TWC authorities claim to know very little... other than that a group of armed terrorists, of *indeterminate number*, commandeered the receiving docks at Ramadas, and reached the ore-ship by piling into one of the hold-modules."

"They know how many men. They know what's going on," said Johl. "They're just not telling...."

Kolenkhov grinned ironically. "Would *you* tell us anything, if you were them?"

"Has Colonel Kemp been told about this?" asked Alvarez.

"That's the worst part, gentlemen. The last transmission we have received from the *Goddard* was that the alien ship had been successfully rigged for course alteration, and that they were bringing it in. Since then, almost twenty-four hours ago now, we haven't heard a thing."

Everyone started talking at once and Nelson Johl called for quiet. "So we have no way of reaching the *Goddard?*"

"No sir," said Gregor. "I'm afraid they're on their own."

CHAPTER 13

THE ILLUMINATOR PUSHED its light down steadily. Even if a scrap of cloud happened to obscure part of it, there was still plenty of hot bright rod showing. Bloody little shade, too, mused Ian Coopersmith as he wound his way through a boulder-strewn pass. And what there was tended to be a jungle area, like being wrapped in a hot, smotheringly wet blanket.

He climbed over a large rock and then turned around to make sure Becky could manage. Though she didn't exactly blithely leap over it, she didn't seem to need any aid. She was handling herself very well, Becky was, considering the fact that they'd been bumbling about in this monster-inhabited world-within-a-ship for five weeks now. Well, not bumbling, exactly, thought Ian. Close enough. At least they were alive.

Becky skipped down, flashed a brief smile and continued ahead of him, all without a word. Nothing unusual, that. They went without words for hours at a time now, communicating through the odd body gesture or expression. It was as though they shared a certain state of mind that opened up an essential telepathy of survival between them. They functioned as a single unit now, in the rhythms of their walking, caution, food-seeking, sleeping, and. . . .

Say it, Coopersmith. Spit it out, he told himself. Dammit, he had to come to grips with it, before it tore him apart . . . and lovemaking.

He rubbed the sweat from his eyes with the back of his hand, and took a deep breath of the strangely tanged air. Dust motes spun before him in their odd, primeval dance of physics. A stray insect buzzed somewhere near, unseen. Coopersmith put his legs into an automatic mode of left-right-left-right and watched as Rebecca Thalberg advanced along the path in front of him. Her movements were fluid, almost feline now. She'd recovered rapidly from the awkwardness suffered at the beginning of their wanderings. Her muscles had hardened, she'd lost ten pounds at least, and clearly she was adapting well to the situation. Oh, sure, she complained a lot, but that was release . . . an escape valve. In fact, at this point she almost seemed to accept their dilemma better than *he* did.

She certainly accepted the sex they'd gotten into better. These modern women, thought Coopersmith . . . particularly the Americans . . . know exactly what they want and when they get it, they have no qualms, no guilt.

Of course, in Becky's case, neither did she have a spouse and kids. That was part of what grated in Coopersmith's mind. He *loved* Leticia. Everytime he made love with Rebecca, he felt, however absurdly, that he was betraying his wife. Marital treason, to say nothing of dispensing with all that his very strict parents had taught him. The fact that he enjoyed the blooming relationship with Becky, indeed *needed it,* did nothing to assuage his uncertainty. Having sex with Becky had nothing to do with survival, no matter what the insatiable woman claimed. If they made it out of this place, what then? He didn't know if he'd want to lose Becky. He was falling in love with her.

One thing truly refreshing about the woman. The race business didn't bother her one jot. Coopersmith had grown up in a warm and loving home with racially mixed parents, whereas Becky's parents had been divorced early in her life. She'd barely known parental love, and she hungered for constant attention and affection of just the sort that Ian was able to give freely and easily. No, it was just the situation that had cleared the way for their love. They were truly compatible.

That they were still alive to share any kind of relationship was a tribute to their resourcefulness and their ability to learn the rules of the enviornmental game as it was played in the late Jurassic. They'd spent three days among the ruins of the three pyramids, but found no clues as to who might have built the structures or to what purpose they might have served. All attempts to find an entrance into the pyramids had been failures. They'd deserted the ruins to make their way across the lowlands of the river valley, following the topography as it gradually ascended to the edges of a great plateau, which was less foliated. Lots of rocks. Mountainous. Coopersmith definitely preferred it.

Becky stopped, and Coopersmith ran into her.

His lack of sufficient reflex action troubled him. What was it? Getting tired, old boy. Getting soft? Old?

"What's that, Ian?"

Coopersmith disentangled himself, and looked toward what she pointed at.

"Goodness gracious," he said, forgetting all his previous preoccupations. "I think we're onto something this time," he added with wry good humor and not a little excitement.

A city.

Or what appeared to be a city, at any rate. Coopersmith stood by her side and stared into the afternoon haze, just distinguishing the collection of rectangular structures in the distance.

"Looks a bit like some South American ruins, Ian. Terraces! Stepped terraces. I can't really tell at this distance, but it looks like they're overgrown with vegetation."

"*Chariots of the Gods!*" Ian intoned gravely. He was grateful that even in uncomfortable situations, he always managed to keep his sense of humor.

"Oh, come off it."

Coopermith folded his arms in contemplation. "No. Really. Do you think that von Danikan chap had something on the ball? Obviously Earth *was* visited by folks from another planet.

The people who made this ship, as a matter of fact!"

"Yes, but that was millions of years before Daniken and the other screwballs say *their* aliens visited Earth."

"But they *were* right in principle, you have to give them that."

"I rather think all this is a little more amazing than what they had in mind." She gestured expansively about the inside of the ship.

Ian glanced about. Yes. It still was a bit mind-numbing, staring at all this. *An entire world on the inside hull of a gigantic starship. A world of dinosaurs, of ruins, of long-kept secrets.* The horizons rolled on up into the haze on either side of them, and the illuminator burned steadily in center of the cylinder like a very long filament inside a very big vacuum tube.

"Just the same," Becky continued. "One comes to accept it, if not grasp it."

"You bloody better accept it, or you become a between meal snack for one of the carnivores," Ian commented.

Becky said, "Do you think we can make it by nightfall?"

"Is that all you think about, woman?"

She stared blankly at him, then hit him lightly on the arm. "You know what I'm talking about, Ian."

"I don't know," said Ian, seriously, as he checked his chronometer. "Hard to say how far away it is. And there's a lot of open territory between here and there. We would have to be very careful."

Becky nodded, then looked back towards the ruins. "I think we should chance it. If we make it, there will be plenty of places for cover. I'm sick of finding the tallest trees, to say nothing of squirming into cracks in the rocks."

Ian smiled. "If you think you're up to it, my girl! But don't say I didn't warn you. We've been lucky so far, you know."

Since they had traveled up from the lowlands, they'd noticed a gradual change in the kinds of creatures which inhabited the highlands. The big Hadrosaurs and the even bigger Sauropods such as the Brontosaurus were not in evidence in this part of the interior because there was a scarcity of large lakes and marsh swamplands—their natural habitat. Consequently, the types of predators which feasted upon them were not seen as much, although Ian had noticed that a smaller species of Gorgosaurus seemed to have no territorial preference. He'd taken note of the prevalence of the more sturdy types of herbivores in the highlands, having seen large herds of Ceratopsians, Ankylosaurus, and other four-legged dinosaurs which affected thick, rhino-like hides and a vast array of spikes, horns, and armor-like plating.

You never get used to looking at those things, thought Ian Coopersmith. Any *kind* of dinosaur was frightening, not merely because of their potential danger. They sparked some primordial fear deep down . . . a very basic instinct. And they seemed so *alien*, even though they did originate on Earth.

He'd read the theories concerning the relationship of lizards and mammals. The smaller, weaker mammals were no doubt prey to the last of the dinosaurs. Hence, to escape from the saurians' night-stalking habits, mammals were thought to have searched out nooks and crannies and caves and high trees, just as Ian and Becky had been doing these past terrifying weeks. There, in partial safety from their natural enemies, they developed a way to keep still for long periods of time. Sleep. At frequent intervals, they needed to rouse, enter a more aware state of repose. Dreams. And what would these first mammals dream about? Why, about the creatures who hunted them, of course. Dinosaurs. Dragons. The beginning of an archetype. Somehow, that archetype, whether genetic or truly part of the "collective unconscious," as Jung thought, had traveled through the eons and lived now in Ian Coopersmith's head. Coopersmith knew it. Traveling through this hellhole with its attendant natural demons was bad enough. When he slept, though, it was truly torture. Nightmares would emerge from the gunk of his unconscious mind, and reach out with razor claws or needlelike talons to tear and rip. Dead, icy, reptilian eyes would glare into his, bloodshot with rage and atavistic hunger. They would chase him across plains, and through swampy jungle, these terrible lizards, and they would catch him and rend him and consume him, just as their brothers had done to poor Huff, and Hagar, and Johl, and Valdone with the wife and the mother and father who grieved. But he would never die. Like an endlessly repeated film clip, it happened over and over, over and over. . . .

Shuddering, Coopersmith realized how parched his throat

was. He took a swallow of water from his canteen. Not too much, since it was hard to say when they'd see their next natural spring or stream with decent drinking water. Though it satisfied his thirst, somehow it didn't do much for the dryness.

Ian Coopersmith had to admit to himself that he was frightened to the very roots of his being. Becky didn't seem to be having as many problems as he was. To begin with, she had no shame about her fears. Her emotions were expressed readily, in tears or screams or whatever. And she had someone to rely on, a caretaker. In Ian she saw a trustworthy father-figure. He was her competent hero, able to take care of all situations at all times. Was that why they were lovers now? If they'd been thrown together in a less dangerous situation, would she have been cold and aloof?

He *did* feel extraordinarily protective of her. Another instinct, or was it love? Where did passion and need end, and true unselfish love begin?

Because of her obvious trust in him, he was afraid to show the fissures of weakness with which he felt himself riddled. Oh, he told her he was scared from time to time, but somehow she never believed him.

He didn't want to die, but he didn't know how much longer he could endure this internal and external pressure. He watched Becky walking ahead of him for a while, almost envying her. He wished *he* had a competent father figure. Somehow, all the responsibility seemed to be on his shoulders to get them out of here, alive.

As they passed a large outcropping of rock which Ian rather fancied looked like a half-finished sculpture of a Stegosaurus (*Dammit, man, stop thinking of the things. You've got dragons on the brain!*), Becky pointed across the plain. "Ian. Look!"

There was a small family of Chasmosaurs within two hundred meters of their position. The group of stocky animals looked suitably fearsome with their heads covered with a large fan-shaped, bony sheath, further adorned with spike-like horns. The largest of the beasts was more than two meters high and twice that long.

"God bless. They're kind of close, aren't they? We'd better lay amongst these rocks until they've put some distance between us."

He grabbed Becky's hand and led her back into the jagged stand of boulders, keeping his eyes on the Chasmosaurs. They climbed the rocks, and Ian could feel the trust in the warmth of her grip. Becky found his hold strong and reassuring. She was falling deeply in love with him, and obviously didn't want to stop herself, despite Phineas Kemp. How easily people followed the whims of their heart despite their commitments. Coopersmith wondered if Kemp would understand. He knew that Leticia would. "Come now," she'd say. "The old deserted island bit. A virile man and a lusty woman. I'd think it unnatural if there wasn't a little hanky panky." But even hearing her reassuring voice in his mind didn't assuage Coopersmith's guilt much.

They'd talked about their respective commitments, and Coopersmith could understand why Becky had fallen so easily for his natural warmth. Apparently old Kemp wasn't a cold fish only in his command duties. One of Becky's pet themes of conversation had been her frustrations with Kemp, and though Coopersmith never failed to stick up for the man, inwardly he was astonished. Did drive and ambition do that to a man's capacity for love and intimacy? Coopersmith wondered if it was worth it. In fact, he questioned the value of his own meager ambitions which had vaulted him to his high level in the IASA, but had also landed him in *this* mess. Perhaps he should have been satisfied with a plain old Earthbound engineering job, living a long and healthy life in comfortable contentment.

They'd spilled much of themselves into each other, he and Becky had, and now he was irretrievably caught up with her. She thrilled with the time and energy he took in trying to understand her from the very beginning, despite the lack of success in their first bout of lovemaking. That had been kind of rough. He'd apologized for seducing her, for letting his drives get the better of him, and promised that it would never happen again. But she *wanted* it to happen again, just as he did. And after a couple of days when guilt had put a barrier between them, she explained that she felt guilty as well, and that perhaps they should work through that guilt, because the comfort they could take in each other, physical and emotional, might be the key to the will to survive. He couldn't argue with that, nor did he want to, and the subsequent sharings of their bodies and minds had proved extremely sustaining for both of them, on certain levels. But the guilt and the doubt remained. He was holding back, he knew, because he realized just how possible it was to fall totally in love with her, and he didn't want that.

Movement in the Chasmosaur herd distracted him from his unsettling thoughts. "Uh oh. I think they've picked up our scent."

The dinosaurs were becoming agitated. The one closest to them had begun to nervously pad the ground with its front feet.

"Damn," said Ian. "I think that big one's coming this way." A thrill of fear raced through him. He was in no state to deal with this.

One of the things they had learned about the Ceratopsians since they'd reached the highlands was the difference in temperament between the tough, rhino-like dinosaurs and the fleshy herbivores of the lowlands. The horned dinosaurs, although plant-eaters, were a scrappy bunch who did not scare easily and who would willingly put up a fight against any predator that threatened the safety of their young within their herd. In fact, Ian and Becky had seen the large males inexplicably charge inanimate objects such as rocks and trees with bone-shattering impact.

Becky looked up at him. "Ian. Are we safe here?"

"God knows . . . but I think we're going to find out. Here he comes!"

The largest of the Chasmosaurs had begun trotting toward their position, gathering speed quickly, kicking up clouds of dirt in its wake. The resemblance to the head-on charge of a big rhino was uncanny, although those mammals were a lot smaller than these bastards.

A knot of fear crawling up his throat, Ian took out his Magnum pistol and flipped off the safety, checking the chamber. The weapon was fine. Coopersmith wasn't. His hands were trembling slightly.

"I'm going to wait until he gets close enough for these slugs to do the most damage," he said, swallowing back his fear.

Steady on, old boy, he told himself. Keep your nerve.

By the time it was seventy meters away, it appeared to have reached its full speed, which was considerable. The air reverberated from the ground-thudding rhythm of its charge.

Suddenly, with incredible volume, it bellowed.

Startled, Ian took a step back, swiftly. He felt the rock behind him dig into his leg even as he lost his balance.

"Jesus!" he cried, tripping over the hard rock. Trying to recover, he twisted around, forgetting his hold on his gun. The weapon flew from his hands into the dust even as he windmilled over into the short drop behind him. He fell a meter and a half, hitting hard on his side. The fall knocked his breath out, and he gasped in pain.

Must get up, he thought, dazed. *Becky. Must watch out for Becky.*

He rolled over. Agony shot through his ribs and up one leg. He tried to scramble up, but he'd sprained his left ankle and he tottered back down again, grabbing hold of the rock that had tripped him. There was the taste of dust and blood and death in his mouth as he saw the Chasmosaur, honking wildly in its unnerving bellow. It was closing the distance rapidly, its head down so that the large horn on its nose was pointing straight ahead. The fanlike sheath of its bony head-crest served as a shield for its softer neck and sagging underbelly. It looked like an armored car bearing down upon them.

Becky was not standing still. She had already dashed over to where the gun had fallen, and retrieved it.

"Stay down, Ian," she said firmly.

"But Becky . . . !" he said, trying to clamber over the rock.

"I said stay down, dammit! No time!"

Becky wedged her right hand between two jagged peaks, taking careful aim down the short barrel of the Magnum.

Ian watched with a mixture of fear and astonishment, forgetting the pain that licked up his leg and his side, ignoring the ache that had begun to pound in his head.

Becky sighted between the rocks, concentrating on the expanding shape of the Chasmosaur's triangular head. Just below two bony projections on its brow were two small black beads— its eyes. She was going to try to put a bullet into its brain through the eye-socket. There was no way of knowing if a Magnum slug would even penetrate the armored skull. Her chances of hitting the tiny eye, though, were slim, especially since the beast was moving so fast.

When it was twenty meters away and closing, Becky fired her first shot. It struck the fan-like sheath, shattering it like a dinner plate. Ian had underestimated the destructive force of an exploding slug. He was shocked to see the beast momentarily stagger as its blood pumped through the wound and down the side of its face. It shook its head and resumed its charge as Becky fired again. This time the bullet entered the thing's mouth just below the curve of its bird-like beak. Bits of bone and a thick mist of blood spurted from its lower jaw. The beast stumbled down upon its front legs, shaking its head violently from side to side. Its bellow reached a higher pitch, and the sound pierced the air, describing the beast's agony.

"Good Christ!" said Ian under his breath as he watched the hulking creature force itself back up to its feet and begin to again move forward. He felt shattered with fear and helplessness. It was all in Becky's hands now. There was nothing he could do.

Nothing.

The Chasmosaur's ugly head was now mottled with blood and dirt. Its lower jaw dangled open helplessly.

But still it kept coming.

Less than ten meters from their fragile position in the rocks, the Chasmosaur's speed had slowed to a fast walk. Still, it was moving with enough power to barrel through the rocks by the force of its own momentum.

Ian watched Becky as she drew a breath, sighted again down the barrel, and waited until the monster's enormous head was thrashing and weaving only meters in front of her. Ian could smell the lizardy reek from the creature, mixed with the dust it had spumed up.

Her face was calm and intent. She fired twice. The first volley struck the horny crest, further obliterating it. The second slammed straight up into the beast's open mouth, which had been thrown back and up by the explosive force of the first slug. The second bullet must have entered the beast's brain through the roof of its mouth, because in the next instant Ian saw the back of its neck, just behind the ridge of its bony crest, explode in a geyser of shredded flesh and vaporized blood. The Chasmosaur's bellowing stopped abruptly as it fell forward, its ravaged head falling into the wedge of rocks where Becky had been firing from. Jumping back, Becky fell and tucked into a tight roll.

Ian cried out and managed to scramble over the rocks and over to her, ignoring the shafts of pain driving through his body. As he touched her, he looked up. The beast's great head hung over them, unmoving, finally stilled. Blood dripped down the rocks, pooling in the dirt.

"It's okay now, Becky," he whispered.

She opened her eyes and stared up blankly.

"You did just fine, darling. You saved our lives." He pried the Magnum from her hands, and switched the safety back on. The thing was hot from firing.

"Ian! Oh God. Ian . . ." she said, reaching up for him.

He held her for a moment, trying to ignore the pain it caused him in his ribs. He just prayed he hadn't broken any. Not likely.

"You were incredible, Becky," said Ian, stroking her hair. "I'm sorry I doubted you."

"What do you mean?"

"Nothing. Let's not talk about it . . . not now. Are you all right?"

"I think so. He didn't touch me. I just lost my balance getting out of the way. What about the other ones?"

Ian stood up and looked beyond the huge head of the dead beast, down to the plateau where the remainder of the small herd continued to graze. He favored his injured leg. "Hmm. Doesn't look like there's anybody else who wants to play hero. Just the same, I think we'd better get out of here. This corpse's going to start attracting scavengers."

"Ian, your leg. . . ." Becky got up, concerned.

"And my side and my head, too."

"Hurt much?"

"You bet. That was a damned stupid thing I did back there. I should have stayed calm. I don't know what the hell is wrong with me, Becky." He looked away, feeling the full burden of his failure.

"Hey. Just a moment here. You fell over a rock. I shot the dinosaur instead. So what? You're not going to do the male ego trip on me like Phineas does."

"It's my responsibility to look after you," he muttered.

She walked around and faced him, hands on hips. "Listen, Ian. We look out for each other here. That's the way we survive. I'm not exactly as strong as you are, and maybe I don't have all the training you do, but I can do my share."

"Obviously."

"And because you didn't get to blow the beast away, your precious ego is stung."

"No. Maybe that's part of it, Becky. But there's more than that. I'm not like Kemp. I promise."

Her voice softened. "Can you walk all right, Ian?"

"Sure. It feels better already."

"Well, we'll never make that city before dark now."

Ian said, "We'll have to work our way across the plateau using whatever cover's available. And find a place to rest tonight. I don't suppose there are aspirin in our survival packs?"

She grinned. "I brought some Midol."

"Not exactly issued medication, but it will do. I wish I had a shot of Scotch to take them with."

"Just think. If we can stay alive, you can have all the Scotch you want."

Ian pursed his lips thoughtfully. "You know, finally I've found something to live for!"

She laughed and took his hand and helped him out of the rocks.

Ian Coopersmith thumped down wearily beside Becky, who lay prone at the edge of the clear purling stream that flowed swiftly down the slope. His chest still smarted, but it was obvious that nothing had broken. There were bruises there, but that was all. It was his ankle that gave him the most trouble, slowing down their progress quite a bit. If they ever had to run. . . . He moved his hands to his forehead as though to push away the remainder of his headache. Becky's tablets had been surprisingly helpful. However, some of the pain still remained.

His jumpsuit top *squished* with his movement.

The thing was sopping with perspiration. He had long since become accustomed to the sting of sweat leaking into his eyes, to say nothing of the aroma that clung to him with the tenacity of the mist that would curl up steadily from the ground after the illuminator began its twelve-hour shift of brilliance. God, how he stank! Growing up with a self-respecting lower-middle class family in the East Acton section of Greater London had drilled into Ian Coopersmith layers upon layers of Western living discipline, to say nothing of English manners. Although in the tidy household by Wormwood Scrubs cleanliness was never next to Godliness—that had a whole upper strata to itself—it was close enough to merit threats of hellfire and perdition if not attained. Even now, should he suddenly be miraculously transported to the bosom of his dear family, his mother would wince and his father would take the familiar pipe from his mouth and point it imperiously toward the spotless bathroom, wordlessly demanding an immediate ablution of his formerly missing flesh-and-blood before hugs and kisses were extended.

Dammit bloody all! he had thought with consternation when his clothes had started to smear with soil and sweat and gritty dirt had begun to swath the bottoms of his trousers. How could a man keep his dignity when filthy and smelly? He would have immediately worried about offending Becky if she weren't having the same difficulty. Still, she had never affected a flossed-up hairdo, nor had she worn any make-up before, so the change in her appearance had not been as devastating as it would have been in some artificially attractive women he knew. No, if anything, her present state—hair straggly and mud-matted, jumpsuit dirty as his—gave her a rather appealing look. "Earthy!" he had pronounced once when she'd asked him if she looked as perfectly awful as she felt, and she'd smacked him playfully, chuckling. Then down they went for one of the many urgent, fearful, and passionate embraces that had occurred during the time before their desperate human *need* for one another had finally broken through their reserve and they'd stayed awake half the night, with sex as company.

"I take it you've decided that the water is not poisonous," he said, mixing his words with a prolonged sigh.

Becky stopped slurping. She canted her head to look at him. Water dripped down her face and hair, back into the stream. "Oh. So that's what I am, huh? Your wine taster."

"Dear Rebecca," he said in his best stentorian baritone. "I'm glad you've found your rightful place in life. Pray tell, how *is* this bountiful vat, vintage 150,000,000 B.C.?"

167

"Here," she replied. "Try some yourself, oh mighty king!" Cupping her hands she splashed up a good pint's worth of water straight into Coopersmith's face. The shock of the cool refreshing stuff left him spluttering comically. Then it reminded him of how very thirsty he was, and how some chill liquid running down his throat might take him away for a while from this dreadful humidity.

He knelt down and drank.

When he rose, quenched, Becky was sitting, legs and feet dangling in the gurgling stream. "Oh, Ian. I could linger here for days."

"Yes, well, may I remind you that there are certain fanged and clawed beasties afoot hereabouts who would just dearly love that, in hope of soon stumbling across us and having some human flesh along with their gulp of fresh water. Very rare stuff, human flesh. I've developed this paranoid notion that the roaring critters have quite a taste for it."

"You really think that we'll discover shelter in that city?" Her eyes were closed, her features the very model of resignation itself.

"I haven't the faintest. But I know we *must* push on." No irony of phrase twist in that; he was serious. He wanted to stay here as much as she did, if only to rest his leg.

She stretched out her arms and yawned deliciously. "Why must you be always right? You remind me of Kemp."

"Becky, we're not in a world of right and wrong now. We're in a world of *alive* and *dead*. I don't think there's any necessity to lecture you on *that* subject."

"You know, I like you."

"That proves you're still alive."

Playfully: "Oh, and if I didn't like you, I'd be dead?"

"Only in spirit, oh thou of excellent taste."

Becky opened her eyes, and suddenly all Coopersmith wanted to do was stare into them for a long time, forget his pains and anxieties. But those eyes were averted now, staring into the stream as though to memorize its pleasures.

"You know, Ian," she said slowly and thoughtfully. "I used to think—oh, *eons* ago, it seems—that without all the paraphernalia of structured civilization about me, without my family and friends, and TV and music . . . well, without all that, life just wasn't worth living. In fact, back ten years ago when the threat of a nuke war with China was about as close as it ever came, I chose to attend school in Washington, D.C., not because I particularly cared for Georgetown University, as nice as it is . . . no, I thought, if there ever *is* a nuclear holocaust that wipes out modern civilization as we know it, with only a few radioactive humans bumbling about left to show for the old gene pool, *I* want to be right under that first bomb and go out"—she snapped her fingers briskly—"just like that. No moaning or mourning. No struggle for wretched survival, no weeping for lost pasts or loved ones. But you know. . . ." She turned to him, and he got what he was hoping for: a chance to stare into her very lovely eyes. ". . . you know, Ian. All that time, I was *wrong*."

"Oh? How so?"

She grappled for words in short movements of hands and fingers. "I mean. . . . I mean, these weeks here . . . with you. . . . Why, they've been *miserable* and horrifying and just dreadful. . . ."

"Oh, thanks."

"No. You see, despite all that, I'm *alive*. And I know I'm alive, I'm aware that I'm alive; not walking through a daydream of work and socializing, hitting other people's keys and letting them hit mine. I'm *alive* and when I eat food I *taste* it, and when I drink water it's the most satisfying drink I've ever had. And when I see you, Ian. . . ."

"Yes?" The feeling in that word was invested naturally.

"Well, I know who you are, more than I've ever known anyone else before. I . . . I . . . . Oh hell, I can't explain, dammit!"

Solemnly, Coopersmith said, "You don't need to explain, Becky. I know exactly how you feel. About all of it."

That excited her. "You mean you were like that too? I mean, so dependent on civilization?"

"I suppose so. I suppose we all are, aren't we? I must admit, though," he chuckled lowly. "If the bomb ever dropped, at no time did I particularly want to be under it."

She didn't notice his sarcasm. Indeed, she hardly seemed to be listening to him at all. "No, I've never felt so alive. And you know, I want to survive. I want to keep on living and living, and growing and discovering. And I know, now, I'll never be bored again. I'm almost glad this happened. Is that a wretched thing to say, Ian?"

"I think you've got illuminator stroke, dearie." Somewhere a strident and hungry cry split the silence of the rocky plain. Coopersmith paused for a moment to listen. "And if you want to keep on knowing what life feels like, we'd better keep moving toward what appears to be our only hope."

Again, she didn't seem to be paying attention to what he was saying. Instead, Rebecca Thalberg was staring dreamily again at the water, sheened with the brilliant reflection of the streak of light that spread from "horizon" to "horizon."

"Becky, dear, are you thinking what I'm thinking?" Coopersmith said slowly, savoring the motion of his words.

Licking her lips, she looked down at the shallow stream. "I don't see any of the usual fauna around this water . . . or under it. Not like everywhere else. . . . Oh, I'd love . . . I think it's worth the chance!"

"Right!" Coopersmith said cheerfully, beginning to unbuckle his belt.

However, Becky paused only long enough to take off her shoes before she leaped, fully clothed, into the water, splashing merrily.

"Oh, hell," said Coopersmith, dropping his gunbelt, shuffling off his shoes, and joining her immediately.

The water that folded over him was crisp and cool, bracing and refreshing.

It felt wonderful.

"Well, at least our shoes are dry," said Becky.

Coopersmith hitched up his backpack for better balance, and grunted in reply. Their clothes were taking an awfully long time drying in this muggy heat. Not a frightfully pleasant sensation, slopping around in wet clothes in this kind of wretched climate. All the same, he had to agree with Becky: the clothes were much cleaner now. And they both smelled better, if that mattered.

They were still keeping to the rocks and the trees, away from the long plain where the bigger beasts roamed. They were making less than excellent time, however, due to Ian's ankle.

Limping was not the best form of travel. By Coopersmith's estimation, they had a good two hours or more of illuminator light left before that great rod in the sky called it a night and the dinosaurs began to prowl in earnest. That gave them an hour and a half more to march, and a half-hour to find some place that looked reasonably safe in which to hole up.

To think that the Earth had been like this for millions upon *millions* of years! From this steaming stew of life had emerged mammals and subsequently human beings. Ian had always felt a gentle *oneness* with nature and physics. His expertise in mathematics gave him the language to express that. But here, in this primeval nature, his own heritage, he felt alien, out of synch. The ecology, though perfectly balanced, seemed to be no place for the more advanced beings that this very environment eventually created. In the middle of a land filled with monsters whose sole purpose in life seemed to be to kill and to eat, he could empathize with the first mammals in their fight to stay on the right side of saurian stomachs.

He hoped his ankle improved. He used to travel with a clean, efficient stride. After a few wearisome days, he'd taught Becky to move with a similar economy of motion. Her aches and cramps gone, she was able to keep up with his normal pace easily. Though her legs were shorter, she was lighter and more agile. Now, trailing behind her, Coopersmith was enjoying watching her. Her movements gave him a certain aesthetic pleasure. The constant reminder of her company displayed lithely before him, feminine sleekness and all, reinforced his own inner supply of security. He'd made sure she knew that. They had learned to give those sort of things to one another, and to accept. The relationship worked smoothly, in that respect.

Through narrow gullies, over stands of scrub-trees, around craggy rocks, they walked, always skirting the plain which afforded no protection. From time to time, Coopersmith caught peripheral but distant glimpses of dinosaurs, convincing him of the wisdom of this path. Only fifteen minutes short of lights-out, they located a tiny crevasse with an overhang they could use to conceal themselves. The entryway was narrow enough to prevent any large head from squeezing through, if its owner was smart enough to find them, which Coopersmith doubted.

With Becky tucked comfortably against him, and their dinner of well-done lizard flesh and fruit digesting with little objection in his stomach, Coopersmith kept the first watch. The Magnum in his right hand gave his mind ease. Rebecca, breathing softly in sleep against his body, however, supplied him with true repose.

She'd always enjoyed ruins.

Since her childhood, Rebecca Thalberg's idea of a wonderfully adventurous day-trip was to seek out some old house or fort and wander. England and Europe had been a trip of perpetual bliss. She'd always felt that houses somehow stored up the impressions of the times and the people they'd been through. To walk amongst the remains of a very old establishment built by human beings was to somehow touch them across the gap of decades or centuries. In the tower of an ancient castle, or in the rocks of the foundation of an old New England home, mossy and blackened with age, there was a feeling of knowing something of the people who'd put them together, who had used them for shelter.

The ruins of the old city were different, however.

Superficially, they resembled some of the assembled stones and mortar that Becky had encountered before on Earth, if only in shapes and material of the structures. But they felt quite alien.

"You think they're all dead?" she asked Ian, surveying the expanse of one of the crumbling, viney pyramidal forms.

"Hmm?" Ian was too busy examining the rune-like carvings in the side of a jutting bit of stone. Pictographs composed part of the message. Characters of some odd written language consisting of what appeared to be claw scratchings made up the rest. Coopersmith had long since given up trying to discern the meaning of the scratches. He was now concentrating on the sequence of sketches, trying to determine if they were supposed to compose a series of related thoughts that would reveal something of the creatures who'd drawn them.

"Whoever built all of this. The species, I mean. Obviously not human."

"What brings you to that conclusion?"

She shrugged. "Oh, just the texture of this place. The feelings I get here."

"Ah! How I love the logic of a woman doctor of science."

Only her familiarity with Ian's brand of understated humor checked her anger. She actually found his statement amusing. Being with him all this time, she'd actually begun to be amused at herself. Just think. Intense Rebecca Thalberg, torpedoeing through life, now able to chuckle at her own inner paradoxes, her absurdities. How that would please her father.

"You know what I mean, damn you, Ian."

"Absolutely. These pictographs, for example." He fingered one of them thoughtfully, tracing the simple, two-dimensional figures. "Obviously they do not depict humans of any kind."

"That doesn't necessarily mean that there weren't—"

"Correct. But notice that these figures are pictured in various poses. They hold things in their hands. Weapons. And these bowls here, with what looks like smoke issuing from them. They know about the uses of fire. Ergo, it's reasonable to conclude that the artists were drawing self-portraits."

"Ian. They have *tails*."

"Quite."

"You think—"

"That these are the creatures . . . or the *sort* of creatures . . . that were responsible for building this spacefaring terrarium?"

"Precisely my conclusion. It's a possiblity. No more, no less."

"Something goes wrong with the ship. It's stranded in our system and those operating it are forced to live in this encapsulated environment, returning to savagery and then working their way back. . . ."

"So where are they now?"

"I was just suggesting possibilities."

"Just so." He squatted down to examine the lower layer of pictures. "Now this sequence here. I don't know if you're supposed to follow it from left to right or right to left or even if it's a *sequence* as we understand the meaning of that word. But it appears to depict some sort of ceremony. The pouring of the fire. This pattern here . . . the two creatures in some kind of dance."

"Religious?"

"Sexual? A fertility rite? A prayer for good crops or to

173

protect them from their less intelligent and more savage coun-
terparts. . . ."

"You know, that may be why the aliens wanted a bit of
Earth as a sample. Perhaps the similar lines of evolution. They
wanted to study. . . ."

"Whoa ho! Just because they seem to have long tails and
snouts doesn't mean that they're lizards, dearest."

"Maybe."

Ian turned his attention back to the inscribed pictures.

"Perhaps it's just a big Saturday night shindig."

Ian glanced at his watch. "Speaking of night, I do believe
we've got one coming on in about an hour. I think we had
better find shelter, old girl."

"Yes, and maybe gather up some wood for a campfire to
cook with. I'm ravenous!"

They had hiked half the day without incident, somehow able
to avoid the other hungry denizens of this ship-world before
reaching the main section of ruins of this ancient city. They
had managed to beat their way through the overflowing vegetation that thrived so well on the remnants of civilization.
They had passed dozens of dilapidated huts and houses, heading
for the nearest of the pyramids, operating on the assumption
that any written remnant of intelligent life would be kept in
what was obviously some kind of monument. And they'd found
that remnant, worn and vine-covered as it was, to Ian's immense satisfaction.

Ian was a bit of a puzzle to Becky. He was as much a mass
of paradoxes as she was. Sometimes he seemed to thrive on
this whole experience, keeping his mind detached enough from
the struggle to survive to concentrate on the sifting through of
all this fascinating information. Other times he just was barely
able to cope. That death could be very close indeed obviously
weighed on his mind, and yet it was also obvious that he was
much more concerned with Rebecca's life than with his own.
That was something that was new to her after her long involve-
ment with Phineas Kemp, who, when not involved with himself, was preoccupied with that holy extension of himself, the
good old IASA.

The love that Ian Coopersmith gave, when he was able to
deal with his guilt, was a natural thing, asking for nothing in

return, only giving. That was a new experience to her. It was only natural for her to respond in kind. The actual easy acceptance of the giving by him was surprisingly satisfying.

No, Ian Coopersmith wasn't like Phineas Kemp at all. She was glad of that.

"What say we climb on up toward the top," Ian said, looking at the peak of the terraced monument. "Even if we don't find an enclosure in which to huddle, I don't believe any of the critters will be able to get at us up there."

"Right."

They gathered some firewood. Then they began to pick their way upwards scrambling over eroded fissures in the stone, scrabbling up the mounds of rubble. At one point, they were forced to use some roughly chiseled handholds to get up the short but steep face of one of the levels, tossing their dried wood up first.

Finally, exhausted, Rebecca said, "Hey. There are only two levels left. Isn't this high enough?" She pointed to a small eroded nook in the face of the structure. "We can even use that. How about it?"

"Sounds reasonable to me," said Ian, stretching. "As a matter of fact—" Suddenly he froze, staring away in the distance, focusing on something that seemed to engage his astonishment. "Holy Je. . . . Well, I do *say!*"

"What is it, Ian?" She turned around to see what he was gazing at so intently. "Oh, my goodness!"

It was perhaps only three or four kilometers away.

That it was not a natural formation of rock was obvious by its uniformity, its symmetry from slope to mist-touched slope of the cylinder. Though it was a little too far away to make out precise details, there was no doubt that it was an artificial structure that appeared to *ring* the interior circumference of the cylinder.

A wall.

And beyond. . . .

In the dim distance, everything *ended*.

That was why the illuminator looked so odd as it tapered off. This was the point at which it stopped, the point where it connected with whatever engine or mechanism that powered it.

Everything else was just dimly blank. A great expanse of grey, non-reflective material, presumably some sort of alloy.

"I do believe that we may have found our intelligent inhabitants of this place," Ian Coopersmith muttered, almost as though to himself.

"How can you be sure? I mean, *this* structure is here. And I don't see any intelligent beings wandering about." Becky remembered her visor. She pulled off her pack, rummaged around inside, found it, and fitted it around her eyes.

Coopersmith followed her example. "Yes. Much better." He pointed, making a sweeping motion with his arm. "Assuming it is a wall . . . or at least some kind of barrier, evidently its purpose was, and hopefull still is, to keep the carnivores of this world out."

"Granted."

"Fine. Now, what do you immediately notice."

"It's *long*."

"Yes, it must be. Actually, what I meant is that there don't seem to be any breaks in it. Any wall that is not maintained will wear away, especially in this kind of climate."

"You're saying that it follows that there must be somebody behind it to make repairs?"

"Absolutely." Ian smiled as he commenced gathering the wood and readying it for the campfire. "And we're going to meet them tomorrow."

Had the Tyrannosaurus Rex been lying on a plain, there would have been no problem, Thalberg and Coopersmith would have given it a wide berth. However because it lay quite still amongst a scatter of rocks and boulders, its thick grey hide camouflaging it perfectly with the surroundings, Becky almost stepped on its tail.

"Oh, God." she managed to stifle a yelp.

Coopersmith fought to control his instinctive panic. This pile of muscular, baleful death was the stuff of nightmares. Only it was *real*.

The behemoth stirred. Two tiny lizards, evidently feeding on parasitic mites and insects that covered the beast's thick, almost corrugated hide, scampered away into the shadows. The great mouth opened with a yawn, revealing a mouthful of ragged, sword-like teeth. It slammed closed with almost a pneumatic hiss. Ian Coopersmith got a whiff of rotting meat nestled uncomfortably amongst the lizardy musk the monster exuded.

Fortunately, the Tyrannosaurus seemed torpid, probably having fed recently; its underside protruded beneath it.

Its proportionally tiny forelimbs were stretched forward and its head laid down so that the jaws rested on the ground. Its eyes were closed. Its great body heaved regularly with bellows-like breathing.

"All right," Coopersmith whispered, cursing their luck. Only about a short distance from that wall, and they had to run into Mr. T. Rex. Still, if they could skirt it, they'd be okay. "Steady, dear girl. Back off slowly, with as little noise as possible."

She obeyed as soundlessly as she could, keeping calmer than he felt. As they moved, Coopersmith unsnapped the holster of his gun.

Suddenly, the great, ugly, veined nostrils flared wide on an inhale of breath. The greedy eyes fluttered open, immediately catching sight of the two backing away from it.

"Oh, shit," said Coopersmith.

Rebecca stopped, paralyzed. "Ian. We can't kill *that*. . . ."

The Tyrannosaurus recovered awareness with astonishing speed. Its vast bulk moved to rise, faltering.

A ray of hope broke into Coopersmith's mind. Of course. There were maybe eight tons worth of dinosaur lying there, prone. Most of its muscle was devoted to its thick neck and haunches. As it moved to get up, though, it was obvious that the forelimbs—about the width of human thighs, tapering down to two clawed fingers—had their definite and very important purpose.

As the massive hind legs pushed hard, the flexed claws were digging into the rocky soil. If not for those small forelimbs. . . .

Even before the final thought entered his mind, Coopersmith raced forward toward the beast, the pain in his ankle awakening.

"Ian!" cried Becky, startled. "Ian! No!"

He stopped about five meters away from the struggling beast. It roared with fury as it saw its intended prey approach and increased its effort to rise, flinging its great tail out to help it balance.

Coolly, Ian Coopersmith brought the Magnum up, switched off the safety, and carefully aimed.

He squeezed off three rounds.

Crack!

The bullet exploded into the nearer forelimb, tearing away a huge section of flesh. Blood pulsed and sprayed.

CaaRack!

Just below the other wound, a larger wound opened, revealing the white of bone.

Caaaa RACK!

The snap of bone was audible, even though mixed with the loud scream of the Tyrannosaurus.

Just as Ian hoped, it instinctively redoubled its plodding efforts to rise. In doing so, it put its eight tons on a shattered limb, throwing it entirely off balance.

With a roar of outrage and pain, it fell to its side.

Ian about-faced and began to run in the direction they'd been heading, wobbling from the raging pain in his leg, but going full speed nonetheless.

"I don't know how long we've got!" he cried to Rebecca Thalberg. "Get the hell out!"

Thalberg needed no further encouragement. They ran as they'd never run before.

The Tyrannosaurus' screams followed them for a long time.

Whether it had finally been able to right itself was hard to say. Becky suspected it had, but by that time they were far enough away for it to have lost scent of them. Just the same, although they slowed their run to a jog, they wanted to get as far away from the giant thing as possible.

"Huge!" was all that Becky could gasp. "Huge!"

"Shut up and *move* it," Ian said, slowing to match her pace. A wave of indignation passed through Becky, but she repressed it. Ian could be as much the macho authoritarian as Kemp, if the time was right. Still, the essence of the advice was sound. She sped up.

After a while they had to slow to a quick walk to catch up on their breathing. Becky often darted furtive looks behind her without catching any sign of the Tyrannosaurus. They struggled on through the land, which had grown a bit marshy with the beginnings of a jungle-like portion nearby. The high trees had long since obscured all sight of the wall they'd glimpsed.

"Wait a minute, Ian. I've got to stop. I can't go on anymore."

"Right," Ian said without objection. He promptly flopped to the ground, chest heaving. "Talked me into it. Just keep your eyes"—he paused for an intake of breath—"focused back the way we came. Should you happen to see a pair of nasty reptilian eyes"—breath—"attached to a body with a mangled forearm, notify me immediately."

Very deep breath.

"Ian." She sat down hard, propping her head up with her hands. Difficult, she immediately realized, because her face was drenched with sweat. "Ian, you saved our lives!"

"Yes, I did, didn't I?"—breath, wheeze. "Entirely automatic. I just *did* it, shot the thing's leg, I mean. No use going for anything else at that point, you know. Thank God I can shoot as well as you can."

"*Better* than I can!"

The two lay there exhausted. Black spots swirled in Becky's vision, swarming up from her dizziness. She was carried off in some reverie of pain, each breath growing less desperate. Shock numbed her thinking; for a moment she asked herself, "Where am I? Why am I here?" as though she had just groped her way from a particularly grim nightmare she could not recall.

"You okay, old girl?"

Reality seemed to coalesce around her annoyance. She managed to prop herself up on a hand and wipe away the sweat dripping into her eyes.

"I told you not to call me that, Ian!"

She was confronted with a grin. "Just checking."

"You!" She rolled over to hit him. He sprang away in time to avoid the weak blow.

"You stay here if you like," he said after a quick kiss to the top of her sopping head! "There's something I want to check on yonder."

He hopped up and limped away.

"Hey! No you don't." She pushed herself up to a stand. "I want to see it, too!"

She followed him, struggling out her canteen. The water

was tepid and bitter—but to her hurting throat it was a balm. Ian marched to the muddy side of a marsh, studded with strands of reeds, weeds, and trees.

He stopped and stared at something out of the range of Becky's sight.

"What is it, Ian?" she said, offering him the canteen. Ian ignored the gesture, staring down into a leaf-shaded bower. Becky screwed the top back on and followed Ian's gaze.

"I thought as much!" Ian said, reaching down and picking up what appeared to be two segments of eggshell. "But I must say, I didn't quite expect this!" Becky followed his gaze into the barrow, her eyes not yet accustomed to the gloom.

"A nest of dinosaur eggs, Ian?"

"Yes, but *look* at it, Becky!" Ian slid down the incline. Snug in the ground was a large mound of what appeared to be cement. Cement with a hole in it. Half an empty eggshell lay by the entrance. "This is a structure made by some sort of intelligent life! To house eggs, yet!" he peered carefully into the dim opening. "A few fragments. No whole eggs or younglings. The hatching seems recent enough, though. Fascinating. One would presume that this is the work of the same civilization behind those walls...."

"And if the shells are fresh, then so is the civilization!"

"Thank you, Ms. Holmes," Ian said, examining the igloo-shaped mound. From its right side jutted a chimney-like device which reached up past the surrounding vegetation. "And my word, unless I miss my guess, this is some sort of temperature-control device, using mirrors! Wish I could knock this apart and see how they solved the problem of thermal-coupling and—"

"Always the engineer, Ian. We haven't got time. We have to meet the people who made this!"

"Quite right. Let's be on our way then. Let's have a hand there, old—" He smiled. "Sorry. My lovely Rebecca. And could I have a sip from your canteen? I'm parched!"

Becky sighed and got the canteen back out.

"Look at that little guy *go!*" Ian said with admiration. "I wonder if he'll make it."

Becky had nothing of her companion's calm concerning the

matter. "Ian, don't just stand there! Shoot the goddamn thing before it catches him."

They had stepped into a clearing and witnessed a scene quite a few yards distant—so that they could not make out details. Some sort of carnivore was chasing something half its size through the underbrush, snapping and snorting. A miniature, stripped-down version of a Carnosaur, Its aspect was fearsome, its speed considerable. The creature it pursued was mostly obscured by weeds.

"What? Waste ammunition on something quite natural? If the prey is to escape, Becky, let it do so on—hey!"

She pulled the gun from his holster, took a few steps away, and fired.

"Stop, Becky!" But Ian Coopersmith wisely did not step forward and attempt to stop her from firing. Why she was doing this, even Becky wasn't entirely sure. The creature being pursued looked vaguely humanoid—or so she imagined—and her move was almost instinctive.

Mother instinct? A flicker of species preservation? It did not occur to her to analyze her actions.

She pushed off the safety, tracked the Carnosaur, fired. The first round missed entirely.

"Becky, that's *not* a long-range weapon. You're as likely to hit the pursued as—"

"Shut up, Ian." She fired again. The Carnosaur was suddenly relieved of its forelimbs and half its chest. It tumbled to a dead halt in a spume of blood and dust. The smaller creature did not stop to discover the fate of its pursuer. It didn't even turn around to look, but rather made a beeline for dense forest. In a trice, it was swallowed into mystery.

"I say! Lucky shot," Ian said sternly, arms folded. "Still you wasted two of our bullets we might be in sore need of at some later time."

Becky grew red in the face. "Has it occurred to you, Ian, that *that* little creature might have been one of the intelligent hatchlings? I might have saved a thinking creature."

Ian's expression changed. "Now there's a thought. What do you think then, Becky? That *could* be the reason why they would lay their eggs out here. Let the newborn fend for themselves. Survival of the fittest. They have to find their way to civilization. Interesting use of the outside wilderness."

"Well, it gave me a certain amount of satisfaction gunning down that Carnosaur on its tail," she said, handing the pistol back. "Sorry I was such a bitch about it, but it was something I had to do."

"Try to restrain yourself next time, though, hey? All the same, perhaps when we get back we can tour the world as Jurassic Annie Oakley and Wild Bill Hickock."

"Let's worry about getting back first."

"Yes, well, the answer lies beyond that wall, so we must push on and—wait a moment. Look yonder! Picnictime for a cannibal, I think! A brother for breakfast!"

Becky turned. Another Carnosaur was slinking in, no doubt attracted by the scent of blood in the air. This one was smaller, perhaps two meters high. It lowered its head and commensed to feast, audibly.

"Fellow wasn't taught proper table manners!" Ian said. "Chewing with an open mouth! Really!"

A movement at the other end of the clearing attracted Becky's attention. A bipedal creature strode out, holding a spear.

A spear?

"Ian! Ian, look over there!"

"What *do* you know!" Ian said after a soft whistle.

"Ian, what's he doing? He can't possibly kill that thing with only a spear."

Ian stepped away defensively, hand firm on the butt of his gun. "Steady on! Let's just *watch* this time. Maybe it's some kind of rite of passage for young intelligent dinosaurs."

"What? Getting *eaten?*"

"Calm down and watch. This could be very instructive."

"You must think I'm trigger-happy, Ian!"

"I'm just glad that now I'm in charge of our weapon, that's all. We can't—" His attention was suddenly diverted. "I say! What the devil is that bugger doing? It's *crazy.*"

The lizard-man had stepped up lightly to the carnivore, Becky could see, and begun bashing it over the head with the blunt end of his spear. At first the Carnosaur almost ignored the rappings, merely letting go with a warning roar, then returning to its more rewarding feast below. But the fellow repeated his rappings, harder, until the Carnosaur was thoroughly maddened. It hopped up to stand on its hindlegs, took a snap at the lizard-man, then advanced toward him, now determined, no doubt, to rid itself of this nuisance and wolf down an extra tidbit in the bargain.

"Why's it doing that, Ian?" Becky demanded.

"God knows!"

Then the lizard-man did the *strangest* thing. He spun the spear around in an apparently ceremonial manner, then flung it. But not at the Carnosaur, Becky saw in astonishment. He hurled it to the side, deep into the forest, where it could not be retrieved.

"Ian! Ian, the gun!" she said. "The poor thing will get torn apart."

"Maybe it's some sort of ritual suicide, Becky. We want to befriend these creatures, so we don't want to interfere with any of their ceremonies."

Then, with a snarl, the Carnosaur attacked, going from a standstill to a sprint in an instant.

The lizard-man stood his ground defiantly, watching the creature charge.

"Oh, Ian, I can't watch," Becky said. But somehow she could not unglue her eyes from the sight.

At the last possible moment, the lizard-man stepped aside, somehow avoiding the outstretched claws, the snapping fangs of the Carnosaur. The lithe carnivore pivoted about. In that moment, the lizard-man made his move, pouncing with incredible speed and agility upon his adversary's back.

The Carnosaur shrieked with fury. It lashed about, trying to bend its head around to bite at its rider. The lizard-man clung with amazing tenaciousness.

Maddened with frustration, the Carnosaur rolled to the ground, turning the struggle into some sort of primeval wrestling match.

Somehow the lizard-man stayed on board.

Becky could see now, though, even through the dust kicking up, that the lizard-man was *doing* something with his own claws. *Digging* into the back of the creature's neck! Bright blood seeped down from the newly opened wound.

The wrestling went on for a full two minutes, partly on the ground, partly in an upright position, the Carnosaur dashing back and forth like a bucking bronco, attempting to unseat its rider.

"Ian! He's shoved his entire hand into the skin," Becky said, clutching Ian's muscular forearm. "Why should—"

Suddenly, the Carnosaur halted its run. The rider twisted his hand in a certain manner, and, in fits and starts at first, then in more of a flow, the mount began to trot away, quite tame and docile.

"What did he *do*, Ian?"

"I have no idea."

"You think we just witnessed some sort of coralling of a wild animal?"

"I don't know. Seemed much too dangerous for that. You'd think that the lizard-man would have some kind of back-up. Or even, if they're civilized, simply lasso the creature. No, I think my first guess was right. Some sort of coming-of-age ceremony. A rite of passage. But come on. I presume that now that the creature has been tamed, the lizard-man is taking it to the nearest entrance to the wall. We should follow."

They discovered the pathway through the foliage that the lizard-man and his new mount had taken, followed the footprints through the undergrowth, pushing past fronds and ferns, careful to avoid any large creatures. Plenty of the smaller varieties winged through the air or scrabbled beside the boles of trees. The humid air was full of their rank smell, combined with the odor of rotting vegetation.

When they finally found their way into another clearing, they were confronted with the spectacle of the wall, less than fifty meters away.

They stopped and stared.

At least ten meters high, Becky estimated, and constructed of wooden planks, stone and mortar. Creeper vines covered parts of it. Other stretches were bare. At regular intervals were cupolas—tower-like protrusions—extensions of buttressing sections apparently thicker than the rest of the wall.

"There's the door, way down there," Becky said, pointing. A sense of relief flooded through her, almost immediately accompanied by a tingling fear of the mystery hidden by that wall. But it was their only hope for safety from the dangers of the wild behind them.

A movement flashed in one of the roofed towers.

"There's something up there!" Ian said. He grabbed Becky by her hand, keeping his Magnum up in his other.

Together they walked to the base of the wall, then strode parallel to it, toward where the tower thrust upwards.

Looking upward in wonder, Ian stumbled on a loose stone. It rattled off into a group of bushes.

Suddenly, something leaned over the tower's side. Its movements were darting with a certain lizard-like gracefulness. Its snout was blunt, with sensitive quivering nostrils that seemed to be taking in their scent. Its head bobbed slowly back and forth as it assessed the intruders...a large head, atop a thin tough powerful neck. The creature was standing upright.

And the eyes....

Much closer to this one than she'd been to the last, Becky could see that the eyes were obviously capable of stereoscopic vision. As they stared down at her, a thrill sped down Becky's spine to see how they shone with intelligence.

Then the creature lifted some kind of weapon in its multi-fingered, obviously articulated hands and pointed it straight down.

The weapon stared at them with tiny beady eyes and began to chitter and squawk.

CHAPTER 14

"STAY VERY STILL," Ian Coopersmith said.

"Ian, what do we do now?" Rebecca asked tersely.

"Something, quickly. That's some kind of weapon he's got there. Looks as though he's ready to use it, too."

They stood in tense silence. Insects droned in the nearby forest. In the near distance, just above what would be the end of this world, water vapor roiled like fog aspiring to become clouds.

The creature at the top of the tower leaned farther over, examining the strange intruders with eyes quite large in proportion to his head. The shape of his skull seemed to indicate a large brain.

Rebecca said, "Take off your clothes, Ian. Right now!" She immediately began to unzip her jumpsuit.

"What? Hey, stop. I'm trying to think of a way to communicate with the thing before—"

"Shut up, you jerk," Rebecca demanded, pushing down the pants, peeling them quickly off. She kicked the clothes away, stood, and stared up to see what the response was.

The creature pulled the weapon slightly back, no longer aiming it. His mouth seemed to drop. A long tongue issued forth, as though tasting their scent. It hissed. His eyes seemed to grow bigger.

"So strip," Becky said, "and let him see the male of the species."

Ian Coopersmith quickly removed his clothes. "We should show we've no weapons," he said, holding up his hands, then slowly turning around. Becky followed his example, turning a complete circle.

"Now what?" she asked.

"Hey," Ian said, "this is *your* strategy. You tell me."

"We're still alive, aren't we?"

"Point taken. Quite a good course of action, actually. I should have thought of it myself."

"Congratulate me later, okay? I'm still scared witless."

"We've found our intelligent life, anyway," Ian said. "Let's just hope they're not much like humans who shoot first and ask questions later."

The lizard abruptly pulled back from the tower's edge and disappeared. "You've offended it!" Becky said, joking. "Maybe you shouldn't have taken your clothes off, after all, Ian."

"Thank goodness Blacks can't blush." Ian sighed. "I guess we should just stand and wait." He collected his jumpsuit, rolled his gun and holster inside it, then tucked it under his arm. "This is the last stop, Becky. We're playing all our chips on this number. Okay?"

"I'm too tired to say anything but 'yes.'"

They didn't have to wait long. Within five minutes, the gate, about one hundred meters to their right, opened. A party of the upright reptiles—some ten in number—issued forth. They strode with a sleek grace, torsos leaning forward, balanced by their tails. As they neared, Becky noted that they carried weapons—spears and wooden swords. Evidently their culture did not use metal. That made sense. There would be no reason for ore deposits in this artificial geology. And the alloy past the soil and on the sides would of course be too hard to chip away.

Becky's only relief was that none of them carried one of those living weapons. That gave her the creeps.

"Becky, this may sound stupid, but—"

"What, Ian?"

"Would you hold my hand?"

She slipped her palm against Ian's, and they laced fingers. "You know, Ian, no matter what happens, no matter if we get saved and go our separate ways or what, I want you to know that I love you. First person always."

Ian sighed deeply and glanced up at the approaching lizards. "I hope all *this* world loves people in love."

When the intelligent lizards reached the naked couple, they formed a wary circle around them, brandishing weapons. They buzzed with conversation. Their language appeared to be a combination of hisses, clicks, and gutteral groans.

Ian raised his hand and forced a smile. "Good afternoon. I want to assure you that we're quite harmless. We need help."

"Ian, they can't understand you."

"True, but they might understand the tone of voice."

"My God, I feel like an animated version of that picture on the pioneer trip."

"All we need now is a little Chuck Berry music," Ian quipped uneasily.

"You know, Ian, they've *all* got those little shirts around their torsos. That's what I noticed about the one in the tower."

"Women. Always fashion-conscious."

"No, really. I wonder what it could mean. Clearly they don't wear it for warmth or protection or modesty."

"Caste symbol?"

"Could be. Could be it's just decoration, although it is a rather plain piece of material. Some kind of faded green plant fiber, apparently. The things can't last long. Look. That one there. He's pointing at us. Isn't he the one from the tower?"

"How can you tell?"

"He's cuter than the rest."

The reptile was jabbering excitedly, looking from companion to companion as though trying to convince them of something. He seemed not to get the positive response desired.

He ceased his talk, then suddenly stepped forward three paces, directly facing Ian and Becky. With a four-fingered hand, he tugged at his little shirt.

"He's trying to talk to us," Becky said. "No. We don't have any of those shirts. We're not *like* you, are we?"

"Now who's whistling in the dark?" Ian said.

With a hiss of what might have been exasperation, the reptile began to tear his shirt open from the bottom. The others screeched with excitement and immediately began to move in on him, brandishing their weapons. The reptile immediately stopped tearing his shirt and held his hands straight up in the air, performing some kind of complicated sign language above his head. The others immediately relaxed, and reformed their circle.

Becky was puzzled.

Ian said, "Very strange. But I think he wants us to put our clothes back on."

Becky shrugged, and complied with the suggestion.

Great hisses and gasps ensued. Evidently quite pleased with his accomplishment, the lead lizard turned back to his companions, pointing at the couple and chattering away.

"Don't look now," said Becky, "but I think that little suggestion just saved our skins."

Two of the braver reptiles sidled up to Ian and touched him. A long tongue flickered. With a strained smile, Ian held out his hand. "Hello, there, charmer."

The lizard put the hand in its sharp-toothed mouth and seemed about to bite it, when the lizard leader saw what was going on. He raced up to the offender and knocked him to the ground. The fallen lizard picked himself up, but in so doing managed to snag his little shirt on an exposed root. It ripped off completely.

Weapons were raised. The two reptiles carrying blunt cudgeis immediately bludgeoned the offending lizard senseless. He lay on the ground, barely breathing, blood leaking from one of his flared nostrils.

"Those shirts appear to be of *great* importance," Ian said, his nervousness still in his voice. "I suggest we keep ours on from now on. No more strip shows unless specifically instructed—okay, Gypsy Rose Lee?"

"Right."

The two lizards with the clubs picked their fallen mate up off the ground. They began to drag him back to the gate. The lead lizard made a quick motion with his four-digit hands. Immediately, two lizards apiece flanked Becky and Ian. The lead lizard executed a neat about-face and began to walk forward.

"I think we've been invited inside," said Ian.

"I don't think it was an invitation," Becky said.

As soon as they walked through the gate, the door was closed and a set of huge logs fitted over its latches. Ian Coopersmith barely noticed. He was too busy examining the cluster of buildings grouped off to the left.

"Evidently, we were lucky enough to stumble upon a city or town of some sort."

They were hustled forward quickly. All of the scurrying lizards stopped with reptilian suddenness as they caught sight of the new arrivals.

"They rather look like ostriches with outsized skulls, don't they?" Ian commented as they strode toward the grouping of buildings.

"*Sauronithoides*, Ian," Becky said excitedly. "I thought they looked familiar. There's been speculation that this kind of dinosaur might have actually developed intelligence if most classes of dinosaurs had not become extinct."

"I thought they'd all become extinct."

"No. For example, birds are direct relations to dinosaurs."

"Well, I guess we're going to meet the rest of the family. They're taking us over to the big stone building yonder."

It was the largest structure of the village, a quonset hut type of building composed of stone and brick and wood. The other houses seemed more like shacks that might have been erected with some sense of alien aesthetics or geometry. To Ian, they just looked ramshackle. Strange tinklings filtered through the air. Exotic and varied scents wafted with the breeze. Some kind of bazaar seemed to be holding forth in what appeared to be a marketplace. Lizards sat behind oddly shaped stalls, engaged in sales and barters. The Music of clanks and rattles and whistles was in the air, beside the tastes of charred meat.

"Oh my God, Ian. Look!"

She managed to point, despite the reptilian hands restraining her arm. Beside one of the stalls was a rack. Upon the rack on wooden hooks were hung dead bodies of saurians.

"They're cannibals," Ian said. "It follows, doesn't it?"

"Yes. Reptiles have been known to eat their own kind."

"You don't think they're going to eat *us,* do you?"

"Unlikely. They *are* civilized, and in civilized cultures curiosity tends to outweigh hunger. If they have leaders, I think they'll want to notify them, if for no other reason than to allow them a look at us before they pop us in the pan."

"Ian!" she shivered.

"If I wasn't so fascinated, I'd be scared shitless."

As they neared the building, a small Iguanodon emerged from its rear, bearing a rider in a saddle that appeared to be part of the beast. The saurian manipulated a series of raised bumps in the back of the Iguanodon's neck. It stopped in front of the party.

"Incredible," Ian said. "It looks as though many of the adaptations that the intelligent lizards have made have been biological. I would bet that since they were not able to advance technologically, they've concentrated on the biological aspects of progress."

"Like the living arrow that cutie-pie was pointing at us."

"Exactly."

"Cutie-pie" scrambled forward and began to confer with the creature atop the Iguanodon. After much chatter and arm-waving, the saurian pushed the neck nodes of his beast, and drew the Iguanodon so close to Ian and Becky that they could smell the beast's bad breath and see the tiny parasitic insects that crawled in the folds of its hide. The saurian leaned over, staring intently at the new arrivals. Nictating eyebrows blinked twice from side to side. Suddenly, it drew back upright in its saddle, and spoke again to the party's leader, pointing one of its digits at the heavily bolted door of the large building.

"Cutie-pie" barked orders.

Three saurians broke ranks with the party and scurried over

to the door, which they proceeded to unlatch. The four saurians in charge of Ian and Becky pulled them forward.

The door swung back. Growls and squawks and hisses issued forth from the dimness within. Becky and Ian were pushed brusquely inside.

Torches shuddered. It smelled musky and dank, of earth and urine and rotting meat. As Ian's eyes adjusted to the dimness, he saw that the whole place was one large chamber, filled with covered stable-like arrangements of cement and brick.

"It's like a prison," Becky said, her voice quivering. "Why are they putting us in a prison?"

"I don't know," Ian responded uneasily.

They were hustled forward. From inside the stalls, Ian could hear the scraping of claws, the gnashings of teeth. Guards patrolled each aisle, holding heavy clubs.

"Cutie-pie" strode forward and talked to one guard. The guard stared wide-eyed at the alien arrivals, then motioned for "Cutie-pie" to follow with the "prisoners." The saurian guard unlatched a door. Wielding his club, he stepped into the darkness. A great din of hissing and growling ensued, abruptly ended by the dull thud of heavy wood against soft flesh. The guard emerged, dragging with it the unconscious body of another saurian. The saurians standing abreast Becky dragged her into the cell.

"Ian!" she cried.

"Nothing I can do," Ian said. "You'll be all right." He sounded as unconvinced as he felt.

After some moments of activity in the cell, the saurians who'd taken Becky inside withdrew. The guard slammed shut the door and latched it.

With no further ado, Ian was shuffled to the adjacent cell. The guard opened the door, and entered. No hisses. No growls. He withdrew and Ian's saurians took him inside.

The smell was terrible. Offal and straw. Vaguely, Ian could make out bowls of some foul stew in the corner beside a trough of water. Roughly, he was seated in a bed of straw. Stone manacles were placed over his hands and his feet. They seemed connected by some ultra-strong vines to the wall. The arrangement allowed him some movement—perhaps as far as the food—but not much.

He hunkered down wearily in the dirty straw, as the door was slammed shut on him. At least he'd get some rest here. He could use some. Yes. He certainly wouldn't mind a few hours of sleep safely tucked away from the constant fear of being eaten by some prowling dinosaur.

Sighing, he shut his eyes as saurian feet stamped away from the cell.

In the quiet, he heard soft, harsh breathing that was not his. It seemed to come from the other corner of the cell. A hiss. A strange mumble, like a sleeper might make.

He was no longer relaxed.

What the devil was going on here? Had they stuck him in a jail cell with a maniac saurian? But why? It didn't make sense. None of it made sense.

At least, it didn't make human sense. He supposed that in order to understand it all, he'd have to think like a saurian.

But how did a saurian think? There could be no comparisons. Or could there?

Ian remembered the biology courses he'd had to take in the University. Requirements for a "liberal" education.

He thought about the human brain. The R-complex. That was the key. That most primitive part of the human bio-computer. Man's inheritance from his reptilian past.

Something scratched on the other side of the wall Ian leaned against. A human voice called. "Ian? Ian, are you over there?"

The creature in the corner stirred uneasily in its straw bed in the corner. Jaws snapped together.

"Becky," Ian said. "Please be quiet. There's something inside here with me that I don't want you to wake up."

"What? Ian, speak up! We can talk to each other. Ian, I'm frightened. What are we going to do?"

"Becky! I asked you to be—"

The creature in the corner snorted. In the dimness, Ian perceived movement. The saurian stood. Straw rustled.

"Oh, God," said Ian, preparing to defend himself.

The saurian bellowed and clicked his strange language. He seemed to be more nervous about being in the cell with Ian than Ian was.

"Ian! Ian, what's going on? Are you all right? Ian, answer me. I'm scared."

"You're scared!"

After a few more moments of the creature's loud calling, the door swung open again. The saurian guard exchanged a few words with the other prisoner, then slithered in.

The former prisoner excitedly pointed at Ian and spoke a few grunts that might have been, "Who or *what* the hell is this *thing* in my cell?"

The guard growled, and led the saurian out, then closed the door.

"Becky," Ian said in a loud voice.

"Ian! What happened!"

"Goodness knows, but I think it's going to take a lot of thought to try to understand this culture."

"If we live long enough to think," Becky answered. "Ian," she said after a few moments of silence.

"Yes."

"I'm not sure, but all in all I think even living with Phineas Kemp would be better than this."

They both laughed.

When Rebecca Thalberg was seven years old, she and a male cousin had wandered one sunny afternoon into the wilderness near the boy's farm. The boy had showed her his private hiding place: a bower, afforded by a gully along which erosion and roots had carved an indentation. There they had settled, she and this nine-year-old, and played "You show me yours, I'll show you mine." Male genitalia had not thrilled her that much upon first exposure, even when he had rubbed it against hers. "To see what it feels like, Becky! This is what grown-ups do!"

"Yucky!" she pronounced, pulling her jeans back on and lying down on the soft ground. "I'm tired. I want to rest."

That seemed okay with Ricky. He was preoccupied with other things off in the bushes. Becky drifted off into a land of pleasant dreams, and when she woke up, Ricky was gone. She hadn't the faintest idea how to get back.

Her first reaction was to cry. Indeed, she could feel the fear and emotion push up from the depths of her being leaking from her tear ducts. But she stopped herself, realizing it wouldn't do any good.

"Fuck *you*, Ricky!" she cried loudly, imitating her Daddy's favorite phrase. Then she set about finding her way back to the farm. Ricky, hiding nearby, disappointed in not scaring her, emerged and grumpily led her back home.

From that point on, Becky Thalberg made sure that she never played "Show me" with anyone who would play scare games with her emotions. That policy served her well over the years to come.

For that reason, when she woke up to darkness and straw and bad smell and reached out for Ian, her first reaction to his absence was betrayal, and then almost overwhelming fear.

But her years of professional—and personal—training keyed into her consciousness and she was quickly in control, at least in control of her feelings if not of her situation.

Claustrophobia and revulsion overwhelmed her for a second as the damp straw crackled beneath her movement. As she held back panic, her first inclination was to call for the reassurance of Ian's voice. But compassion checked her. He deserved whatever rest he was getting. She should not be selfish, just because she could not sleep now.

She breathed deeply, calming herself, and tried to meditate.

Just as she was approaching something resembling tranquility, however, a couple of saurians barged in and dragged her out.

As she stood, blinking in the light, the process was repeated on her companion. Ian emerged yawning and vacant-eyed.

He *had* been sleeping.

"Good God! Can't a man get a decent night's sleep in this world?" Ian griped, his attempted cheeriness strained.

"Maybe they've decided to change the sheets."

The saurians babbled away at one another like a bunch of excited kids, then began to hustle their guests out the entrance.

"They've obviously decided that we're not of the same mindset as they," Ian said, squinting in the daylight as they walked outside.

Becky took a grateful breath of the fresher air. "What do you mean, Ian?"

"Well, obviously they were observing our behavior by placing us under controlled conditions."

Becky looked down at her filthy clothing, felt her matted

hair, and sighed. The saurian party surrounded them, but allowed them to walk unhindered by restraining hands. Becky put her head on Ian's shoulder as they walked. "Oh, Ian."

"Awful. I know. I'm glad to see you, too. I don't think I could have made it without you." He put an arm around her.

"God, I'm sorry, I must smell terrible."

"You haven't exactly been bathed in perfume in there. But then neither was I, dear heart. As I was saying, I did some thinking in my cell. We apparently showed them that we didn't do anything violent when we turned off our neocortex in sleep."

"You mean that's what the saurians do?"

"Apparently. And when they do, they revert at least for a while, to their purely reptilian nature. An interesting balance, eh? One that must make for a fascinating sort of society. *If* you can figure its more Byzantine aspects."

"Maybe something will dawn if we watch the locals."

They skirted the more populated sections in weary silence, just watching the inhabitants go about their daily tasks. Unfortunately, any part of the city they walked through was soon abuzz with chatter and excitement. Crowds would gather to gawk. Not exactly the proper atmosphere for sociological observations, Becky mused, when the watchees were just as fascinated with the watchers.

However, she was able to begin to appreciate the architecture and the general alien air of the clustered structures. Everything had a certain strange symmetry. Things seemed to be displayed either in twos or threes—two parallel towers, each a different color, or three columns, or two humps to a building's roof, or three windows in a wall. Tall buildings alternated with squat buildings, jeweled minarets rose beside plain dun huts in a peculiarly homogeneous yet clashing mix of styles and designs.

"Rather like a nut mix," Ian commented.

"Only thirty percent peanuts."

"I just think we're hungry."

"Let's not think about it, okay?"

Bright colors flowed or fluttered all about in odd paterns, shapes, and sizes like the scales of some gigantic coiled rainbow snake. Acrid and sweet odors surrounded them. From time to time, strange creatures that were not saurians scampered through the alley. Here and there saurians who were not interested in the new arrivals were involved in antic dances or frantic claw-waving or were playing whistlings and faint flutings through wind instruments stuck in their nostrils.

The saurian party—ten members, Becky counted—led them from the city and up a hill toward a huge, ancient structure that squatted like some old mouldering wart. A tracery of vines covered it like veins. Multicolored banners danced when the faintest of breezes blew. Candles fluttered in windows. Smoke issued from pipes. It was a very large building.

"The Capitol!" Becky said.

"Or Parliament."

"Or the Palace."

"Or the Kitchen."

"Complete with the recipe book, *To Serve Man?*"

"Let's sincerely hope they don't use garlic. I hate garlic."

"I like garlic. I didn't see any growing in the jungle, though."

"What a relief."

The huge building was surrounded by a wall. Being used as a door to this was a particularly large Triceratops.

The saurian escort party halted before the dozing Triceratops, chittered at one another. One of their number seemed to draw a figurative straw and was pushed out reluctantly toward the slumbering monster.

Carefully, the saurian approached the behemoth and climbed up the rough fold of skin behind its bony headgear.

The beast's eyes opened.

The saurians screeched warning.

The climbing saurian speeded his ascent, hopping up the back and jamming his hands underneath the crest. Suddenly, the annoyance in the beast's eyes faded to dullness. Lethargically it rose and waddled off, allowing Ian, Becky, and company to enter.

"I've known a few doormen like that," Ian said.

"Probably because this culture hasn't invented tipping."

They were taken through a more normal door on the building's side. Trails of incense wound through the hallway. Strange hieroglyphs were scribbled on the walls. They passed through a large chamber where saurians—*robed* saurians, Becky saw—were sitting in crouched positions in various portions of the room, eyes glassy.

"Ommmmmmm," said Becky.

"I do believe we are seeing signs of some kind of religion here."

"I don't think, though, should we get out of here, that we're going to need deprogramming."

In the distance, faint echoes of chants sussurated like the sea surging through a cove. Strange clicks and grunts sounded, an alien symphony. It all gave Becky the shivers.

The saurians guided them to a small room, covered with finely woven tapestries and cushions, all woven from an odd fiber that had a faint sheen. Sconces held phosphorescent globes to light the place. The saurians chittered, gesturing that they should enter.

"Looks more comfortable than the cells they chucked us into," Ian said.

"At least we get to stay together."

"Hmm. Quite!" A gleam crept into Ian's eyes. "Lots more comfortable than jungle floor, too."

"I'm sorry, Ian," Becky said. "You're just going to have to start using a new deodorant soon."

"Hey, you're not exactly Princess Sweet Scent, old girl. All the same, we could both use a bath. Reptilian pheromones, civilized or not, aren't exactly my cup of tea."

"You take that side, I'll take the other," Becky suggested, "if *that's* how you feel about things!"

She settled in a corner. The pillows were stuffed with soft foam-like materials. After weeks of using the ground and tree-limbs for beds and pillows, these felt awfully good.

Ian obviously agreed. No sooner had the door closed than he was sawing logs in his corner. She drifted into a kind of half-awake reverie, the sounds of Ian's snoring somehow comforting.

Footsteps. Outside the door. Coming this way. Somehow strange and shuffling. Instinct drove fear into Becky Thalberg.

"Ian!" she whispered.

Ian was already up, crouched by the side of the door. He

put a finger to his mouth to silence her.

The door opened. Immediately, the saurians saw Coopersmith. They chittered excitedly, motioning him to stand back. Reluctantly, Ian obeyed, arms raising in the classical stance of surrender.

One of the robed saurians entered. He was taller and heavier than the others, but he was bent. His red-and-blue robes were slightly worn and tattered. The skin of his exposed face and arms was an unhealthy, mottled purple, streaked with veins. But his eyes burned with intelligence, curiosity, and life.

The creature hobbled forward, staring at the humans with unbridled wonder and excitement. Then he lost his footing and tumbled to the ground, making squawking noises.

Becky had to laugh at the comical sight.

Immediately two saurians jumped from the door and helped the robed one up. Something like humor shone in the fellow's face as he looked to the humans, as if in apology.

He shook off assistance and wobbled the rest of the way to Becky. His hands rose. He stroked her long hair. Something like an "Ah!" of appreciation issued from his mouth.

He stepped over and inspected Ian Coopersmith.

Then, eyes brimming with tears and happiness, the robed saurian stepped back and commenced to caper.

Four of his companions—those in robes—began to pipe an alien song as the saurian danced and skittered like a man trying to do the hornpipe on the deck of a storm-wracked ship.

"I think he's actually happy to see us!" Ian said.

"Do you think he's King or something?" Becky asked.

"Something special around here, certainly. Clearly he's the one that's supposed to figure out who we are. He does seemed pleased."

The robed saurian cavorted and pirouetted in an ungainly display of awkward moves. Finally, apparently unintentionally, the creature tripped on his robes and fell flat on his face with a squawk of pain. Clicking and hissing in disgust, he raised himself and began to simply stare at Ian and Becky.

"He seems to expect something." said Becky.

"What?" wondered Ian.

"A dance from us, perhaps."

"I can't dance, Becky!"

"Ain't you got rhythm, boy?" she said. "We don't have to waltz or anything!" Thereupon she commenced singing her favorite old Motown song, "Dancing in the Streets," with accompanying jumps, twists, and gyrations.

Ian tried to follow her lead, but he looked more like he was exercising than dancing. Close enough for rock 'n roll, Becky thought.

Improvising some of the lyrics, Becky finished up. Ian shambled to a halt.

"Well, what did you think?" Becky demanded of the robed saurian, who was, at this point, simply staring blankly at his guests.

The creature jumped about and then began jabbering, making strange gestures.

"No, no, sorry, friend," said Ian, pointing to his mouth. "We mainly communicate with these—and we don't know your sign language, I'm afraid, so we'll just have to get along as well as we can, okay?"

The robed saurian pointed at his mouth and nodded. He then made a gesture that seemed to indicate that he wished for the humans to follow him.

Tail flapping on the floor behind him, he executed a shaky turn and strode from the room.

Ian looked at Becky and shrugged.

They followed.

"Books," said Becky. "Piles and stacks of books."

"Yes, *their* versions of books. They look more like dino skin than paper."

They were in a large room stocked with manuscripts, all sprawled in a disconcertingly unkempt fashion on odd shelves which were apparently carved from the same material from which the building was fashioned.

With excitement shining in his eyes, the lizard-man grabbed an armful of the scrolls and dumped them on the ground in front of the human couple.

"An obvious invitation to examine, I'd say," Ian Coopersmith said. "Shall we?"

They knelt and spread the leathery material.

"Hieroglyphs and drawings, Ian. Quite like what we saw out there on those ruins."

"Words. Too bad we don't have some kind of translation device. This stuff is fascinating."

"Copies of their version of a bible, don't you think?"

"Most likely. Or some kind of record of what they think their origins are. Every culture has to have that, either in their religion or in folklore."

"I can't make heads or tails of it, Ian."

"We should gaze at it reverently, though—and with interest, to show that we appreciate its importance."

While they did just that, the saurian bustled into a corner, sorting through the clutter. He muttered enthusiastically as he pulled out what he needed and carried it back to his guests with an air of urgency.

Carefully, in front of them, he laid out a blank piece of plant-fiber—bluish in tinge—and produced a thin piece of modified charcoal. Carefully, his tongue flickering with concentration, he marked out a couple of hieroglyphs. He pointed to one of these, then indicated that this symbolized himself.

He then put the writing utensil on the paper and took a step back.

"I think he wants us to write something," Becky said. "Go ahead, Ian. Do your best."

Pursing his lips, Ian looked at the robed saurian, then picked up the piece of charcoal. Watching the deftness with which Ian manipulated the writing utensil seemed to excite the saurian immensely. When Ian copied the hieroglyphs, then mimicked the pointing ceremony, the saurian was beside himself. He gave a brief spastic dance, then settled down, motioning for Ian to continue.

Ian then commenced to write the word "humans." With his finger he tapped this, then the appropriate hieroglyphs, then himself and Becky.

He then wrote down "saurian," tapped it, and pointed to the robed lizard-man.

He drew a map of the solar system, complete with the cylinder. In the diagram's representation for Artifact One, he lettered in the hieroglyphs that the robed saurian had first written. Then with an expansive gesture, he pointed all around him.

The saurian's expression seemed puzzled.

Ian tapped his chest, then tapped the circle he had drawn for the planet Earth, then traced a pathway from Earth to the ship.

Understanding leapt suddenly into the saurian's eye.

For a few moments, he seemed stunned. Then he seemed to faint, sprawling out onto the ground as though this were too much to take.

"Watch out, Ian! He might revert to his primal reptilian behavior and kill us both!"

But the creature, though clearly unconscious, did nothing of the sort. He just lay there.

"As I thought," said Ian. "We're dealing here with a more advanced kind of saurian. Part of the ruling class. Philosopher? Scientist?" He paused. "Is he still alive?"

"I don't know. There's something wrong with this guy, I've noticed. His skin. He seems very sick—while the other robed priests or whatever they are seem perfectly healthy. The sickness is not a sign of their class. Let me just have a look. . . ." Rebecca leaned over the fallen saurian. "God. He does look bad. It doesn't look like he's. . . ." She touched a tentative hand to the creature's chest, then passed fingers over the mouth. "No! He's not breathing! He's *dead!*" Rebecca Thalberg backed away from the fallen saurian, blood draining from her face. "I hope the others don't think we killed him!"

"Should we call the others? Maybe they can help."

"Hello! *Hello!* Help! We've got a dead—"

"Rebecca! I thought you said he was dead?"

"He wasn't breathing."

"He seems to be rousing . . . that or advanced rigor mortis!" The saurian twitched and jerked, as though attached to a live wire.

"Some kind of strange catatonia?" Ian suggested.

"*Lizard*tonia, more like."

The saurian got up, tottered about for a few moments, getting his bearings, then returned his attention to the humans.

He walked up to the astonished Becky and pronounced a gutteral word, tapping her lightly on her head. Something like

"Snashish." Then Ian: "Zashist."

Becky and Ian pronounced the names as well as they could.

Then the saurian tapped his chest, indicating that they were welcome to name him.

Becky smiled and pointed to the saurian. "Thesaurus!"

And that was the creature's name from that point onward, though Thesaurus never quite managed to pronounce it properly.

"You know, I think I'm actually used to it by now," Ian Coopersmith said.

"I don't think I could *ever* get used to it!" Becky snapped.

They were riding an Iguanodon, Thesaurus at the bio-controls, Becky and Ian in a saddle arrangement farther down the back. There were no other guards. No need for that. Thesaurus and the saurians quite trusted them by now . . . as far as any saurian trusted anyone.

"Do you think we're almost there?" Becky said, holding Ian around the midsection, trying to compensate for the jouncing, bouncing ride. Clouds and folds of mist hung from the end of the cylinder, which they were approaching.

"I think I make out something in the mist up there, Becky."

"Thank *God*."

Two "days" and two "nights" had passed since they had met Thesaurus. For several hours after their mutual renamings, they had been immersed in the job of translation. The task had not gone smoothly. Even now, only a few words and a few gestures were truly understood. Nonetheless, there was a bottom-line kind of communication, particularly between Ian and the saurian, perhaps simply because both were straining so very hard at it. The two had developed a strange kind of camaraderie. Becky was almost jealous.

After their first session, they managed to ask for and receive water to bathe with—and the food served to them, fried meats mostly, garnished with fruits and chopped vegetables, was actually edible, if hardly spiced to their tastes. It was a vast improvement on scavenging and Becky figured she had already put on about two pounds.

Even now, as she bounced three meters above the ground, holding onto Ian for dear life, the images of the preceding twenty-four hours flitted through her head.

At Ian's request, Thesaurus had taken them on a tour of the city, shown them the things that were important. By that point, Ian's conjecture that Thesaurus was a member of an elite group was borne out—in fact, he was apparently rather like a philosopher-king.

He showed them this, rather than told them this, in context with his tour.

An alien society indeed—and yet, Becky had once read that if the dinosaurs had not died out, they would have been the ancestors of human beings—and what *were* human beings, anyway? What gave them their unique difference from lower animals? Certainly not social habits or ties, or anything like that. Intelligence? The saurians had that. Self-awareness? Yes, they had that as well.

All this was too much for Becky. She just welcomed the rest and the comforts provided after weeks of harrowing nightmares. She absorbed what Thesaurus showed them docilely, not focusing on the implications of the details as did Ian Coopersmith, but rather trying to understand the race holistically, ecologically.

Apparently, they had already witnessed a telling part of the society's structure. Although there were no families as such—after all, nuclear families were a mammalian invention—young and old were supported in a rough, communal sense.

The first thing that Thesaurus had taken them to see was a public mating, which seemed to be some kind of spectator sport. Each of the participants—a male and a female—had been selected for various reasons, and were both on the brink of sleep, thus allowing their feral, reptilian natures to take them over fully. The ritual was conducted in a pit, over which ranks of seats were mounted for many saurians who hooted, hollered, and hissed in what Ian at first interpreted as bawdy encouragements. But then, as the male and female tore their shirts off, the sound blended into chants of an unmistakable religious and ritualistic nature.

The actual mating was something to watch indeed.

"Ian! It's...it's got *two*—"

"Yes. A hemipenis. Certainly significantly larger proportionally than other reptiles. I say! They do seem to be rather enjoying themselves, don't they?"

"It doesn't turn *me* on, I can tell you that."

"Thesaurus indicates that the participants "go away." Transcendental transport, I suppose he means—'outside this universe, with the Gods.' Pantheists."

"Well, we know where they lay the results, don't we?"

This, also, Thesaurus showed them, along with an explanation for the rite of passage they had witnessed. And he showed them the bio-breeding centers.

Those had been almost beyond Becky's ability to comprehend. Although these creatures' technological abilities were of necessity limited, they were geniuses with genetics. Flesh and nerves and blood in breeding looms . . . fascinating.

Now Thesaurus was about to show them something which he considered quite important.

The mists parted before them. There, stretching up and up, was the end of the cylinder—the thing they had been shooting for, hoping to find their way out of the cylinder's dangerous parts.

At the base of this was a temple.

Thesaurus stopped the Iguanodon in front of the portal and made a bleating yell. Immediately, five priests in flowing robes streamed from the portal, calling welcoming songs.

"Old Thesaurus seems well-known here, I'd say." Ian commented.

The Iguanodon knelt and the riders dismounted. They went into the temple. The walls were crammed with saurian hieroglyphics, complex tapestries, and altars.

But Thesaurus did not stop here. Rather he led them down the passageways to a room absolutely bare of ornament. Several other priests followed them.

"My God! This wall is—"

"Metal!" Becky finished for Ian.

There were heavy drapes hanging over one section of the wall.

"Ian! It's an entranceway into the next section of the cylinder!"

"What are we waiting for?" Ian said, stepping forward.

Thesaurus barked an order to the other priests, who gently restrained both Ian and Becky.

"No!" hissed Thesaurus. "No . . . my . . . my Snashish, my Zashist." He pointed to the entrance. "My Snashish, my Zashist. . . . Thesaurus know you there. *Good!*" He pointed to himself. "Thesaurus. *Bad!*"

Slowly he lifted his robe up to his chest.

"Oh, Ian. No wonder he doesn't look so good," Becky said.

Ian whistled softly.

On the saurian's body were a number of faint radiation burns.

CHAPTER 15

KEMP BENT DOWN to pick up the discarded ration-pak. It was lying by the long-dead ashes of a fire-pit near the entrance to a small limestone cave. "Anything in there?" he asked of Mikaela Lindstrom, who was still inside the cave.

There was a pause before he saw her blond hair coming out of the darkness. Her bright green eyes were shining like a cat's as she appeared, carrying a small object. "This must be what set off the metal-detector," she said, handing him a small communications unit. The metallic surface was already showing signs of corrosion from the fierce humidity of the interior.

"At least *somebody* survived," said Phineas. "Long enough to get this far, anyway."

Looking up into the surrounding treetops, and the bright hazy sky beyond them, he was again reminded of the scope of the ship's interior. Despite his anxiety, he could not deny his sense of awe and dread when he thought about the beings who had *built* this place.

"Presuming that they could not find their way back to the entrance hatch," said Phineas, "why would you suppose they would be making camp this far away from the general area. They couldn't be *that* lost."

"They?" said Mikaela.

"I'm assuming, and hoping, that there was more than one survivor. Anyway, it seems like they were moving away from the general direction of the base camp."

Mikaela looked up at the illuminating rod, high in the sky. "They were heading towards the aft section of the cylinder?"

"Maybe. If Coopersmith made it, I'd bet that he was trying to reach the part of the ship where the engines are located. And then maybe find a way into the alien crew-quarters."

"I wonder if they made it...."

"Hard to tell how long ago they were through here. Going through this forest on foot must be hell. But we know now at least that we should be out looking for them." Kemp looked back to the omni-terrain vehicle, where Richards, the driver, and Nordman, the weapons specialist, both kept watch with razer rifles. "And we're going to need something a little faster than the OTV. Too damned slow."

"The ornithopter?" asked Mikaela.

"Yes, I've got them bringing the thing in in pieces now. As soon as we can get it put together, I'd like to get started."

As they began walking back to the OTV, Mikaela touched his arm, and Kemp felt his pulse jump a bit. "Phineas?"

"Yes?"

"I know this might sound out of line, but would you mind if I went along with you in the 'thopter?"

"Part of the search party? I don't know.... I've been thinking about that. If you didn't come, I would miss your company, but I don't want to put you to any unnecessary risk. It's not your responsibility, you know."

"I know that. But I could use the chance to survey more of the environment. I won't get in the way, I promise...."

"I wasn't worried about that," said Phineas, managing a small smile, but feeling awkard doing it. He was attracted to this woman, and now that he had renewed evidence that Becky might still be alive, he didn't know how to deal with his new feelings.

Mikaela smiled back. She *was* a pretty woman. "Then it's a deal?"

"It's a deal."

Richards stopped the OTV, waiting for the guard on duty to deactivate the perimeter-field, then guided the ungainly vehicle into the base camp. As they approached the main dome, Phineas saw Doctor Robert Jakes waiting for them.

"Colonel!" said Jakes over the dying whine of the OTV's engines. "I've got to see you right away."

Kemp opened the door and jumped down, then guided Mikaela down, before turning to face the engineering specialist. "What's up, Doctor?"

Jakes looked at Mikaela Lindstrom and the two others climbing down from the OTV. "I'd like to speak with you privately, Colonel. . . ."

Kemp looked to Mikaela for a moment. Mikaela grinned, and began walking towards the lab-dome. "I've got some work to do anyway," she said with no apparent hurt feelings. "See you later, and thanks for the ride, Colonel."

Phineas wanted to say something, but she walked away quickly. It was an awkward moment, and he felt some resentment towards Jakes.

"Please, Colonel. It's important." Jakes's thin face looked even more dour and grim than usual.

"All right, what is it?" asked Kemp as they began walking toward his offices in the main dome.

"The communications modules," said Jakes.

"Trouble?"

"Bad trouble. They're damaged so badly that I'm not sure we can fix them."

"What? What could have happened to them for it to be *that* bad?" Kemp stopped and looked at the engineer, while his mind wrestled with the idea that the operation might be totally cut off from Copernicus Base.

"I tell you what *did* happen, Colonel. Somebody sabotaged them. They knew what they were doing, too. Everything's fouled up pretty good. Used a magnetic-driver and welding torch. . . ."

Kemp did not speak right away. His mind was reeling with

211

added knowledge, and the attendant implications. *Sabotage. Christ, what else can happen?* But for what reason? He couldn't believe that anyone would want the alien ship destroyed. . . . What the hell was the purpose in cutting off their link with Copernicus Base? And who did it?

"Colonel, are you all right?"

"What? Oh yes. . . . Sorry, Jakes. And you say there's not much chance of getting things fixed?"

"We can try . . . I don't know."

"How many people know about this? Anybody see anything?"

Jakes shook his head. "I had two of my men down there to check out the problem right after it happened. They didn't see anybody. I told them to keep their mouths shut, and *I* haven't said anything about it, other than that communications are down for the moment."

"I can't believe this," said Kemp. "Everybody on this mission's got top-level security clearance. . . . It's almost impossible that they could get somebody on board, presuming that they knew about the mission in the *first* place."

"Who's *they*, Colonel?"

"The Third World Confederation, who else? It's obvious what this ship represents, and if they do know of its existence, they would want it for themselves—just as badly as *we* want it."

"What do you think their next move is?" Jakes rubbed his chin and cast a quick paranoid glance about the camp to see if anyone was watching them speak.

"That's hard to say. They don't have any ships fit for Deep-Space Operations . . . but they must have some kind of large plan involved. Damn it, I just don't believe this is happening, that's all!"

"I'm afraid it is, Colonel."

Kemp shook his head, rubbed his eyes. "All right, Doctor, why don't you see what you and your men can do about patching us up? Check back with me later."

Jakes nodded and walked towards the entry hatch. In the clearing just below it, some of the crew were working on the ornithopter. It was almost completely assembled and looked like a giant mosquito with large gossamer wings and a pair of helirotors above its thorax.

Colonel Kemp stood watching the work on the ornithopter for a moment, knowing that he also had responsibility to whomever might still be alive out in the interior, but his mind was getting jumbled. Too many things happening too fast. He walked to his headquarters wrapped in thought.

"Will that be all, sir?" asked Captain Marshall, who was standing stiffly before Kemp's portable work-table. The man was a model underling—efficient, trustworthy, and ultimately boring. Kemp knew that Marshall would follow his instructions to the letter because of his lack of imagination to do otherwise.

"Yes, I suppose so, Captain." Kemp did not look up from the notes he had been making to himself on a small pad. "Oh, one more thing. Has the ornithopter checked out for flight yet?"

"Yessir. It's fine. Lieutenant Zabriski's taken her up. It'll be ready when you are."

"Very well, Captain. Have it loaded up with the gear, and tell the others we'll be lifting off in about ten minutes."

Marshall saluted laxly and left the room, shutting the door and leaving Kemp alone with his thoughts. A small air conditioning unit hummed in the background.

Phineas should not have been surprised to know that Marshall was aware of the sabotage, but he *was* angry. Apparently the men who had discovered the mess had opened their mouths, and now the whole crew was looking at one another, wondering if they were staring into the eyes of a traitor. That kind of tension wasn't good, but Kemp was powerless to do anything about it.

The only good thing he could be certain of was that the outrigging operation had gone smoothly and Artifact One (even now, he clung to his original name for the alien ship, disdaining the more popular *Dragonstar*) was being gently but inexorably shifted out of its cometary orbit and onto a course which would intersect with the Earth-moon system.

But everything was ganging up on him. Not knowing if Becky might still be alive; his feelings for Mikaela; the lack of contact with Copernicus; an espionage agent loose among the crew; and the growing feeling that the TWC had more tricks up their sleeves.

As a precaution, Kemp had Fratz and Bracken monitoring the long-range detection scanners, in the event that anything might be approaching them as they drew closer to Earth orbit. Even if it was an IASA vessel, Kemp wanted to know about it way ahead of time. He wanted a safe margin in which to operate, especially if he might be out in the 'thopter when more trouble started. Damn it, he thought. If it wasn't for Becky, and his conscience, he wouldn't be taking personal command of the search party flight. . . . Sometimes he didn't know *what* he was feeling.

For the first time in his career, in fact, he considered taking something for his nerves—one of the little green capsules which were standard issue in all Mission medkits. He reached into his desk drawer, where he kept a small pack of them, opened the container, and looked at the capsules. He wondered why they were called "little green monsters" by everyone.

No, not now, he thought. *If I've gone all this way without them, I'm not going to start now.*

Slamming shut the drawer, he got up and went outside.

The ornithopter's engines whined softly behind the cabin, just loud enough to make everyone speak loudly without really yelling at one another. Including Kemp and Lindstrom, there were three others on board—Zabriski, the pilot; and Michaels and Nordman, who were both expert marksmen with a razer-rifle.

"Ready to lift off, Colonel," said Zabriski.

Kemp nodded, and the odd-looking craft leaped into the air. It was a mechanical hybrid, combining the actions of a helicopter and a bird, and was exactly the kind of craft needed to operate in a closed air-space that was full of tricky flying conditions, such as the rotating, vortices-full atmosphere of the *Dragonstar*.

As the base camp dwindled in size, and Zabriski headed for the aft end of the cylinder, Mikaela began studying the terrain below with a pair of electronically-magnified and adjusted binoculars. She carried a small recorder on her lap, and occasionally she recited a particularly important observation. Kemp watched her at work, and was pleased to see that she was one of those people who were truly dedicated to their jobs. There simply weren't enough people around like that anymore.

Zabriski remained hunched over her controls, a tense expression on her homely features. "We've got to watch ourselves in here, Colonel. . . . There's a gravity gradient which increases sharply as we increase altitude. Also some funny air currents. Doctor Jakes said it has something to do with the atmosphere not rotating at the same speed as the land mass."

"Stay as low as you can," said Phineas. "I want to keep an eye out for any sign of them down there."

Zabriski gave a thumbs-up signal and continued staring straight ahead. The view was spectacular, even from the relatively low altitude of a thousand meters. The mind was continually trying to reject the image of the upward curving landmass and the lack of horizon. In addition, when you looked down the length of the cylinder, the lines of perspective closed in, and gave the impression that you were falling down a bottomless well. But Kemp knew that more than two hundred and fifty kilometers distant, this particular well *did* have a bottom, and they were betting on the logic and ingenuity of the survivors to have headed for that spot.

Several times the ornithopter would buck or dip as it passed through a thermal bank, or the residual wash of an atmospheric vortex. Kemp wondered if the heat-energy of the illuminating rod in the center of the cylinder was heated to varying temperatures so that gradients would be produced to create artificial weather. If that were so, it would help explain the turbulence experienced by Zabriski.

"Everything all right, Captain?" Kemp leaned forward with his most serious expression setting his features.

"Yeah, Colonel, but I'll tell you . . . this is the damndest ride I ever took. I've flown everything there is to fly, just about, but this is one hell of a ride! I don't recommend airspeed much above a hundred klicks per hour."

"That'll be fine, Captain. Just take it as it comes. . . ."

The craft continued to pitch and dip occasionally, but Zabriski seemed to be learning some of the interior atmosphere's tricks, and she was having less difficulty as the flight progressed. Phineas hardly noticed any of this.

At least he was *doing* something now. He had never been the kind of person who could sit still, letting somebody else get all the action while he directed things from an armchair. He had considered staying back at the base camp, now that the sabotage was known, and it was a good bet that the TWC would be trying something else. . . . But he doubted if he could have withstood the *waiting*. The sheer tedium of simply sitting around waiting for something to happen would have brought him that much closer to the little green monsters in his desk drawer.

They flew on for another two hours, passing over three areas which had Lindstrom so excited she almost fell out of her seat. The discovery of stone-block ruins, their peaks above the green carpet of the forests, was a surprise to everyone. Lindstrom insisted that they land and investigate. Kemp agreed, thinking that it was possible that the survivors might be there, or that some sign of their presence might at least be found.

The first set of ruins, simple post-and-lintel constructions, yielded little except the ideas from Mikaela that there was intelligent life in the cylinders. Kemp countered with the idea that the building might be the work of survivors from the original alien crew, or perhaps their descendants, who had worked their way out into the cylinder once all the supplies within the crew section had been exhausted.

Later on, they landed at a group of three pyramids, where Kemp and his men found evidence of a campsite. Once again, he felt hope rekindled in his heart. The feeling that Becky and probably Coopersmith were still alive was growing stronger. Mikaela Lindstrom wanted to stay long enough to make some sketches of the pyramids, but Kemp was getting impatient, so much so that he did not want to land at all when they passed over the remains of an ancient city. Mikaela was upset with the decision, but something else had just become visible in the distance ahead of them. The flat end of the giant cylinder was now becoming clearer, even though parts of the sky at the distant end were obscured by patches of water vapor.

Mikaela had been talking about how many of the dinosaurs so far observed exhibited discrete changes in their somatotypes when compared with the fossil records. She said that it was most obviously due to genetic mutation and the continuing evolutionary process, despite the constant, controlled environment of the *Dragonstar*. She felt that over the hundred and fifty million years or so, it was possible that evolution had produced some intelligent species, although it would be difficult to predict whether there would be representatives from the saurian or mammalian families in existence.

"... and you'll have plenty of time to test out your theories," Kemp was saying in response, when Zabriski cried out excitedly.

"Colonel! I've got something coming up down there. Looks like a mountain range or something . . . see it?"

Kemp looked down and ahead of them to see a long low ridge stretching across the landmass, extending through the thick forests, and curving upwards as though endless. As the ornithopter dropped down to a lower altitude, and drew closer, the definition of the ridge became more clear.

It was not a mountain range. Nor was it any kind of natural rock formation.

"I don't believe it," said Zabriski.

"Phineas," said Mikaela. "Do you know what that *is?*"

Kemp did not reply for a moment, but continued to stare in amazement at the structure looming ahead of them. It was undeniable now. It was a gigantic *wall*, perhaps ten or fifteen meters tall, which made the great wall of China look like something made from a child's block set. A barrier, with buttresses, and towers spaced at even intervals.

The ornithopter slowed and hovered over the incredible wall, as everyone looked down upon it, and what lay beyond it.

A city.

A living city.

CHAPTER 16

"HELLO, PHINEAS," Rebecca Thalberg said. "We've been expecting you. That's why we suggested that the saurians bring you here."

She was sitting on the floor opposite Ian Coopersmith. All about them, the floor was littered with charts and pictographs: alien symbols. Coopersmith gazed up casually and grinned at the newly arrived party. "Afternoon, Colonel. Have we got an alien culture for *you*."

"Shit on alien cultures," Kemp said, striding forward, and hauling Becky up from her crouch. "I'm just glad to see you two *alive*." He embraced Becky fervently. She responded only as a sister might to a long-lost brother. There was no passion in the hug, no ardor.

Puzzled, he embraced her and looked down to Coopersmith. Coopersmith cleared his throat as he rose and went over to speak with the five saurians sitting nearby, dressed in flowing, colorful robes. Or he made an approximation of speech, anyway, filled with gestures.

Kemp didn't pay too much attention. Emotions twisted and roiled inside him. Joy soured to jealousy, relief to anxiety. He turned to Becky. She confronted his searching gaze with an honest, open expression that said, *Yes, Phineas. Things have changed between us.*

He stepped back a moment and gazed about the hall as Mikaela Lindstrom stepped over to Ian Coopersmith and began babbling excited questions. A dozen armed saurians stood guard in various places. They spoke their high-pitched chitter to one another, occasionally turning toward the party and simply staring with reptilian astonishment.

Coopersmith excused himself from Mikaela's questions and guided one of the saurians over to meet Kemp.

"Colonel Kemp, I should like you to meet Thesaurus, who has been seeing to our needs and communicating with us. Thesaurus is sort of a scientist-ruler."

"Uhm, hello Thesaurus," Kemp muttered. He was shocked that Coopersmith's nearness didn't produce a strong urge to throttle him. Only a mild urge. "Your friend doesn't look so good, Coopersmith."

"No. A little too full of scientific curiosity for his own good. There's some kind of hole in the wall at the end of the cylinder. Full of interesting things, from what I can gather."

"You've been there."

"Yes. Didn't go in, though. Apparently, it's got a high radiation level."

"That would explain the shape the poor fellow's in."

"Yes. The price of knowledge is steep."

"We'll have to get radiation suits and explore."

"The request was on the tip of my tongue," said Coopersmith.

Phineas Kemp breathed deeply twice and let all his emotions go with his final exhalation. He carefully fitted on his professional veneer, and he turned to Nordman. "Raise Michaels and Zabriski on the com. Make sure they're still okay."

"Check, Colonel."

Kemp and his crew had landed near the city, and immediately been surrounded by the saurians. Lindstrom had almost burst with ecstasy. "These must be *Sauronithoides,* Phineas," she cried. "We're looking at intelligent creatures who might very well have been the big wheels on Earth, if they'd had the chance. Intelligent dinosaurs, Phineas. Imagine!" After a period of extreme caution on the humans' part, as the saurians executed various odd dances and capers which appeared to be some kind of proclamation of peaceful intentions, Kemp had allowed the saurians to lead them away, leaving Michaels and the pilot to guard the ornithopter and serve as relay for communications between them and the base.

The com unit squawked, and a voice said, "Roger. Zabriski here. We've got about a hundred of the things milling about, forty-five meters away. Tamed and astonished, I'd say. Treating us a though we're gods."

"Get that, Colonel?"

"Got it," he turned back to face Becky. "The question is, will they let us go?"

"I don't think there will be any problem with that, Phineas, as long as we make our intentions clear, and promise to come back. At first they didn't know what to make of us. But once their priest-class got ahold of us ... well, we started getting treated like royalty. I've managed to figure out a few words and gestures in the days we've been here. Ian's done a lot better than I have, haven't you, Ian?"

Because he's a reptile, too, a snake in the grass, Kemp thought, but as soon as he realized the irrational nature of that thought, that feeling, he suppressed it. "So. We've much to talk about, then." Not a quiver or a shake to his voice. But Phineas Kemp found no pleasure, no self-righteousness in his display of pride.

"Yes," Ian Coopersmith said. He rose. He was wearing a robe similar to the ones that the lizard-priests wore.

"Nice outfits, huh?" Becky said, spreading her own and performing a mock curtsy. The robe was like a piece of a rainbow. "Needless to say, our suits were a trifle dirty and ragged after our expedition here." Her hair was newly washed. Soft and smooth, shining in the light from the window. On a very deep level, Kemp knew that he would never be able to touch it the way he would like to again.

Even though he hadn't lost her to the dinosaurs, he'd lost her.

He glanced over at Mikaela, and took some comfort in her presence. He could hear his father's voice say: *You've become an old softy, Phineas. The women have finally got you right where they want you, one hand on the gonads, one gripped on your heart. Say goodbye to your dignity.*

And Phineas thought, *Yeah. You're right, Dad. Now shut up.*

Ian Coopersmith stood, brushing off his hands. "So, we've got lots of time. What do you want to hear first? How we got here, or what we've found?"

"In any order you care to give it," Kemp said. "Only we really don't have that much time, Ian." He looked at him sternly. "Our problems aren't over yet. Looks like the TWC is going to make a military play for this vessel. When, we don't know, but we have to be prepared. There's no one between them and us. We're on our own." He told them about the sabotage.

"Damn," Ian said. "And I thought we were home free."

"Home's a long way away, Ian," Kemp said resignedly. "And there are some big obstacles in our path."

CHAPTER 17

CAPTAIN FRANCIS WELSH sat in his quarters of the *Andromache*, drinking his fourth beer of the morning, when the TWC expeditionary leader entered.

"'Lo, Jashad," Welsh called cheerily, holding up an unopened bulb of beer. "Have yourself a cocktail."

"I am sorry, my friend. My religion forbids the consumption of alcoholic beverages." White teeth showed through a dark beard.

"Oh yeah. Well, smoke a joint, then." Blearily Welsh leaned over and procured a recently rolled marijuana cigarette for his captor. The man called Jashad accepted it graciously and lit it with his own lighter.

"Everyone has his weaknesses," the handsome, fortyish man explained, blowing out his words with an exhalation of smoke.

"Everybody's got his drug, you mean," Welsh said, laughing. He took a gulp of his beer. "Even if they only manufacture it for themselves in their brains." He coughed. "Yeah. I can see the shelf of the stuff in the average TWC peon brain. A gallon of the elixir of stupidity. A vial of arrogance. A beaker of misinformation. And a whole crock of the bullshit you fling for propaganda!"

Jashad laughed heartily. "You misunderstand us, Captain Welsh."

"Really?" He crumpled his beer bulb container, tossed it into the trash receptacle, and reached for another full one. "I understand you killed a lot of people to get my ship. A lot of my friends. I understand that you would have killed *me* too, if you didn't think I might be useful in your mission . . . whatever the shit that *might* be." Welsh snorted. "What are you here for? Another game of chess? Never thought you'd find an infidel who could actually beat you once in a while, did you, Jashad?"

"I admit, I do enjoy our games." He took another casual draw from the cigarette, holding it in his lungs for only a second or two. "But I have not come here to engage in that activity."

"Yeah, well, like I told you, I'm not going to help you navigate, or anything. I swear to God."

"That's not necessary, Captain Welsh. Our own men have proved most effective in that capacity. And we have nearly reached our destination."

"So now you're going to kill me, huh? Can I finish my beer first?"

"Please, Captain Welsh. You are too bitter. Your company has been most welcome on this trip. I have grown most fond of you. No, you may yet be of service. And besides, even if you had no potential for service, I would still not have you killed. You have proved yourself harmless enough, if provided with"—he pointed to the trash can full of empty beer bulbs—"enough cocktails."

"I have *that* to thank you for, anyway," Welsh admitted grudgingly.

"You were the one with sufficient supplies," said Jashad. "We merely allowed you . . . access." He sat down in a chair, which was bolted to the floor. "No, I am here, Captain Welsh, neither to play chess with you nor to kill you."

"Cheers then."

"I'm here to try to explain."

Welsh almost spit out his beer. "Explain! What good is that going to do you, Jashad! Explain *what*, anyway?"

"Exactly why the drastic measures we've taken have been necessary. Captain Welsh, you may not be aware of this, but the fate of the world lies in the balance now."

Welsh listened to the story of Artifact One with something approaching disbelief. "Holy shit," he said, finally. "No wonder you folks want it. You want to know about its stardrive, so that all the star colonists will be good little Moslems."

"You are being simplistic, Captain. We are mostly concerned with the present balance of power on Earth. Already, the other forces of the world have outstripped our collective nations not only in outer space accomplishments, but in affairs terrestrial. We do not wish to become the leaders of the world, Captain. We merely wish a balance of power. We wish for our various cultures, beliefs, and world-views to have an influence on the destiny of mankind. We wish for the children we bring into the world to have a *place* in that world. We wish, in short, for an identity. As holders of the keys to the universe, perhaps we might find that identity, Captain. We regret our tactics. They are all we know. Besides, what *other* tactics might we use to obtain that which we *need* not only to survive, but to maintain our self-esteem, our integrity? Too long have we suffered. We have to take these measures, can't you see?"

"And so, to maintain all that shit, you've murdered the crew of this ship and are about to slaughter our people who've taken over what you call Artifact One."

"Only if that is necessary, Captain."

"In other words, if they don't surrender upon demand. Which you bloody well know isn't very likely."

"We don't want to kill them, Captain," said Jashad. "And we doubt that we can persuade them to give up. Ah—perhaps, if you explained the situation to them, they might better understand."

"Up yours, Jashad. I told you, no go. Kill me first."

Jashad sighed heavily. He stood and thumbed the door control.

Welsh stiffened, expecting his death to enter.

"Gentlemen, if you will!" Jashad called.

Two men entered, holding more bulbs of beer. They set them down beside Welsh, then departed.

Jashad made a mock-Islam bow to Welsh. "Drink up, friend Welsh. I want to beat you in this afternoon's game of chess."

He left.

Mumbling to himself, Captain Francis Welsh popped another top.

CHAPTER 18

"...and so we took our clothes off," Becky said, lounging casually on a mound of leaf-stuffed pillows.

Kemp choked on his strong, lukewarm tea. "What did you do that for?" He looked over to Ian Coopersmith, sitting with a fat smug grin on his face. He had to hold back the irrational feelings of jealousy that still flooded him at the thought of Coopersmith and Becky together. Even his warm feelings for Mikaela provided scant comfort in this situation.

"It was Becky's suggestion," Coopersmith said, "and quite a brilliant one, I must say."

"Why, Becky? To show you were discarding your weapons?"

"No. Principally to show the saurian that we were intelligent beings, that the stuff we wore *wasn't* skin. As it turned out, Ian had the common sense later on to realize that we'd better put the clothes back on, and *fast,* or they'd club us senseless."

Kemp blinked. "But why? I don't understand. Surely all this around us"—he swept his hands around, indicating the room they sat in, with its rugs and its intricate mosaics, the scattered manuscripts on the floor, the windows offering views of other buildings—"surely this suggests rational minds."

"You forget, Phineas," Mikaela said, "that we're not dealing here with human beings. The rationality of these creatures is most likely based on an entirely different set of circumstances, to say nothing of environment and bio-social necessities."

Phineas shook his head, confused. "So continue, Coopersmith. What happened then?"

"Well, they dragged us to what we thought was a prison and locked us in separate cubicles. Previously, we'd seen really bizarre behavior. One of the saurians accidentally got his shirt torn off—that's all the middle class of the society wears, you know—and the others just clubbed him into unconsciousness, as though it was an automatic response. They're evidently not exactly gentle with one another here in Saurian Land. So they stuck me in my cubicle, manacled me—"

"Me too," Becky said, "only they clubbed the previous occupant of my cell, who'd been in a real lather."

"Right. But the occupant of my cell was asleep in the corner."

"Pleasant," Kemp said, wishing they could go outside. The reptilian musk of this place was getting to him.

"Yes. But you know, when this particular chap woke up, all he seemed to do was scream to get out. And they *let* him out. All calm and civilized as you please when he exited. Well, to make a short story shorter, they kept us there for a few hours. Then they brought us here and introduced us to Thesaurus, who's become quite a friend. Near as we can reckon, Thesaurus belongs to the upper class. The priests. Or the philosopher-kings, if you will. Plato would love it here. Evidently, they've got three classes, just like in his *Republic.* They've got a warrior-class, a worker class"—he nodded over to the guards—"a sample of which you see yonder. And the priests, who serve as religious and community organizers as well as governors. But this is not a political system, Phineas. It's more a *biological* system. In the days that we've been here, Becky and I have been pretty much able to sketch out the scope of this civilization. Of course, there are details and nuances we'll *never* be able to understand, unless we could know what it's like to *be* a saurian. We think, though, we've got the basis."

Mikaela said, "What about families? They wouldn't have families, would they? Being reptiles."

"You put your finger on one of the keys," Becky said.

"Let me guess the other one," Mikaela interrupted with great excitement. "They probably don't have any limbic system in their brains. Just the R-complex, blending into their version of the neo-cortex."

Becky raised an eyebrow at Ian. "It took us *days.*"

Ian snorted playfully. "Yes, well she's a paleontologist, isn't she? We're just laymen on that subject!"

"Hey! Wait a moment," Kemp said with irritation. "You're leaving *this* layman way behind. Fill me in."

"Okay," Mikaela said. She turned to Coopersmith and Thalberg. "Do you mind?"

"You're the authority," said Coopersmith, smiling.

"Deep down, we've still got a reptilian heritage," Mikaela said. "Mammals are descended from reptiles. The part of the human brain that is still reptilian is a group of massive ganglia. The corpus striatum, the globus pallidus—"

"You don't have to get so technical. Just the essentials, okay?" Kemp said.

"Ah. Very well. Essentially, there are three parts of the human brain. From bottom up, there is the R-complex, which plays a vital part in our instincts. Aggression, ritual, and territoriality—these are all things that are controlled by the serpent inside of us. Including sexual display, I might add. Now, atop this, with an entirely different chemical system, is the limbic system, our mammalian heritage. This might be called the seat of our emotions, our tendency to form social groups, to be angry, to despair, to love, to nurture, and to continue the species and the culture. Quite a bit more complex than our reptilian natures. Following that is the neo-cortex, which is the home of reason. This is where we think. Again, an entirely separate system. Current psychotherapeutic thought is that if you can get all these systems into harmony, you've got a well-adjusted human being. But if any of them gets out of control—which they often do—you've got trouble." She turned to Coopersmith and Thalberg. "I presume that you've supposed this by the behavior of the saurians."

"Yes," Coopersmith said. "From what we can tell, the system is this. The warrior class does not actually live within these walls. Apparently, whatever serves for their version of a neo-cortex is only used occasionally, most likely in times of danger for the species. How they know about danger, I've no idea. Some kind of ESP? God knows. At any rate, the others don't want them around, anyway. Too dangerous. Now, the middle-class, the *workers*, are a pretty strange bunch. In their normal, shall we say, 'waking' stage, they are perfectly rational individuals, easily organized by the leaders and by traditional social dictates. In short, good citizens. The good citizens wear that little shirt, for a very good reason. You see, they've not developed the same kind of sleep system we have. When their neo-cortex—or the analog for that in their brain—turns off to do its data storage and processing, this allows the R-complex to take over. Since the actual body and brain need only a couple of hours to actually sleep, these middle-classers are essentially schizoid beings. You never know if your neighbor is going to kill and eat you. Not quite so drastic, but harmful. Jekyll and Hyde, don't you know? So, the system is simple. From infancy, just before the individual realizes he's 'falling asleep,' he or she is trained to tear off his or her shirt, thus signaling others to get the individual in check if there's trouble. Generally, though, when the saurians get tired, they check into one of the cubicles we were thrown into. When mating time comes, they just throw a male and a female in the same cubicle together just before their bedtime."

"Only it's a public spectacle! We were shown one. It's supposed to be a mystical as well as biological ceremony. I'm struggling to try to figure out their religion now."

"What about the philosopher-kings?" Kemp wanted to know.

"Evolution at work. Apparently, at some stage in evolution, saurians who were better integrated began to emerge," Coopersmith continued. "These became the organizers, the leaders, the thinkers. Through intellect, these few began to organize a viable society. Apparently, it's quite a history. Absolutely incredible. For example, you might have noticed ruins on the way here."

"Yes, we did," Kemp said.

"Right. Relics of the civilization before the leaders got together and said, 'Hey. Let's build a wall to keep the bad critters that want to eat us *out*. Voilà. The great wall. Towers. Guards. Systems of defense that include some really marvelous manipulations of symbiosis. I could go on for hours. Specially bred reptiles raised for the sole purpose of being *weapons*. Then there are the Watch Beasts, a species of carnivores they've just recently been developing to patrol the perimeter of the wall!"

"Wait a moment now. You say there's no family. How are the creatures raised?" Kemp asked.

"That was one of the areas that I explored," Becky said. "The female lays her eggs in special heat-controlled huts *outside* the wall, oh, a kilometer or so. Then she goes back to normal life in society. The eggs hatch. The more intelligent hatchlings manage to survive and find their way back to civilization, where they are welcomed with much ritual. A board of review composed of the priest-kings decides exactly what state of being these youngsters are. The warriors are given rigid instruction—almost behaviorally conditioned, as a matter of fact—and then kicked back out into the jungle. The ones judged sufficiently advanced to belong to the workers are trained, and then allowed to join society. Very rarely, a new priest-king candidate arrives, which is the occasion for great joy. The system is by no means smooth, or so well-divided. For example, there are stories of the occasional supposed philosopher who 'falls asleep' and commits some dreadful act. And there are those priest-kings whose R-complexes are used to further their own political ends. Apparently, this *can* be a kind of Machiavellian heaven. There are whole intricate structures of deceit."

"I can imagine," said Mikaela. "With no family network to work within, each individual owes allegiance only to the social fabric—and himself."

"Gaming appears to be a way of life, here," Becky said. "To say nothing of ritual. *Unbelievable*. Incredibly complicated. You know, there's even a ritual method of smashing a rogue saurian's head. One of the great jokes you can play on a friend, for example, is to trick him into 'falling asleep' outside of a cubicle. If you can get a pair of handcuffs on him so that he can't do any harm, it's great sport."

"And quite embarrassing for the friend when he wakes up, I dare say," Kemp commented. He licked his lips and studied the two. "It looks like you've been enjoying yourselves. I'm sorry to break up the party with my bad news." He nodded at their dress. "I can imagine that Thesaurus was pretty excited to find that you don't have a reptilian stage."

"Yes. He identifies with us, as do his fellows. The curious thing about him is that he seemed to *expect* us."

"Something to do with whatever is inside that opening you describe at the temple by the wall. These things may well be a deceitful lot. How do we know we can trust them?" Kemp said, glancing at Thesaurus and his group of priests, still involved in their heated discussion.

"Well, my friend, if you're correct about the TWC being on their way, let's hope that you can make friends with them," Ian Coopersmith said. "We're going to need all the help we can get. Oh, and Phineas. . . ."

Kemp wished the man wouldn't be so familiar with him. The situation was grating on him.

"The indications I've received from Thesaurus and these manuscripts from the temple are that this culture is aware of . . . I guess you would call them beings . . . or *gods* who 'created' their world. The pictographic tapestries show lots of primitive creation-myth scenarios that back this up. They also appear to have a messianic myth that—"

"That says the gods will be coming *back* someday?" asked Mikaela, cutting him off.

Kemp looked at her, unable to hide his surprise. Coopersmith and Becky smiled lightly.

"That's right," said Ian. "And guess who I think *they* think these god-creators are?"

Kemp shook his head. "This is incredible. Are you sure, Ian?"

"Of course I'm not *sure,* but there is a lot of evidence which points to this, and I'm no trained archeologist. I think it would be wise to let Doctor Lindstrom have a look at the depositories."

"I'd love to!"

"Just exactly how well are you able to communicate with them?" asked Kemp.

Ian shrugged. "Not much, really. I started out by noticing

that their numbering system is based on the number eight—to be expected since they have eight digits on their hands, right?—and I tried to establish some of their letter symbols and number signs by describing some basic mathematical concepts—you know, geometric formulae, good old pi and the circumference of the circle, that sort of thing."

"And did it work?" asked Kemp.

"Yes, after a lot of trial and error, of course. Thesaurus worked very hard with me. He's got the personality of a true scientist, Colonel. He's like a kid playing with a new toy. We seem to get on fairly well communicating, as I'm sure you've noticed."

"You're actually making progress?" asked Mikaela.

"Very little, actually, but it's a start. I think we're going to need a team of linguists in here to do the job right."

"That will be some time off, I'm afraid," said Phineas. "What about this 'divine' status which has been bestowed upon us?"

"You know, I don't believe that Thesaurus subscribes totally to that. He's a bit in awe, certainly, but he doesn't think we've come down from Olympus. The others are not so sure about that."

"And where have they gotten all these myths from that made them expect our arrival? That hole in the wall you mentioned?"

"I believe so, Colonel. But then, we'll just have to have that checked out when we can get those radiation suits, right?"

"How do you know that the saurians might not be looking forward to the arrival of the TWC representatives as well?" Kemp asked.

"I would imagine, Phineas, that *that* depends entirely on how the TWC comports itself in the situation." He shook his head sorrowfully. "But they don't have a very good reputation of behaving themselves, do they?"

The pictographs on the bottom level showed, with remarkable clarity, two saurians in sexual congress.

Mikaela Lindstrom took her magnification lens, adjusted its lights, bent over, and examined the picture. Remarkable! Etched into the stone was a fainter ghost image of the couple rising above their copulating physical forms, detached.

That must mean, she thought, that the next level, with its more abstract images, indicates some higher state.

Of mind? That would certainly jive with what Ian Coopersmith had learned. Different states of consciousness!

Behind her, she heard Jakes shuffling about.

"Pacing again, Doctor?" she asked. "How can you be so antsy when there's this wonderland of new knowledge around you? You're a scientist, man! Expand your horizons!"

Jakes moped over, took a look at the wall of the temple Mikaela was poring over, then went back to his pacing. "What I'd like to know is what is keeping the blasted ornithopter with the supply of specially-rigged LS suits that Kemp promised for me and my men. We've been waiting *two days* since we found this temple. *Two days* since we determined that yes, there *is* a dangerous radiation level past that hole. I mean, why couldn't he have just fixed up one suit, right away? It would have only taken a few hours!"

Mikaela Lindstrom studied the abstract forms. Funny. Some of those shapes *could* be almost human. God-like, bigger than the ethereal representations of the adrift saurians. . . .

"And I can't possibly guess who that suit would be for, Doctor," she said sardonically.

"Well, can't you *understand?* You've got your heaven. You've got your dinosaurs and this saurian culture." Mikaela turned. Jakes's long thin face was slightly red with emotion. "You're a paleontologist. I want to see those starship engines."

"Yes, I know. You're an engineer. But surely you can't restrict yourself to one area of inquiry, Doctor. You have to see the universe as a holistic enterprise, each segment a microcosm of the macrocosm. Believe me, I've faced plenty of bio-engineering problems in trying to understand how dinosaurs were structured from the mere evidence of a few *bones.*"

"You don't understand at all," Doctor Jakes said, mopping his brow with a handkerchief. "We're talking FTL, my dear. We're talking impossibility. We're talking about the dreams of astronomers and astrophysicists and little kids who stare up in the sky and want to go to the *stars.* How would it work?" He pointed toward the control area. "The answer is just *yards* away from me, Lindstrom. And the only thing between me and *it* is a little radiation."

"And look what it did to poor Thesaurus over there." She pointed to the saurian leader taking a nap on a mat. The poor thing had been *so* tired after all the excitement. She and Thalberg had tried to figure out what kind of medicine or treatment might help it, but so far they were afraid to try anything before they understood more of saurian biology. "Look what the radiation did to him."

"Over a period of *many* trips inside! And he accepts that, can't you see? Besides, he can go only so far, apparently. I'm the one who can figure out how to go all the way through, I *know* I can."

"Come on, Jakes. With all the men that Phineas has lost with this business, he doesn't want to lose anymore. The special LS suits will be here in due time. He wants a lot of them, anyway, so that anyone who wants to can go inside."

Jakes sighed and sat down against a wall. "Yeah. I guess you're right. Pardon my unprofessionalism."

Jakes probably felt left out because he wasn't with the second expedition to see this Temple. That had occurred later in the afternoon of the big reunion day. During their tour, Ian Coopersmith had pointed out some of the artifacts and records that had led him to his fantastic set of assumptions. She had been surprised at how many of Coopersmith's notions seemed valid in light of the saurians' cultural artifacts, and had asked to be allowed to do more research in the next few days, with the help of Thesaurus.

When they returned to the main hall of the temple by the wall, Kemp summoned Zabriski and her crew by radio, guiding them in to their present location with a homing beacon. Then he reported to Captain Marshall a detailed summary of what he had uncovered. Following a discussion with Ian Coopersmith, Kemp decided to send the ornithopter to pick up Doctor Jakes and some of his men to determine the radiation level that might prove to be a barrier to investigation past the portal.

Marshall replied that the scanners on board the *Goddard* and *Heinlein* had so far detected nothing within range, and that the outrigger engines would presently begin deceleration of the *Dragonstar* as it approached the Earth-moon neighborhood. Estimated arrival in L-5 orbit was still two and a half weeks away, but considering the velocity of the alien ship and the time needed to alter its course, gross course corrections and deceleration were already beginning.

The ornithopter had departed, leaving Kemp, Mikaela, and the two other astronauts with Ian and Rebecca. Later that evening they were treated to the equivalent of a 'state dinner,' which many members of the ruling caste of saurians attended. A fine time was had by all, with Ian's and Thesaurus's amusing attempts at communication the showcase.

Mikaela could not help but notice the coolness between Phineas and Becky Thalberg. Indeed, it had interested her tremendously. She could imagine that Thalberg and Coopersmith hadn't exactly been playing tiddlywinks for amusement in the wild, while they were alone. How long-lasting would the romance be, though?

Oh well, she had thought. Only time would tell. And if there was one quality a paleontologist had to cultivate, it was patience.

The next two days passed quickly as the ornithopter made several flights from the barrier to the base camp and back. The radiation level was quickly ascertained, and adjustments to some space suits were begun. Ian Coopersmith continued to establish a more meaningful system of communication with Thesaurus and his comrades, while Jakes cooled his heels waiting for his suits. Theoretically, normal spacesuits could have been used but, not with nearly the protection Kemp desired, or with the optimum degree of maneuverability. No, old uptight Colonel Kemp wanted to make sure that there was no rushing anymore, without absolutely stringent preparation.

The walled-in civilization had been established quite a few centuries back, Mikaela Lindstrom surmised, since it was the only way the saurians' ancestors could cope with the savage realities of the Mesozoic world. The system of guard towers and maintenance crews which were constantly patrolling the great wall was a revered tradition. Well it should be, since it represented the very survival of their society. This society was largely agrarian, stemming from the obvious habits of their ancestors. There were urban centers evenly spaced about the interior circumference, serving as places of economic and cultural exchange.

236

Jakes looked around the hall for a moment, then chuckled to himself. "I guess I am champing at the bit, aren't I? Part of it, I suppose, is that this place, this culture, gives me the creeps."

Mikaela turned to him, honestly surprised. "Why is that, Doctor?"

"I don't know. Ancient mammalian response. Somehow I don't quite trust these fellows. Behind the respect they're giving us might just be fear, and that's when you have to be a little nervous, for safety's sake if nothing else.

"Also, you have to realize that I come from a fundamentalist family."

"Pardon?"

"Back in my church in South Carolina, they used to teach the Bible as literal truth."

"You were a creationist?"

"That's right. Even through much of my college prep for my Ph.D. It took God six days to create the universe and the Earth, and on the seventh day he rested. Amen. No argument, son, or you'll go to hell. Well, not that bad, I suppose. Still, there was that existential threat inherent in the whole schematic of belief."

"What made you change your mind?"

"Maybe I *didn't* change my mind, Doctor Lindstrom." He laughed at Mikaela's double-take. "No. Just kidding. I think the change was gradual starting when I understood that the whole universe, including myself, was a process. And when I understood, as a physicist, the tricky nature of time itself. My mind just opened up, and I've kept it opened stubbornly. Still, old fears seep up occasionally. Like now."

"Everyone has to have some kind of religious system to hang his head on, Doctor. Whether they call it science or politics or whatever, people settle on systems of thought around which they structure their universe. Take these saurians, for example. Thesaurus is not the only saurian leader to have wandered past the portal. Each generation, as far as I can tell, *selects* one member of their number from a large group of volunteers. They call him the 'Messenger from the Gods.' As far as I can tell, a lot of what they do, what they believe, hinges on what these Messengers find behind that wall."

Doctor Jakes smacked his fist into his hand. "And all I need is that suit!"

"Suits, my friend. Others are coming with you. Including yours truly."

"Coopersmith says that Thesaurus doesn't have much knowledge of any control section. I just hope that we can get through all the way."

"I'm sure that you'll find a way, Doctor Jakes."

"You have such faith in me, my dear." The engineer's eyes twinkled, and he sat down. "Okay. So tell me a little more about our saurian benefactors."

"Well, as this picture here seems to show"—she pointed up at what she had been examining—"explicit in the belief system—or religion, if you will—is the concept of something *beyond* this world. An outside. The saurians believe that when they are in their R-complex stage of sleep, they somehow mystically drift into this state of being. They don't *remember* this—save for abstract dreams, represented *here*. Quite often, during these trips . . . into levels as well labeled as any Hindu pantheon, I assure you . . . insights will occur to the creatures. Personality shifts."

"Do they believe in an afterlife?"

"I'm not sure. There's a hint, though, that they think they get a glimpse of their afterlife during these somnolent periods."

"The universe in a grain of sand, huh? Eternity in a day."

"I don't really think we can begin to totally understand, but it's something like that. As more biologically aware creatures, they sense their place in the gene-flow of things."

"I think Thesaurus over there senses we're talking about him," commented Jakes. "He's rousing from his visit to the afterlife." Jakes stepped over and helped the struggling saurian up from his nap. "Up you go, my friend."

Thesaurus began to chatter, but Jakes shook his head. "I'm sorry, pal, but we don't understand that lingo yet."

Thesaurus pointed down the corridor. "Go? Go?"

"Not yet. We need radiation suits. . . . Lindstrom, you think you can make Thesaurus understand?"

"Thesaurus." She made motions of putting something on.

"Yes! Yessssss!" Thesaurus's eyes gleamed with understanding. Apparently Ian Coopersmith had already filled him in. He lifted his robes and pointed at his skin and said, "Bad."

"Yes. I daresay you've lost a bit of your life to the cause of science, haven't you?"

Mikaela made good use of the time she had with Thesaurus, requesting him to show her the most important of the pictographs. She was deeply involved with this when the ornithopter flew in, bearing the special LS suits.

Jakes called his two men together. They went through the fifteen suits, looking for their right sizes.

"Hey, Zabriski!" Jakes called. "Where's that one we requested for Thesaurus?"

"Yeah, well, Morton and his detail—they're the ones who worked on this stuff" Zabriski said after a bit of hemming and hawing, "Well, they weren't too successful. They're hoping to have it finished by tomorrow."

"Well, I guess we'll just have to go in without him," Jakes said. "You think you can make Thesaurus understand that, Mikaela?"

"Of all the *stupid*—" Mikaela said.

"Look, we just didn't have any LS suits fitted with a *tail*," Zabriski said, defensively.

Thesaurus was walking out expectantly, excitement in his eyes. "Go! No hurt!" he said in his peculiar hissing voice.

"Get those things on, guys," Jakes said, beginning to slip his on.

Mikaela turned to the saurian. "Thesaurus go . . . tomorrow. No suit." It took a bit of doing until Thesaurus was made to understand he had no suit.

The gleam died in his eyes, but finally he nodded.

"Thesaurus no go. Thesaurus show."

He beckoned them to follow. Mikaela followed after hastily donning her own suit, feeling very bad that the saurian would not be with them when they stepped into the control section of his world. He knew, and they knew, that he couldn't afford that extra bit of radiation.

"How did your chess game go, Commander Jashad?" the pilot asked as Jashad entered the cabin.

"The drunken fool lost again. He is becoming quite boring

I am no longer amused. Perhaps we should kill him."

"You should do it quickly. We are approaching rendez-vous."

Jashad sauntered confidently up and examined the readout screens. "All is prepared?"

"Yes. I don't think they have a chance. We are too well-organized."

"Excellent. But we cannot afford swelled heads until our mission has been accomplished. I will remain here until we dock, according to plan."

"And Captain Welsh?"

"He is much too drunk to worry about. Besides, we may well have the opportunity to put him to use."

Colors still parading across her vision, Mikaela forced her attention away from the alien mural to where Jakes and his two men were examining the side of the wall.

"It's . . . it's *incredible*," she said. "I can see so many things in it. I could just study this . . . forever. This is what *taught* the saurians! But this just doesn't jive with—"

"Right. We'll figure that out later," Jakes said. "Right now, though, I want to get through to the control section."

"You and your goddam FTL drive! You're obsessed, man!"

Thesaurus had directed them, emphasizing that there was nothing to harm them past the curtain. Leaving the saurian behind, putting on their special hoods, they had stepped into the chamber. Immediately, as though detecting their presence, the wall to their left had come . . . *alive!*

Or so it seemed. Holographs—a tank shielded by some clear substance—filled with wonder. Mikaela wasn't quite sure what it was, exactly.

"That's right." Jakes said flatly as his men used their equipment to examine the wall. "I've a few theories about what such a drive would look like—call it a hobby, if you like. I've even got engineering diagrams. There would have to be some kind of field generator, I theorize—"

"Doctor!" Morton said in an excited tone. "I just tapped this bit of wall. And a panel opened! There's a lever inside."

"Thesaurus didn't mention anything about any lever!" Jakes said.

"I don't believe he's looked. Or maybe. . . ."

"Maybe what?"

"Maybe he wasn't intended to *find* it."

"Well, I guess there's nothing else to do but pull it." Jakes said, unable to hide his eagerness. "Pull away, Morton. Let's see what happens."

Morton pulled. Nothing happened.

"Just goes to show you that levers don't necessarily mean—" said Jakes.

He was interrupted by the sound and sight of a doorway opening in the wall. Beyond was darkness, here and there streaked by traceries of phosphorescense-like light.

"Don't go in," Jakes said, visibly forcing himself not to rush through the opening. "Sommers. Check it with your sensors."

Sommers worked a few controls, scrutinized the results on his machine. "No traps, as far as I can tell."

"Check again. We don't want another repeat of the Snipe incident. Especially since its *our* lives at stake."

Sommers obeyed. "Nothing bad but radiation."

"Excellent. I'll go first." Jakes squared his shoulders. He stepped through the newly opened portal. "Morton, hand me your flashlight, would you?"

The instrument was transferred.

"Me next, please?" Mikaela requested.

"Certainly," said Jakes, turning the flashlight on. "I—"

All around, lights glimmered on, providing spooky multicolored illumination to their surroundings.

Jakes caught his breath. "My God. It's like nothing I've ever seen."

"Why'd the lights come on? You hit a switch or somethin', Doc?" asked Morton.

"Just his presence did it, I think," Mikaela returned. She stepped through and realized just what Jakes was talking about.

There were shapes here . . . shapes and geometrical forms here she had never seen, blending together in impossible ways. It was all like something from an Escher print—only in three dimensions.

The lights crept up to either side of the cylinder. In the distance, Mikaela could make out the gigantic end of the cylinder—not smooth, but bulbed and dented with forms of machines modeled after an Alice-in-Wonderland mushroom garden.

Jakes blinked at all this through his specially treated visor. "I never quite expected anything like *this*. Up there, though"— he pointed to the aft end of the cylinder—"something seems to be missing. I can see I'm going to have my hands full investigating—"

Suddenly there was a loud snapping sound. A gigantic flashbulb seemed to explode in their eyes.

When they recovered, they saw that one of the machines had blown itself apart like a burst poppy.

"What was *that?*" Morton had just stepped through the portal.

"God knows," Jake said. "We'll have to put our sensors to it. It was something triggered by our entrance, there's no question about that. Later, though. Right now I want to find that startship drive."

"Right now, *I* just want to *stare*," Mikaela said.

"I can't blame you," said Jakes.

"I hope you can tell what these machines are, because I certainly haven't the faintest."

"That's what I'm here for."

Some meters away, something caught Mikaela's eye. Something slowly coming alive with particolored light, like some neon sculpture crossed with a thousand lavalamps. This, blended with holographs like shivering ghosts caught in some trap.

"That—" Mikaela said. "It looks like the thing in the other room. I *have* to go and—"

A form stumbled through their number, walked several meters ahead of them, and then halted. Reptilian eyes looked all around, taking in the wonderful sights. Arms reached out as though to grasp everything it could get.

"It's Thesaurus!" Mikaela said. "He *knows* he shouldn't be in here! It might kill him!" She moved toward the saurian, but Jakes stopped her.

"The damage is already done, Lindstrom. Thesaurus knows what's he's doing."

"He's *killing* himself, that's what he's doing," Mikaela said.

"No. He's already done that. It was all just a matter of time.

It was his price for knowledge."

"But he could have waited till tomorrow for his special suit!" Tears had come to Mikaela's eyes.

Thesaurus was staggering ahead, touching surfaces, cringing with either pain or pleasure—or perhaps both.

"Tomorrow? He might have died *tonight*, Mikaela. There's no telling with radiation poisoning. No. I know exactly how he feels. He wanted to see it *now*."

"I can't take it," Mikaela said, breaking away from Jakes's restraint. She ran up to Thesaurus, who was staring up, eyes gleaming. "Thesaurus," she said. "You have to get back. It's not good—"

Thesaurus turned and looked at her. A gutteral click and hissing emerged from his mouth, but it was gentle, not hostile at all.

She pointed back. Thesaurus said, "Yessss," and began to walk back.

Halfway back, the creature keeled over, and lay still. "Jakes! Morton! Sommers! Help me get him *out* of here!"

The men came running. Together, they carted the unconscious saurian through the two portals, back into the temple chambers.

They laid him down on his mat, where he breathed shallowly.

"That dose of radiation really did it to him this time," Morton said.

"Maybe he could feel something coming on anyway," Jakes commented. "That's why he figured he couldn't spare the time."

Sommers said, "God. Coopersmith and Kemp are gonna be some kind of pissed. We shoulda watched this thing!"

Angry, Mikaela turned to them. "Would you loudmouths shut up and get on the radio to Thalberg. She might actually be able to *do* something!"

Thesaurus spasmed. His eyes shot wide. The saurian grew rigid. Then relaxed.

"I think. . . ." Mikaela said. "I think he's dead."

"Oh, that's just great," Morton said.

"Certainly it puts a pall on things," Jakes said. "But it's not as if we killed him. He's been killing himself for years. But he was the first . . . the first Saurian to see the Other Side in physical form. And that is what he wanted, I'm sure. Come on, Mikaela. You can't do a thing. We need you in there."

Mikaela wiped away her tears and nodded.

CHAPTER 19

"ARE YOU CERTAIN it's on intersect?" asked Phineas as he spoke to his second-in-command by radio.

"Yes, Colonel. Commander Fratz has been tracking it since the scanners first picked it up. At first he thought we might just be passing through shipping lanes, but there's no denying it now. It's coming in for an intersect." Marshall looked up from the headquarters intercom at Commander Bracken and Ross Canter, one of the flight engineers, who had volunteered to remain as part of the skeleton crew at base camp.

"It's possible that Copernicus has diverted it from its course to investigate our radio silence," said Kemp. "How's the work going on the communications problem?"

"No luck, so far, sir."

"What's the ETA on that ore-ship?"

"At present velocity I would estimate within the hour," said

Marshall, watching Commander Bracken nod his confirmation.

"I want you to keep me informed on the status of that ship, Captain. Secure the main entry hatch and alert your men to be ready for anything. I'm coming back to the camp by 'thopter as soon as possible. Carry on. . . . Kemp out."

The intercom radio clicked off and Marshall looked over to the two men in headquarters office. "You two heard the man. . . . what do you think?"

Bracken shook his head. "I don't like it, Captain. I can't put my finger on it, but something doesn't *feel* right to me."

"I think we should just play it by ear," said Canter. "The Colonel has no way of knowing what's going on. I, for one, think it's quite natural to assume that Copernicus has sent that ore-ship out here to investigate. I don't think we have anything to worry about."

Marshall nodded slowly. "Well, I hope you're right, Canter. We can't afford any mess-ups at this stage of the game."

"Captain, I'm supposed to be relieving Fratz on the *Goddard* bridge. I think I'd better get going," said Bracken.

"I'll go with you," said Canter. "See if I can help the crew that's working in the service module."

Marshall nodded and sat down behind his work-table. "All right, keep me informed. I don't want Kemp calling back here and me not having anything to tell him."

Canter and Bracken chuckled at the small joke, and left the room. They walked to the entry hatch, and descended down the ladder to the airlock, where they suited up for EVA to the *Goddard*. Once on board the ship, Bracken headed for the bridge and Canter made his way down the main corridor to the service module. The ship was deserted aside from two of Jakes's men working on the damaged communications equipment and Bracken at the Command console. *It's going to be easier than I figured,* he thought, as he paused outside the entrance to the Module. Taking over the base camp would be a simple matter with the bulk of the *Goddard* crew at the end of the cylinder, but Canter realized that controlling the base camp would be of little help to them. If Jakes succeeded in gaining access to the control section of the *Dragonstar*, Kemp would be in the driver's seat, quite literally.

Canter needed a contingency plan. He only had an hour or

so before the ore-ship rendezvous, so he would be forced to work quickly.

Walking back to the airlock, Canter climbed into his EVA suit, and radioed Bracken on the bridge. "Commander, this is Doctor Canter. . . . I'm getting an unstable reading on one of the outriggers. I'm taking one of the work-scooters down to the aft end and check it out."

"Okay, Doctor," said Bracken. "Be careful out there. . . . I don't have anybody to back you up if you get yourself in a jam."

"Affirmative, Commander. I'll check in by intercom if I find anything interesting."

Canter flicked off his helmet-mike and cycled the airlock. With the shining expanse of the alien ship below him, he coasted over to one of the work-scooters—little more than a frame, cockpit, and naked engine—and climbed aboard. Accelerating away from the *Goddard-Heinlein*, Canter headed down the length of the immense cylinder toward the stern. From Jakes's most recent reports, the saurian wall was located approximately forty klicks from the engines. He would have to estimate distances since he did not have the time to get a precise location. He would also be limited to placement of an entry hatch in the side of the cylinder.

That, in fact, was the key to his plan—there would *have* to be another entry hatch near the aft-end. . . .

The little scooter picked up speed and he was topping four hundred KPH when he started to decelerate, finally slowing to a crawl, and dropping his altitude to ten meters above the surface of the hull. He had the sensation of flying in a hovercraft across a vast desert plain.

It was difficult to believe that you were actually flying across the surface of a *ship*. Without instruments to give him a precise amount of distance covered, Canter was forced to guesstimate when he was within forty kilometers of the end of the cylinder, where he began scanning the surface for the distinctive markings that indicated an outerhull airlock.

Ten minutes later he found one, somewhat smaller than the one the IASA was using. He was not sure of its exact position, but it would have to do, since he was running out of time. Using the razer-torch on the scooter's tool-rack, he burned through the plate which housed the lock's manual override panel, then carefully opened the outerlock door. To mark its location, he took an electronic work-flare from the scooter's rack and attached it magnetically to the hull by the lock. Its low-frequency beeper would serve as a beacon to anyone trying to locate the lock.

As he climbed back aboard the scooter, he checked his chronometer—less than twenty minutes before the ore-ship would arrive, at the latest. He would have to hurry. He fired the scooter's engine, headed back toward the *Goddard-Heinlein* link-up, and radioed in to Bracken.

"Commander, this is Doctor Canter.... I've located the problem on one of the impulse engines. I can rectify, but I will be tied up for about another hour or so. Do you have any problem with that time-table?"

"Affirmative, Doctor. ETA with the ore-ship is coming up soon. I don't know if you should be out there while all that's going on."

"I don't *want* to be out here, Commander, but if I don't get this engine stabilized, it's going to fail sooner or later. I'd rather save us the trouble of course-correcting for the loss of directional thrust when it goes...."

"All right, Doctor. I guess you know what you're doing, but be careful. Bracken out."

Canter smiled as the radio went dead. The scooter accelerated until he was at top speed. He held it there for a few minutes, before reversing thrust and slowing down for rendezvous.

The minutes ticked past. As he approached the *Goddard*'s airlock, he could see the ungainly configuration of the ore-ship closing in on their position. Dwarfed by the size of the *Dragonstar*, the approaching vessel looked like a flying insect, hovering with wings blurred into invisibility. It had already pulled alongside the *Goddard-Heinlein*, but Canter could see no external activity as of yet.

He switched frequencies, tuning in on the base camp intercom. Someone was talking, and Canter eavesdropped.

"...like they're close-approaching for docking," said Bracken. "I've tried reaching them on the intercom but I'm getting no response...."

"They must know we're having a communications problem," said Marshall. "Probably don't have their own equipment tuned to our specific frequency. Proceed with docking, Commander. . . ."

Canter slowed his scooter as he approached the ships. The ore-ship was nestling in beside the *Goddard*, lining up its docking collar with the Deep-Space cruiser. He watched as the two ships became joined, siamese-twin-like, at the waists, and listened on the intercom.

"Ore-ship docking completed," said Bracken. "Their airlock is recycling. We should know what's going on in a minute. . . . Stand by, Captain. . . ."

After securing the scooter to the hull, Canter drifted across to the open-lock of the *Goddard*, on the opposite side of the fuselage from the docking collar. He cycled the lock, stepped inside, and pulled off his EVA helmet, hoping that someone on the boarding crew would recognize him. This was no time to get himself shot.

The main corridor was silent as he entered. Then he heard footsteps to his left. Looking up, he saw a crowd of men wearing olive-green jumpsuits, LS-helmets, and visors, and carrying weapons. The man in the lead turned and raised his rifle to his waist, aiming it. Canter threw himself against the wall, raised his arms in the bulky EVA suit, and started screaming to identify himself.

The lead man hesitated for a moment, and two others joined him, walking slowly up the corridor, their guns trained on him.

"It's Canter! . . . Rassim! I'm *Rassim!*" He felt a knot growing in his throat, and he feared that soon no words would come. They were going to shoot him, he was certain.

The lead man stopped, gestured him to move into the center of the corridor with the barrel of his weapon. "Rassim *who?*" he said softly.

"Pierre . . . Pierre Rassim! I'm with the *Jiha!*"

The leader lifted his visor. He was olive-skinned and wore a neatly trimmed, full-face beard. He smiled ironically. "Why are you here, Rassim?"

At first, Canter did not understand the question, but suddenly, the correct answer came to him: "I'm here for Ahmad Nesrudah. . . ."

The leader's shoulders dropped perceptibly as he relaxed

his grip on his rifle. "All right," he said to the other men. "It's all right." Then, turning back to Canter, he said: "What's the situation here?"

"One man on the bridge. Two back this way in the service module. They won't be any problem. Nobody on board the smaller ship, and one man inside the entry hatch on a security post. There are only four men at the base camp. Everyone else, including Kemp, is at the other end of the alien ship." Briefly Canter explained the situation, and told the commando leader about the beacon at the aft-end, which marked the entry hatch.

"You suggest that we take the men in through there?"

"That's where they can control this ship, don't you see that?"

"What about these . . . lizard-men? Will they be a problem?"

Canter shook his head. "I don't think so . . . from what I understand, they have no technology to speak of. Listen, you'll only need a handful of men to secure the base camp; I can contact their headquarters and tell them that IASA people are coming aboard, and they won't suspect a thing. You take the rest of your men down to the other end of the *Dragonstar*, follow the signal from the beacon, and enter the same way as you were briefed on this entry. You should come up inside the saurian civilization. I'm sure you can take it from there."

The leader grabbed Canter by the front of his EVA suit and pushed him against the wall. "This was not in the briefing . . . it sounds crazy to me!"

"No!, listen . . . no one expected them to move the base camp! We had no idea that they would have access to the control section of the ship! We've *got* to change our plans, or this whole thing is a waste of time. Now, you've got to take out the man on the bridge so that I can use the intercom . . . !"

The commando leader was going to speak again, but he changed his mind. He released Canter and returned to his lieutenants, whom he briefed quickly. Twelve men remained on board the *Goddard* while the others were ushered back into the ore-ship by their bearded leader.

"This way," said Canter, leading a lieutenant and six men toward the bridge. The other six went back toward the service module.

Bracken did not even have a chance to turn around before he caught two bursts of fire. He fell from the chair in a heap, and Canter took his place, flipping on the intercom. "Captain Marshall, this is Doctor Canter. . . ."

"What is it, Doctor? Where's Bracken?"

"We've got Doctor Kolenkhov and some of the Copernicus Staff on board, Captain. They hitched a ride on the ore-ship to investigate our radio silence. They request permission to enter the *Dragonstar*. . . ."

"Doctor Kolenkhov?! You're kidding! Where's Bracken?"

"He's down at the airlock preparing to escort them through the entry hatch."

There was a pause before Marshall replied. "Why didn't Bracken notify me of all this?"

"He was kind of taken by surprise, Captain. I can't really blame him." Canter paused, forced a chuckle from his dry throat. "I mean, if you've ever met Doctor Kolenkhov, I think you'd understand. . . ."

Marshall paused, then replied. "Hmm, yes, I've heard stories about him . . . supposed to be quite a character. All right, Doctor, tell Bracken I'll be expecting him. Marshall out."

Canter turned and nodded to the commando lieutenant, who turned and led his men from the bridge to the airlock, where Canter passed out EVA gear to the half-dozen men. As they suited up, the other six commandos arrived and began pulling on their own suits.

Once outside the *Goddard*, Canter led them through the outer chamber of the lock, took them through, and had them discard the EVA gear and start up the ladder.

When they reached the platform below the hatch, Canter climbed up, opened it slowly, and saw Captain Marshall standing just down the knoll, waiting for him with another man. He waved as he stepped out onto the spongy ground, and Marshall raised his hand to return the greeting. At that moment, three of the TWC commandos appeared and fired their automatic rifles. Marshall and his underling were cut down by the hail of slugs in an instant.

"Let's go!" cried Canter as he began running towards the headquarters dome.

Across the clearing, near the generating station for the force-field, stood another man, ostensibly on guard duty. He was shocked into momentary immobility by the sight of the two men being shot down before his eyes, then took cover behind a rack of equipment and started spraying the area with razer fire. Three commandos were lanced by the heat-beams and cooked from the inside out, dead before they hit the ground. Everyone else dove for cover and pinned down the lone sentry with concentrated automatic weapons fire.

The only other man alive at base headquarters was Commander Douglas Fratz, who had been on break in the headquarters dome. He heard the gunfire, and ran to the window, and he was shocked to see the olive-green troops scampering across the clearing, led by Doctor Canter. As he watched, he realized that it was only a matter of time before they countered the sentry's position, whoever they were. And Fratz knew what he must do.

"This is base camp, calling Colonel Kemp! Come in! This is Commander Fratz...! Come in, please!" Fratz waited by the console, expecting the commandos to come bursting through the door any moment. *Come on, Colonel!*

"This is Colonel Kemp.... What is it, Commander?"

Fratz summarized the events in a few quick sentences while the sounds of gunfire continued outside the dome.

"Jesus Christ!" said Kemp. "I'm about five klicks from landing the 'thopter there! Can you hang on?"

"Negative, Colonel! They've got ten, maybe twelve men out there. Heavily armed. Get out of here while you can! Get some help!"

"Try to hang on, Commander. We're heading back. Good luck, man...."

Fratz flipped off the radio, and noticed that the sound of gunfire outside had stopped. *I can't believe this is it*, he thought. *I can't believe I'm going to die like this....*

As he turned to take cover behind the work-table, the door to the room flew open. There were three men wearing olive-green jumpsuits. Fratz didn't see their guns until the barrels flashed.

He never heard their report.

CHAPTER 20

FLYING AT THE highest velocity that Zabriski would risk, the ornithopter struggled against the atmospheric caprices of Artifact One's interior. Phineas Kemp's mind was experiencing a separate turbulence. What *else* could go wrong? He felt like some biblical character being tested by a malevolent and wrathful God. *How could the TWC have gotten control of one of our ore-ships?*

Hell. It didn't matter *now*, he told himself. What mattered was that they were inside the ship. The base camp had been wiped out. Kemp was certain that the commandos wouldn't stop there. If they knew where the majority of the crew was located, how would they get across the more than one hundred and fifty klicks of hostile territory? How did they intend to take over Artifact One?

Well, he thought, unconsciously tightening his seatbelt, feeling the throb of the ornithopter's engines under his boots.

253

They'd probably change the course of the gigantic ship. Now that they had overrun the *Goddard,* the *Heinlein* and the base camp, they certainly controlled the new engines that the IASA team had tacked on to guide Artifact One back into an accessible orbit around Earth. No doubt, there waited more TWC ships in the place to which they intended to redirect the alien ship. Once there, the game was entirely theirs. They could explore Artifact One at their leisure. Its secrets would be theirs to unlock.

However, Kemp and the IASA still had two wild cards to play, as desperate as their situation seemed.

First, they had the protection of the saurian wall, and hope-fully the friendship and esteem of the saurian culture. In normal circumstances, that would not bother the TWC commandos. They could simply fight a war of attrition, with Kemp and his men the inevitable losers once the new destination was reached and the TWC could bring superior weaponry and numbers of troops into play.

And second, for all practical purposes, Kemp's team still had control of the prized engines of Artifact One. Not only control, but *access.* It would take a while to get the mammoth ship to exactly where the TWC wanted it. Any time during that period, the IASA team could stumble not merely onto the secrets of the *Dragonstar*—but onto the controls and the guid-ance system as well. If they *used* them—well, that would be an entirely different ballgame, with the TWC the inevitable losers.

There was no question that the TWC commandos would realize this.

No question that they would try to do something about it.

Kemp wondered what kind of weapons they had. How many men? All that made a great deal of difference.

He'd gone over the questions with Coopersmith when he'd contacted him by intercom, right after Fratz had warned him away from the base camp. It would be at least an hour before the 'thopter would reach the saurian wall. A lot could happen by then.

The radio beeped. Kemp flicked on his helmet-mike.

"Kemp."

"Coopersmith here, Colonel. Doctor Jakes and two of his

men and Doctor Lindstrom, are in the aft-end—"

"*Now?* Ian, for Christ's sakes, we're under attack!"

"I know that, and *you* know that. I don't think the saurians really understand. I could have spent another two days explaining exactly what is going on with the TWC, and just *who* they are."

"Yes. That's probably for the best. They must know about everything, if Canter was their inside man, as Fratz had said. They must realize that in order to have full control of the situation, they have to take over this section as well. So, we have to assume that there're coming, eventually. If they come across the interior, we've got plenty of time to prepare."

"But Phineas, you know that we found other access points from the *exterior*. Some quite close to the saurian civilization and the engines."

"Quite true. And they'll be in a hurry, won't they? You know, Coopersmith, I think we may well be in trouble. Set up some defensive emplacements immediately. Oh, and Coopersmith. In the saurian mythology, is there anything about a coming Armageddon?"

"I could ask, Phineas."

"Well, you tell them that it may well be here, *now.*"

The entry shaft and hatch design were virtually identical to the one leading to the IASA base camp. Marcus Jashad, the leader of the ninety-man commando squad, stood on the platform below the hatch, preparing to manually turn the gearwheel that would free it. He signaled to his men below, then opened the large, rectangular panel.

Bright light spilled down.

He climbed up and onto the vine-covered ground, into the strange and rich smells of the interior.

Something was wrong.

Jashad could see no sign of any saurian cities. No saurian wall. Nothing at all that Canter had told him about.

Surrounding the clearing near the hatch were thick stands of primitive forest. Even though Jashad did not know the difference between a cycad and a gingko, he was aware of the strategic obstacle that enclosed his men.

Where *were* they?

He glanced up towards the center of the cylinder, checking the direction of the illuminating rod in an attempt to get his bearings. Behind him, the remainder of the assault team poured out of the entry hatch, each man momentarily stunned into immobility as he paused to stare at the hostile surroundings.

As his lieutenants gathered about him, the leader turned to one of them. "Get Canter on the radio. IASA frequency at the base camp...."

"Fatah, here...."

"Get me Canter," said the leader. "The so-called 'Rassim.'"

There was a pause while the leader waited. The forest around him and his men was alive with sounds: scurrying in the ground cover, insect-buzzings, an occasional cry of hunger or agony.

"Rassim here."

"This is Jashad," said the leader. "What have you done to us?!"

"What's the matter? What're you talking about? Where are you?"

Jashad related their predicament angrily.

"All right," said Rassim/Canter, explaining that he had not had time to properly locate an entrance within the saurian barrier. "Continue to broadcast a distress-call with your radio, and I'll use our scanning equipment to get a fix on your position. Stand-by...."

Jashad held the radio tightly, trying to hide the frustration and fear he felt. Some of his men were anxiously guarding the perimeter of the small clearing, while others were pointing skyward, where a group of Pterosaurs glided by like large, burnt-orange kites.

The radio crackled, and Rassim/Canter's voice was heard once again. "Rassim here.... Sorry for the delay. The instruments placed you along the same longitudinal axis as the base camp, and you are within sight of the flat end of the cylinder. Can you see it from where you are?"

"Yes," said Jashad. "It is partially obscured by clouds and haze, but it is visible."

"Proceed towards the flat end, and you should be able to see the barrier within five klicks, and be careful.... there's supposed to be some rough customers out there."

Jashad laughed. "Rassim, it is *we* who are the 'rough customers!'"

256

"Whatever you say.... Anything before I break off?"

Jashad paused. "Yes, there is one survivor on the ore-ship. The Command pilot, a miserable drunk named Welsh. Have him taken to the base camp and dry him out. We may be needing him to ferry our troops back to Ramadas Khan. Can you take care of that, Rassim?"

"No problem. He's on the bridge, right?"

"Locked in with one of my men. We are going in now. Jashad out."

"Good luck. Rassim out."

The bearded assassin assembled his men, briefed them quickly, and struck out into the forest. They employed a point man, followed by a two-man file which snaked through the maze of trees cautiously. Before they had covered the first kilometer, the men were feeling the effects of the muggy, warm temperature. Perspiration soaked their fatigues a deep, dark green. It was at that point that Jashad noticed something *different* about the surrounding forest.

It was silent.

Abruptly the insect-sounds had disappeared. There were no small things rustling in the undergrowth. Jashad signaled for the column to halt. "Listen," he said to one of the men standing close by. "Something's coming this way...."

The silence was broken by the distant thrash of branches and the barely audible *whomp* of heavy footfalls. Something was closing in on their position, and it moved boldly, without fear of detection.

"Keep moving!" cried Jashad, as he tried to locate the source of the intruding sounds. It seemed to be approaching the rear flank of the column, but he could not see very far within the lush green weave of the forest. "Double-time!"

The commandos slipped into a half-jog, bobbing and weaving, through a makeshift path. Suddenly a ravenous scream cut through the humid air like a blade. Turning, Jashad and his men were horrified to see a beast emerge from the tapestry of fronds and broad leaves not ten meters from the men at the rear of the column. It was at least six meters tall, boldly contrasted to the forest by its tan hide, accented by light yellow stripings. Thick hindlegs moved like giant pistons as it surged forward. Its huge head dropped low; its great green eyes and grinning jaw were riveted upon the commandos at the end of the column. Jashad did not recognize the Gorgosaurus for what is was, nor did he care. Before he could shout any commands, the column had broken ranks and scattered into the forest.

Automatic weapons' fire filled the heavy air with a steady ratcheting clatter as the Gorgosaurus charged, catching one of the men in its jaws like a power-shovel scooping up a chunk of earth. Raising its head, the beast tossed the man slightly and closed its jaws upon him. Two quick snaps, and the man disappeared as the beast paused upright to work a distended bulge down its gullet. Its belly and flanks were peppered with scarlet wounds as the commandos' slugs ripped into its hide, but still it lowered its head and resumed its attack. Apparently driven to a feeding frenzy by the first taste of fresh blood, the Gorgosaurus had no care for its safety. Another man stumbled as he ran from the beast, and was crushed beneath its splayed hindclaws. The Gorgosaurus paused to pick the corpse from its foot, worrying the body with its forelimbs and eagerly snapping it up with its jaws.

The men closest to the carnivore continued to fire .40-caliber slugs into its thick body. Although it showed no signs of injury, as the Gorgosaurus raised its head and attempted to move forward again, it stumbled and fell forward. It gave out a bellowing cry as it thundered to the ground, its heavy hindlegs twitching violently, it tail thumping the earth in a series of shaking death throes.

Finally the beast was still. As the commandos slowly crawled from their hiding places, grouping about the huge body, the scavengers of the Jurassic world began to appear. Little four-legged lizards scuttled out of the undergrowth to swarm about the Gorgosaurus' carcass to nip and gnaw. Clouds of insects materialized, descending on the still-warm flesh to feed and lay eggs. Eat and eventually be eaten. That was the law of this world, and the commandos stood watching the display in a state of profound shock.

In the distance, there was the renewed sound of bellowing and thrashing. The smell of blood and fresh meat was in the air and the scent was attracting other carnivores. Jashad marshalled his forces and cleared out of the area at double-time. *Damnable Rassim!* he thought as he ran for his life. *He was responsible for this travesty.* The *Jiha's* finest men being eaten like dogfood! Someone would pay for this, thought Jashad.

The forest blurred past them as they ran, spurred on by the unknown terrors behind them and the growing fury of revenge that was welling up in them. Jashad tripled-timed to the point of the column, inciting his men with slogans and quasi-religious exhortations. The men screamed jingoistic responses as they ran, getting psyched up, forgetting the horror that had almost destroyed them.

The trees began to thin as they moved closer to the barrier. Jashad lost all sense of time as well as distance as they rushed toward their objective. Behind them, the forest was alive with the sounds of the beasts. Suddenly, beyond the stand of redwoods and conifers, the leader saw the high, featureless expanse of the wall. Even from a distance it looked formidable, and immediately, he was considering the best way to get over or through it.

"Spread them out!" he called to his squad leaders. "Take cover near the edge of the trees."

They moved forward, fanning out to face the wall and a short clearing which had been worn smooth by lumbering and what appeared to be a fairly heavy concentration of dinosaur activity. As Jashad reached the cover of a large-boled tree, he studied the wall's composition—an ingenious combination of wood and stone and earth. There were buttresses at certain points along its length and at larger, even distances, crudely built guard towers rose up even higher than the wall itself. Within the tower closest to their position, Jashad could see two lizard-like creatures, holding what might be crossbows, staring out at the forest. They did not appear to have detected the commandos.

Jashad took a deep breath of the humid air, then signaled his explosives men. They scrambled through the undergrowth to his side: five of the best in the business, backpacks jingling softly. Jashad wiped a frond out of the way and addressed the men. "Think you can put a hole in that wall?"

The leader grinned, his white teeth contrasting with his sweaty, dark skin. "No problem." He nodded over to the guards. "If you take care of those two . . . creatures, we'll blow half the wall down."

Jashad glanced over at the saurians again, rubbing his beard, which irritated him in this environment. "I truly regret that we have to operate in this fashion. Would that we were the first to contact this extraordinary race! But amends can be made later. We have no time to waste; we must move forward immediately, and anything—human or alien—that stands in our way must be removed. I've never seen conditions in which the ends have more justified the means."

The explosives team poised at the dense edge of the clearing, waiting for the signal to run.

Jashad gave the signal for his sharpshooters to take their places, indicating what their targets would be. He watched them with pride as they inched forward, then aimed.

Such a shame indeed, thought Jashad as he put his binoculars over his eyes and focused them on one of the guards. Such an interesting looking creature, slightly taller than the average human, with large, bright eyes. Three fingers across from the opposable thumb. How fascinating! He hoped that, after this battle, when the TWC was in control, when they had crushed or captured Colonel Kemp and his men, and penetrated the engine section of this mammoth starship, they could come to terms with these lizard-men. With a well-trained will, Jashad pushed any regret or guilt from his mind. Then he signaled the snipers.

Bullets exploded.

Jashad watched as they slapped into one of the guards. The blood which splattered was certainly red enough. The saurian jerked back, took another round in the face, then toppled over the side and thudded onto the ground. With a downward gesture, Jashad signaled for the explosives men to advance. Then he called out for the sharpshooters to cover them.

The explosives men jogged forward, almost as one, their timing was so practiced. Within seconds, they had split up and taken their places at five-meter intervals along the wall. Quickly, bars of C-7 plastic explosives were slapped against the rock, cement, and wood. An explosive cap was immediately embedded in each one. These would be triggered by radio, once the commandos were away and out of danger.

All was going well, until another of the saurians appeared at the left tower. This one had a different kind of crossbow, Jashad noted with surprise. On this one—slightly bigger—the quarrel seemed to be *moving*.

The explosives team was already on the way back.

Jashad called out to the sharpshooters.

High-powered rifles cracked, bringing down the saurian guard.

But the quarrel had already been unleashed. It slashed down toward one of the men.

"Watch out!" Jashad screamed, quite unprofessionally.

The men quickly did zig-zags. The quarrel swooshed past the man on the left end, just missing him.

Almost immediately, it sprouted wings, swerved around in a tight arc, and buried itself in the man's abdomen. The commando gave an agonized scream. The quarrel's tail seemed to lash about like the tail of a snake. Blood flowed onto green khakis.

By the time that the realization that the arrow was a living thing dawned upon Jashad, the thing had already chewed halfway through the commando. Jashad cursed, then yelled for the others to hurry back.

The stricken commando writhed on the ground for a few seconds, and then was still. Sounds of tiny teeth snapping carried on the slight breeze.

Stunned expressions on their faces, the others returned to cover.

"Well, don't just stand there," Jashad cried. "I want that wall down!"

Immediately, the explosives team leader took off his backpack and picked out his radio control box. He selected the proper frequency, then pushed the button.

With the sound of rolling thunder, huge holes were torn out of the thick wall. Dust and rock spumed. Smoke and fire licked up. The top of the wall caved in. When the debris finally settled, there was a quite adequate opening in the saurian wall.

"Advance!" Jashad cried, gripping his own weapon with renewed intensity. Quickly, the guerrilla force scrambled through the clearing to the edge of the rubble. Jashad peered over fallen masonry and shattered wood beams. Two hundred meters away was the city that Canter had spoken of. But there were also quite a number of frenzied saurians advancing toward the TWC commando force. Some were riding their dimmer and *bigger* cousins, beasts that snorted as they slowly stamped toward them. "I know it's hot," Jashad called. "But we'd better erect our fighting suits." Quickly, he pulled his own from his back-pack, wishing that his men had the sophisticated fighting suits employed in honest-to-goodness wars. But since with a ter-rorist/guerrilla team mobility was the deciding factor, each man carried only a standard defense: an oversuit, strategically rein-forced with bulletproof plastics in vital places. Jashad slipped this on quickly, then pulled his LS helmet down, adjusting the gas mixture to medium-level performance. In normal actions, *swift* actions, the setting was *peak*. But who knew how long this business would last?

Without having to be told, the men carrying rocket launchers loaded their first rounds. Rifles were raised.

Jashad, feeling heady with the rich oxygen mixture flowing into the LS helmet, chinned his communication unit and was about to call for advance, when an alarmed voice blared into his earphone. "Commander! Behind! Look behind us!"

Jashad spun around. Emerging from the forest swarmed a group of about twenty unclothed saurians, armed only with clubs.

With frenzied screams, they raced toward the destroyers of the wall.

"Unit B!" Jashad cried. "Turn and open fire!"

Twenty men swiveled, aimed, and sent a volley of rifle fire into the ranks of the saurian attackers. Most of the lizard-men were cut down mercilessly, but two managed to avoid the bullet spray. They leapt upon two commandos. One was quickly dispatched by speedy knife work. Before the other could be killed, however, his club had smashed a commando's helmet and sharp claws had torn out the man's throat.

"Unit B, cover our rear," Jashad said. "The rest, advance. Get those rockets going at the biggest defenders!"

This was *not* going to be so easy, after all.

They charged forward. At a range of fifty-meters away from the saurian defense force—an impromptu one at best, Jashad noticed—the launcher men kneeled and aimed their rocket tubes. Smoke flashed. With a boom and a thud, the first rocket penetrated the chest of a Triceratops, literally blowing it apart. Methodically, each of the burden beasts were so disposed of.

At the range of twenty meters, the other commandos flopped to the ground on the order of Jashad. Rifle cracks ripped the air. Within minutes, perhaps a hundred saurians lay writhing or dead on the plain.

More, however, swarmed from the city, carrying wooden swords and crossbows fitted with their living bolts. Soon Jashad was swatting away the persistent creatures trying to bore their way through his suit. Several of his men were killed in this fashion, when their suits were penetrated. It was a slow and agonizing death. The things more than unnerved Jashad, but his years of training put him into kind of an automatic control of the situation.

Suddenly, he heard fierce roaring from behind him, loud to him despite the helmet. "Jashad," the voice of Unit B's leader cried over Jashad's earphone's. "Rocket launchers!"

Jashad turned.

Emerging from the forest were the most fiercesome beasts he'd ever seen. An Allosaurus was slinking forward, mouth open wide anticipating a feast. Following it closely was a Tyrannosaurus Rex. Both had no doubt been attracted by the scent of blood. Growls of other creatures echoed their bellows in the distance.

The party had been announced, the feast proclaimed.

Jashad swore violently as he crouched and chinned the com control. "Unit C. Lower numbers, up to Five. Detach from ranks and cover rear."

With practiced speed, the specifically numbered men with rocket launchers broke ranks and ran back to join Unit B. Even as they did so, Jashad saw with dismay that other unclothed saurians were slipping around the sides of the broken wall, dodging the roaring carnivores.

A rocket fired. A chunk of Tyrannosaurus blew away with a blast of smoke and blood. The monster paused only a moment, then forged onward. Another rocket, fired recklessly, missed entirely.

With a prodigious leap, the Tyrannosaurus attacked the closest of the rifleman, snapping him off at the thighs. The disconnected legs wobbled a moment, then teetered over. The Tyrannosaurus chomped quickly mechanically, ignoring its wounds. Bullets splattered its chest to no apparent affect.

Jashad cried, "Advance through the town!" The defenders had been thinned out, and if they could break through, they would have the shelter of the city to assist their efforts to stay alive. He could see that the rear defense would soon become a bloody carnage. He hadn't counted on the place's fauna to come to the aid of its beleagered intelligent cousins. But then, to a hungry dinosaur, it didn't make any difference if it were eating a human or a saurian. If the invaders moved through the saurian army, or whatever had met them, the saurians would have as much of a problem with the invading monsters as the commandos were having.

Losing about ten men in the process, they managed to do just that.

Sweating profusely, Jashad stopped to catch his breath. His bayonet dripped with saurian blood.

The sound of engines came to his ears. The sounds of whir-ring propellers. . . .

Jashad looked up. An ornithopter flew over his head, maybe a hundred meters high. His first inclination was to order it shot down. But when he realized that the flying machine was passing without attacking the commandos, he decided to let it pass.

Already, a possible alternative plan was forming in his head. There *had* to be an alternative plan. . . .

This one was not working well at all.

He wasn't half as drunk as they thought he was, thought Captain Francis Welsh, as he lay back in his command chair, set to the reclining position. These fucking A-rabs had no idea how much beer Fran Welsh could pound and still walk the line. His single guard sat somewhere behind him, presumably with a gun still trained to his general vicinity, but Welsh did not want to chance anything.

He had played along with that vicious bastard, Jashad, be-cause he wanted to stay alive. It was that simple. But the beer and the dead-time on board the ship were starting to wear thin on him. Plus the fact that he knew that his crew was dead and other IASA people were probably getting killed all around him. . . . He was beginning to feel guilty, and a little itchy.

Perhaps it wasn't so simple after all. Simply saying *screw it* wasn't going to make him feel any better in the long run. Always the short run, always the easy way out. That had been his motto of late. Just putting in the time till that pension would take care of him. Shit, how could he lay there thinking about his goddamned pension when there were guys getting wasted all around him? That stank, plain and simple.

His thoughts were interrupted by the compartment hatch opening. Playing up his drunken bit, he lolled over the edge of the chair to cast a moonish, glazed eye toward the new arrival. Some guy wearing an IASA jumpsuit carrying an automatic rifle. Welsh didn't recognize him but the guard did not seem upset to see the uniform of the opposition. Something funny going on here.

"Orders from Jashad," said the stranger, and the guard stood up, keeping his own weapon at the ready. "I am Rassim—you were expecting me?"

"Yes sir," said the guard.

"The *Goddard* and the *Heinlein* are secured, and so is the enemy's base camp. We are to escort the prisoner from the ship to the base camp. Let's go."

The guard turned and approached Welsh, who remained limp in the chair trying to look as foolish as possible as he ogled Rassim and the guard.

"What the hell's the matter with him, drugs?" asked Rassim.

"Drunk," said the guard. "All he *does* is stay drunk!" He laughed.

"Then we'll have to carry him. You on that side, I'll grab him under this shoulder."

All right, thought Welsh. This is where it happens or it doesn't. Either I let them take me out of here, or I make my move. Let's see what happens....

The one called Rassim shouldered his weapon, slinging the strap over his arm, and bent down to firmly grasp Welsh under the armpit. The guard, surprisingly enough, tried to do his part with one hand, still holding his rifle in his left hand. Welsh let his head roll to the side, where his nose was inches from an automatic handgun in the guard's thigh holster. Now isn't that interesting? he thought. But as long as he's got his rifle ready, I'm screwed. Of course, I might be finished anyway, seeing's how I haven't handled a weapon since basic training twenty years ago....

Welsh went completely limp and let his eyes becomes slits. Dead weight, and the guard could not handle him with one hand; it was that simple. There was a pause as the guard reluctantly shouldered his weapon and grabbed Welsh more securely. He felt himself being lifted, half-dragged from the chair towards the hatch. All three of them would not be able to squeeze through the entry at once and there would be more jockeying of position. It would be then. Or not at all.

Waiting for the right moment. A turn of the head, and pressing of the guard's thigh up against him. It had to be timed right. . . .

It was.

As they hefted him sideways to slip through the hatch, Welsh's flailing arm brushed the guard's waist, then fell into the trigger-well and he yanked it free, pointing it upwards. He squeezed the trigger and the sound of the shell exploding that close to his own face shocked him. But not nearly as badly as the guard. In a moment of suspended time, Welsh saw the man's lower jaw catch the slug in its upward ascent and dissolve completely into a scarlet blossom. Then bullet passed through the roof of the mouth, and he watched the man's scalp explode outward.

Stunned by the gun's report and the instantaneous death of his comrade, the man named Rassim still held onto Welsh as the guard collapsed lifelessly. Almost calmly, the captain swung the automatic towards the traitor in the IASA uniform and pulled the trigger twice. Ignoring the loud bark of the shells, he watched almost with fascination as two dark holes opened themselves in the man's chest. One of the slugs must have hit something vital because a veritable fountain of blood shot from the tiny dark pit and Rassim was thrown violently through the hatch, his hands still reflexively grabbing Welsh and carrying him along.

Die! You bastard! Die! raged the Welsh, silently, as he pulled himself from the doomed man's hold. Rassim lay on his back, his head thrown askew, his feet drumming out a death-tap on the deck as the fountain of red now ebbed to a trickle.

Slowly, Welsh took cover behind a bulkhead and waited to see if the shots might have attracted any more of the Arab terrorists, but after a few long minutes, he was certain that he was now alone on the ore-ship. To be absolutely positive, he forced himself to scour the corridors and the decks, then secured the outer hatch and deactivated the airlock, sealing himself in.

When he returned to the flight deck, he activated the frequency scanner and monitored various channels until he heard the voice of Colonel Kemp of the IASA. Locking in, he interrupted the broadcast. "Breaker, breaker...this is Captain Welsh on board the *Andromache*....Mayday and breaker here...."

He repeated the short message until he heard the voice of Kemp acknowledge. "We copy, *Andromache*. What is it, Welsh? I'm afraid we've got our hands full right now...."

Fran could hear the sound of confusion and explosions in the background, and the *whomping* sound of ornithopter's rotors. Quickly he relayed what had happened, and that the oreship was now secure. What followed surprised him, but certainly did not displease him. Kemp told him to remain aboard until he was contacted, and then quickly radioed out.

Captain Welsh smiled, satisfied that he had done his part, and returned to the stash of beer on the bridge.

Colonel Phineas Kemp peered through the bubble of the ornithopter as he replaced the radio mike in its clasp. "Stay at this altitude," he said to his pilot. "They might try to take a few shots at us...though I do have to admit, they look pretty busy down there." Zabriski nodded and kept a steady course over the saurian territory.

"Now get down to the left, towards that temple-like building. Two of our people are down there and I want to reach them before the guerrillas do." Phineas reached again for the communications mike as he surveyed the chaos below. He saw a whole detachment of saurians with no clothing, and wondered if they might be of the warrior-class Coopersmith had mentioned. There were so many things to learn about the intelligent reptiles, but there would be time for that later.

"Coopersmith, Kemp here! We're coming in! Where are those emplacements I requested? Those saurians could use some help!"

The radio crackled with Coopersmith's voice. "On the way, Colonel. We thought they'd be hitting the barrier farther down the line."

"Well, get them back here, quick!"

"Already done."

"And get ready to go. Tell Becky we're taking you out of here!"

"No objection, Phineas. The fighting sounds pretty heavy out there."

"It *is*, Coopersmith. Over."

Phineas Kemp took one more look behind as the battlefield was lost to sight. His last image was that of an Allosaurus tromping through a group of TWC commandos, while holding one in its jaws like a limp cigar. The Tyrannosaurus had been felled.

"My God," Kemp said, shaking his head. The ornithopter began to lower, coming to a final rest by the temple of the philosopher-kings. "I wonder if the TWC would have come if they'd known what was waiting for them."

"I wonder if *we* would have, sir," Zabriski said. "From that Snipe onward, things haven't exactly been rosy with Artifact One."

"It will all work out, Zabriski. It will be worth it all."

"Right now, I just want to get out of here alive."

The ornithopter rocked to a halt. Kemp slid the door back, hurled out, and raced for the temple steps, which he took two at a time.

Coopersmith was in the hallway.

"Where's Becky?" Kemp demanded.

"She's collecting some of the saurian manuscripts. She doesn't want them destroyed by the TWC."

"Damn the manuscripts! Ger her, *now!* I'm going to raise the troops on the way here. Then we're going to get the hell *out!*"

The clattering and booming sounds of the conflict were rapidly drawing near. Kemp drew his pistol, then began to pace nervously. To have come so *far*, despite all the obstacles— and then to lose it! The thought was almost too much to take. He was almost ready to abandon Coopersmith and Becky. They'd made it in the wilderness, hadn't they? This business was more important than a couple of lovebirds. . . .

He shoved the thought from his mind, realizing that it was born as much of perverse jealousy as impatience.

A minute later, Becky came racing out, scrolls under her arm. Kemp glared at her angrily, and was about to yell at her when Coopersmith, his own pistol drawn, bounded out athletically. "Okay! Let's go! I saw a detachment moving down the street from a window. No time to waste!" They ran out to the waiting ornithopter.

Funny, thought Kemp. Why had Zabriski opaqued the polarized glass?

Unless. . . .

"Coopersmith, no!" But Ian Coopersmith was already hauling at the sliding door.

The handguns bristled from the cabin, held by men in battle suits. "Ah, Colonel Phineas Kemp," a man with a beard said. "I suggest that you put your weapons down. We have much to talk about."

Zabriski called, "I'm sorry, Colonel. They just stormed in before I knew what was happening."

Frustration clenching his gut, Phineas Kemp sighed and threw his pistol in the dirt.

CHAPTER 21

"So, JASHAD," Kemp said sourly. "You're just leaving your men to be scarfed up by dinosaurs." He gazed through the bubble's glass at the land streaking past below, watching the shadow of the ornithopter flow unsteadily over forest and saurian grain fields and saurian buildings. He'd never felt so low, so *beaten* in his life.

"The fighting men of the TWC were aware of the danger," the dark, bearded man said. "They have always been willing to give their lives for our cause."

"Bloody well drilled into them, I don't doubt!" Coopersmith spat sarcastically. "Is that all you people know? Violence?"

"We were well taught by your peoples of the West, my friend. After so many years of oppression, we learned the ways of survival."

"Political tommyrot!" Ian Coopersmith said. "Propaganda! I'm part West Indian. My ancestors knew *real* oppression, and

271

I know the difference between efforts to survive, to maintain dignity, and a full-scale power play by a world cartel. You're just a puppet, Jashad. A puppet."

"I can see the strings moving your mouth, Ian Coopersmith," Jashad said, undisturbed. "Perhaps we are all pawns. But the game is interesting and worthwhile, is it not? The keys to the universe? I wish that *this* pawn's masters had those, and not your side. That is an honest emotion, I assure all of you."

The TWC commandos had tied them all up, except for Zabriski, who was flying the ornithopter. They did not want to fire a gun in the cabin, and therefore, one of the commandos, to emphasize their determination, held a knife to Rebecca Thalberg's throat.

Jashad knew about the temple with the portal into the aft end of the ship. Jashad had demanded to be taken there immediately.

"My men can take care of themselves," Jashad continued. "There will be many casualties, true. But once they take up a fortress position in the city, they will be able to endure long enough to be aided."

"You *hope*," Becky said defiantly.

"Yes. I do hope," Jashad said. "I also hope to be at this temple soon. How long, pilot?"

"Just a minute more," Zabriski answered. "The end's coming up."

Already shreds of mist had begun to envelop them. This part of the cylinder was shrouded in a permanant light fog, due to the air currents and collected water vapor. Zabriski leaned forward, and pointed. "That's it, right over there." So saying, she tilted the ornithopter toward the structure.

Backed by dull grey alloy, the temple stood in bright contrast. White pillars reared over a long series of steps, its only resemblance to Earthly temples. Otherwise, the architecture, like that of the other buildings the saurians had built, seemed based more on organic principles rather than geometric, as though to celebrate the aesthetics of biology. Thus, the temple had all kinds of cupolas, towers, mounds, and protrusions, linked by vein-like passageways.

"Set us down right by the steps," Jashad said. Then a thought seemed to occur to him. He swiveled to Kemp. "Are there guards?"

Coopersmith answered for him. "Only at the actual portal inside the temple."

"How many?"

"Four."

"Will it be necessary to kill them? Or would you people be so kind as to extend your carte blanche to your esteemed captors?"

"I don't want to see any more people killed, human *or* saurian," Kemp responded immediately. "We'll see that you get through."

"Excellent! I must admit that when possible, I abhor violence."

The ornithopter dropped down. The prisoners were untied. Prodded by pistol barrels, they led the way through the entrance of the saurian temple. The place smelled of musk and mystery. Coopersmith led them down a series of tunnels, footsteps echoing eerily.

The corridor ballooned into a large chamber, filled with light. At the other end, Doctor Robert Jakes was trying to communicate to the guards, waving his hands with frustration.

Upon spotting the new arrivals, Jakes hailed them and proceeded to run toward them excitedly. "Colonel! The door at the end opened for us. You should *see* what's inside. I'm afraid I've some bad news as well." Halfway there, he noticed that Colonel Kemp had company. He was about to turn and race back, when Jashad brandished his gun.

"Please. I wouldn't run away," Jashad said. "You must show us what you have found. I am very excited. Very excited indeed."

"Colonel Kemp?" Jakes said.

"May I introduce Mr. Jashad of the TWC, Doctor Jakes. He and his hoodlums are in charge now."

Jakes sighed. "Colonel. Thesaurus is dead."

Becky cried out, "What? What happened?"

"He was supposed to stay out. His radiation suit wasn't ready. He couldn't stand the suspense."

Coopersmith's voice was choked with emotion. "He saw it, though . . . he saw the other side?"

"Yes, Coopersmith. He saw it. We've been studying it now for quite a while."

"And Mikaela?" asked Kemp.

"Doctor Lindstrom is in good health and has been invaluable to our investigation." He turned suddenly to Jashad, a strange smile creeping to his face. "So. Political monsters have reared their heads. You've come for the stardrive, haven't you?"

"You are a very intelligent man, Doctor," Jashad said. "We have come for all the secrets, all the *power* that this vessel holds. It is rightfully ours."

Jakes nodded, his expression growing stranger. "Oh, I'm sure you'll get a big kick out of what's waiting for you back there, all right."

Coopersmith said, "What do you mean by that, Doctor?"

"I believe there are enough suits for everyone. I suggest you put them on. Of course, Mr. Jashad and his friends—being righteous and on a holy mission—probably would not need them."

Jashad grinned. "We are practical fanatics, Doctor Jakes."

"Very well. They're stacked this way. Come with me, we'll put them on, and I'll take you for a tour."

They put on the suits. It took only a few minutes to convince the guards not to give the TWC commandos any trouble. The saurians seemed quite as excited as Doctor Jakes. Something *had* happened, Kemp thought. Something big.

The doors were opened for them. They passed through the curtain. Immediately, it became apparent that the new corridor was not constructed by the saurians. The walls were of the same metals as the cylinder end. Electric lights shone from their placements in the walls. The corridor stretched straight ahead.

"I am curious," Jashad said, his features losing some of their tension lines as they were melted with awe. "If the saurian culture has had access to this section of Artifact One, as you call it, all this time, why are they not more advanced in technology?"

Doctor Jakes explained, uneasily, after getting a nod of permission from Kemp. "Apparently, all this time they've only had access to this particular passageway. When they first showed it to us, we were astounded, and you'll see why when we turn around this corner up here."

They executed the turn, the commandos still keeping their handguns trained on the captives. When he saw what awaited,

Jashad obviously had a hard time keeping his attention on his proper TWC duties. He muttered an exclamation of astonishment in his native language.

Kemp, who had not seen this section of the corridor, was equally impressed. "I can see now why this is a holy place. No wonder these creatures have such a rich mythology."

Stretching along one wall for a length of fifty meters was a panorama in three dimensions that, in pictures and sounds and smells, described the life and death of the universe in symbolic terms.

Doctor Jakes tapped the glass cover of it. "Unbreakable. They couldn't get inside to see how it works if they *wanted* to. Now. If you'll notice, the middle section here is a complex symbology—almost a mandala—of biological cycles. As far as I can tell, these permutations that the streaming pictures go through are *teaching* methods to explain a non-technological method of genetic control. Hence, the saurian's mastery of bio-systems—to a certain extent, at any rate. I suspect that there's more represented here than they can yet understand." Doctor Jakes walked along toward the end of the moving mural.

Kemp, despite his sense of defeat and his anxiety, was dazzled. Colors flowed in intricate patterns. Representations of life forms, chemicals, genes, and molecules moved in a majestic dance that was beyond his comprehension. Strange music filtered through the air. The principal motifs of the symbology were pictoral variations of the saurians themselves.

"This was *placed* here! On *purpose!*" he said. "To teach . . . to teach the reptiles that found it."

"Not only that," Doctor Jakes said, voice brimming with excitement. "Come have a look at *this.*"

At the far end of the mural, was a holographic miniature of the solar system. Included in the holograph was a representation of the very starship they were on now. The final depiction in the array was that of a creature, metamorphizing from one variation to another.

"My God," Becky said. "It looks kind of like a man, now. Could it be, do you think, the creatures that created this ship?"

"No," Jakes said. "No, what you're seeing is a mathematical projection of all the possible ways that evolution might have produced intelligent life on the planet Earth." He breathed a sigh and shook his head with something like incredulity. "I know that because of what I've seen beyond the final portal. Believe me, this is just the beginning."

It took a good deal of will power to pry themselves from the dazzling wonders displayed on the wall mural, but eventually Doctor Jakes persuaded them to continue.

The corridor stopped dead in front of them.

"This is the end of the road for saurians," Jakes said. "At least for a while."

"What do you mean?" Kemp asked. "Why isn't it the end of the road for human beings?"

"There's no way to analyze the reasons now, but I suspect they are complicated. And yet—watch." He stepped up to the wall. A panel opened, almost magically. Jakes pulled a lever.

With a click, a door opened.

Subtle shadings of bright colors streamed through into the comparative dimness.

"Your eyes will accustom themselves soon," Jakes said. "Come. My assistants are on the other side, taking readings."

Wordlessly, the party shuffled through the opening into wonder. The handguns of the commandos were nearly forgotten by both captors and captives.

The theory had been that this section of the ship would not only hold the stardrives that powered this mammoth vessel, but also the control section as well as the crew quarters. There had been excited conjecture that if the alien race that had built this ship had enough technological sophistication to recreate a reconstruction of the Earth's Jurassic age within the main part of the cylinder, then they might have created a recreation of their home planet's environment in the aft end.

Nothing could be further from the truth.

Machines.

All the way around the circumference of this section stretched alien machinery. Large and small machines, oddly shaped machines, differently colored machines. No illuminator burned above a thick rod stretched the kilometer distance between the walls. A part of the generator, no doubt, Kemp supposed. Much of the machinery was no doubt for enviornmental maintenance, but still. . . .

"It was dark when we came in here, Colonel," Doctor Jakes

said in a subdued tone. "But as soon as we walked just a few steps, these lights came on. All around the periphery. We immediately did just as you ordered, Colonel. We searched for the stardrive."

Suddenly, Jashad's eyes burned with intensity.

"Yes, Doctor Jakes. By all means, tell us about the stardrive!"

Jakes broke out in light laughter.

Angrily, Jashad waved his gun. "I am not to be mocked, Doctor Jakes, nor is our holy purpose to be mocked!"

Jakes sobered a bit. "Well, it looks as though our whole concept of this ship has been mocked. As best as *I* can tell, from an hour's examination, based on all I know of physics and engineering, there is *no stardrive* on Artifact One. The propulsion engines, in fact, are quite similar to the ones *we* use. Only bigger, of course." He sighed. "This, gentlemen, is most definitely *not* a starship."

Kemp had never been so stunned in his life.

He felt the stars dwindle away out of reach. His hopes crumbled and his wonder funneled back into despair.

Jashad, however, was furious. "You're lying, you Western scum. You're *lying!*"

Jakes shrugged. "Take my word for it, I'm not. I assure you, however, that there's plenty of knowledge to be had within this section. There are more computer banks here than in the Eastern seaboard. From the feeling I get, though, there is nothing here that will give the domination of the universe, Jashad." He could not suppress a wide grin. "Sorry."

"How do you know these things?" Jashad demanded. "How can you be sure?"

"I've just taken the alien's word for it," responded Jakes.

"They're here?" Rebecca said, her grief for Thesaurus washed away by excitement. "There are extraterrestrial beings here, now, *alive?*"

"No. There aren't even any signs of our hypothesized crew quarters. In fact, as far as I can see, there is absolutely no evidence of exactly who or what the creatures that created Artifact One really were. We might run across a few tantalizing clues as we examine the evidence. Nothing more, however."

"Okay, Jakes. Come clean. How do you know so much

after being in here only a few hours?" Kemp was irritated.

"Quite simple, Colonel," Jakes said. "You know that holographic mural outside? Well, it's clearly intended to instruct the intelligent reptilian life that the—the ETI's, let's call them—that the ETI's foresaw or even *manipulated* into their eventual form millions of years ago. Influenced, no doubt, by specifically measured radiation emission from the illuminator. But the saurians not only had to find it first, they had to understand it. Apparently, the ETI's left something similar for us human beings. For similar reasons." He coughed. "You see, this is not just the only entrance that the lizards could use. It's the only one that humans could use."

"Wait just a moment, Doctor!" Coopersmith said. "Are you implying that they knew we were coming! That doesn't correlate at *all* with the theories about this ship. I mean, no *stardrive?* What you're saying is that this ship was put here in orbit *on purpose!*"

"But why fill it with dinosaurs, for God's sake?" Kemp demanded. "It doesn't make any sense!"

"It does if you start thinking about Artifact One in a different sense. A different system of thought, gentlemen. A different approach. Now with the givens I have presented, what conclusions would you come to?"

"A gigantic ship filled with dinosaurs in their natural environment," Becky began, running down the facts. *"No* stardrive. A saurian culture purposefully nurtured and educated by the mechanisms of this vessel, but unable to pierce this far into the ship's control section. A door that opens automatically upon the presence of human beings—creatures *anticipated* by that mural outside, in some form. . . ."

"One last thing of importance," Doctor Jakes said. "Come here." He led them past a smooth, large mound of metal. On the other side stretched a mural of similar scope to the one in the corridor, yet obviously much more complicated. Instead of explicit symbols, computations and equations seemed to flow in a never-ending cycle. Lights flashed in various configurations of form and color. "As near as I can guess, it's not only a teaching tool, but a kind of catalog of the systems and computers and other machines in Artifact One."

"I don't understand," Kemp said. "I don't understand at all.

You mean to tell me that whoever created this ship *knew* we would find it?"

"Not only that," Becky said in a somber whisper. "They also created us. Can't you see, Ian! The *Dragonstar* is some kind of gigantic test-tube! A discarded test-tube!"

"If this is a test-tube," Coopersmith said, "I sure would like to see the laboratory!"

"No," Jakes said, shaking his head emphatically. "I studied this—this primer, shall we call it. That is not the indication that *it* presents. The ETI's did *not* create life on Earth."

"Well, then, what *did* they do?" Jashad demanded. He seemed every bit as enrapt with the unfolding explanation as the others. His followers did not seem to understand English. However, they seemed hard-pressed to keep their attention on holding up their guns, so fascinated were they by the whorls and swirls of color upon the mural.

"From what I've gleaned from the information presented here—along with some intuitive leaps of mind, I must admit, my conclusion is that they *shaped* life. They used this artificial environment to test life-forms. Or perhaps what we have here is the *reason* that dinosaurs became extinct upon the Earth. The shapers decided to opt for the evolutionary pathway that led to the development of mammalian intelligence rather than reptilian. Perhaps they themselves were family folk, and favored the development of the limbic system."

"Wait a moment!" Becky said. "I thought that the creatures here were from the Jurassic age. Didn't the extinction come later?"

Kemp said, "Funny. Mikaela just mentioned to me a few days ago that *her* conclusion was that there were creatures from the Cretacious period as well, which would jive with Doctor Jakes's theory."

"You mean to tell me that the ETI's spent millions of years hovering about Earth, shaping?" Becky said. "That doesn't sound very likely to me."

"Who said that they had to hang around all that time?" Doctor Jakes said. "They could have set things in motion, then come back to check how things were going every two or three million years. In other words, this ship is a *lot* older than we thought. But let me start from the beginning.

"I suspect that the ETI's mission, initially, was to scout out the proper beginnings of life. According to modern theory, this solar system is about five billion years old, with Earth essentially being 'born' about four point six billion years ago. About three billion years ago, large amounts of oxygen began to be produced on Earth from the ultraviolet dissociation of water molecules and also perhaps from green plant photosynthesis. Things we might call plants thus produced their own nourishment from sunlight. The seas became a veritable broth of just the right chemicals. With electrical storms, there became enough variations, *mutations* if you will, that the first amino acids and other favorable conditions for the beginnings of animal life developed. Rather like the theory that if you stick a hundred monkeys in front of typewriters, they would, given enough time, eventually produce the works of Shakespeare. There are just so many combinations possible before life is formed. The amino acids, of course, are the basis of protein and also the essential chemicals involved in the DNA code. One-celled animals came into being. Changes in the DNA occurred, and so the cells changed, and then they joined into colonies . . . and, well, you know the rest. This took billions of years. We've some fossil relics that prove this. So, essentially, the ETI's stumbled onto the Earth at about the end of the Permian age— and began their shaping. Inside of Artifact One, they developed a similar environment to the Earth's surface and began accelerated experiments to determine just what the ecology should be in order to eventually evolve life. Do you notice that there *aren't* any mammals here? You know, at one time, I suspect there probably were, but they were all transferred to the Earth's surface. When the ETI's were eventually satisfied with the programs they had keyed into the evolutionary and ecological computers, they set Artifact One into elliptical orbit. They left behind their teaching device for the developing saurians. And they prepared the mural we see here for the express purpose of educating any creature intelligent enough to key the brain scanners. Evidently, we fit that description, as I suspect the ETI's thought we would, if we could *find* this ship, and get to it, and into it."

"But why was our first ship blasted? Why all the death and pain it took to get here?" Kemp demanded imperiously.

"I suspect that was our own fault. After all, it was because of our stupidity that the Snipe ran into trouble with what, after all, were merely devices to protect the hull from meteors and asteroids. And we were stupid enough to enter through the middle of the cylinder, rather than near one of the ends! I strongly suspect that we barely passed the brain scanner test!"

"Well, we *did* make it," Kemp muttered grumpily. "And what good is it going to do us? The TWC has got the secrets."

Jashad grinned.

Jakes sighed. "Oh, you militarists, you politicians, you stupid fuggheaded twits!"

Jashad frowned. Kemp frowned. Coopersmith couldn't help but chuckle. Becky rolled her eyes.

Jakes continued. "Don't you understand what I've been telling you? The ETI's certainly weren't going to leave anything here that would tell us how to kill each other, or how to gain power, or whatever. The stuff here is for *all* mankind. What we have here is not so much the keys to the stars as the keys to our own planet, to unfolding the potentials of the human race in our own environments. Now, that very well may lead to ventures into the stars, but only after we get our heads straightened out. The fact that the ETI's exist tends to suggest that there are plenty of advanced civilizations in the galaxy. You don't think that they're going to put up with an Earth civilization typified by fascist, arrogant, anal-retentives like you, Phineas Kemp; or merciless barbarian terrorists like you, Jashad."

Both Kemp and Jashad bristled, but said nothing.

"No. And as a matter of fact, my friends, I suspect that we start examining this storehouse of wisdom fast, so we can get our act together as soon as possible," Jakes said.

"Why do you say that, Doctor?" Becky asked.

"When Mikaela, my men, and I first entered the portal, not only did the lights begin to go on all about, but this happened." He pointed to the burst mound.

"Looks like a blown fuse," Coopersmith said.

"Something like that. It's the remains of a one-shot tachyonic transmitter. Evidently a signal was beamed to the universe when we entered.

"Folks, the ETI's know we're here now. I suspect they'll

be here sometime in the future to see how their little project has progressed. I wonder if they'll be pleased to see what we've done to the Earth and to ourselves." He turned to Jashad. "If indeed you do claim this ship, you and your holy TWC, you will also be the ones who will have to answer to those that come, Jashad. Do you think that the TWC is ready for that responsibility?"

Jashad said, "It is our holy responsibility! It has been prophesized that our races shall lead the peoples of the world, under the leadership of Allah!" But the man seemed to invest no confidence in these words. Indeed, he seemed nervous, unsure.

"And you're calling *me* fascist, Doctor Jakes," Kemp said, trying not to sound arrogant. That little comment had hit home hard. "So, Jashad. What are your plans now? Clearly, this is not what you're after."

"I must confer with my fellows," Jashad said softly.. "Doctor Jakes, call your other helpers in immediately!"

Jakes did so. Morton and Sommers had to be cautioned not to do anything stupid. Mikaela looked at Jashad and company in astonishment, then moved to Kemp, who put a protective arm around her.

"I'm so sorry about Thesaurus," she told Becky and Ian. "We had no idea he would rush in—"

"My fault," Kemp said bitterly. "I should have had his suit fixed immediately. If I'd known."

"Would you quit forever shouldering the bloody responsibility, Kemp?" Coopersmith said. "It's nobody's fault. I'll miss him very much."

"Other things to worry about now, both of you," Becky said.

Jashad repeated, "I must confer!" He waved his gun toward the exit. "Come!"

Prodded on by the weapons of the three commandos with Jashad, they turned away from the gallery of alien technology and headed back through the passageway to the humid atmosphere beyond the entrance to the temple.

As they stepped out into the clear, facing a set of declining steps, Kemp heard the crack of automatic rifle fire. In the next instant, the three commandos were convulsing away from them, parts of their scalps and faces blown away by sniper fire. Only Jashad remained as he turned his weapon toward Becky.

Coopersmith reacted first, but he and Kemp smashed into the man together, deflecting the shot from his handgun, knocking the weapon from his grasp. The assassin lunged and caught Ian in the jaw with his fist and broke for the entrance back into the temple. In the moments that followed, Kemp saw that Jashad's bullet had indeed grazed Becky and there was wound across her thigh which looked like the slash of a sword's blade. Down below, beyond the steps of the temple, an IASA OTV was trundling toward them. The snipers had cleared their concealed positions and were also running up the steps.

As Kemp lowered Becky to the floor of stone, Coopersmith joined her. His look of concern was genuine. The reinforcements reached them and Kemp assumed command of the situation.

"Good work, Lieutenant," he said to the first man who reached them. "What's the status of the operation?"

"The guerrillas didn't fare too well with their little plan, sir," said the lieutenant, wiping some sweat out of his eyes. "We rounded up what was left of them. What the dinosaurs didn't take care of, the saurians did. Those guys are a tough bunch of fighters! One of our point men had spotted you come down with those TWC guys so we figured the best thing would be to wait until you were brought out so that we could ambush them with the sniperscopes."

"Yes, well ..." Kemp began.

"I know it was risky, sir, but that's all we could do in the situation, and it looks like it worked out okay."

"Take Doctor Thalberg down for someone to look at her leg," said Coopersmith, helping Becky to her feet.

"Yes," said Colonel Kemp. "A good job, Lieutenant, but I'm afraid we have one more thing to take care of."

"Jashad?" asked Coopersmith, a grin beginning to play at the corners of his mouth. He took the automatic rifle from the Lieutenant, then regarded Kemp. "Allow me, Colonel?"

Kemp smiled. "By all means, Ian. He couldn't have gotten far."

Without saying another word, Ian turned back into the temple entrance and retraced the steps he had taken only minutes before as a captive. It was an eerie sensation to walk through alien corridors which had a tinge of familiarity, still knowing that he was inside a chamber designed by minds so far more clever and superior to his own. His footsteps resounded with faint echoes as he advanced, watching for any place where the terrorist might be hiding.

And *hide* he would bloody well have to do, thought Ian. The black-hearted son of a bitch! He had known that men such as Jashad existed, but he had never dealt with his ilk until now. There was only one thing they understood, and if he had to, Ian intended to speak the assassin's language.

Past the mandala and the panorama of spectacular images he walked, entering the final chamber. He saw that the lights were already blazing and he knew that Jashad had come this far.

"First," came a voice, "I suggest you not move."

Ian froze in his tracks. Because of the echoey nature of the voice, he could not pinpoint its origin.

"You thought I was weaponless, O brave warrior?" Jashad said. "I, weaponless? How amusing. No, you shall make a worthy hostage. I presently have trained upon you a very deadly handgun I kept in a holster on my shin. . . ."

Ian swept the area with his peripheral vision. He spotted a set of combat fatigues, illumined by the glow of information screens all blazing with their own spectral light.

"Now, please. Place your weapon on the floor slowly. Kick it away from you. Raise your hands above your face, then face me. In *that* order, please."

A sudden turn would be no good. This was a trained assassin he was dealing with. Finely honed reflexes. . . .

Coopersmith realized he had to buy time.

He began to lower his weapon.

From the corner of his eye, Coopersmith saw a form coming toward them, saw Jashad, panicked, swing his weapon, fire.

In that instant, Coopersmith swung around and squeezed off an entire clip from his rifle, panning the barrel back and forth. The volley of slugs ripped through Jashad's midsection, lifting him off his feet and stitching him to the wall behind him. His eyes still open, his face still recording that final shock, he slowly slid to the floor, leaving a crimson trail of his progress on the polished surface of the wall.

Dead by the sword he lived by.

Coopersmith ran to the form that had distracted the assassin. Blood spattered one shoulder. Thesaurus the saurian struggled to get up, eyes glittering in the light of the information screen, transfixed.

"I'm glad to see that the rumors of your death were entirely exaggerated," Coopersmith said, letting him lean against his side.

Something garbled emerged from the saurian's mouth.

"But then, how would they know if a saurian's dead or not, what?"

Thesaurus's eyes remained on the screen.

"That's right. Apparently we've got one to teach us, too. But I'd better get you back. Who knows—maybe you'll be around long enough to help us learn what that thing there says." Coopersmith lifted the saurian up, and began to carry him toward the exit. "I sure hope so, pal. You just saved my life."

"Good," the saurian said. "Good."

His eyes remained wide open all the way to the temple and the waiting others, taking in whatever they could.

CHAPTER 22

REBECCA THALBERG HANDED Phineas Kemp his cup of coffee.
"One sugar. Just a dash of cream. Lukewarm."

"I'm touched," Kemp said wearily. "You remembered."

She ignored his implicit sarcasm. "Are you sure you want this? Maybe you should just turn in. It's been a long day." They were in the mess hall of the *Heinlein*.

"How's your leg?"

"It smarts a bit. That's all. I'll live."

Kemp sighed. "You know he's married, don't you, Becky?" He didn't look at her.

"Men like Ian usually are."

"You love him?"

"Very much."

Kemp sipped at his coffee. Absolutely perfect. Better than he could have made himself.

"What about *him?* Does he feel the same way?"

287

"Look, Phineas. We were two lost people. We needed each other." She shook her dark hair. "Oh. That's right. You don't know what it's like to *need* someone, do you, Phineas?" There was no rancor in her voice.

"So then." Kemp could not look at her. He held his emotions in rigid check. "Is he going back to his wife?"

"Our relationship is over, Phineas."

"Oh?" Kemp looked up, unable to keep the hope from his eyes.

"And I'm afraid that that part of *our* relationship is over as well, Phineas."

Kemp was stunned. "But Becky. If it's that way with Coopersmith. . . . Why?"

"Because I know the sort of man I want now, Phineas. And I'm afraid that you just don't fit the bill. I'll always be fond of you. We can't help but be friends. This is, if your pride allows."

"God," Kemp said bitterly. "What a way to end the day."

"Things *have* been twisted around a bit, haven't they?" She went to him and gently put her arms around his neck. "Our whole concept of where we came from, where we're going— as a race, and as individuals. . . . I've changed, Phineas. You have to understand that. I have to get my own life together before I can minister to someone else's."

"I never—"

"Shh. You're upset now. You're fatigued. We can talk about this later. We'll have plenty of time, Phineas. I have the feeling that the rest of our lives are going to be quite exciting. This is just the beginning."

"I think I've had enough excitement for a long time."

"You don't blame yourself, do you, Phineas?"

"Well, let's just say that ever since we first caught sight of this ship, my self-esteem has been knocked down a few pegs."

"You'll live." She patted him on the shoulder. "Ian estimates about another week and a half before we get back to Earth orbit."

"Yes. Thank God we can at least rely on our technology." She leaned over and kissed him on the forehead.

"Good night, Phineas. I'll see you at breakfast."

"Good night, Becky."

She sauntered out, pausing for a moment at the exit, as though she had something else she had to say. Mikaela Lindstrom, carrying a tray with a sandwich and a glass of milk atop it, brushed past her, with a mild greeting. Becky smiled to herself, then left.

"I should have asked you if you wanted something to eat," Mikaela said as she set down the tray. "Want half of a tuna fish on rye?"

Kemp shook his head. "Hungry work, realizing the truth about your universe, isn't it?"

Mikaela said, "It still hasn't sunk in yet." She took a swallow of her milk.

"I'll tell you the one thing about it all that bothers *me*," Kemp said. *"Why?"*

"Why what?" Mikaela asked.

"Why did the aliens do it? It just doesn't make any sense."

"Well, perhaps it is irrational. But you know, Phineas, there is more to existence than the strictly rational view." She was thoughtful for a moment. "Okay. Let's take an example. Human beings. When people get to be of a certain age, a certain *maturity*, when they see that they can't continue on indefinitely, isn't it their natural inclination to begin a family, to have children who will carry on after them . . . and so on? How do we know that when a civilization reaches a certain maturity in the cosmos, its natural inclination is to spawn another, *different* civilization? That's what this one did, evidently, with the raw materials that were available to it. I mean, Phineas, doesn't it feel good to know that somewhere out there are our *parents?* And they may well be here anytime to say hello. It's staggering, that's what it is."

"I suppose I'm just a bit homocentric. I always dreamed of being part of the spearhead to the stars myself." Kemp said.

"This is paradise for me, Phineas. I *love* it here. All the things we're going to discover . . . have *already* discovered. It makes me grateful I'm alive." She munched her sandwich. "It gives me an appetite. *You're* certainly cheerful, Phineas. Come on, brighten up! Everything has turned out at least reasonably well." She put down her sandwich, and looked at him. "Oh. I suspect that Becky's pretty much told you how things stand with you two."

"That's right."

"I pretty much saw it coming."

"Oh, did you?"

"You must admit, scaled against the rest of what's happened today, it's pretty unimportant."

"She's alive, and she's well, and she's doing what she wants to do. I guess that's what's important, isn't it?" Kemp said. "Well, at any rate, Mikaela, I just can't help feeling that my relationship with Becky is just one more thing I've screwed up in my life."

"You feel cast adrift, I bet. Unable to relate to what's happened, or to who you used to be. You've changed, Phineas. It happens to us all. You'll grow because of it, I assure you."

"You've been through things like this before?"

"Oh, all the time. I've had a few fairly traumatic things happen to me in my life that seemed to leave me out in the cold. I survived, though."

"I didn't realize. You'll tell me about them sometime?"

"Certainly," she answered. "We'll have lots of time, Phineas." Her voice had a warmth that went beyond friendship. Slowly, she ate the rest of her sandwich, staring frankly at Kemp. She gulped the rest of her milk, then licked her lips.

Kemp blinked, surprised.

"You know, Phineas. This has been a pretty tense day. How about coming over to my cabin for a drink? There's no reason to end a day like this so dourly."

Her blond hair shone softly in the light. The invitation gleamed mischeviously in her eyes.

Kemp felt uncomfortable. "Why, uhm, that sounds . . . quite nice, Mikaela."

She stood, and as she walked around the table toward him, he noticed the lithe lines and curves of her body beneath the tight jumpsuit flow, exquisitely feminine.

She stood behind him and slowly began to rub his shoulders. "We Swedes are famed for massage, you know."

"Ah." Already he could feel his tension dissolving under the graceful touch of her fingers. He chuckled to himself.

"What's so amusing?" Mikaela asked.

"I'm just wondering why you like me, I suppose. I'm not so sure I'm so crazy about myself any more."

Mikaela's laughter was musical.

"Dear, dear Phineas. Haven't you guessed? I'm a paleon-tologist. I've always wanted a dinosaur of my very own."

From the creator of the bestselling *Silistra*
series, a temptuous odyssey to the farthest
reaches of the human imagination...

Janet Morris's
THE KERRION EMPIRE

*"Not since Dune have we witnessed a power
struggle of such awesome intensity...
A literary feast!"* —Eric Van Lustbader

____ **Book I: DREAM DANCER**   06334-8/$2.95
____ **Book II: CRUISER DREAMS**   06453-0/$2.95
____ **Book III: EARTH DREAMS**   05658-9/$2.75